THE (UN)POPULAR VOTE

JASPER SANCHEZ

KATHERINE TEGEN BOOKS
An Imprint of HarperCollins Publishers

Library of Congress Control Number: 2020951698
ISBN 978-0-06-302576-9

Typography by David DeWitt
21 22 23 24 25   PC/LSCH   10 9 8 7 6 5 4 3 2 1
❖
First Edition

For my grandfather,
who did not throw his bike at Hitler,
but taught me the story's in the telling.

The (Un)Popular Vote contains depictions of transphobia and homophobia. This book is about queer characters and details their struggles as well as their joy. This book is *for* queer readers, but please read with care. Your well-being comes first.

ONE

"POLITICS," MY DAD USED TO TELL ME, "IS sleight of hand." Smoke and mirrors. The art of the steal, rather than good old-fashioned hard work. Democracy, he said, is an elegant, elaborate distraction.

Take this scene playing out on C-SPAN. It's a real performance. A Republican congressman from a tiny, gun-toting district in rural Maine is giving a heartfelt soliloquy on the joys of hunting New England cottontails, which he'd like to see removed from the endangered species list. It'd be a rousing speech, if everyone's minds weren't already made up. The real wheeling and dealing happens behind the scenes, in the cloakrooms C-SPAN's cameras can't see. When the vote comes, it won't be based on rousing speeches or public opinion. It'll come down to whose money greases whose palms and who owes favors to whom.

This speech is a parlor trick. Pageantry in the name of polite society. I've heard it all before.

My laptop streams on my desk as I go through the motions of my morning routine. The sun's up, but its rays haven't yet breached the sill of my second-floor window. I rummage for clothes in the dim. Moments like these make me miss my old school's uniforms. I'm still not used to picking out clothes for myself. Even outside of school, femininity was another dress code I didn't want to follow. In the end, I keep it simple. Binder, packer, trunks. Dark jeans. A mildly rumpled Oxford, the sleeves artfully cuffed. My tried-and-true red hoodie. Pomade through the floppy part of my dark blond hair. It's another kind of uniform, but it's one I choose.

I keep one eye on the screen as I labor in front of the mirror. The congressman's still going. His tinny voice rattles through my shitty laptop speakers. Every so often, the feed cuts away from the three tiers of podiums at the center of the House Chamber. Another camera pans around the room, taking in the rings of seats and ugly blue carpeting.

I know that room. I know the name of every scholar and philosopher whose face graces those walls, and I know there are bullet holes in the ceiling from a 1954 shooting. I've been *in* that room. I did a summer program in middle school. They called it a leadership conference, but it was really a glorified summer camp. They herded us into the House Chamber before the crack of dawn, before the session started, to listen to retired congressmen extol the virtues of public service in staid, nonpartisan platitudes. Half the kids fell asleep, but I was transfixed, my white knuckles gripping the edges of my sticky leather seat.

Most of those seats are empty this early in the morning. It may be three hours later in Washington, but the session's only just started, and this is a low-profile bill. Most representatives are in their offices. Some are still in their beds. Some aren't even in Washington. There are no assigned seats in the House. But Democrats tend to sit stage right, Republicans stage left. Ironic, I know. That means I can narrow my search down by half. The camera keeps panning, and I keep scanning. The bird's-eye angle doesn't help, not when half the men are balding and the other half seem to favor the same Don Draper–wannabe hairstyle. Still, I can rule out the gray- and white-haired. Focus on the first few rows. Search for broad shoulders on a slim man—

There. In the second row, near the center. A blot of neatly styled blond hair, green and grainy under the harsh, energy-efficient lighting.

Congressman Graham Teagan, Democrat, from California's Second District.

Or, as I know him: Dad.

Motion sensors switch on cool fluorescent lights when I pad downstairs. Everything here is automatic, from the lights to the heat. It's smaller than the house in Marin, but it's not small. This is a McMansion compared to a real-deal, old-money mansion. That place was Dad's taste, old-fashioned and ostentatious enough you could see it from space. Sometimes I think Mom picked this house out of spite when they covertly separated last year. They couldn't make it formal, let alone *public*; Dad didn't want the scandal, let alone the speculation. So they have an agreement. Mom and I moved forty miles north, where I have the freedom to transition and Dad has the freedom to ignore me. Mom dutifully plays the part of the good wife, making public appearances and countless other sacrifices to spare me from having to do the same.

This house—this town—is supposed to be my safe haven.

The kitchen's empty, though a half-full carafe steams under the brushed chrome coffee maker. A note hangs from the fridge, pinned under a Harvard magnet. In loopy cursive that adheres to every stereotype about doctors' illegible handwriting, Mom informs me she was called in early and she loves me.

My athletic socks slip and slide on the hardwood floors. Monty, our Jack Russell terrier, noses at my calves. I pour the rest of the coffee directly into a thermos. No cream; no sugar. The microwave whirs, then chirps when it finishes thawing my breakfast burrito. I lean over the granite island, still watching my laptop. Mom hates it when I eat without sitting down, but it's a burrito. It may be smothered in locally sourced organic hot sauce, but it's still a burrito. Ergo, finger food.

I love Mom, and I appreciate everything she's done for me this past year, of course I do, but I like the mornings when she heads to the hospital early. Whenever she catches me watching C-SPAN, she gives me the look she gives patients with terminal cancer. When I put up a better front, she stares at me over the brim of her mug in a way she never did when I left for school in a uniform skirt. Sometimes she straightens my collar or smooths my cowlick with her thumb, but it's worst when she just looks at me. Because I can never name the emotion that storms up behind her eyes, whether it's pride or wistful nostalgia. I just know she's measuring every inch of me against the man I'm trying to be. When she looks at me, she still sees the doorjamb where she used to mark the height of the girl I was, and I never know how this version of me measures up.

This house may be manned by artificial intelligence, but it doesn't judge me. Not for spilling hot sauce on my shirt. Not for wearing a silicone dick in my boxer briefs. Not for watching C-SPAN on my laptop at five a.m. just to catch a glimpse of my dad's face.

Pablo texts when he's outside. He honked precisely once, the first morning of junior year, and never again. Not after the informal reprimand Mom received from the neighborhood association, which strictly prohibits "noise nuisances."

I hurry outside, red high-tops in hand, while Pablo

Navarro's Range Rover idles in the driveway.

"Hey," he says as I hoist myself into the passenger seat. The rising sun burnishes his adobe skin in gold. He's got more facial hair than just about anyone in the senior class, and he wears it proudly. Even though it's pushing seventy degrees already, his blue-and-red letterman jacket hangs over his broad wrestler's build—*fat*, he'd correct me without an ounce of shame.

"Hey." I yank the door shut, and Pablo winces, as if he can feel his car's pain. He loves this thing like it's his own child.

Taylor Swift's latest single spills from the speakers; Jenny calls Pablo's Taylor obsession his only character flaw. The car smells like oil and leather polish. Underneath, it still has that new car scent, too, even though his parents gave it to him before I moved here.

"Did you watch CNN last night?" I ask as I stuff my heels into my shoes.

"Dude," Pablo says, shooting me a skeptical side-eye. "I don't know why you stay up for the pundits. If anything major happens in geopolitical events, you'll get a news alert."

"I'd rather be the first to know."

"I'd rather bundle up in a blanket cocoon and catch some sweet, sweet shut-eye."

"Sleep's a social construct."

"No, it's not. Your go-to argument won't win this debate."

"Sleep's overrated, then."

"You'll take that back as soon as we start getting homework."

I roll my eyes. "Class is the easy part. It's the extracurriculars I'm worried about." My GPA is literally perfect, but that won't be enough to get me into Harvard, not when my extracurricular roster is so spotty.

Pablo knows what I mean. He's heard me complain about it enough to know the tune of my anxieties by heart.

He expertly navigates around Hythloday Court until we're heading downhill. Mom and I live on a respectable hill in the Utopia Heights neighborhood of Santa Julia, California. All the hills signify upper-middle-class social status, but the Navarros live up on Olympus Crest, which is adorned with private roads and gated estates.

Pablo notches down the volume, which signals he's about to say something Serious. "So I've been thinking," he says, low and conciliatory, which means he knows it's something I'm not going to like. "Maybe you should join JSA again."

My laugh comes out as a hoarse bark. "Yeah, no. Not gonna happen."

"It's been a year, Mark. The state leadership you knew have all graduated, and the rest have short memories. They're not going to recognize you."

Pablo is one of precisely two people at Utopia High School who know the truth about my DNA, both my chromosomes, and where they come from. Which is why he should know

better. I may have built my life around the Junior States-
men of America at my old school—it's where I met Pablo
and Jenny, after all, and it's why they know everything about
me—but I made a deal. Cutting ties with JSA and everyone
in Marin was the price of moving here. It didn't feel like a
sacrifice at the time. I didn't exactly have friends at St. Anastasia's, and the promise of living as myself transcended every
other consideration. It wasn't until I started at UHS, knowing only Pablo and Jenny and cut off from the prospect of
rejoining the regional debate club that I loved, that I realized
how much I missed it.

"All it takes is one person." My throat's dry, so I reach for
my coffee. "Just one person recognizing the freckles on the
bridge of my nose or the cadence of my speech." That's all it
would take to destroy the life we've built in Santa Julia, one
wrong brick pulled from a Jenga tower.

Pablo edges another glance at me. "What about founding
a chapter of Model UN or something?"

The idea's already crossed my mind and been summarily
rejected. "Everyone who'd be interested in joining is already
in JSA."

"I'd join. And Jenny."

"I can't ask you guys to do that." Not when Pablo has
wrestling, and Jenny has student council, and we're all IB
seniors at the brink of the hardest year of our lives.

We're down in the foothills, where the houses are smaller

and closer together. Gas stations and strip malls border the residential neighborhoods. It's a Monopoly board, Small Town Edition. Go straight to Utopia High School. Do not pass Main Street; do not collect $200.

Pablo's not giving up. He likes to think he's the levelest head in any room, but unless it's literal calculus, he's not a problem-solver. That's Jenny's job.

"What about volunteering for a campaign?"

"What, like my dad's?"

Pablo grimaces. "No, of course not. But there's plenty of other stuff. The county supervisor race?"

"No one's campaigning this far ahead for local races."

We pull into the school's deserted parking lot. We're early, even for zero period. Pablo parks and switches off the engine. The synth pop beat cuts out. Pablo won't look at me, but I can tell he's frustrated I won't accept his help.

I reach for my backpack straps.

"Well," says Pablo. "At least you have French Club."

"Ouais," I reply, just this side of dour. "J'ai Club Français."

The squeak of my sneakers against the checkerboard linoleum must give me away because ZP calls out—calls *me* out, to be exact—before he even turns around.

"No, Mark, *shoo.*" He punctuates the gesture with a flick of his Cal mug, acrid teachers' lounge coffee sloshing over the brim. I try to protest, but he barricades the classroom door with his body. "I'm not letting you spend yet another morning conjugating verbs for my actual students."

"But I can help—"

"They need to learn to do it themselves, so they can test out of Latin. Just like you did. Last May." He shakes his head. "You really need a hobby."

"I have plenty of hobbies," I huff. "In fact, I have multiple books in my backpack that are totally unrelated to school."

He squints like I'm speaking ancient Greek. "Which books?"

"*Das Kapital, What's the Matter With Kansas?*, and *The Man in the High Castle.*"

"So, light reading, then." ZP nods. "You know, I read comic books."

From anyone else, the quip would come across as a barb, but Jesse Zielinski-Pak is known for his acerbic chalkboard manner. Somewhere between teaching government, student government, Theory of Knowledge, and zero-period Latin, he styles himself as the Cool Teacher. And, okay, maybe he is. He doesn't mind that we've all dropped the "Mr." and abbreviated his name to two letters. He's young and married to a local folk-rock icon. He slicks his hair back and wears skinny ties and shows off his Korean mythology–inspired sleeve tattoos.

He's also the only teacher who treats us like adults.

"The library doesn't open until seven thirty," I reason

10

with him. "I'll be quiet and let the freshmen screw up declensions all on their own."

"Fine," he relents, "but we really do need to work on getting you a life."

So ZP writes out names of the Founding Fathers on the whiteboard as his actual students start to stumble in, and I sit up on the counter in the back, balancing my tablet on my lap. I'm thinking about the life ZP thinks I need while I wait for the school's glacial Wi-Fi network to load the Google News alerts I check every morning.

Graham Teagan makes headlines more often than most third-term congressmen. But he's on Ways and Means, the committee where the movers and shakers sit, so his vocal opposition to the Republican tax plan is showing up on a few political blogs. The California papers, meanwhile, keep featuring will-he-or-won't-he profiles, speculating as to whether Dad's going to announce his candidacy for next year's gubernatorial race. As if they don't already know governor is the next stop on Dad's road map to the White House.

No new results for *Madison Teagan*. The most recent result is from last fall, the morning after the election. Under a photo of Graham and Greta Teagan, backlit by spotlights, clasped hands raised in triumphant victory, a rabid Bay Area blogger notes the conspicuous absence of their daughter, Madison. Why isn't the girl who started canvassing for her father at thirteen at his victory rally?

Finally, *Mark Adams*. Results litter my screen—an artist's exhibit in Santa Fe, a dentist's malpractice suit in Albany, a taxidermist's estate sale in Provo—but none of them are me.

Because Mark Adams is no one. He's not a politician's son or a transgender icon. He's not making a name for himself. He's just a high school senior, living under the radar.

Just like I promised.

TWO

I HAVE FRIENDS, I PROMISE. IT'S JUST THAT today is Tuesday, and they have shit to do. Pablo and Jenny have JSA. Rachel coordinates Key Club's creek-cleanup project. Nadia attends planning sessions with the yearbook staff.

That's how I end up alone with Benji in ZP's room. It's kind of our group's home base when we have nowhere else to be. Nerds hanging out in a classroom at lunch—sounds pathetic, I know. But really, it's strategic. There's air-conditioning, a stronger Wi-Fi signal, and, most important, no bees. Technically teachers aren't supposed to leave students unattended in their classrooms, but ZP trusts us.

Besides, I like this classroom. Laminated copies of the Declaration of Independence and the Constitution hang side by side. The back wall has blank butcher paper for student government to use, as soon as they're elected. Wide windows open out onto the school's central square. We have a view of the senior steps, where jocks and cheerleaders congregate.

Alternative kids chill by the sundial. Preppy underclassmen sit on the ledge of an overgrown planter.

Benji Dean and I don't really talk. We work in companionable silence. He huddles behind his beat-up, sticker-clad laptop, his spine curved like a question mark. His meticulously messy peroxide-blond hair hangs down over his eyes. He's tall, thin, and the kind of pale you'd expect from someone who's spent his formative years becoming a Tumblr-famous Social Justice Warrior—and, no, I don't mean that as a pejorative. His hands fly over the keyboard, his nails painted pink.

Benji is technically a sophomore now, though we all still think of him as the Freshman. After Madame Lavoisier drafted me to run Club Français last year, the club became a glorified hangout for my friends, regardless of whether they knew any more French than "Voulez-vous coucher avec moi?" One day, Benji walked in, and we didn't know why. We baked croissants and sold crêpes and watched pretentious arthouse films. We weren't exactly advertising that Club Français had become a cover story for an unauthorized queer club. Maybe gaydar sent him our way, because Benji chose us over the actual Gay-Straight Alliance, emphasis on the *straight*. Ever since, our token freshman has been an honorary member of our group.

Meanwhile, as a senior IB diploma candidate, I have to focus on my graduation requirements. For the uninitiated, the International Baccalaureate program is the more intense, international version of AP. Beyond the exams and the Theory of Knowledge course requirement, we're supposed to do 150 hours of community service and write a four-thousand-word so-called Extended Essay. I asked ZP about advising my essay last spring, when it was still in the abstract, and he said he'd be happy to work with me. I'm perfectly on track for the January due date, in the abstract. In reality, I need to pick a topic besides "something political science–y." I'm playing Wikipedia Roulette, clicking cobalt-blue hyperlinks at random in the hope of stumbling upon the perfect topic.

"Have you heard of the Overton window?" I ask Benji between sips of my lukewarm coffee.

"The what?" Benji peers over the brim of his laptop.

"The Overton window."

"Why are you asking me about architecture?" He has a Southern accent, but only just. I think he tries to hide it.

"I'm not. It's a political theory."

"What kind of political theo—" He stops himself short, lips twisting like he's swallowed something sour. "No, no, I'm not falling for that."

Okay, maybe I'm kind of predictable. I swipe one of Benji's Flamin' Hot Cheetos and take a crunchy, satisfying bite.

"Fine." Benji pushes his laptop shut a moment later. "I'm listening."

"The Overton window refers to the range of political ideas

that seem socially acceptable at any given time. It's about mapping discourse. So, on the left, for example, universal healthcare was a socialist fringe proposal a few decades ago. Now most Democrats support it. So on one side, the window's shifted farther to the left."

"While the other side's lurched to the right."

"Yeah. Neo-Nazis went from being an extremist group to marching proudly through the streets as the alt-right."

"The marvels of good branding," Benji says wryly.

I laugh in spite of myself, in the slightly crazed, hysterical way people laugh about politics these days. We have to laugh because there's no other way to release the hurt. "Do you think there's an extended essay somewhere in there?" I ask.

"About the emergence of the alt-right as a quasi-legitimate political movement?"

"Maybe. There's something really interesting about what constitutes socially acceptable discourse."

"As long as the range of socially acceptable discourse includes punching Nazis."

We're laughing again, but it hurts a little less like this. "Always."

Thanks to my free period, I'm done with class by lunch on Tuesdays and Thursdays, and Tuesday afternoons, I see my therapist. She and a few other adolescent psychologists rent some extremely overpriced square footage in Hearst Village so they can be close to the school that houses their clientele. I started seeing Eleanor for gender dysphoria. That's what you do when you're a transgender teen looking to start hormone replacement therapy. You jump through the psychiatric hoops before they let you jump through the medical ones. I read so many horror stories online about trans kids being denied medical care for not being the right kind of trans, but Eleanor wasn't like that. I never had to *prove* my transness to her. My testimony was enough, just like it is for any cisgender kid. I said I was a boy, and Eleanor believed me.

I kept seeing her after she signed off on HRT because I had a pesky undiagnosed mood disorder. Bipolar, which I might have been able to ignore if not for the expiration date on Dad's promise of unconditional love—and the major depressive episode it provoked. Eleanor helps. So does the psychiatrist I see once a month downtown. So does the little pink pill I take every night.

Sometimes it works; sometimes it doesn't. I'm still a work in progress, and sometimes I'm okay with that.

My session runs late, and the waiting room's not empty when I leave. In the armchair closest to the door sits a familiar face. Ralph Myers, twin brother to my friend and Club Français comrade Rachel. We're in the same classes—all the IB kids are—but I don't really know him as anything other than "Rachel's twin brother." They're cut from the same genetic cloth—pale skin, wavy brown hair, freckles—but that's where the similarities end. Rachel's bold to the point of brazen; Ralph's quiet to the point of weird. I know he's smart, at least as smart as his pre-premed sister, maybe even smarter. He never raises his hand in class, but he always gives the right answer when teachers call on him. He's a man of few words, but they're always exactly the right ones. He's always there, at the edge of the frame, the blurry edges of the photograph. I know Rachel invites him to hang out with us, but he never does. I wish he would. I never know what to make of him, not his elbow patches or bow ties or stoic silence. He's an enigma, and now he's sitting here waiting to see Eleanor or one of her colleagues.

His posture is painfully straight, like he's been called to the principal's office. His hands are in his lap, and he's picking at his cuticles. When he looks up at me, his eyes are clear-water blue behind his thick black-rimmed glasses.

I look down at him, petrified in place, fists clasped around my backpack straps. We stare at each other silently, guiltily. We've caught each other in the commission of a crime. I'm not ashamed of my bipolar diagnosis, therapy visits, or mood stabilizers. Still, stigma makes secrets of the truths inside my skull. It's not my shame that's the problem; it's everyone else's. I don't want them to look at me like my diagnosis is a CDC warning label branded on my forehead.

I don't know why Ralph's here any more than he knows why I'm here.

It doesn't matter. That's another lesson Dad taught me about politics. When you have dirt on someone and they have dirt on you, neither of you can make a move. Stalemate.

So I nod, and Ralph nods, and I try to smile, but I'm pretty sure it looks like I'm having a stroke. I know I should say something, anything, but I don't have a clue where to start.

I'm saved by my buzzing phone. Pablo's waiting for me.

Twenty minutes after the final bell, campus is already a ghost town. Only a handful of stragglers haunt the halls.

I jog through the empty breezeways. Posters for student council candidates flutter in the wind. One has already fallen to the ground. Shoe prints emboss the yellow construction paper.

Pablo parks near the football field, which is, conveniently, located on the exact opposite side of campus from Hearst Village. The shortest distance between two points takes me across the quad, into jock domain. The gym floods my field of view. I'm about to round the corner when I hear voices.

At first they're nothing more than indistinct hisses, a trick of the wind. I'm sure I've imagined them. Still, I stop short, palms braced on my thighs. My lungs heave and shudder. It's quiet. Calm. Still as the surface of a freshwater lake.

"What did you say?" A deep voice. Husky, angry.

Fabric rustles, then someone coughs.

"I asked you. What did you say?" Louder this time.

"Just leave me *alone*." Higher pitch, but still in the typical cisgender male vocal range. There's something about the cadence of his speech, the barest hint of an accent, and—

When I peek around the corner, I see Benji, cornered by a trio of jocks. They're all uniformed in the same letterman jacket Pablo wears. The only one I know is Henry McIver, who hangs back from the others, surveying the scene with impassive eyes. He's IB, but even if I didn't know him, I'd still recognize him from the hundreds of student-body-president flyers leafleting the corridors. Henry's got a quarterback's build. He's not small, but he looks it next to his linebacker friends. His red hair stands out like a bull's-eye.

"We can't do that, Benny," says the linebacker with the husky voice. He has a crew cut that screams "JROTC."

"You're a fag, Benny," says the third guy. A San Francisco Giants baseball cap cloaks his features.

"The worst part," says Crew Cut, "is you don't even try to hide it. That prissy shirt. Those limp wrists. You paint your fucking nails. You're asking for it. You're begging for it, aren't you? Just begging"—his fists clench in the floral linen of Benji's shirt—"for any attention we'll give you."

"Isn't that right?" asks Baseball Cap, leaning in close.

"What the fuck are you doing?" I yell, because I have no sense of self-preservation.

Three sets of eyes turn to me.

There's a blur of dark, a gash across the screen, and something snaps. Squelches. Crew Cut and Benji are a tangle of limbs, throwing punches that I hear rather than see.

I sprint forward, but the brawl's over by the time I reach them. Henry's got his arms hooked through Crew Cut's, holding him back. Crew Cut is cradling his face, hiding the damage, but there's murder in his eyes.

"Benji." I reach for his shoulder and tug him toward me. "Benji, are you okay?"

He turns, spots of red splattered over his skin. His lip is split, but he's smiling. Blood dribbles down his teeth. "I'm great," he says, and suddenly, I understand why.

Benji threw the first punch.

THREE

THE CITY IS FULL OF NOISES. COUNTERINTUI-
tive, I know. Santa Julia, California, is barely a city. Despite
being the largest semi-metropolitan area between San Francisco and Sacramento, it feels like the kind of small town
Mark Twain would've written about. Suburban sprawl
stretches the city thin, rawhide pulled taut over the face of
a drum. There are cows here, too. People forget that: wine
country isn't just a checkerboard valley of vineyards. There
are dairy farms full of happy California cows and bleating
sheep in fluffy white coats. North of the Bay Area, California
is still mostly frontier country. Santa Julia is something in
between.

I catalog the ambulance shrieks and wolf howls long into
the night. I lie on top of my comforter in my trunks and my
undershirt and stare up at the ceiling. Every so often cars
careen by on the street below, and their headlights project
searchlights on the screen. Shadows wink in and out of focus.

I give up eventually. The glow-in-the-dark hands on my watch say two a.m., but it feels later. Maybe the battery's dead; maybe time's stopped. Maybe I'm stuck.

I've been moving in slow motion since the fight. Since I took Benji by the hand and marched him over to the main office. Since he ducked into an unlocked classroom and begged me not to tell anyone. Since I agreed.

On my free ride home, Pablo asked what took me so long, and I laughed it off. He didn't see through me. After all, I have years of practice from hiding my dysphoria. I know how to wave and smile and pretend I'm not gritting my teeth. I'm good at faking it. Later, Mom and I ate Chinese take-out, and we made small talk about the newest Shondaland show. Mom pretended not to mind that I ordered the kung pao chicken extra spicy, and I pretended nothing was wrong. I went upstairs and did my homework and watched CNN political analyst Don Lemon systematically dismantle the Republican tax plan.

But I can't sleep, and there's no point trying. I don't turn on the lights because Mom might notice. I let Monty into my room, and he licks my hand and curls up at my feet on the bed. I blink against my laptop's pale blue glow and stare at my Google News alerts, which haven't changed since morning. On Messenger, all my friends are offline except Jenny. Reliable, kindred-spirit, night-owl Jenny Chu, who may well be plotting world domination in her bedroom two streets over. The little green circle beside her profile picture is luminous, radiant. It would be so easy to click and type and spill.

Except Benji asked me not to.

I need a distraction—something, anything—so I try looking up Ralph on social media, but he's not on Twitter or Instagram. There's just a perfunctory Facebook profile, bare-bones facts. Hometown: Santa Julia. Education: UHS. His wall consists entirely of links from his mother, their subjects ranging from college rankings to unconventional babka recipes. He doesn't have photo albums; there's just the photos Rachel's tagged him in over the years, group shots at school where he's always in the background. Then there's his profile picture. It's a few years old. He's riddled with acne, braces threatening to break through his broad smile. There's a middle-aged man beside him, and aside from the receding hairline, the resemblance is uncanny, right down to the cashmere quarter-zip. They're out in nature, surrounded by fat, ancient redwoods, wind whipping Ralph's longer curls. That's when I close the window. Even though it's a public profile, I feel like I did in the waiting room, like I've glimpsed something illicit through a cracked door.

An hour wears by like acetone through paint while I read academic articles about the Overton window without absorbing a single word.

So I put on my noise-canceling headphones and turn on *The West Wing*. Comfort bingeing. Monty jumps up on my

24

legs and dozes off while I watch smart people work together to make real change. It's cheesy and dated and embarrassingly nondiverse, but it never fails to remind me that somehow, somewhere, in some universe that's not entirely removed from this one, it is possible for ordinary people to make the world an extraordinary place.

I keep on watching until dawn.

UHS doesn't have a school newspaper. Not anymore. The journalism program was a victim of California's vicious budget cuts fifteen years back. At least, that's the official story. There's a conspiracy theory stoners like to tell behind the bleachers that the administration shut the program down after a power-hungry staff writer with Ivy League aspirations orchestrated an elaborate coup to overthrow the paper's editor in chief.

I'm pretty sure that's just a myth.

What we do have, in place of a school-sanctioned publication, is a blog. Although junior Amber Carr styles herself as an investigative journalist, it's *Dystopia High*'s salacious blind items that have garnered her a coveted verified checkmark on Twitter. All anonymous tidbits on who's dating whom, who's cheating on whom, and who got wasted at Dante Gomez's party last Friday night and vomited all over the topiary. That kind of stuff. I don't know most of the players who populate the UHS rumor mill, but I still follow the blog on Twitter. Everyone does.

That's where I see it. On Twitter. Loitering in ZP's room on Wednesday morning, I scroll past political commentary, puppy pictures, and queer culture memes in a sleep-deprived haze. Then the photo blows up like a mushroom cloud on the horizon. *Dystopia High* has Crew Cut's headshot, his splotchy pink face swollen and mottled with purple. Stitches lace one eyebrow. His nose is distended, distorted. The headline reads "AFTER-HOURS BRAWL: TREVOR DALTON TELLS ALL."

I click the link, but I can barely read the post. The words swim together. Trevor Dalton's saying Benji Dean punched him viciously, maliciously. Trevor Dalton's playing the victim, and fellow football teammates Kevin Guo and Henry McIver are backing him up. "Benjamin Dean," Amber writes, "did not respond to requests for comment."

FOUR

THE NEWS DOESN'T BREAK. IT *SHATTERS.*

Thanks to the bureaucratic hell of block scheduling, it's lunch before my friends and I are all in the same place, out in the campus boondocks for our weekly Club Français meeting. The thermostat broke last spring, and our overworked custodian still hasn't had a chance to fix it. Which means it's sweltering, and we're all simmering.

Except Benji, who isn't here.

I hold the floor. Kind of. I'm standing at the front of the room, but I'm not leading the meeting. I haven't written out an agenda. All thoughts of recruitment drives and crêpe bake sales have evaporated. Instead, I'm pacing, because I can't sit down when my body's vibrating like a tuning fork.

I'm not the only one. Jenny perches atop a desk. Her black fishtail braid hangs over her shoulder. Her tweed dress shorts and button-up chiffon tank reveal large swaths of skin. Her knee jiggles up and down like a jackhammer. She's my best friend, but you wouldn't know it from the way she's looking at me now. "You knew?" she asks, her eyes perilously dark. "You were there, and you didn't see fit to, I don't know, *tell anyone* until Amber Carr's gossip column was calling for Benji's head?"

"Benji asked me not to tell."

"Benji got punched in the face," says Jenny, direct as always. "He might not have been thinking clearly."

"Technically, he came out of it with cosmetic damage," says Rachel Myers. She's sitting cross-legged on the floor, fanning herself with a flattened raisin box. Sweat glues strands of her short, wavy brown hair to her face. "Trevor has a broken nose and five stitches."

"You're not on his side, are you?" asks Nadia Kadir, Rachel's girlfriend. They're still in the honeymoon phase of their promposal-turned-something-more, but Nadia's expression implies Rachel's flippant comments could change that.

"Babe." Rachel tugs on the hem of Nadia's hijab to straighten it. "Of course I'm on Benji's side. I'm just saying, it's not like he had a concussion. He knew what he was asking Mark."

Nadia's cheeks flush. Of course, it could just be the heat. Athleisure leggings and a long-sleeve shirt sheathe her curvy figure. I'm not sure how she does it. I'd be burning up in her modest garb. "Mark," she asks, "what did Benji say when you checked in with him?"

"Um." Guilt rattles through me. When Benji begged me to leave it alone, I thought he wanted me to leave *him* alone, too. I never second-guessed that impulse. Even this morning, when I saw the article, my gut told me to set the record straight with Amber or run to Principal Flynn or just beg Jenny to help me fix this. I can tell myself I was honoring my promise to Benji, but maybe I was wrong.

"Ya Allah save me from the emotional illiteracy of teenage boys," Nadia mutters.

"I tried texting him after wrestling," Pablo says. "No reply. But don't you have art with him second period?"

"He wasn't there."

"Has *anyone* actually talked to him in the last four hours?" Rachel asks.

"It's not like him to miss a meeting," observes Jenny.

Now that I think about it, Benji has *never* missed a Club Français meeting. We see him once a week like clockwork and sporadically outside school-sanctioned Club Français events. He's our friend, yes, but we don't invite him to our boozy coed sleepovers. We say it's because he's fifteen, but those nights are when we get our most intimate. When we tell secrets too fragile to survive in the light of day.

Honestly, I'm not even sure I have Benji's phone number. We're friends on Facebook, of course, and Club Français has a group chat. But Benji and I aren't the kind of friends who talk, except to exchange small talk over the hoods of our laptops.

"Fuck," curses Pablo, and we all turn to look at him. True to his all-American letterman jacket, he's usually a total goody two-shoes. He never swears. "Did anyone know this was going on?"

There it is. The question that kept me up last night. My legs give out, and I slide down the wall and hug my knees to my chest.

Since we realized last year that everyone in Club Français was queer, we've treated it as an underground pride club. Our safe space. We don't fly a rainbow flag in the window. Madame Lavoisier doesn't know. But *we* do. We talk more about queer issues than the actual straighter-than-the-hyphen-in-the-name Gay-Straight Alliance. We've talked about coming out and PDA and every flavor of queer erasure. But we've never talked about bullying at UHS. On a national scale, sure. But never in our own halls. Never once did Benji tell us he was being bullied.

We exchange guilty glances, and I know we're all thinking the same thing:

Maybe we never gave him the chance.

Then the door bursts open. Blinding sunlight obscures the shape in the doorway. Tall, thin, gangly—

It's Ralph, Rachel's quiet-weird twin brother, and he's pink in the face. He looks nothing like the skittish, reserved boy I crossed paths with in my therapist's waiting room yesterday. I've never seen him look so determined. "Rach," he huffs. "Why aren't you answering your messages?"

"Because the reception out here sucks?"

Ralph shakes his head. It's only then that he steps fully

into the room, and Benji steps out from behind him.

Benji, in a black turtleneck unbefitting of California summer, with berry bruises coloring his cheeks and jaw. He smiles, then winces when the motion stretches his split lip. "Sorry we're late."

"Where the heck have you been?" Pablo exclaims, going full mother hen. His muscles are tense, hands twitching at his sides, only barely keeping himself from hopping off the counter and going to check for himself that Benji's all in one piece.

He's standing at the periphery of our circle, close enough to lean against the wall or run out the door if he needs to. Ralph stands sentry, hands stuffed in his pockets and concern furrowing his brow.

"I was *summoned*," Benji says, gesticulating wildly, his nails free of polish, "to the main office before zero period was over. I spent the first hour waiting in the lobby with sympathy hot chocolate from the secretary while Trevor cozied up to Principal Flynn. Then Flynn questioned *me* for an hour, guilty until proven innocent, like she was just waiting for an excuse to use the interrogation techniques she learned in the Marines. Then, just when I thought I was up for bail, they brought in Trevor and his parents and put my mom on speaker since she can't just up and leave the office like other parents. So we rehashed the whole thing *again*. Flynn declared me persona non grata on campus until I make a decision, so I was just killing time in Hearst Village until

Ralph here decided to smuggle me back on campus to talk to all of you, and—"

"Stop," Jenny says, and Benji does, because it's Jenny, and she could probably get the earth itself to stop turning if she wanted. "What decision?"

Benji blinks, like he's only just now remembering the rest of us are here. "Flynn gave me an ultimatum. Apologize to Trevor or take a one-week suspension."

"Apologize?" Pablo asks, a sharp edge to his voice. "Apologize for *what*?"

"You know what for. I punched first. So, obviously, it's my fault. All of it."

"Bullshit," I say, keeping my voice even, despite my shaking fists. "You didn't start anything. Trevor and Kevin did, with their threats and slurs. You were fighting *back*."

"Hard to say I was 'fighting back' when I started it. And I did."

"Words are their own kind of violence," Nadia says intently. "And Flynn knows that."

Benji shrugs. "Doesn't matter. All Flynn has is my word. It's a he said—he said, and there's three of them against one of me. But the fight? There's incontrovertible evidence."

"It's in the student handbook," Jenny lectures like a professor to a class of kindergartners. "Zero-tolerance policy for fighting."

"But there are . . ." Rachel sputters. "Mitigating circumstances!"

"'Zero-tolerance' means the circumstances don't mitigate a damn thing," Benji mumbles. "Not without proof."

Rachel, bless her heart, has never been political. She still believes in the system. Hell, she thought Pete Buttigieg was the height of queer politics until Nadia sat her down and gave her the Talk—about neoliberalism, that is. She just absorbs everything Benji says and nods. "Okay, so no apology. I mean, I never understood why schools thought being suspended was a real punishment, anyway. You can just stay at home, watch old seasons of *Project Runway*, and finish those *Queer Eye* recaps where you talk about, what was it—"

"How *Queer Eye* imposes a homonormative model of LGBTQ identities that isn't particularly 'queer' at all." Nadia nudges her girlfriend, smiling as she turns to Benji. "Which you're *wrong* about, by the way. Just because they're focusing on *trends*—"

Benji looks up to the ceiling, trying to hide whatever's going on behind his eyes. "Those essays won't matter when colleges see the word 'suspension' on my transcript in two years."

"Oh," Rachel says softly.

Because maybe, to some other kid, suspension would sound like a paid vacation. But we're the IB kids, the nerds, the ones who started studying for the SATs when other kids were studying for spelling bees. Having a pristine transcript is *step one*. I'm not sure a letter of rec from a Nobel laureate would be enough to get you past a cutthroat Ivy admissions committee with a suspension for fighting on your permanent record.

"I—" Benji turns, helplessly, to Ralph, who's been so inconspicuous this entire time. Ralph nods encouragingly, and Benji admits, "I don't know what to do. I don't want to apologize, but y'all don't get it. I can't afford to screw up. I don't—"

I'm about to cut in. The safety's off, and the words are loaded like bullets in my throat. I'm about to tell him he didn't screw up, I was there, I saw everything, Flynn should be suspending Trevor *and Kevin* outright—

But Jenny beats me to the punch. "It's simple," she says, and I breathe easier, knowing she's got this. "Take the deal."

"What the fuck?" I ask—or maybe yell.

Jenny shoots me a disapproving glance before returning her attention to Benji. She sounds every bit the jaded, dispassionate defense attorney when she says, "Think of it as a plea bargain. Suffer this minor indignity, which everyone will forget by the end of the week, and you'll protect your transcript. That's all that matters."

"Indignity?" I protest. "What about *integrity*? How is any of this fair? What kind of fucked-up system makes a victim choose between apologizing to their bully and serving time like they're the one who did something wrong?" I turn to Benji. "You didn't. And you shouldn't have to choose."

"No one said the system was fair, Mark," Jenny replies.

"But it's the one we're living in."

"What if there were another way to work the system?" Nadia asks. "Trevor has to apologize for his part in the fight, too, right? What if you take the deal, make your apology, but don't accept Trevor's? That's a reasonable compromise, right? You can protect your integrity and your record."

Benji shakes his head. "Anything short of full-throated display of reconciliation isn't going to cut it."

"Then," Rachel tries, "you accept Trevor's apology with your fingers crossed behind your back, and we'll all know you don't mean it."

"Wait, babe, that's totally it." Nadia presses a quick kiss to Rachel's cheek. "Benji, what if you accept the apology, but go to Amber and tell your story?"

"That kinda undermines the point of a full-throated display of reconciliation."

"*Dystopia High* is an independent publication."

"Freedom of the press!" Rachel adds.

"It won't matter." Jenny shrugs. "The librarians let Amber use their office as her HQ. The blog's effectively published on school property, so Flynn would argue that that makes any statement admissible to the disciplinary board."

Nevertheless, Nadia persists. "Pablo, what if you called your parents' lawyer? Maybe they could do something, put pressure on the school, I don't know—"

"I don't want that," Benji insists. The way he's hugging

his arms around his chest makes him so small. So young, too young to be looking up YouTube tutorials on how to cake concealer over bruises.

"Benji," Pablo says softly. "The first thing you said was that you don't want to apologize. So don't. We'll help you figure out college later. Maybe that's when we'll talk to the lawyers—or at least some counselors—but for now . . . don't let Flynn intimidate you into confessing to a crime you didn't commit. Don't apologize to Trevor for having the audacity to be yourself. Don't let them take any more from you than they already have." He clears his throat in the perfect quiet. "Mark, back me up here?"

I open my mouth, summoning up the speech. It should be easy. I know what I believe. Indignity at the cost of integrity isn't worth the price of salt.

Don't let them take any more from you than they already have, Pablo said.

Take what you can get, Dad sneered when he sat across from me at that mile-long dining room table in Marin, dictating the terms of our agreement. My name, but no legal name change. Hormones, but no surgery. A new life, but no ties to my past. So many compromises so I could live as my true self. Except . . . is it really the truth if all the details are redacted for the sake of homeland security?

Staying stealth isn't lying, but sometimes it feels like it. I'm proud of being trans, and it's not even that I'm ashamed of being closeted. I just wish I'd been able to choose for myself. Instead, I let Dad take my decision away. Who am I to lecture anyone about indignity?

"I'm sorry," I say. "Jenny's right. You have to think about your future. If that means gritting your teeth through a fake apology, then—we all know the truth."

The way Pablo's looking at me means he's going to blast all of Taylor's revenge songs on our drive home, but Rachel and Nadia are both murmuring their assent. Jenny's perfectly still, not smug in the least. And Benji—

Benji's shaking. Head hung, dejected and defeated, he looks like he really did go through those enhanced interrogation techniques and barely made it out alive.

Ralph steps forward and puts a steadying hand on Benji's arm. He surveys the rest of us, the corners of his mouth pinched and drawn. This can't be what he expected when he snuck Benji back on campus to get our advice. His gaze settles on me last and lingers. His disappointment smarts more than it should.

Finally, he turns back to Benji. He tilts his head down close to Benji's ear, but he speaks loud enough for all of us to hear. "You have to do what's right for you. None of us can tell you what that is."

Except, we just did.

And the unredacted truth of it is, however disappointed Ralph may be in me, I'm more disappointed in myself.

FIVE

THEORY OF KNOWLEDGE IS EPISTEMOLOGY FOR beginners. TOK, as we call it, is the capstone course for IB diploma candidates. Half philosophy and half rhetoric, it's all about what we know and how we know it. Or whether we actually know anything at all.

Today we're talking about rationalism. Or, ZP's lecturing us about rationalism.

As opposed to empiricists, who believed you could only trust your own five senses, rationalists argued that other forms of knowledge—logic, math, morality—were also innate. ZP goes on and on about Descartes and Kant, and normally I'd be all in, but it's his reference to Leibniz—the guy who invented calculus contemporaneously with Newton but gets none of the credit—that snags my attention. Because God fell under the umbrella of innate knowledge for the rationalists, Leibniz made a further inference. God makes no mistakes, he argued, and God made this world. Ergo, it must needs be the best of all possible worlds.

Here's where I'm calling bullshit.

I'm on the fence about God, personally. Dad was raised Catholic, and he made sure I went to catechism, also known as Sunday School: Deluxe Edition. I don't know about God, but I know I don't believe the rest of it. God sure as hell isn't infallible.

If God were infallible, he wouldn't have put me in this body. He wouldn't have let hate dictate the course of human civilization. He wouldn't have made us creatures who prey on difference.

If this were the best of all possible worlds, I wouldn't have to hide the fact that I'm trans. My identity wouldn't be a death sentence for Dad's political career. Dad's love wouldn't be contingent on whether I'm an asset or a liability.

If this were the best of all possible worlds, Benji wouldn't be bullied for being gay. He wouldn't feel like he has to hide it from his friends. He wouldn't have to choose between indignity and integrity.

If this were the best of all possible worlds, I wouldn't get a *Dystopia High* news alert announcing Benji's suspension.

BREAKING NEWS: STATEMENT
FROM BENJAMIN DEAN
[Editor's Note: At the author's request, comments have been disabled. —AC]

If you follow this blog, then you've seen Trevor Dalton's allegations against me. I'm writing this post to confirm them.

Yesterday, shortly after the final bell, I ran into Trevor and two other members of the football team. They engaged me in conversation. A few minutes later, I punched Trevor. He punched back. His teammates and another witness helped break up the fight—but not before I deviated Trevor's septum.

That's how Trevor tells it, and I don't dispute these facts. But there's a difference between facts and truth.

The *truth* is that Trevor "engaged me in conversation" by pushing me against the gym wall and spitting homophobic slurs in my face.

This isn't the first time Trevor Dalton, Kevin Guo, and others have engaged in this behavior. I've been subjected to a pattern of bullying as long as I can remember. I've been victimized for my size, my wardrobe, my makeup— and all the assumptions these facts invited about my sexual orientation before I ever came out. For years, I've been taunted, shoved into lockers, and harassed with thinly veiled threats of sexual violence.

Trevor claims that he was defending himself against my aggression. Well, I was defending myself against his.

When I explained all of this to Principal Flynn this morning, she blamed me for not coming forward sooner.

If only I had "proof," she said, maybe the administration could have done something. Maybe then, she told me, this "mess" could have been avoided. While she's deeply sorry for any suffering I've endured on school grounds, she says it's clear I acted beyond the bounds of self-defense.

So she gave me a choice. Apologize to Trevor, or accept a suspension that will go on my permanent record.

It's an easy choice, right? Craft a few delicate words. Grin and bear it until this all goes away.

Except it won't just *go away*. Apologizing would say that Trevor's actions are excusable. I'd be giving him and his friends permission to keep on terrorizing kids like me.

Here's my message to Trevor, and to anyone else who takes issue with a high-femme fag walking these halls:

I'm not sorry.

After class, I corner Henry in the hallway. "We need to talk."

Henry doesn't even look at me. And why should he? We've never exchanged a single pleasantry beyond class debates about the constitutionality of gun control or symbolism in *Crime and Punishment*. He's the star quarterback of our losing football team, and merely deigns to grace IB classes with his presence. I'm the new kid who turned out to be a giant leftist nerd. Not worthy of his notice. He rocks his head from side to side, working out a crick in his neck. "Sorry, Mark. I've got football practice."

I catch him by the pleather sleeve of his letterman jacket. "No."

He glares at me, finally seeing me as something other than a speck of dirt on his cleats. He doesn't like what he sees.

Even though I'm the one with him in my grip, I'm pinned. My heart rate ticks up, marking me as prey in the presence of a predator. My body still remembers what it's like to be a girl in a room full of men, the threat of violence a constant knife at the hollow of my throat. It never mattered that I wasn't a girl; the girl the world saw was proof enough.

Now Henry's looking too closely. I'm afraid he'll see my pecs are too swollen to be muscle. My hips are too wide. My feet don't fill my shoes. My body is a minefield.

"Fine," Henry growls, shaking off my hand, "but not *here*."

We're still in the hallway. The crowd flows around us, oblivious to the tension between us.

Then Henry ducks into the boys' bathroom, and I follow him, bewildered. A skittish freshman flees at the first wave of Henry's hand. We're alone in here, among the tiny gray tiles and graffitied slurs. The stench of urine clogs my senses. I avoid this place in favor of the single-stall restrooms near the office whenever possible.

The squalor doesn't faze Henry. He leans back against a sink, his arms crossed over his chest. "Well?" he demands. "What did you want to talk about?"

That's when I get it. Henry doesn't see me as prey; he sees

42

me as a fellow predator. I pass. Henry doesn't doubt my masculinity. He has no reason to doubt it. Everyone is cisgender
until proven guilty. Of course I'm a man. I grabbed him by
the arm, as if I were entitled to his time. Only a man would
dare wield such casual violence.

My hands are slick, grimy. I wipe my palms on my jeans,
but the guilt doesn't go away. "You know exactly what we
need to talk about, Henry."

"There's nothing to say about that." Except, if he really
believed that, we wouldn't be here.

"You were there, same as me. You know Benji doesn't
deserve to be suspended."

His eyes flash. "I know what I saw."

"Which was?"

"That sophomore punched Trevor. They fought. I broke it
up. You helped."

"I helped." My mouth is dry; the words are salt on my
tongue.

"You helped," he agrees, nodding, as if he's doing me a
favor and I should be grateful for his judicious retelling of
events.

"What about what happened before the fight?"

"What happened?" Henry shrugs. It's a taunt. He asks it
the way he asks existential questions during TOK. "There
was a conversation."

"That's what you're calling it."

"What would you call it?"

"Bullying. Harassment. Provocation."

"That's a matter of opinion."

"It's a matter of record," I argue. "Benji's statement is perfectly clear."

"Yes." Henry nods, shocking me off-balance. "He confirmed the facts. Motive doesn't matter when you indict yourself, which he did. That sophomore hit a fellow student."

"*That sophomore* has a name, and your homophobic meathead buddy hit back."

"You know UHS has a zero-tolerance policy for violence. *Benjamin* knows that. And even so, he chose suspension."

"Only because he didn't have another choice."

"He could've apologized." Henry shakes his head. "It's a stupid loophole in the handbook, really. An apology wouldn't *unbreak* Trevor's nose. It's not fair."

"*Fair?*" My fists twitch at my sides.

"When I'm student body president, I'll make sure that 'zero tolerance' means no excuses. No apologies. No mercy for instigators." He's not looking at me anymore. His gaze is fixed on the bare bulb dangling from the ceiling. It flickers and buzzes in clear violation of the school's safety code.

"But you'll make sure your friends on the football team get leniency for their infractions. You'll let bullies roam free and terrorize anyone who dares to be different."

"Like I said, Mark, I'm sure you mean well, but you don't

44

know what you saw."

"I saw enough," I say, reckless against all reason. I'm closer to him now. Close enough to smell the faint residue of Irish Spring. Close enough to see the hole near the collar of his T-shirt. Close enough to see the whites of his eyes. "I saw enough to know you stood by while your buddies bullied my friend. I saw enough to know you don't deserve to be student body president."

"Sure," he scoffs. "What are you going to do about it?"

I don't know. I barely know why I said it. I meant it as a schoolyard jibe. I didn't expect to have to back it up. But if there's anything I've learned about masculinity, it's that you have to show bravado even when you've got nothing to back it up.

So I smile at him. Bare my teeth. And say, "I'm going to stop you, Henry. I'm going to make sure you lose the election."

SIX

JENNY'S WAITING ON THE FRONT STEPS WHEN I get home. Her dad's faded Dartmouth sweatshirt slopes off one shoulder. "Hi," she says.

"Hi." The lights are off, which means Mom's still at work. We could go inside. We could sit in my room, on the bed I didn't sleep in last night, and let those four gray walls close in. "Do you want to take a walk?"

Jenny opens her mouth to point out that she walked *here*, thank you very much, but thinks better of it. "Sure."

"Let's take Monty."

She smiles then, because even though Jennifer Chu's career ambitions can best be described as Olivia Pope, she still can't resist that furry face.

Monty runs up to me as soon as I unlock the door. He brushes against my legs, whining and keening and slobbering all over my hands. Jenny distracts him with tactical head pats while I clip on his lead.

The three of us walk up the hill. Monty barks at cars, but Jenny and I don't say a word. We make our way to the end of the cul-de-sac, where the sidewalk leads to Hollis Park's upper playground.

This one's empty, like it usually is. There's a nicer complex down near the entrance, with a nice gazebo for parents and nannies to take shelter in. That's where the kids usually go. Sometimes I think the city has forgotten about this place. The grass is wild, overgrown. Rust varnishes the metal play structures. One of the picnic tables is missing a plank. This park is imperfect. One of the only places in Utopia Heights that hasn't been plucked and groomed and fussed over until it's picture-perfect.

That's why it's my favorite place in Santa Julia.

I let Monty off his lead on the lawn. He promptly finds a squirrel to chase. He woofs in glee, while the squirrel appears more annoyed than concerned. Even though he's fully grown, Monty is still tiny. Hard to perceive as a threat.

Jenny's hands are in her pockets. Her gladiator sandals are out of place in the dirt.

"Swings?" I ask.

"Yes, please."

We march through sand of questionable cleanliness and claim the twin swings. The chains creak under our weight, and my exhaustion sinks into me.

The sun is impossibly high in the sky. This day has gone

on for years, empires risen and fallen since I woke up yesterday morning. I don't know how it isn't sunset yet.

Jenny pumps her legs like a pro, bending and straightening her knees at precisely the optimum rhythm for maximum aerodynamic potential. I'm more clumsy. I'm clumsy at most things involving my body, thanks to years of strategic dissociation. It doesn't help that I'm going through a second puberty right on the heels of my first.

"I think I owe you an apology," I say to the bright white sun.

"You think?"

"I should have told you what happened. I didn't realize what could happen. What *would* happen. You would've known. You always know what to do."

Jenny falls back, gravity yanking her down to earth. "I couldn't have predicted this."

Maybe there's a law of physics I've neglected to account for. Maybe small town plus queer kids always equals bullying. Maybe I've been naive to think this far-left, granola-obsessed hippie haven in Northern California was immune.

Maybe there's no such thing as a safe space in a world like this.

"Did you know?" She didn't say anything earlier, but maybe she couldn't, in front of everyone. It's different when it's just the two of us; she knows everything about me.

She's quiet for so long, I assume she didn't hear me. The

48

wind howls. Monty barks. Birds and cicadas chirp to their own beat. The park is alive with noise. "No," she murmurs. "But I should have."

"Jen."

"Can you honestly tell me you're not thinking the same thing?"

My silence is indictment enough.

"Yeah," she says, her voice low and rough. "Benji's not like us. We're all birds of a feather, but the rest of us fly as a flock. We're in all the same classes; we're always together. There's security in that. We may be the nerdy queer kids, but we're the nerdy queer kids, plural. Benji's alone. He's doesn't have friends in the sophomore class. And the rest of us, maybe we hide it better. You're stealth; you pass like any other cisgender guy. No one knows I'm aromantic because I still hook up with guys, even though I don't date. No one knows Pablo's asexual because he *does* date, and they figure he's just too modest to engage in locker room talk about his *conquests*. Nadia and Rachel are discreet because of Nadia's religion. It's different for Benji. There's a bull's-eye on his back."

Just because Benji has the audacity to break a few ironclad male gender stereotypes. Difference adheres to his skin like flypaper. It makes him vulnerable, and we should have known. Should have asked. Should have watched out for him. Should have done anything other than pretend scenic wine-country vistas and white picket fences meant we were safe.

49

I slow to a halt. Dust coats my throat. "We have to do something."

"Benji made his choice."

"It was a false choice—one he never should've been forced to make."

"It's the choice the student handbook gave him."

"I know," I say. *"I know."* I've read the student handbook. I know the bylaws; I know them well enough to know they're shit. "That's why we have to do something."

"Mark, don't torture yourself by relitigating this."

I shake my head vehemently. "We were wrong earlier. Telling Benji to apologize and just . . . move on. He was right. Appeasement makes us part of the problem. We can't just stand idly by and shut our eyes and stick our fingers in our ears and pretend everything's A-OK. That's the Dan Savage model of political progress. Nothing gets better if we all just pray for the day we can get the fuck out of this place. That's the attitude that enabled Trevor and Kevin and who knows who else. It's the reason Benji didn't feel like he could come to us. If we do nothing, if we sit back and wait for the world to change, it won't. It'll happen again. If not to Benji, then to the next gay kid who walks the halls alone. When it happens then, it'll be on us, for not doing *anything*—"

"Mark," Jenny cuts in, her urgency the only thing that breaks my feverish monologue. She drags her legs through the sand until she comes to a stop. She leans toward me like

she wants to reach out, but there's too much distance between our swings. "Railing against structural inequality isn't going to help Benji."

Jenny's right about one thing. Benji made his choice. He stood up against the system, and I—

I start swinging again, listless. Yesterday, Trevor pushed Benji against the gym wall. Today, I grabbed Henry's arm, hard enough to bruise. "I may have done a stupid thing," I confess once the bile in my throat has settled.

Jenny quirks an eyebrow. "May have?"

"Okay, I definitely did a stupid thing."

"Are you going to tell me, or do I have to guess?" she asks, just this side of sardonic. "This could be fun. Did you slash Trevor Dalton's tires? No, wait. Did you confront Flynn? Did you rant at *her* about structural inequality? Please tell me you're about to go viral."

I suppress a full-body shiver, because Dad can't disown me over a viral video of a confrontation that never happened. "I kind of threatened Henry McIver."

"How do you 'kind of' threaten someone? Did you wag a plastic knife at him?"

I wrap my hands tighter around the chains. When I close my eyes, I almost mistake the tang of rust for blood. "Henry was bragging about what happened. Talking shit about Benji. Saying he got what he deserved. Then he had the gall to start *campaigning.* He said that when he's student body president, he'll make sure our zero-tolerance policies get tougher, but bullying? That's subjective. Too difficult to enforce, you know?"

"Mark, did you slash Henry McIver's tires?"

"I told him I was going to tank his campaign. I *vowed* to tank his campaign, to be exact."

"How, exactly?"

"I didn't get that far."

"So you just threatened him and then made a dramatic exit?"

At least I have the common sense not to tell her my Frank Underwood moment happened in the boys' bathroom. "Pretty much."

Jenny fixes her eyes on the horizon. "When I talked to Dante after Spanish, he said he feels for Benji but can't change Henry's mind."

"I wouldn't have expected anything less from Henry's veep."

"Dante tries. Henry just doesn't care what he has to say."

"If Dante really cared, he would've said no to Henry to begin with."

Jenny shakes her head. "People don't say no to Henry."

"That's the problem." I sigh. "I guess that means I'll be helping you and Clary campaign for the next two weeks."

"About that," says Jenny. "I caught Clary on her way to cheerleading practice. I said she should do an interview with Amber immediately. Position our ticket, so to speak, as antibullying. Remind the voters that Henry just stood and watched. Clary agreed to the interview. She didn't agree about what she should say."

Dread spoils my stomach like sour milk. "What does she want to say?"

"That Benji should've apologized. Because violence is wrong, whatever the circumstances, and an eye for an eye makes the whole world blind."

"She's pulling the 'both sides to blame' card on bullying? She's president of the GSA!"

"Well," says Jenny, "as we always say, the only kind of gay in the GSA is gay-as-in-happy because they're all self-congratulatory allies patting themselves on the back for doing the bare minimum."

I shouldn't be surprised. Clarissa Cabrera only founded the GSA because she thought it would look good on college applications. That's Clary in brief. Good on paper. A padded résumé printed on heavyweight card stock, but not a lot to back it up. She takes enough IB classes to look impressive to outsiders, but opted out of the full diploma. She's all about the optics. Her approach to politics is to shake hands and smile for the photo op and leave the rest to anyone else.

Clary and Jenny are reluctant allies, or, in common parlance, frenemies. It's always been in their best interests to collaborate on student council races because they have more in common with each other than they do with Henry McIv-er's ilk. Until now.

"You have to convince her to come out in support of Benji."

Jenny snorts. "Have you met Clary? She's never more stubborn than she is when she's dead wrong."

"Change her mind. Handle her."

"You know it's not that easy."

"Then run against her."

Jenny lurches forward and almost topples off her swing. She regains her grip at the last moment, but comes to an abrupt stop. "What?"

It's the obvious solution, and Jenny solves problems. Cheating boyfriend? She'll spread a rumor he has chlamydia. Adderall addiction? She'll get a profile in the *Santa Julia Herald* highlighting your academic achievements. Slut-shaming victim? She'll write an op-ed hit job for Amber's blog about what fourth-wave feminism really means. So if the problem is that there's no good candidate, then Jenny's the person to solve it.

"If Clary's on Henry's side," I say, "we can't let her win, either. We need a third-party candidate."

"Student government isn't a two-party system, Mark."

I stall my swing. "Yeah, it kind of is. The popular kids versus everyone else. The problem is, even though the popular kids are never going to let her into the inner circle, Clary still wants to be a popular kid. She's sure as hell campaigning like one. Which means there's no candidate representing *everyone else.*"

"Even if you were right, and I'm not saying you are, I can't run for president."

"Why not? You're already running for veep. You've got nearly universal name recognition. You're the logical choice, Jen."

Jenny glances at me over her shoulder. "The papers are already filed, and even if they weren't, I'm running for veep for a reason. I don't have *time* to be student body president. I'm already running our chapter of JSA, and I have responsibilities on the state level. That's not counting IB or French Club or, you know, any semblance of a social life." She shakes her head; her braid whips in the wind. "I can't do it."

"You have to," I insist, "or else it's one of them."

She looks at me and looks at me. There's a quarry behind her eyes, her mind always working, mining, churning. "What if I had a better option?"

"Who?"

Jenny smiles. "You."

"I think I'm running for student body president," I tell my reflection that night. The full-body mirror is a new addition to my room. I used to avoid mirrors, puddles, and windows— any and every surface that betrayed the dissonance between the signal in my mind and the static on the screen. It's easier now. Not easy, exactly, but closer. Since I started testosterone, I've been able to face myself. I'm watching my body become the one I only dared imagine in the darkest hours of the night.

Tonight, I'm imagining that body telling my dad something he's not going to want to hear.

I haven't seen him in person in months. Since my birthday, back in February. I'd only been on T for a few months then. Not long enough for anything to have changed except my attitude. We FaceTime precisely once a week, but it's not the same. The pixels elide the sharper line of my jaw. Three thousand miles of fiber optics conceal the drop in my voice. Each week Dad looks right at me but ignores the facts that don't fit his chosen narrative. Dad deals with my transness the way Republicans talk about global warming: complete and categorical denial. Like most of those Republicans, it isn't about religious objection so much as political self-interest.

That's the thing about denial. Once the damage is done, intentions don't matter.

When I tell Dad what Jenny and I decided, he's going to hear me. He's going to look at me. He'll have no choice but to see me. Really see me. The son he's tried to deny.

I need to get it right.

"I'm thinking of running for student body president," I say again and immediately purse my lips. Jenny would slap me on the wrist for prevaricating like that. *Man up*, she'd say. Ignore the socialization that taught me to make myself small and take up as little space as possible. Say it again, and be sure about it. "I'm running for student body president." Be declarative. Definitive. Bluster with bravado like only a cishet white man can. "I am. I am running for student body president. I *am* running—"

"Mark?" Mom's voice, soft and plaintive.

I clear my throat. "Yeah?"

My door pops open. Mom peers in, platinum-blond hair up in a wispy ponytail, dressed in sweats and slippers even though it's still summer. "Do you have a minute?"

Technically, I should be reading *Richard II* for English, but I've read it before. "Yeah, sure."

"Come sit with me downstairs. I have a pot of cocoa on."

I follow her downstairs. Monty springs from his slumber and bounds after us.

I sit at the granite counter while Mom finishes pouring our hot cocoa. She makes it from scratch with bitter dark chocolate, cinnamon, and a hint of chili powder in mine.

Monty runs laps around the island before I toss him his favorite stuffed elephant chew toy, which he always manages to misplace. He has a donkey, too, among a veritable zoo of plush options, but he likes the elephant best. The traitor.

Mom shoots me an amused glance but doesn't point out that I'm maybe taking the symbolism of partisan politics a little too seriously.

I wrap both my hands around the mug, heat seeping through to my palms. The cocoa is too hot to drink, but I breathe it in. Sugar and spice waft up to meet me.

"So," says Mom. She taps her index finger against her mug, and I brace for impact. "What's this about you running for student body president?"

My cheeks flush crimson. "You heard that?"

"You were using your debate voice."

"I was not."

"Honey, you were *projecting*."

Okay, maybe the only way I know how to project confidence in my personal life is to imagine myself on the public stage. After all, I used to be good at it. There's a row of Best Speaker gavels on the shelf above my desk to prove it. "It's not for sure. It's just something Jenny and I were talking about."

"I thought Jenny was running with that other girl. The one who goes by a nickname from that Cassandra Clare series."

"Clary," I reply, more surprised that Mom can't conjure up the name than that she knows Cassandra Clare's, "and yeah. At least, she was until Clary proved she's a terrible candidate."

Mom sips her cocoa. She's so calm about this, while I'm as tense as a government shutdown. "Would this have anything to do with the phone call I received from the school today?"

Panic lances down my spine, but I shouldn't be surprised. I was there. Of course Benji or Trevor would've said something. "They called you?"

"Of course they called. You witnessed a fight. The real question is why I had to hear about it from Moira Flynn instead of my own son."

"It's complicated."

"Yes, everything is complicated when you're seventeen and the world is brand-new. But some things are simple. When someone draws blood, you tell your parents."

I can't meet her eyes, so I study my hot cocoa. Tiny bubbles detonate and leave craters in the foam. "I'm sorry."

"Mark, honey. I'm not angry, just concerned. That woman said Benji hit another student."

"He was provoked." In my head, I'm there again, on the dark side of the gym, watching from afar as those assholes pin Benji against the wall. Fear wells up in my chest, my lungs, my throat. When I speak, my voice comes out small and weak. "They pushed him around. Called him names. Taunted him. All because—" Saltwater fear bubbles up my trachea. "All because—"

"I know. Honey, I know."

I'm grateful I don't have to say it. I raise my mug to my lips. Let the liquid heat warm me from the inside out.

Mom watches me drink. "But I do have to ask," she adds, almost regretfully, "about your role in all of this."

Guilt. So much guilt. An avalanche of it, burying me alive. "I tried to stop them. As soon as I realized what was happening, I yelled at them to stop. I was too far away, and I pulled Benji back, but I know it wasn't enough—"

"No, honey, that isn't what I meant. I'm so proud of the man you're becoming, Mark, but I worry about you."

"Mom . . ."

"No, hear me out. I worry about you making yourself a target. When those boys decide getting Benji suspended wasn't enough, they're not just going to go after him. They'll go after his allies, too. They'll go after you."

"That's why—"

"No, Mark. You don't understand. They'll go after you for speaking up for him, but what happens if they do some digging? What if they figure it out?"

"That's not going to happen," I say with more of that false bravado. "You can tell Dad—"

"This isn't about the deal you made with your father. This is about what happens if these homophobes realize there's a transgender kid on their campus."

"I can protect myself."

"Like Benji did?"

"No," I say. "By challenging the system. That's why I want to run for student government. The current candidates aren't going to do anything to address the school's bullying problem. Clary's going to ignore it, and Henry's going to enable it.

Maybe the president's just a figurehead, but at least they have a voice, even if it's just on the PA for the morning announcements. And that's something. Because someone needs to speak out against the school's victim-blaming policies, and it shouldn't always have to be the victims themselves. Especially when they're punished for even trying. The rest of us need to do more. So, this is me doing more."

"Mark," Mom says, soft despite the warning in her voice. "Your father—"

"I know what you're going to say," I cut in. "I get it, okay? It's not just the bullies. If I run in a campus-wide election, sooner or later, whether it's blogs vetting me or candidates doing oppo research, someone will figure it out and out *me*, and that will nullify the deal with Dad. So you're going to tell me I can't run. Not now. Not like this."

Mom raises an eyebrow. "No, you really don't know what I'm going to say."

"Then what?"

"I was going to tell you that your father won't be pleased, for all the reasons you just enumerated, but his opinion doesn't matter. You have to do what's right for you. *That* is what I was going to tell you."

"Past tense?"

"I changed my mind. Now I'm telling you to *run*."

SEVEN

"IT'S ABOUT DAMN TIME," SAYS PABLO WHEN I tell him the next morning.

"What are you talking about? Were you running some illegal gambling ring for the student council races? Isn't that kind of unethical, considering you're running?" Pablo is running unopposed for treasurer, mainly as a favor to Jenny, who has a way of getting everyone to owe her favors and never owing anyone in return. "I literally hadn't even considered running until Jenny brought it up."

Pablo looks at me, longer than he really should while he's driving. Then he says, *"Dude,"* like it's supposed to convey a whole treatise on human emotion.

"If there's a translation key to homosocial invectives in some chapter of the Bro Code, I still haven't received my copy."

Pablo rolls his eyes. "Dude. The first time I ever saw you was in the political fair at that JSA overnight. Fall of freshman year. I was overwhelmed by all the people in that room. All the passion. I went from table to table, taking some pamphlets and a few buttons. I smiled and nodded when the volunteers asked me questions. Then I got to this one table, and I couldn't even see the sign because there was a whole mob crowded around it. But I could hear this kid, clearly fresh out of middle school, arguing with a grown man. You took one of the pocket Constitutions they were giving out and held it in the air for the rest of us to see. Then you started quoting from Article One, Section Eight, without even looking at the darn thing. You used the John Birch Society's own swag to drag their entire philosophy of limited government. I'd never seen anything like it."

"It was the Elastic Clause," I say, chagrined. I remember that day. I was impulsive and unprofessional. I ranted at the chief Bircher for ten minutes until one of the girls from St. Anastasia's pulled me away and made apologies on my behalf.

"It was badass, is what it was." Pablo summarily ignores me. "That was when I knew. You weren't at JSA because you thought it would look good on your college applications or because you'd heard how lit the dances were. You were exactly what it said on the tin: a statesman. That's the truth, Mark. You were born for this."

That's what I always hoped Dad would say when I told him I wanted to follow in his footsteps. Harvard, law, politics, manhood. I look out the window. Ignore the prickling sensation at the corners of my eyes.

"It was a tragedy you didn't join JSA when you moved here. It's such a waste that your only outlet for talking politics is the classroom. So, yes, Mark. It's about time you run for student body president and show this town what you've got."

Pablo and I part ways in the parking lot. He heads off to the gym, and I take the scenic route to the history room. The one that doesn't force me to walk past the gym. Instead, I pass the strand of bungalows devoted to the arts. The lights are on in the band room, warm and orange through the open door. Dissonant chords from disparate instruments reverberate through the air. They're out of tune. A cacophony. Just warming up.

I walk faster. I need to do this before I lose my nerve.

I'm later than usual. Half a dozen kids are already in Latin, none of them working. With drooping eyes, they make idle conversation, full of ellipses and false starts. No one wants to be awake before the sun.

I make my way straight to ZP's desk. My heart is pounding. I wouldn't feel this much trepidation if I were approaching the *Resolute* desk in the Oval itself.

ZP looks up from the graphic novel he's reading. "Mark." He smiles. "Are you here to tell me you've finally found a teenager-appropriate hobby? Drafting drinking games for the State of the Union doesn't count."

"Well, maybe." I take a deep breath. Tap into that debate-voice place Mom noticed last night. "Hypothetically, if I were interested in running for student government, would there still be time to get my name on the ballot?"

ZP's smile stretches into a full-blown grin. "Mark," he chides, "why didn't you tell me you wanted to run?"

Candidates don't exactly inspire confidence when they say they decided to run impulsively, so I lie. A tiny little white lie. A political fib. The first of many, if I want to make a go of this. "I needed to be sure I could fit it in my schedule."

"Can you?"

"If I give up my free period, yeah."

"Use zero period as your free period. I'm begging you. Since, you know, you're not actually enrolled in a zero period class."

"You're talking like I'm going to win."

"There's a place for you in student government, win or lose. Which reminds me, what did you want to run for? Elsie's running unopposed for secretary. Or there's class historian—"

"President," I say, loud and clear. Bold as I want to be. "I'm running for student body president."

In English, we break into groups to read *Richard II* aloud. The way Shakespeare's meant to be experienced, as Ms.

Polastri puts it. She fancies herself a matchmaker, which is why Jenny and I always end up in the same group. Nadia jokes that she's just there to cockblock us.

Polastri sends us outside, where we claim the senior steps. It's a rare opportunity, because they're the universally acknowledged capital of jock domain. They're supposed to be a symbol of the senior class's unity—of the heights to which we've climbed together—but the steps belong to the senior class only in name. They're a forbidden kingdom, except at times like these, when the guard's away. So I sit on the top step and breathe in this rare air.

Nadia sprawls out on the concrete, fresh paint already distressed after two weeks of sneakers and heels scuffing it up.

Jenny's lying down, too, her head in my lap. If Polastri looks out the window, she'll see exactly what she wants, even if it doesn't mean what she thinks it does.

We're supposed to assign parts. Read the play like normal people, but the sun is shining overhead, one of the last sterling mornings of summer. So we make a show of switching off after every single line, rather than reading by character. It slows the pace, strips the verses of their rhythm and ease.

It's Jenny's turn. We both see it in the copy we're sharing. She looks up at me instead, upside down.

I know what that means. I tug the paperback from her fingers and toss it aside. Nadia groans, probably because we were only ten lines from the end of the scene. But the fate of dead kings is insignificant in the scheme of our lives. Here, on these stolen steps, this sacred ground, our invasion has already begun. "We need a game plan."

"A war plan," Jenny amends. She sits up. Stretches her arms far above her head. Her shoulder blades shift, tectonic plates beneath the surface of her skin. There was a time, when Jenny and I first met, when Polastri's speculations weren't totally off-base. Now our relationship is entirely platonic and stronger for it.

"We have to file the papers by first bell tomorrow," I say. "I finished everything I could, but there's still the petition."

"One hundred signatures," says Jenny. "Give it here."

I pluck the goldenrod envelope from my backpack, and Jenny snatches the paper right out of my hands, lips pursed. They straighten out when she sees a dozen signatures already adorning the grid. Real signatures, too, not lewd blow-offs. Trust me, I checked. "Where'd you get these, stud?"

"Latin. There's a fifty-fifty chance they signed because they're glad I won't be hanging around every morning. Someone muttered something about how I make them look bad even when I don't say a word."

Nadia laughs. "Talk about a winning platform."

Jenny pulls the pen from behind her ear and yanks the cap free with her teeth. She signs her name in purple ink. "Lucky thirteen."

"Just eighty-seven to go." I sigh. "In twenty-two hours."

"Eighty-six," says Nadia, swiping the petition from Jenny. She inks her name in bold copperplate letters, the same way she signs her art. "And you don't need to worry about the rest."

"It's doable," says Jenny, numbering off tasks on her hands. "We'll get all the IB signatures next period. We'll make the rounds at lunch. After school, Rachel can take it to soccer. Pablo can get the wrestling team tomorrow. Have it back to you before that bell rings. It works; we can make it work."

"Jenny," Nadia cuts in, "chill." She folds the paper twice, then tucks it into her camera bag. "No need to tap Rachel and Pablo. I can get it done myself. No problem." She offers up Jenny's pen while looking over to me. "As long as that's okay with you, Mark?"

I nod.

Jenny takes her pen, bewildered, though she tries to hide it.

Nadia smiles. "Yearbook staff, remember? We get shit done."

At lunch, we make lists.

Jenny didn't wait for ZP's permission before she erased his entire whiteboard, and she has a dozen bullet points written before anyone else shows up.

Nadia's out shopping my petition. Jenny asked for text updates every five minutes, and Nadia complies—with a different GIF of Olivia Pope saying "It's handled" each time. By the third GIF, Jenny curses and tosses her phone in my lap, as if it's my fault.

Rachel comes in late, a smudge of dirt on her cheek and a twig in her hair. "Sorry. Bio lab. What do you need me to do?"

Jenny hands over the marker and lets Rachel play scribe. Rachel's handwriting is usually way too neat for a doctor-in-training, but Jenny talks faster than she can manage. Rachel's script shrinks and crimps while Jenny rattles on about policy points and social media blitzes and voter out-reach.

I sit on a desk and watch, in awe, as my campaign finds its own staff. I'm about to insist, *We really don't need an advertising budget, do we?* when the door slams shut. We always keep it open, at ZP's request, so the slam isn't a shot across the bow; it's an act of war.

There, like a stock villain from a '90s teen movie in her plaid sweater set, is Clary Cabrera. She's five-foot-nothing, but her patent-leather pumps click with determination as she marches right up to me. "Mark Adams," she seethes. "What's this I hear about you running against me?"

"It's not about running against you," Jenny answers on my behalf. Hands on her hips, she has more gravitas than half of Dad's colleagues. "It's about representing the people. You know, the queer students who feel disenfranchised by your policies."

"Jennifer," says Clary, her pin-straight black hair swishing as she whirls to face down her former running mate.

"Clarissa," Jenny returns in kind.

"I should have known you were behind this. Brutus."

Jenny rolls her eyes, unimpressed. "This isn't a coup, Caesar. Three terms as class representative may have gone to your head, but this is still a democracy. I'm not stabbing you in the back on the Ides of March; I'm backing the candidate I think the people will choose on Election Day."

"The candidate you think people will *choose*?" Incredulity drips from her words like ice cream melted from a cone on a midsummer day. She swishes back to me. "You think you've got a shot at my crown?"

"Again," says Jenny, "not a crown."

I should be terrified. I should feel small and afraid. I should remember every time the mean girls at St. Anastasia's made me feel small and afraid because they didn't like how butch I dressed, or how little makeup I wore, or how I acted like a dyke. But I'm not in the vaulted halls of that false cathedral anymore. I'm not the girl they thought I was.

I square my shoulders and steel my spine. "That's your problem, Clary. You're making this election about you. That's why all your posters are just larger-than-life selfies. Your slogan is literally 'Yes, Clary Can.' People vote for you because they don't have another choice. It's you or Henry, who's the closest thing to a Republican this school has. There's no one listening to what the people actually want, because I guarantee it's not a figurehead in a crown with a scepter in her hand."

"So what, Mark? You think you can be what the people want?" She looks me up and down, from the blond of my hair to the red of my high-tops. "The people don't know you any better than they know themselves. You've been here for what, a year? You have no life outside of IB. What do you even know about Utopia High School? What do we know about you?" She leans in, close enough that I can smell her jasmine perfume. "Let me give you some advice, candidate to candidate. The best thing you can do right now is lose your candidacy papers. Burn them. Save yourself some dignity, and drop the hell out now."

"Or what, Clary?" It's the same threat I made to Henry, before I had the barest bones of a plan to back it up. "What are you going to do?"

She sneers up at me. "You better pray you don't find out."

EIGHT

THURSDAYS ARE GYM DAYS, BUT PABLO AND I skip our workout routine to hit up a tiny indie art store in the Village—and Costco when the tiny indie art store fails to meet our campaign supply needs.

Two hours later, we reconvene at Rachel's white stucco ranch house in the foothills. When Nadia comes in an hour late, we're all spread out over the Myerses's butcher-block table, debating poster-board colors. She drops a stack of papers in front of me with a shocking thud.

"What the heck?" Pablo asks.

Chin on her hands, arms on the table, Rachel sighs. I don't know if she's more relieved that Nadia's here, or that her interruption has stopped the debate on whether red poster board will make prospective voters think I'm a communist, and whether that will make them more or less likely to vote for me.

The top sheet in Nadia's stack is the candidacy petition. Every line is full, and when I thumb through the subsequent college-ruled pages, I see name after name I don't recognize. "Nadia, this is . . ."

"Amazing?"

Jenny snatches the papers. "This is . . . significantly more than one hundred signatures."

"What'd I tell you about yearbook staff?" Nadia smirks. "We get it done."

Jenny drops the papers and looks up. If I didn't know better, her shark-toothed smile would scare me shitless. "And you know *everyone*. Every demographic. The yearbook targets every potential voter group."

Nadia settles in next to Rachel, kissing her on the cheek before focusing on Jenny. "Sure. Does that matter?"

"It means you're pretty much the best petitioner in the history of petitions," says Rachel. She has a thousand smiles, one for every occasion, from ZP's cheesy jokes to Megan Rapinoe tweets. But her smile for Nadia is this discreet, dimpled thing, closed-mouthed and demure, and when Nadia grins back, I have to look away.

"*It means*," Jenny cuts in, "you know this school. You've got your finger on the pulse of the electorate. We can use that."

"Sure." Nadia looks from Jenny to me and, when I shake my head, back to Jenny again. "How, exactly?"

"We need you to do a poll of likely voters, broken down by demographics. Year, gender, academic track, clique. All of it. Ask them what they know about Mark Adams. Figure out what would persuade the undecideds and how we can chip away at Henry's and Clary's respective bases."

Nadia pulls out a notebook. "Got it. What do you want me to ask?"

While Jenny and Nadia iron out how to get voters to reveal their hearts and minds without feeling like they're being cross-examined on the witness stand, the rest of us are back to debating poster board.

"Mark," says Pablo, swatting my arm to get my attention. "This is your campaign, okay? You have to decide what it's all about."

"It's about justice for Benji," I say instinctually. "Changing the system. Giving a voice to disenfranchised students."

"Is it?" Pablo squints. "Are you running as a populist?"

"Isn't he?" asks Rachel.

Nadia looks up from her notebook to point out, "Populists are all about representing the interests of the so-called everyman. Mark knows maybe fifty UHS students by name. He can't run as a populist."

"Thanks, Nadia," I say, sarcasm a cheap reflex. "What do you think it's about?"

"Making the school a safe space. For everyone. We need a slogan that reflects that."

"We should poll on it," says Jenny, without looking up from her legal pad. "Actually, Nadia, organize a focus group."

"Slow down, Olivia Pope," says Pablo. "Mark, what do you think?"

74

They all look to me, their fearless leader.

Which. Well. I kind of am. I'm the candidate. I'm the one whose name is going on these posters. I'm the one putting it all out there for the world to see.

You have to decide what it's all about.

Pablo's right. This is my campaign. I can't just sit idle and let my friends make these decisions for me. I can take their advice, especially when they know better, but at the end of the day, it comes down to me. My message. My politics. My vision.

Yesterday, I told Benji to exonerate his bullies because I was scared of my own. Benji turned around and told the whole school to make space for "a high-femme fag" because he isn't going anywhere, no matter how hard the system tries to box him out.

This is the same scholastic ecosystem that accidentally enrolled Pablo in ESL in kindergarten because he was speech delayed, and they just *assumed*. That demanded a doctor's note in order for Nadia to be excused from strenuous activities in PE during Ramadan. That told Rachel maybe she just doesn't have what it takes to be a doctor, before her ADHD was diagnosed.

The system doesn't want to make space, and no one who benefits from it wants to cede theirs. The only way to change the system is to stand up and claim your own.

I meant what I said. I want to show this administration

and everyone else that marginalized kids deserve space in the halls of UHS; I want to follow Benji's example.

"I'm running as a populist," I announce, looking at everyone in turn. "And I think I've got a slogan, too."

MAKE YOUR MARK

We're all elbow-deep in glitter paint when the Myerses's front door clicks unlocked. Rachel said her mom would be working late; it's the whole reason we decided on her house. When I look up, the afterimage of glitter sparkles at the edges of my vision.

It isn't Mrs. Myers at the door. It's Ralph, and he's juggling three cardboard takeout trays stuffed with iconic red-and-white In-N-Out bags. "Hi," he says, teetering in his blue brogues.

"What's all this?" It's possible Jenny thinks of dinner in the same way factory foremen view humane working conditions: unnecessary.

"I heard you guys might need sustenance," replies Ralph, stiff and formal.

"Always," Pablo says, getting up to help Ralph with the bags.

"You didn't have to do all this." I cross my arms over my chest, self-conscious in more ways than one. I slipped my binder off in the guest bathroom an hour ago, in accordance with binding safety guidelines. I'm mostly flat in a high-compression sports bra, but *mostly flat* is still a mine-field waiting to blow. "We invaded your house. You didn't have to feed us."

Ralph scratches the back of his head. His chestnut curls, already tousled, rustle into further disarray. "Rach told me what you're doing for Benji."

There's a funny thing about the word *you*. It doubles as a collective noun. The greasy bags and the context clues suggest Ralph's using the collective *you* to encompass the whole of Club Français. But he only looks at me when he says it, and I feel the weight of his attention.

Still, I don't understand Ralph's stake in this. He isn't in Club Français. He isn't a sophomore. I have no idea how he knows Benji, though he clearly does. He brought Benji to us in a panic when Benji needed our advice. He told Benji to do the right thing when the rest of us didn't have the guts to say it. And now he's bringing us classic California comfort food after we've pulled eminent domain on his house. This means something to him.

That's why, when Ralph says there are milkshakes and sodas out in the car, I volunteer to help carry everything in.

Out in the driveway, I recognize the practical Prius Rachel sometimes drives. On the passenger seat, there are a few cardboard drink holders painstakingly wedged between the door and the center console. Four drinks to a carrier, white paper cups lined with red and green palm trees. "You got more drinks than there are of us."

The tips of Ralph's ears tinge pink. "I wasn't sure what everyone would want. Rach and I ostensibly keep kosher, but I've heard the shakes are good."

"You've never had one?"

"Like I said, kosher. Ostensibly."

"That doesn't mean you can't have a milkshake, though, right? Just that you can't have it with a burger?"

"Well, the dietary restrictions include guidelines about cross-contamination in food preparation, too, but we're pretty lax about that part. But, more to your point, what would be the point of going to In-N-Out and not ordering a burger?"

"Oh my God, Ralph"—I put on my best show of mock indignation—"the *fries*. The fries are the entire point."

"But they get cold and soggy if you let them sit—"

"Heresy. Complete and total blasphemy. The fries are perfect, hot or cold."

He smiles. "Next time, I'll order fries and a milkshake."

"Chocolate. It has to be chocolate."

"I think I'd prefer strawberry, actually."

"Heathen," I say, without heat.

"You goys are technically the heathens here."

It takes me a minute to dredge up the shards of Yiddish I've picked up from Rachel and remember "goyim" is the term for non-Jews. Then I get it, and I have to laugh, because I'm not sure I've ever heard Ralph tell a joke before.

Actually, I've heard him say more in the last two minutes than the last year. It's nice, hearing him talk about something other than bee imagery in the poetry of Sylvia Plath or the causes of the Cuban Missile Crisis.

Inside, the table's been cleared, all of our precious campaign cargo safely stored in the living room. The food's spread out in its place, and the Myerses's kitchen smells like meat and cheese and grease. Everyone's parceling out paper-wrapped take-out on vibrant turquoise plates. Hamburgers for Ralph and Rachel. An off-menu grilled cheese for Nadia. Animal Style for Pablo. Ralph passes me a chocolate shake. He takes iced tea instead of a soda.

We all sit around the table, breaking bread and meat and cheese together. Jenny starts listing all the campaign stops I'm going to make around campus next week, until Pablo literally clamps a hand over her mouth. Rachel mentions how much she's dreading the oral commentaries we're doing in English. Nadia tries to kiss Rachel quiet, and I start to bring up the Extended Essay abstracts that are due at the end of next week. Everyone's groans drown me out. Nadia flicks a fry at my face. Pablo invites us to his open-mic night at Atelier tomorrow night.

So we make plans. We stuff our faces with junk food. We laugh until our faces hurt. Outside the night may be cool and dangerous, but here, in the Myerses's well-lit dining nook, we carve out a space for us, small but safe, and undeniably *ours*.

NINE

MY RINGTONE YANKS ME FROM MY PEACEFUL slumber at four a.m. When I wrangle my phone, the screen blinds me with an unknown number. I jam my eyes shut. "Mmph," I grunt by way of greeting.

"Mark?" I can't identify the voice, but whoever they are, they're entirely too perky for this ungodly hour.

"Who is this?"

"It's Amber."

"Amber," I repeat, to buy myself time. The only Amber I know is Amber Carr, gossip blogger extraordinaire, but I don't really know her. I've never actually had a conversation with her before now. Not that you could call my half-conscious grunts a conversation. "How did you get this number?"

"I have my sources." You'd think I'd asked her to reveal the identity of a whistleblower.

"Right. Why are you calling me?"

"I need a quote—"

"No, I mean, why are you calling me at four in the fucking morning?"

Amber heaves an exaggerated sigh. "I'm on a deadline, Mark."

"It's a *blog*. That you run."

"My blog is where it is today because I run it with high standards of professionalism and journalistic integrity."

I'm pretty sure Amber's readership is limited to the student body, helicopter parents, and drama-thirsty teachers living vicariously through us.

"Sure, but doesn't professionalism also mean conducting business during business hours?"

There's sharp intake of breath on the line. "Mark, you want to be very careful what you say to me right now. You're making your political debut, and you don't want to make an enemy of the Fourth Estate."

"God, Amber, no one's trying to make the press an enemy. Just hang on a second."

I sit up and frantically wave my free hand until the motion sensor above my night table catches sight of me. The lights power on, harsh and antiseptic. "Okay. I'm awake." Another political fib. "What did you want to ask me?"

"Rumor has it you're joining the race for student body president."

"That's not a question, but yes. I'll be filing the papers this morning."

"Would you care to tell prospective voters why you're launching a desperate last-minute bid when there are already two qualified candidates in the race?"

"Wait a minute."

"Would you say your candidacy is a ploy for popularity?

"No, of course not."

"What would you say to critics who view your candidacy as a desperate ploy for popularity?"

"Do those critics have names, or are you using your blog—erm, *platform* as a soapbox for your own opinions?"

"This is about you, Mark, not me, and frankly, your weak attempts to deflect criticism only reflect poorly on you."

"Christ, Amber, slow down."

"The news slows down for no man. Or woman. Or enby."

Something bright and gaseous burns in my chest at her use of trans-inclusive language. Maybe it's hope. Maybe it's fear. Maybe it's indigestion. "Okay, look. Can we start over?"

"You can't start over when everything's on the record," Amber explains as if she's teaching journalism to a toddler.

I've watched enough shows about Washington politicians navigating the journalist swamp monsters living in the Potomac that I should know how to fix this. I just have to give her something she wants. "What if I give you an exclusive interview?"

"Exclusive?" Amber scoffs. "Who else were you planning to sit down with?"

I hand over my candidacy papers first thing. ZP goes through them one by one, initialing and dating the corner of each while I hover over him. "Congratulations, Mark," he says with a genuine smile. "You're officially running for student body president."

I match his smile in kind.

"Go forth," he says, shooing me with both hands. "Campaign. Win this thing."

"Aren't you supposed to be impartial?"

"Of course. I'm the Supreme Court."

"Are you forgetting *Bush v. Gore*?"

"The FBI, then."

"J. Edgar Hoover literally blackmailed presidents."

"How about the FEC?"

"You're really not reassuring me here."

"Well, reassuring you isn't my job. But hey, at least you found a hobby, right?"

TEN

"THERE'S GOOD NEWS AND BAD NEWS," SAYS Nadia when she swans into ZP's room halfway through lunch.

"Okay. Give it to me," says Jenny. She's sitting in ZP's rolling chair, her feet up on his desk. "The good. The bad. The grotesque."

"ZP is going to kill you," Rachel says when she catches sight of Jenny's languid pose. She tagged along on Nadia's polling expedition.

Jenny flicks her wrist, unconcerned. "Polling data. Now."

Nadia fishes a cable out of her camera bag and hooks her tablet up to ZP's projector. Pie charts and bar graphs in primary colors overlay the list of philosophers on the whiteboard.

Pablo asks, "How . . . ?"

Rachel switches off the lights. "Don't ask."

"Okay," says Nadia. "I polled two hundred likely voters, which is ten percent of the UHS student population. I tried to hit every major demographic group, but there were a couple that weren't interested in speaking with us."

"She means the Christian Club," Rachel explains.

"And the football team." Nadia shrugs. "Anyway, let's start with the headlines. If the election were held today, only ten percent of students would vote for Mark." She enlarges her first pie chart. The largest slice, about two-fifths of the pie, is ruby red. The second chunk, maybe a third, is canary yellow. A wedge of emerald green outweighs the tiny sliver of sapphire blue that must be me. "In a bit of an upset, Henry would win the election by a double-digit margin. Clary's the one who hemorrhages support by your presence in the race, but it's worth pointing out that seventeen percent of voters are still undecided."

"So what you're saying," Pablo says slowly, "is we're screwed."

"*I'm* not saying anything," says Nadia. "The numbers say we're facing an uphill battle here."

"Uphill or scaling a cliff face?"

"There's a graph for that!" Rachel exclaims. She seizes Nadia's tablet and swipes to the next screen.

"Or a *series* of graphs," corrects Nadia. "I asked a few questions to get a sense of how firm Henry's and Clary's support is. What, if anything, could convince their voters to change their minds? So, Henry's base is ironclad. His voters don't just like him—they worship him. He's the hero of our otherwise dismal football team. He's cool. They all want to be him. Or do him. Or whatever. Our only opportunity is this quarter, the reluctant Henry voters." She reclaims her tablet and circles the appropriate sector in white squiggles. "These voters plan to vote for Henry because they're sick of Clary. They don't think it's fair she's been class rep for the past three years, or they don't think she's done anything worthwhile. To them, Henry represents change. He's antiestablishment."

"Even though he was prom king last spring. He's the top of the social food chain," Jenny seethes.

"Apex predator," I agree. "What about Clary's supporters?"

Nadia swipes to the next screen. "Although Clary's still the favorite without you in the race, her supporters are soft. They're not voting for her; they're voting against Henry, or the elite jock-patriarchy. That's why her numbers dip when your name's on the ballot. There's a real opportunity there to convince her so-called supporters, especially the issues voters, that you're a better option."

"There are issues voters in a high school student council election?" Pablo asks, skeptical.

Jenny glares. "We *make* them care about the issues."

"What issues?" asks Rachel. "Clary talks about vegan school lunch options. Henry wants ritzy pep rallies before every football game. Isn't antiqueer bullying kind of a special interest issue?"

"Not if we frame it as a wedge issue between the establishment and the political outsiders."

"But," Rachel starts, "aren't you the definition of an insider, Jenny?"

"No more of an insider than Henry is."

"It's not about objective truth," I add. "It's about what people believe."

"Which is *malleable*," Jenny says.

"What I'm hearing," Pablo says, "is that this is a contest of personality. We need to appeal to the people who hate them both."

"Which is a voting bloc that exists!" Nadia interjects. "A whopping forty-five percent of the electorate think both options suck. If we can convert the majority of those voters, while hanging on to everyone who's in your column now, we have a chance of winning a plurality in a three-horse race."

"I'm sensing a 'but' coming," says Pablo.

"Well. That's where the bad news comes in."

"This wasn't the bad news?" I ask.

"The worse news, then." Nadia swipes to a new pie chart, one slice blue, the rest a gnawing shade of gray. "Name recognition. Only twenty-one percent of students have heard the name 'Mark Adams.' What's worse, a third of the students who know your name aren't confident they could pick you out of a lineup."

There's a part of me that hears this and thinks, *Oh, thank*

God. Because for fifteen years, all I wanted was to blend in with the kids they made stand in the other line on the playground. People always noticed me, if not because I was the politician's daughter, then because it was a part I couldn't play convincingly. I didn't fit in with the girls, and I wasn't one of the guys. I was always the odd one out. The queer kid, in every sense of the word, even before I knew what it meant.

Dad made me swear to blend in here, but maybe I wanted to disappear, too. Maybe there was more comfort than I realized in moving to this town, telling everyone I was just one of the guys, and having them believe me. In being able to slide into white male privilege and live under the radar for once in my life.

But the adaptations I learned to survive as a trans boy in a cis society won't serve me now. They won't get me elected, and they won't make UHS a safer place for kids like Benji.

Or kids like me.

"We knew this was going to be a problem," Jenny says. "It just means we have to introduce Mark to the student body. It's precisely the right climate for that. Everyone wants a new face."

"An actual political outsider," Pablo adds.

"The Amber Carr interview will help with that," Rachel says. "It's an opportunity to get Mark's story out there."

"And Benji's," I add.

Jenny nods, and I'm sure she can see the spin in her mind's

eye. Hell, it's probably in neon signage. My face on a bill-board. All of this in a history book fifty years from now, claiming *this* was the campaign that forged us.

We're all quiet for a moment, trying to see what she sees. Trying to imagine that narrow, precarious, rocky path up the cliff face to victory, and what the view must look like from that rare summit.

"Well." Jenny claps her hands together and kicks her feet off the desk. "Let's get started."

After school, Jenny and I end up lying side by side on my bed watching *Veep* on my laptop. We have the house to ourselves, and Jenny's parents would be horrified, even though Mr. Chu definitely still has a Pinterest board planning our wedding. Mom would just remind me there are condoms and dental dams in the bathroom, even though I've told her it isn't like that anymore.

"Do you think that'll be us in twenty years?" Jenny asks.

I look at the screen, where former president Selina Meyer's bartering away her principles for four more years in the White House. "I think you mean thirty."

"Psh, we can do it in twenty. What do you say? You could be the youngest president in US history—with the help of a badass chief of staff, of course."

"What about your K Street corner office?" Because that's always been Jenny's plan. Georgetown, law school, a cushy consulting job where she can pull the strings from behind the scenes. We're both policy wonks, but she's never wanted to be the face of change.

"I think I could be persuaded. Besides, who else is going to teach you to compromise?"

"I know how to compromise. Maybe not like that"—I gesture back to the laptop—"but."

She shifts up onto her side, resting her cheek on her hand as she looks at me. "Mark, you believe in everything so much, but sometimes you can't see the trees for the forest."

I mirror her posture so we're face-to-face. "Isn't it supposed to be the other way around?"

"Not for you," she says. "Do you remember how we met?"

"You mean the debate about abolishing the Electoral College where you were so convincing as devil's advocate I really thought you believed in that archaic, undemocratic—"

Jenny cuts off my tirade. "After our opening arguments, during the Q&A, someone asked if you thought the National Popular Vote Interstate Compact was a viable alternative to a constitutional amendment. But you insisted on the principle of the thing, even though the NPVIC is a practical workaround."

"It's not the same thing. Getting every state to pledge their delegates to the candidate who wins the popular vote would negate states' electoral votes, sure, but it doesn't negate the symbolism—"

"You just said it! The NPVIC puts the winner of the popular vote in office, Constitution be damned."

"It's not that simple. You can't just say 'Constitution be damned' when there's debate as to whether the NPVIC is even constitutional—"

"Do you even hear yourself right now? The fact that we're still having this debate after nearly two years proves my point. You're ignoring the practical good that would come out of it because it doesn't pass some arbitrary ideological purity test. You're so caught up in the idea of the thing that you forget about the two hundred fifty million eligible voters the policy would empower. Forest, meet trees."

"I—" I really don't have a counterpoint here.

She grins. "This is the part where you're supposed to concede and say, 'Yes, Jenny, you're right. I understand the error of my ways. Please promise you'll manage all my campaigns because I'd be lost without your wisdom.'"

I think back to that JSA overnight convention, in a business hotel across from a roaring theme park in the South Bay. I remember the dance after the debate, finding Jenny in a room full of sweaty nerds pretending they knew how to twerk. I remember her pulling me close with a playful smirk, then leading me up to the roof. I remember the chill of the November night and the taste of cinnamon gum when she pressed her lips to mine. I remember her hand teasing the bottom of my shirt as she whispered in my ear that she'd never hooked up with a girl before. I remember flinching back and telling her *I wasn't* before I had a chance to think it through. And I remember the look in her eyes when she sat down with me on the edge of the roof, watching neon roller coasters race across the street, and listened to everything I didn't know how to say. She was the first person I told.

"You're right," I say, throat dry. "I'd be lost without you."

ELEVEN

ATELIER, OUR FRIENDLY NEIGHBORHOOD BOOK-store/bakery, hosts a biweekly open mic. They rearrange the café tables and set up a microphone near the gardening section. They lower the house lights and switch on the string lights. The aroma of freshly ground coffee and freshly baked pastries percolates through the room.

When Jenny and I get there a few minutes before show-time, Nadia has already pushed two tables together, stolen a few extra chairs, and acquired a platter of assorted croissants and a carafe of coffee.

We all know Pablo's hiding out in the pantry, meditating like he does before a wrestling match, but there's another conspicuous absence.

"Where's Rachel?" Jenny asks Nadia.

Nadia looks up from her phone, where, presumably, she's in constant contact with Rachel. "She's going to be late. She can't leave until after Shabbat dinner, and there's some top-secret pit stop she has to make on her way here."

"Sounds ominous," I say. Knowing Rachel, it could be anything from a snack run to a liquor run.

"It's probably harmless." Nadia glances back down to her phone. "Probably." She might be remembering Rachel's promposal, which started with Virginia Woolf and ended in a dove attack.

"Is this thing on?" Akash, an older guy with graying hair, a well-groomed mustache, and a Fair Isle sweater, takes the stage, tapping the microphone with his index finger. It's on, and he knows it. Akash dreamed of a career in stand-up before attending the Culinary Institute in Napa. "I'd like to welcome you all to Atelier's open-mic night!"

The crowd's mostly twentysomethings, all hipster-coded students from the community college with neckbeards and glasses of questionable utility. They snap while the rest of us clap.

"First up is an Atelier regular, Pablo Navarro."

Nadia whistles. I attempt a poor facsimile of a wolf howl. Jenny keeps clapping like a normal person, but no less enthusiastic for it.

Pablo comes out dressed in a Hawaiian shirt and espadrilles, ukulele in hand. He smiles as he settles down on the stool and lowers the mic. He's so calm, confident in a way I've only ever felt on a debate stage.

Surprising absolutely no one, he plays a stripped-down cover of an old Taylor breakup ballad, and he's terrible. Of course he is. But in true biromantic fashion, he doesn't change

94

any of the pronouns. He's singing with the kind of sincerity that comes from experience, and I wonder if he's thinking about the guy from JSA who ghosted him after one otherwise swoon-worthy mini-golf date because Pablo wouldn't "put out." He's dated too many people who don't understand the difference between romantic attraction and sexual attraction, and his heart's always the one left in the gutter. Maybe that's the reason he likes Taylor so much; she knows what it's like to watch someone toss her love in the trash along with the tabloids.

When the final chord wanes, we all scream loud enough to drown out the hipsters' obligatory snaps. Pablo beams with pride. We welcome him to the table with open arms, high-fives, and fist bumps.

But there's a reason Akash always books him first, and that's to guilt us into staying for the ensuing hour of spoken-word pieces, poorly penned breakup songs, and a vexing mime performance.

When intermission comes, Rachel sneaks in through the side door.

Except, she's not alone. Benji's there at her side.

He's got a jean jacket on over a floral-print shirt, and a black instrument case tucked under his arm. He smiles at the sight of us, lips stretching wide until he winces. His split lip must still be healing.

Everyone rushes over to hug him. I'm last in line. My movements are stilted, my arms stiff. I can't get them to tighten properly. To an outsider, it probably looks like I'm cleaving to toxic masculinity.

If only it were that simple.

"Hey, man." The words are small and inadequate, a leak in the ceiling against the torrent of things I should be able to say but can't.

Benji smiles at me as if nothing is wrong, even though I can see the purple splotches set in his skin. "It's good to see you, Mark," Benji says, either oblivious to my awkwardness or polite enough not to mention it.

Pablo asks Benji how he's been. Nadia asks if he's doing his homework. Jenny asks when he'll be ready to do a real interview with Amber, at which point Pablo punches her in the arm.

"What?" asks Jenny, genuinely miffed. "This campaign started because of Benji. He's an asset, and we need to use everything in our arsenal if we want to win this thing."

I feel sick. My stomach is a washing machine on a heavy-duty spin cycle. I'm probably well on my way to a stress ulcer. Because Benji is here, and Jenny is talking about the campaign we started *because of him*, and I'm forced to face the fact that I'm no better a friend than I was before this.

It's been two days. Two days that Benji has been suspended, and I haven't reached out once. I never asked anyone for his phone number. I haven't texted, called, or gone to visit him. I don't have the slightest idea where he even lives. But the worst part—the unforgivable part—is I never stopped to ask what he wanted. He made me swear not to tell anyone about the fight, but now I've turned his trauma into a platform. Sure, I can justify it. Say he started it. Made the story public domain with his statement. I can claim he *inspired me*, but that doesn't change the fact that my entire campaign hinges on his pain. I did this because I wanted to be a better friend. I wanted to make up for all the ways I'd let him down, but now I see I've made the same mistake twice.

When the seas part, I realize Ralph has been tucked behind Rachel and Benji this entire time. Everyone else is chattering about school, the campaign, and Benji's upcoming French horn solo, but Ralph is staring at me.

Ralph has this habit of fading into the background. I'm not sure how he manages it, because he doesn't exactly look like someone who can disappear. He dresses like a seventeen-year-old professor, always wrinkle-free button-downs and grandpa cardigans. On anyone else, bow ties and elbow patches read "hipster affectation," but Ralph wears them so effortlessly, like he genuinely doesn't care what anyone else thinks. He has a face most people would call "interesting" rather than attractive and the bone structure of a Dickensian waif. He should stand out, but so often, he fades away.

Except right now, I'm the one who's gone invisible in a crowded room, and Ralph is the only one who can see me. We see each other.

Then Akash toggles the house lights to signal the end of intermission.

We go back to our tables, and even with two of them, there's too many of us. We all scoot in closer together. On one side, Jenny's knee knocks against mine; on the other, Pablo's shoulder.

Benji takes the stage, his French horn balanced on his knee. Polished brass gleams under the spotlight. He plays a moody jazz piece, dark and sultry and full of deft improvisation. I don't know much about jazz, but I know enough to recognize Benji's talent. I can't believe I've never heard him play before.

But I've never thought to listen.

Friday night still means "date night," even for the nerdy queer kids, so everyone disperses after the open mic. Pablo has plans to catch a late showing of some new romantic comedy with a girl he met at the gym. Nadia and Rachel are driving up to Redwood Ridge. Jenny has been furtively texting beneath the table all night, though she won't even hint who she's planning to hook up with. Benji's mom picks him up because, well, he's fifteen and has a curfew.

Jenny offers to drop me off before her mystery date, even though she's running unfashionably late for a booty call.

"I can give you a ride," Ralph offers, stepping up beside me. He pulls the Prius keys from the pocket of his khakis and dangles them so they catch the light.

"Oh." I muster a half-hearted excuse. "I'm not really on your way home."

"Where do you live?"

"North, up near El Dorado trailhead."

"I don't mind."

When I tap Jenny on the shoulder, she brushes me off with an absentminded kiss on the cheek. I tell her to have fun and be safe, but I'm not sure she hears me.

So I get in the passenger seat of the Prius and buckle up. Moody indie rock comes on over the speakers, a husky voice crooning lovesick pleas over the building frenzy of fervent string instruments.

Ralph reaches out to ratchet down the volume, looking at the dashboard rather than at me. "I can turn it off."

"No, I like it."

"Okay." Ralph checks the rearview mirror and looks over his shoulder as he backs out. It doesn't surprise me that he's a diligent driver. I bet he always looks both ways before crossing the street, too.

It's quiet as we drive through the foothills. Just the steady thrum of the music.

Ralph keeps his eyes fixed on the road. I look ahead, too.

"Don't you have anything better to do on a Friday night?" I ask, restless.

"Don't you?"

"Fair point. I'm just going to claim the couch and watch CNN. Catch the West Coast rebroadcasts."

"Don't you already check the news on your phone every ten minutes?"

"I like the commentary." And maybe I have a bit of a crush on Anderson Cooper. Look, I know it's a cliché, but . . . He's usually so calm and restrained, but then there are those rare moments when the pressure builds up, and he drops all pretense of journalistic neutrality because he's not afraid to denounce wrong—usually when it comes from the right.

Also, the glasses. I rest my case.

"Well," Ralph says, "my late-night plans start with making tea and end with bingeing *Star Trek* until I fall asleep with my laptop on my stomach."

"Kirk or Picard?" I ask, because I know enough to know that's what I'm supposed to ask.

He sneaks a glance at me. "Are you a fan?"

"Not really," I admit. "I've only seen a few episodes, but I respect the sociopolitical enterprise of the franchise, you know?"

I catch the corner of a smile before he turns back to the road.

"I know," he agrees. "And to answer your question—Kirk." If it weren't so dark, I'd swear he's blushing.

"Really? I thought you'd go for Picard's stoic leadership style."

"They say fortune favors the bold, and when is that more true than when you're 'boldly going' to the outermost reaches of the cosmos?" Another car's taillights glint off Ralph's glasses. "But my favorite series is actually *Voyager*. It's the one I grew up watching. Reruns, after school. With my dad."

Soon we reach the turn for my subdevelopment.

"El Dorado, you said?"

"Yeah. It's the next left."

We wait at the intersection, the Prius's turn signal ticking like a metronome, and I'm thinking about the question I've been meaning to ask Ralph for the past two days. "So, how do you know Benji?"

"Oh," says Ralph, surprised, as if he's forgotten he doesn't usually come out with Rachel on Friday nights. "I'm in band."

"Oh," and maybe I'm surprised, too. I still have trouble thinking of Ralph outside the mold of Rachel's quiet-weird brother, who's smart but doesn't feel the need to show it. This is the Ralph who exists outside the confines of IB classrooms. He goes to therapy in the same office I do. Of course he has hobbies and does extracurriculars. He likes *Star Trek*; he's in band. I wouldn't be so surprised if I'd ever thought to ask. "What do you play?"

"Clarinet, since fourth grade."

"Do you do jazz, too?"

Ralph laughs. "No, just classical. I'm not really good at improvising."

I can't tell whether he means that metaphorically as well as literally. "It's another left past the streetlight."

Ralph turns, his hands steady on the wheel. "I know you know Benji through French Club, but . . ." He trails off, his hesitation a palpable thing. "Why are you doing this?"

I look at him, his silhouette backlit by headlights. "What do you mean?"

"This thing you're doing, with the election. Stepping out of relative obscurity to campaign on an antibullying platform."

I know he's trying to clarify, but I still don't understand. "What happened with Trevor," I say, "never should have happened. It shouldn't happen anywhere, but especially not at UHS. I didn't realize—" I unclench my fists. "We can't just let this happen at our school. Adults say we're just supposed to wait it out, you know? We're supposed to grow up and leave our small towns. When we're in college, they say, when we're in the city, it gets better. But the world doesn't get better unless we make it better. We have to fight to make it better." We drive past well-lit homes, full of Rockwell families. Some of them probably go to our school. "Benji's my friend," I murmur, "even if I haven't been a very good one to him. I did what anyone would have done."

"No," says Ralph, looking at me, "not anyone."

I look away, seeking out rooflines in the dark. "It's the third house on the right."

TWELVE

I CAME OUT TO MY PARENTS ON MEMORIAL DAY, sophomore year.

I'd like to say I had a plan, but I didn't. Or, I did—a glorious ten-point plan to be carried out exactingly over the next two years—but I didn't follow it. I meant to drop subtle hints to gauge their reactions, like the polls Dad had already started commissioning for the gubernatorial race he *still* hasn't officially entered. It was supposed to be careful and calculated and—let's face it—political.

But I screwed up. I went off script.

Dad was home for the long weekend, which was a first. He usually spent holidays in DC so he could hit up press-worthy events. The year before, he spent Memorial Day at Arlington National Cemetery with a gaggle of other Congressmen trying to bolster their credentials with veterans. This year, he spent the morning speaking at the local VA clinic and was home by noon. He switched off his phone, traded his business casual for shorts and a polo, and joined Mom and me in our sprawling backyard.

Mom was reading a paperback urban-fantasy novel on a chaise lounge by the pool. Dad was heating up the grill.

Charcoal briquettes smoldered red hot, and hickory smoke clouded the patio. Late-afternoon light bled through the American flag that fluttered by the screen door. *People have died for this*, I thought.

I had a ten-point plan, but I hadn't seen Dad alone in weeks, and that morning he'd given a speech about the men and women who'd given that last full measure of devotion so the rest of us could live free. I'd watched him live on the local news. His hazel eyes glittered in the harsh fluorescent light, and his dark blond hair took on a greenish tinge. It looked gold outside now, in the afternoon glow.

People never said I looked like him because people never say daughters look like their fathers.

That's when I told him.

And that's when he told me to stop joking.

He doesn't tell me much of anything anymore. Not even on Sundays.

Although Dad kept the house in Marin, no one really lives there anymore. Sure, Dad goes home for donor dinners and the occasional town hall, but he actually lives in the Georgetown brownstone he bought when he was first elected five years ago. It was a pied-à-terre then, a place for him to stay while Congress was in session, but never more than a house away from *home*. Everything changed after the separation. Dad lives in DC full-time now. I don't think he'd bother coming back to California at all if he weren't planning to run for governor.

Every Sunday, Dad goes to Mass at St. Matthew's cathedral. In 1963, that palace of Romanesque architecture hosted Kennedy's requiem. Each year, the day before the Supreme Court begins its term, the cathedral hosts Red Mass—attended by the justices, members of Congress and the cabinet, and often the president himself—to request guidance from the Holy Spirit in legal matters. It's a premier place of worship for Catholics in DC, a cathedral for politicians and those who aspire to the Oval. And Dad? Dad's got his sights set past the statue of Lady Freedom on the Capitol dome, all the way down Pennsylvania Avenue. So, no, Dad doesn't go to Mass because he believes. He goes because that's where the cameras are, and taking Communion under Washington's watchful eyes is a way to raise his national profile.

Every Sunday, after he comes back from Mass, we have our weekly FaceTime date. These are the only sanctioned conversations we have, and he wouldn't even have agreed to these conversations if Mom hadn't strong-armed him.

Every Sunday, I sit at my desk and wait, dressed as if I went to Mass with him, and when he makes it home from the service and socializing with whatever Washington bigwigs happen to show up that week, he calls me for a video chat.

He keeps me waiting longer than usual today. There must've been someone important at the cathedral, maybe a cabinet member or a foreign ambassador. But, if I'm being honest, there's a long list of people Dad would rather talk to than me, and that list is about to get a lot longer.

It's my own damn fault. My fault for violating the terms of our agreement. My fault for being the kind of problem child who needed to make an agreement with my own father so he wouldn't disown me. My fault for still needing his approval, even after all this time.

God could create a thousand universes in the time it takes for my computer to ring. *Incoming call from Graham Teagan.* I accept immediately. Too quick; too eager.

I see my face, clean shaven, blond hair neatly parted to the side. My collar is starched and straighter than I am. I look like a preppy teenage boy. Mostly. Maybe my face is a Rorschach ink blot or an optical illusion. The young girl and the old woman. The blue-and-black dress or the white-and-gold. You blink and you squint and you see what you want to see.

Dad's portrait replaces mine, crystallizing into something painfully familiar. He's in his study, a wall of books in the background, rich leather and spines embossed in gold.

I'd like to say Dad is what I'll look like in thirty years, but maybe that's wishful thinking. I'm a work in progress, and he's fully rendered. Mom always says Dad has a face for politics. She used to it say it with a smile, a nudge, a wink, but now she says it with the resentment of a reformed good wife who refused to let politics tear her family apart—so she did it first.

"*Dad*," I say, and I hope he can't hear how weak I sound. How relieved I am to see his face. "Hi."

He smiles, he does. It's small, but I can tell myself he's happy to see me, too, right up until he says, "Hello, Mads."

The lights go out in my heart, and I remember. I remember everything.

When I called him on it, months ago, Dad claimed there was nothing wrong with calling me "Mads." It was a childhood nickname, he said. I was overreacting. He didn't see the issue with using a diminutive derived from my deadname. He's never once called me Mark, but I'm supposed to be grateful he stops short of Madison. I'm supposed to be grateful for a lot of things that don't even begin to constitute the bare minimum of decent parenting.

"How was church?" I ask, because that's what I'm supposed to ask, and asking polite, inane questions is what I am supposed to do. Making a fuss about what Dad calls me when Mom was barely able to convince him to call at all—making any kind of demands when Dad thinks I'm holding his world to nuclear ransom—is off-limits. After all, Dad doesn't negotiate with terrorists.

"Good," says Dad. "I ran into Senator Díaz, and we had a

long talk about how best to oppose this tax plan that's coming to the floor next week. You remember Senator Díaz, don't you? We had dinner at his house in Alexandria." He sighs, and something dims in his eyes. "He asked about you."

"What did you say?" I shouldn't ask, not when I know there's no answer that won't hurt.

"I said you were starting your senior year. Applying to Harvard. You are still applying to Harvard, aren't you?"

"Of course." It's been my dream as long as it's been his.

"Have you started the application?"

"My essays are done." They've been done for months. Everything has been done for months. "I'm just trying to decide who to ask for letters of rec."

"Good," he says. "Good."

That's the extent of his commentary, because he doesn't know enough to comment. He makes sure I keep up my GPA, and he asks enough questions that he can disparage the state of California public schools, but never more than that. He doesn't know my teachers' names. He doesn't know what I wrote my college essays about. He wants to know as little as possible about the life I lead under a name he can't say aloud.

Maybe the resentment clouds my face, or maybe his own neglected paternal instincts get the better of him. "How is school going, then?"

This is where I should say, *We read Leibniz this week in TOK*. I should tell him, *I've been brainstorming ideas for my*

Extended Essay about how we frame the idea of progress in political discourse. Hell, I could even ask him, *Remind me again how you feel about punching Nazis?* Instead, I square my shoulders. Set my jaw. Say, just like I practiced, "Dad, I'm running for student body president."

He blinks, once, then twice.

For a moment, I think he must have misunderstood. I open my mouth to say the words again, but then I remember. This is what he does when I tell him something he doesn't like. It takes time for him to process the words that don't compute with his carefully ordered worldview.

After all, this is what he did when I told him I was trans.

"You're *what?*"

There it is. The indignation. The rage. I knew it was coming, but that doesn't make it hurt any less.

"Something happened, Dad. My friend was suspended for defending himself against a bully. The principal enforced a flawed policy. Benji spoke out about it, but that won't change the policy. Someone has to challenge the system—like you taught me. So I'm running for student body president, and when I win, I'm going to—"

"When you *win?*" Dad echoes, voice rising. The vein in his temple throbs. "Who told you you could even run?"

I never used to understand how he could carry that much anger. If his body were a vessel, he would be poised to overflow. But then I started testosterone, and I started to understand. All that bullshit about how men's and women's brains are wired differently is just that, but there is some truth to the claim that people feel things differently. Not because of a false chromosomal binary, and nowhere near as clear-cut as essentialists would have you believe. But hormones impact how we experience emotion, and testosterone? Testosterone makes my anger quicksilver.

Except I'm not angry now. Everything in me hurts, but this isn't the time to catalog my pain. "I don't need your permission, Dad."

"Yes, you do. Despite what you may believe, you're still a minor, and as such, you're still subject to my rules."

"Mom gave me her blessing, but I would have done it anyway. Because it's the right thing to do."

"We had a deal, Mad—"

"I'm still following the letter of *your* law. I haven't legally changed my name. I haven't interacted with anyone who could recognize me from before. I haven't done anything to out myself or hurt your career, even though it hurts *me* to keep up this charade."

"You say you haven't done anything to out yourself, but do you realize what an election is?"

His face is unnaturally red, hypersaturated on the screen. The color of the crimson on the flag.

"An election is an invitation. You are rolling up the curtains and opening the doors to your house for every single voter. You are giving them permission to dig through your dirty laundry and search every closet for every last skeleton you have buried. You are inviting them to set up camp in your kitchen, your living room, your *bedroom* for the duration of your tenure as their representative. Because when you run for office, *Madison*, any office, even student body president, you cede your right to privacy. Because you are a public figure. The public *owns* you. They own your time, they own your agenda, and they own your body. You do not get to keep secrets from them, and when you try, you will surely fail. Someone will find you out, and your constituents will punish you for ever having tried to deceive them."

I feel it now. My blood stampedes through my veins. Anger claws at the walls of my rib cage, something feral fighting to break free. "Then what are they going to do to you, Dad? When your constituents find out about me? How do you think they're going to feel when they find out you lied about the separation? Do you think they're going to reward you by electing you governor?"

"You don't have any idea," Dad says, "how politics works. If you think your classmates would elect you if they knew the truth about you, you are sorely mistaken."

"That's the thing, Dad." I smile, even though I don't feel anything but hurt behind the mechanical stretch of my skin. "Everything I know about politics, I learned from you."

* * *

Mom takes me out for brunch.

She sees the way my lip wobbles when I head downstairs after the call and gets her keys before I say a word.

We go to Railroad Square, the old, picturesque part of downtown. Red brick faces every building. Wrought-iron grates adorn the windows. Old-timey cars are parked in parallel along the storefronts. A family of ducks waddles over the cobblestones.

Mom and I get a window booth at Sunnyside Express, Santa Julia's premier locomotive-themed diner. They give us oversize menus with photos of the most popular entrées, but we already know it by heart.

I order coffee, and Mom surprises me by ordering a mimosa. I'm not sure I've ever seen her drink before noon. Normally, I'd fill the booth with idle chatter, but I don't have it in me today. So Mom sips her mimosa and talks enough for both of us. She tells me stories about the hospital, and it's good. It's easy.

Our food comes, sizzling and gleaming with grease. My plate is a riot of color, bright yellow egg yolks, red fire-roasted salsa, and dark green jalapeño slices. I douse my huevos rancheros in Tabasco sauce.

Mom drowns her Belgian waffles in maple syrup, and I shake my head.

"Hush," she says, though I haven't said a word. "I know you're a pancake purist, just like your—"

She stops herself, but the damage is done.

I poke my egg yolks with the tines of my fork until they break, viscous yellow flooding the craters and valleys between vegetables and beans. "It's okay," I say, even though it isn't.

"Oh, honey." Mom sighs. "Mark, would you look at me, please?"

I look at her. Her heart-shaped face, her platinum-blond hair, her dark brown eyes. I used to hate it when people said I looked like her. Now she has wrinkles she didn't have before I came out and she went to war on my behalf.

"Whatever your father said, whatever he told you about your election, I want you to know I'm proud of you. For standing up for Benji and queer kids like yourself. For doing the right thing, even when it isn't the easy thing."

I can't look at her anymore because tears have started prickling at the corners of my eyes, that thin membrane between everything I feel and the outside world threatening to tear.

"Mark," Mom says, then again, when I don't respond, "*Mark*, what did he say to you?"

"It doesn't matter."

"It does," she murmurs, "but you don't have to tell me. Just know that he's wrong." Her eyes are shining in the dim electric light, her hand shaking ever so slightly as she grips her water-stained knife. "He's wrong about this, and he's wrong about you."

And *God*, I wish I could believe her.

THIRTEEN

JENNY ASSIGNS EVERYONE ELSE POSTER DUTY while she and I sneak off campus to do interview prep. And eat real food for lunch. Except we spend ten minutes driving around Hearst Village arguing about where to go, only to end up at Atelier.

We settle in at the wobbly table near the window. It's hard to beat this stunning view of the parking lot. Across the street, St. Julia's Cathedral always has topical, punny witticisms on the sign out front. Today it's "HE'S NOT GOD'S PRESIDENT."

Jenny picks apart her croissant with her fingers. "So, I talked to Amber."

"How'd that go?"

"About how you'd expect." She licks a dollop of raspberry jam from her index finger. "I may have underestimated her disdain for student government."

"You mean, her disdain for the student council as a mostly ineffectual body of government, or her disdain for your three years of unchecked power?"

Her lower lip curls. A smudge of chocolate masquerades as a mole on her chin. "The latter."

"Let me guess. She cried censorship and insisted a free press must exist free of government interference."

"I tried to explain I was talking to her as the campaign manager of Make Your Mark, but she didn't recognize the distinction."

"Well, it is kind of tenuous."

"Not really. Student government isn't even in session until after the election, which means my term as junior class rep is over. I'm a lame duck. I can't authorize a spirit day, let alone a gag order. I explicitly stated this was about you, not my own bid for veep."

"You're on my ticket, though."

"God, Mark, it's a high school election. We don't have *tickets*. What we have are symbolic alliances, which only have power because they're universally acknowledged as alliances."

"That's the problem, though. Amber's acknowledging your symbolic place on my ticket."

When Jenny shakes her head, her aviators teeter on her forehead, threatening to topple down to her nose.

"So, I'm guessing she didn't give you a sense of what she's going to ask during the interview?"

"She's very tight-lipped. You'd think she has the scoop of the century, like she was about to break Watergate or something."

"Well, we *are* trying to keep a scandal under wraps."

Jenny squints. "Which scandal are you referring to?"

"We have more than one?" I lower my voice to a whisper, "My gender identity."

"Right." Jenny exhales through her teeth. "I'm more concerned about your gender identity as it relates to your hidden heritage. If your secret parentage comes out, Clary will call you out for profiting off your sizable social capital, and Amber will eviscerate you for lying to the American public. And yes, I mean the *American public*, writ large, because she'll drag your dad's constituency into it, too." She wipes her lips with a napkin, only succeeding in further smearing the chocolate fudge. "Even Henry would find a way to use it against you."

"Henry?" I scoff. "Henry's got white male privilege written all over him."

Jenny shakes her head. I'm missing something. Some crucial piece of intel I'd have if I weren't the perpetual outsider. That's the thing about being the new kid: some kinds of native knowledge you never pick up.

"So what am I supposed to do about the interview?"

"Reschedule?" Jenny says blithely. "Preferably for after the election."

It figures that we end up debating "the natural temperament of man" in TOK. Our crash course in Western philosophy has made it to the Enlightenment, which is the one school of thought we're already supposed to know by heart. Namely, Locke and Hobbes.

"The fundamental question," ZP says, kindly summing up the reading for anyone who didn't do it, which, let's be honest, is everyone, "is whether the human condition is a state of reason and kindness or abject selfishness. Is man a rational animal or a senseless beast?"

"Well, I think the answer's obvious," Clary declares without bothering to raise her hand. "Men are definitely senseless beasts. Women, on the other hand, are the rational subset of the species."

Laughter detonates like grenades. When I look around the room, even Rachel has joined in. From her seat behind me, Jenny's laser vision bores holes in the back of my head. She's heard me rant enough times about how transmasculine people get thrown under the bus in this kind of totalizing discourse, where any and all masculinity must be sacrificed at the altar of entry-level feminism, but I can't say anything now. Any nuanced attempt to deconstruct toxic masculinity would be condemned as mansplaining. Clary would snicker *not all men* before I got a full sentence out, without a thought to how masculinity harms men and nonbinary people, too.

"Right," says ZP, more diplomatic at distilling teachable moments from snark than most teachers. "Thank you, Clary, for reminding me to use gender-neutral language. Let me rephrase. Fundamentally, are humans rational animals or senseless beasts?"

Papers shuffle. Shoes scuff the carpet. Someone coughs.

ZP looks straight at me, which, okay, is fair, because we've had this conversation before. "Rational animals," I proclaim, without a second thought.

"Okay, great. What makes you say that, Mark?"

It's what I believe, but I don't have a teleology of my proof lined up. So, of course, when I try to compose an answer, my brain presents me with every possible counterargument. Have I considered war, famine, and genocide? How can I possibly believe the best in people when the world is littered with evidence of humanity's cruelty? This isn't the best of all possible worlds. "I have to believe that," I say, far more earnest than any class discussion warrants, "because the alternative is that we're going to keep destroying ourselves until we cause an extinction-level event."

"Circular reasoning." On the other side of the room, Henry leans forward, bracing his elbows on fake wood. "You can't say you believe people are good just because you want them to be good. You're implying that the evidence supports the opposing argument."

"Is that what you believe, Henry?" asks ZP.

"I'm following the bread crumbs of Mark's own argument." Henry shrugs charitably. "I think he has a point, actually. About the evidence. If people abuse power when it's handed to them, that implies people are naturally brutish."

He's staring straight at me, something hawkish in his gaze. "The truth is, Mark, when you peel back the lacquer-thin veneer of civilization, the heart of mankind is dark and rotten. We're driven by our instincts. We want food and shelter and sex, and we'll do whatever it takes to survive, even if it means stepping on someone else."

"So what's the solution, Henry?" I ask. "The Thomas Hobbes brand of authoritarian regime? A police state with a Hammurabi-esque code?"

Henry juts out his chin. "If that's what it takes."

Clary raises her hand, but no one's paying attention.

"So what would that look like, for student government?" I press. "A band of roving hall monitors, imbued with the authority to punish anyone whose look they don't like?"

"Well, it's better than the custodial nanny state you're proposing," Henry snaps. "Better than anyone who can't take a fucking joke reporting to Principal Flynn that someone hurt their feelings. This pandemic of political correctness—"

"Hey," ZP interrupts, arms outstretched, ready to stop the two of us from lunging across our desks and starting an all-out classroom brawl. "That's enough. Let's watch the language, guys, and keep it civil." He looks from me to Henry and back again, concern flitting across his features. To the rest of the class, he asks, "Now, does anyone else have an opinion on the fundamental state of human nature?"

It's my fundamental opinion that Henry McIver is a douche.

* * *

The final bell cues a mass evacuation. I stuff my books in my backpack and flee the scene before ZP can ask me what the hell I was thinking. Or, worse, whether anything is wrong. Through the hall and into the breezeway, I catch sight of chambray and khaki ahead of me and immediately seize upon an escape plan. "Hey, Ralph," I call, exhaling sharply when he turns to blink at me. "Have a second?"

"Um," he stammers, "yeah, sure."

I step off the beaten path. "I was wondering. Do you have Benji's address?" It's a question I can't bear to ask Rachel or anyone in Club Français for fear of the judgment in their eyes.

Ralph's glasses wobble when he scrunches his nose. "His physical address?"

"Yeah."

"Then no, I don't."

"Oh." I should have known. It was a stupid idea, anyway. A stupid, harebrained scheme to assuage my conscience.

"But I know where he lives."

"What?"

"I don't know the street number. Or the street name." He sounds chagrined, as if he *should* know those things. "But I know how to get there, and I'd recognize the house on sight."

"Could you draw me a map?" My mental map of Santa Julia sucks, mostly because I didn't grow up here, yes, but also because I don't drive. "Or just describe the part of town? What the house looks like?"

"I can take you there," he blurts, then immediately follows it up with a logical explanation. "I'm supposed to drop off some new sheet music, anyway."

"That'd be great, actually." Maybe I shouldn't take advantage of Ralph's overly polite offer, but desperation breeds, and all that.

The Prius is parked at the far end of the lot, near the football field. Which doesn't make sense, because band is a zero-period class. Until I realize Ralph probably parks this far away on purpose to minimize the risk of fender-bender-by-newly-licensed-driver. That seems like something he would do.

Not that I really know him well enough to make that kind of assumption. I barely know him at all. We have mutual friends and maybe a mutual therapist. He spontaneously offers me rides. But what I do know about Ralph makes me want to know more. He holds himself apart, on purpose. He's the quiet-weird kid not because other people have labeled him as such, but because he's chosen it for himself. Ralph keeps his curtains drawn and his lights out; you can't see anything from the sidewalk. I know why I've had to cordon off whole wings of myself, under orders from on high, but I don't know why someone would do it so intentionally to themselves.

We get in the car. Ralph lowers the volume on the radio

but doesn't turn it off completely. Lush, moody instrumentals settle on my skin like dew. I wedge my backpack between my knees. Ralph expertly navigates through the labyrinthine lot. That's the other upside to parking this far from civilization: we're closer to the exit.

Every so often, Ralph drums his fingers against the steering wheel to the music. There's a pattern to it, and I wonder, absently, whether it has any correlation to the keys on the clarinet.

Which gets me thinking about band, the reason Ralph knows Benji. The reason I'm in this car with him, on the way to a house I've never been to, in a neighborhood I can't even name. "Do you and Benji hang out a lot? Outside of band, I mean."

Ralph squints, as if he's staring into the sun. "Kind of?"

"Is that a question?"

"It's contingent on how you define 'a lot.'"

"On a regular basis outside of an academic context?" My voice hitches up at the end of the sentence.

"Now that was definitely a question."

My laugh comes out of left field. "Okay, let me try that again." I pitch my voice as low as it goes, which is a bit of an adventure because it's still dropping, and imitate my favorite unreliable narrator. "'A lot' is an adverbial phrase meaning, in this context, 'on a regular basis outside of an academic setting.' If two world leaders see each other a few times a year at global summits, only to smile politely for the press corps, no one would accuse them of hanging out 'a lot,' or, for that matter, at all. However, if the same two world leaders arrange clandestine closed-door meetings and destroy the translator's notes, we might consider that 'a lot.' In fact, we might consider that *a lot* more than 'hanging out,' a term which here means 'social intercourse without nefarious aims.'"

"Oh my God." Ralph snickers. "Okay, it's definitely not safe to laugh like this while driving."

"Probably not," I concede, but regret nothing. There's something illicit in watching buttoned-up and bow-tie-wearing Ralph laugh without self-consciousness, like I've snuck out of the house on a night I was supposed to be grounded. "You still haven't answered my question, by the way."

"Okay," says Ralph, coming down, "in that context, yes. We don't hang out outside of school very often, but we eat lunch together sometimes. Most days, I hang out in the chem lab. It's quiet there, so it's a good place to read or get started on homework."

"Please tell me you don't do homework during lunch on a regular basis."

Ralph's whole profile goes pink, from the shell of his ear to the expanse of neck visible above his collar. "Only sometimes. If I run out of things to read on my Kindle, or I can't find a fic to read online. Benji always has good recommendations. He's the one who got me into reading fanfic, actually."

Looking at Ralph, thinking about what I know about fan fiction, considering what I know about Benji, I have a whole new slew of questions I want to ask but definitely shouldn't. Instead, I say, "You should join French Club."

"Rach tried to get me to join once, but I told her it didn't make sense. I don't take French."

"Ralph, you may not have noticed this, but almost no one in French Club speaks French."

He frowns. "You and Nadia do."

"Yes, but Jenny and Pablo take Spanish, and Benji's in the pilot Mandarin program."

"How'd you convince them to join?"

I need something to do with my hands, so I fiddle with my sleeves. "At first, it was just because we were friends. Or maybe it was because Madame Lavoisier brought Atelier croissants to the first meeting, where we then organized a crêpe sale to raise money for an unspecified excursion."

"You guys went to San Francisco, right? Rachel talked about it last spring."

"Yeah, we went to the Legion of Honor, then we spent the night at a hotel in the city." It's not a lie, but it's only half the truth. Once we were reasonably sure Madame Lavoisier was asleep, we snuck out and headed to the Castro with an assortment of very bad fake IDs. They got us into a divey gay bar but were confiscated when we tried to order drinks. We did get to dance to dubstep remixes of '80s pop hits

124

before they kicked us out, though, and I swear it took me weeks to get all the glitter out of my hair.

"That sounds fun."

He has no idea. "The thing is . . ." I bite my lip, unsure whether I should tell him this. But if I want to make Club Français a safe space for queer kids, it can't stay an insular secret club. It needs to *come out* and into the light. Even if it means I'm about to do something monumentally stupid. "French Club may have started as a place for our group to hang out, but it kind of turned into something else."

"Kind of?" Ralph asks intently.

"Yeah. Once we realized we were all"—and here it is, the moment of truth—"queer, French Club became an unofficial queer club." Once I've said it, I can't leave it at that. Every inch of my skin is burning, and rambling is the only thing I know how to do. "Because the actual GSA is basically shit. As far as we know, the alliance is one hundred percent allies, so-called. Or, at least, no one is out. Not that being out is the be-all and end-all of queer politics, because it shouldn't be. But if you're going to run a high school GSA, it shouldn't consist entirely of straight students. It's insulting. And we were all already in French Club, so it just . . . made sense. It didn't change much. We still do the same vaguely Francophile activities, which, if I'm being honest, revolve entirely around French cuisine, but we talk about queer issues when Madame Lavoisier isn't around. We're part support group and part advocacy group.

Or, at least, I thought we were."

Ralph stays quiet all through my babble and after it's done. The voice on the radio sings mournfully, adamant that he *should have known better*, and God, I know exactly how he feels. This was a bad idea. Among other things, I've effectively outed half the club based on a stupid assumption about why cisgender teenage boys read fan fiction. I keep saying I'm going to stop doing this stupid, selfish shit, and then I keep on doing it.

Then Ralph says, "Maybe I should join, then."

"Oh." I have to stop myself from lowering my forehead to the dashboard, because *oh* is literally never an appropriate response to someone coming out, however obliquely. I should know; I've done it enough times. "I'm sorry if that was weird. Telling you that. I didn't mean to put pressure on you to come out. I shouldn't have . . . Fuck, I'm sorry."

"No, it's . . ." Ralph sneaks a glance at me, worry lines etched above his brow. "I don't mind. It's not a secret or anything. I'd say I'm out, but there aren't many people who would care. I'm gay, but it's mostly theoretical. Rachel knows. Mom doesn't, but she also doesn't make assumptions. If I ever went out with a guy, she wouldn't be surprised it was a guy. She'd be surprised I was going out with *anyone*."

That kind of confession deserves to be met in kind. It's the most personal thing Ralph has ever said to me, and despite his claims, I shouldn't have led him into it. The least I can do is be honest. Except, of course, *being honest* is a complicated proposition when Dad is a heartbeat away from never speaking to me again. I wanted to tell the rest of Club Français the night we all came out, too, except I couldn't. As much as I'd like to tell Ralph, that's not a choice I can make. It's an illegal move on the chessboard of my choices. It's the move that means I'd never play chess with the man who taught me ever again. "I'm pansexual, by the way. Since we're talking about this."

Ralph looks at me again, just out of the corner of his eye. "Are you out?"

"I try to be. My mom knows. She's totally cool with it." Something clenches in my chest, and the space where I should mention Dad goes unfilled. "Obviously French Club knows. Other than that? As Nadia's poll numbers suggest, no one outside the IB bubble has any idea who I am, let alone what my sexual orientation is."

"Do you think it will come up?"

The farther we get from school, the smaller the houses get. Older, too, chipped paint on cracked wooden siding. We're still in the school district, but near its border.

"Why should it?"

"You're doing an interview with Amber, right? If you talk about why you're doing this—this school's not-so-hidden homophobia problem—don't you think Amber's going to ask you why you're so invested?"

"Maybe." I run a hand through my hair. "Probably."

"What are you going to tell her?" Ralph turns down a narrow street. His eyes tick up to the sign for Mulberry Lane, and I can see him memorizing and filing it away.

"It would be hypocritical not to come out," I say, feeling hypocritical even for saying this. I know I shouldn't owe anyone my sexual orientation *or* my gender identity, but knowing isn't the same as believing, and being a public figure isn't the same as being a private citizen. It fills me up like heartburn, every awful thing Dad told me about elections rushing back. *An election is an invitation.* You open yourself up and put everything on display, and if you don't, they'll cast you out. Pelt you with stones. Exile you from the only land you ever called home. "I want to be honest," I say, and I do. I do.

FOURTEEN

RALPH PULLS INTO AN EMPTY DRIVEWAY. THE house is small and blue, freshly painted, yard brimming with poppies and marigolds. On the front porch, a wooden swing with striped cushions sways in the wind.

"Is this it?"

Ralph nods. I follow the line of his gaze to the gold numerals bolted beside the door. He turns the key, and the engine goes dead. The music cuts out. Complete and total silence, except for the tumult of my breathing. Ralph watches me, but he doesn't say anything. He doesn't ask me why I'm so afraid to talk to someone I call a friend.

Eventually, I get out of the car. I walk up the porch steps. I stare down the royal blue door and pitch my knuckles against the wood. The memory of Benji's knuckles, glittering with blood, stops me cold.

The door swings open, and there's Benji, as dressed down as I've ever seen him in UHS sweats and a T-shirt. "Mark."

His still-healing lip hangs open, surprise he can't quite hide. "What are you doing here?"

"I was hoping we could talk."

Benji looks past me, to where Ralph's standing beside his car, shifting his weight from one foot to the other. They nod to each other, and Benji looks back to me. "Yeah, of course we can talk. Do you want to come in, or . . . ?"

"I don't want to take up too much of your time."

Benji laughs, something sharp and jagged, and I realize my mistake. He's been suspended for five days; he has nothing but time. Still, he makes the decision for me, taking a seat on the swing. He curls one leg up under him and angles his body toward the space he's left for me.

I look over at Ralph, who still hasn't crossed the driveway, promises of sheet music seemingly forgotten. His hands stuffed in his pockets, he hazards, "Listen, there's a Starbucks around the corner. I'm going to get an Earl Grey. Text me, okay?"

He retreats before I have time to point out I don't actually have his number, a fact I should probably rectify if we're going to be hanging out on a regular basis outside of an academic context.

Benji rests one hand at the back of his neck, his posture open, expressive. Patient, though I don't deserve it.

"I'm sorry," I start. I mean to follow it up, but the words have dried up, a drought I don't know how to quench.

"For what?"

"For not reaching out. About what happened last week. Or, before."

Benji leans back, the swing rocking with him. "It sounds to me like those are two entirely different things."

"Maybe."

"Which one's keeping you up at night?"

"Why didn't you tell us?" My voice cracks, coming out higher than it has in months. I hear myself as the scared girl I used to be. "In your statement, you called it a pattern. You said it'd been happening for years."

Benji nods.

"Then why didn't you say something? To any of us? I know . . . I know I might not have been the most approachable person, but I hope you realize—" This isn't the time for the Mark Adams Vanity Exhibition. "Why not Pablo? Why not Ralph?"

Benji turns to me, and in the afternoon sunlight, the fading bruises are clearer than they were in the dim of Atelier. "I was ashamed."

"Benji, it wasn't your fault. You *know* that. What happened—it's on them. You have nothing to be ashamed—"

"I wasn't ashamed it happened," Benji cuts in. "I was ashamed I didn't do anything to stop it. It kept happening, and I just . . . let it."

"Benji," I say, helplessly treading water in an ocean far

too deep. I don't know how to offer a drowning man my arm when I can barely stay afloat myself.

"You know I don't regret what I did." Benji's dark eyes harden like flint. "My only regret is that I didn't do it sooner."

"You didn't do *anything* wrong. *I'm* the one who was wrong. I never should've told you to apologize."

Benji shrugs. "It was a rock and a hard place. It's not like either of us had a crowbar."

"Still, you were right. Speaking out is the only way to stop them."

"Stop them?"

Across the street, Benji's neighbors have a sprinkler running, watering a half-dead lawn. A couple of kids in cutoffs run through it, laughing, without a care in the world. They're so young, and it's still somehow, inexplicably, summer. They have no idea what the world has coming for them, how it will try to twist and rend them into formation, how if they dare step out of line, a whole army will come for them in broad daylight.

"When you come back"—I swallow hard, a full glottal stop—"I want you to be safe."

"Mark." Benji shifts his weight again, and the swing rocks back and forth. "You and I, we don't go to the same Utopia High School. Not really." His accent comes out when he's like this, his vowels stretching out like his limbs. "You're upper-middle class. We both have single moms, but yours is an oncologist; mine's a paralegal. Meanwhile, you're convention-ally masculine and conventionally attractive. You wear hoodies and leather jackets in muted, lumberjack colors. You've never dated a guy, or anyone, for that matter, so you pass for straight. I'm not saying that's right. I'm not saying it's easier to be pan than gay in a heteronormative society. But high school's a jun-gle, and sometimes camouflage is the only thing separating the prey from the predators. Guys like Trevor and Kevin, they look at you, and they see a guy like them. You're straight until you give them a reason to doubt you."

Even though I know, intellectually, that I pass, hearing Benji talk about me as a normal cisgender man jars some-thing loose from me, a bone pried from my rib cage. Under any other circumstances, the thought of passing so effort-lessly would electrify me, but Benji's words instill only guilt. Because the thing is, he's not wrong.

"I don't get to hide," Benji continues. "The clothes I wear, the things I like—I don't *want* to hide, and even if I tried . . ." He shrugs. "It wouldn't matter. They'd still take issue with the drawl in my voice or the way I hold my wrists. Those are facts. Indelible. I know what you saw upset you, Mark. It opened a door to a whole bigoted underworld of Utopia Heights you never knew existed. It shocked you, and now you're on a crusade to change it. But it's not an underworld to me. *This* is the Utopia Heights I live in; this is my normal."

Guilt scratches at the walls of my throat. "Benji—"

He holds up a hand. "No, I'm not finished. What I'm trying to say, Mark, is that if you want to weaponize your privilege to try and make things better, then go right ahead. But don't pretend I'm going to be safe when I walk through those double doors on Thursday. Nothing you promise me now is going to make that possible."

"I'm not making promises."

"You're campaigning."

There are a thousand protests on the tip of my tongue, a lawyer's arsenal of objections and redirections. But Benji's asking me to *listen* to him, so I nod, the motion feeling clumsy and unpracticed. "I should have asked you. Before I decided to run."

"If you're running solely because of what you saw last week, then yes, you should have," Benji says, solemn. "I don't want to be your mascot. I'm not a cause or a crusade."

"It's not like that," I insist. "I'm not running because of what happened to you; I'm running because of what you *said*. Your statement was—"

"Don't you dare call me brave."

I try to smile, but only half my mouth goes along. "I was going to call it 'inspiring.' Flynn didn't care which option you chose as long as you went quietly and let everyone pretend they'd never heard anything go bump in the night. But you didn't go quietly. She gave you two shitty choices, and you didn't accept either."

"Nah." Benji sweeps his arm, encompassing everything from his sweats to the sky. "I still got suspended. It just felt better to go down fighting." He pauses, blushing behind his bruises. "So to speak."

"That's why we need to keep fighting," I say. "You're right. I was upset and surprised. I had no idea, and that's on me. But I know, now. The system is full of false choices—two shitty options, just in different packaging. Suspension or apology. Henry or Clary. A rock or a hard place."

"Your campaign speech isn't exactly filling me with optimism here."

"That's the point. We need systemic change. The crowbar to move the rock, avoid the hard place, and forge another path. That's why I'm running. I'm trying to do my part. Not just because the system failed you, but because it's failing everyone. Every kid who doesn't feel safe to come out. Every kid who's questioning. Every kid who can't even start to question their sexuality or gender because UHS isn't safe. And no one's doing anything. The administration doesn't care. The GSA doesn't care. So maybe this is a lost cause. Maybe I can't start a political revolution by running for class office, but I know things can be better than this. Because I can see it, Benji."

Those kids are still running, laughing, on that lawn that isn't quite green.

"Or I can imagine it. We can build a better UHS. One

where students are educated and empowered. Where hate speech and hate crimes alike are prosecuted to the fullest extent of the disciplinary code. One where we're a real community rather than a clique-centric hierarchy. Maybe that's naive. Maybe it's a fever dream, or a foolish delusion rooted in privilege. Maybe it goes to the etymology of *utopia*, the nowhere land, the good place that doesn't exist."

My eyes are shut, and I see it. Rachel and Nadia holding hands without guys catcalling them. Benji dressed head to toe in florals and pastels without anyone snickering. Me, wearing a T-shirt with a catchy trans slogan without the world ending. "But I need to believe in that promise. I need to believe that things can be better, and that we can make them better if we put in the work."

I need to believe it, because I don't know who I'd be without that hope.

When I open my eyes, Benji's watching me. His eyes have softened in the afternoon light, no longer sharp or stone. "Go on, then." He nods like he's been waiting on me all day. "Tell me about the campaign."

FIFTEEN

THE DESKS ARE GONE WHEN I GET TO ENGLISH first period. No telling if this is a premature senior prank, or whether Ms. Polastri has graduated our Shakespeare renditions from reader's theater to interpretative dance. My campaign team is already arranged in a tidy circle on the floor. Ms. Polastri's nowhere to be found, but I pick up the stage directions and squeeze in between Pablo and Nadia.

"Good," says Jenny. "You're here. We need to talk about this interview."

"All we do is talk about the interview," I protest. "I'm as prepared as could be."

"In two hours, you are going to eat those words."

"Jenny." Nadia rests a solemn hand on Jenny's shoulder. "It's not halal to threaten your running mate."

"Aren't there multiple arcs of *Scandal* devoted to vice presidents attempting to usurp the presidency?" Pablo asks.

"Speaking of *Scandal*," Jenny says, and that's my cue to

groan because Jenny has a way of turning every *Scandal* plot point into a teachable moment. "Oh, shush, you televisual elitist."

"What could the so-called deep state possibly teach me about an interview for a high school blog?"

"A lot, actually. OPA excelled at PR."

"All right. Fine. What are you trying to handle today?"

Jenny levels with me. "You have a Mellie Grant problem."

Pablo snorts out a laugh before he can stop himself, then covers it up by fake-coughing into his fist. He always claims Jenny strong-armed him into watching the show, but we all know he's a total sap for Fitz and Olivia.

"What?" I ask, baffled. "Jen, I'm pretty sure I'm not a brunette Hillary Clinton analog who faces an uphill electoral battle due to rampant sexism and a history of sharing headlines with sordid sex scandals."

She waves her hand, as if my point is nothing more than an insubordinate gnat flying in her face. "You know that's not what I mean. When Mellie's running, she comes across as too smart. Too knowledgeable; too competent."

"What you're describing," I point out, staid and stately and not at all overreacting, "is a Jed Bartlet problem. It comes up during both his campaigns, especially the reelection bid when he's running against a Bubba type. That makes more sense as an analogy, because I'm white and Catholic, and his Nobel Prize in economics loosely corresponds to the IB diploma candidate thing. Not to mention his whole backstory, how he gets involved in his private school's politics when his father's secretary brings the injustice of the school's gender inequality to his attention—"

"*Mellie*," Jenny continues, "alienates voters, not only because she comes across as a cold fish, but primarily because she constantly feels the need to prove she's smarter than everyone else. She's always *performing* that she's the smartest person in the room."

"I don't need to be—"

"Mark, come on." Nadia sighs. "You just mansplained Jenny's contemporary pop culture reference with Aaron Sorkin."

Okay, so, maybe Jenny has a point.

Rumor has it the head librarian still hasn't forgiven the administration for cutting the journalism program, so she's let Amber turn the library into the unofficial *Dystopia High* HQ. The building smells of ink and must. Shelves of cellophane-jacketed books line the walls. A gray-haired deputy librarian smiles at me. I weave through the mostly empty tables, past a row of sad computers that look older than I am. The office is behind a glass wall, just past the checkout counter. That's where I see Amber, five feet of dark brown skin topped by six inches of buoyant black curls. She's seated on a wheelie stool, and when her pirouettes bring me into view, she waves me in.

I slip behind the counter and through the sliding glass doors, all the while feeling like I'm sneaking into the staff-only section of the Louvre.

"You're late," Amber hisses, her gaze flicking to her smartwatch. "We only have twenty-six minutes left."

I convinced Amber we could do this during our midmorning study hall period rather than lunch. She put up a fight because Guided Study's half as long, but with only a week to go before Election Day, I need every last lunch hour for campaign stops.

I don't roll my eyes, because rolling your eyes at the beginning of an interview is a good way to guarantee it's going to be a hatchet job. "I'll stay during break if you need me to."

"Fine. Just hurry up and sit down so we can get started."

I sit and fold my hands to stop myself from fidgeting. And I smile, as well as I know how.

Amber has a mustard-yellow blazer over her blouse, which seems overly formal for a blog interview, but what do I know? Maybe I'm the one who's underdressed in my Henley-and-hoodie duo. Amber certainly looks at me like I'm worthy of about as much attention as the gum on the bottom of her ballet flats. She has her laptop out on the table between us, surrounded by mounds of file folders. "Do you mind if I record this?"

"Yes, actually."

She looks up from her laptop. "It's standard procedure,

140

Mark. I'm not going to quote you out of context. That would be unprofessional."

And God forbid Amber ever do anything unprofessional.

Jenny told me under no circumstances to let Amber record me, but Amber's glaring at me like she's already started writing that hatchet job in her head. "Okay, sure."

"Perfect." She flashes a photo-worthy grin, then taps her trackpad. "Please state your full name for the record."

"Mark Adams."

"Age and occupation?"

"Seventeen. I'm a senior and a candidate for student body president."

"Great." Amber looks up again. "According to my records, you started at UHS last fall. Can you tell me a little about your upbringing?"

"I'm not sure how that's relevant." Or how she has *records* about me. I can only imagine what secrets her laptop holds.

"I'm just trying to paint an accurate picture. So the voters will have all the information they need to choose the best candidate."

"Right." My hands are clasped so tight I can feel my bones. "I grew up in Marin. I went to a private Catholic school. After my dad—" Nope, can't go there. "Last summer, my mom got a job offer up here, so Mom and I packed up and moved to Santa Julia."

"But not your dad?"

"Off the record?"

Amber nods and pauses the mic.

"My dad's not in the picture anymore." It's a white lie, white like the fabric on the flag. It's my patriotic duty to tell this lie. Or my filial duty. When you're a congressman's kid, there's not much of a difference. "It's hard for me to talk about him."

If Amber's face was a papier-mâché mask of indifference just moments ago, the glaze has begun to crack. "Then we'll move on. Back on the record." Another click. "So, what was it like being the new kid at the start of your junior year?"

"Nerve-racking." Kind of like this interview. "I knew a couple of the people in my class from, um, a conference."

"Which people?"

"Jenny Chu and Pablo Navarro. They were great. They welcomed me with open arms. Their friends became my friends."

"So, the IB diploma kids in your grade."

"Pretty much, yeah. I have all my classes with them, so we probably would've become friends anyway."

"You're an IB diploma candidate, correct?"

"Correct."

"I take it you know that less than six percent of each graduating class does the full diploma."

"I hadn't done the math, but that sounds about right, I guess."

"And only a third of students ever takes a single IB class."

I'm sure there's a line of reasoning I'm supposed to be following, but right now all I see is a scatterplot.

"How," Amber continues, "are you going to represent the entire student body when you've spent your entire time at Utopia High sequestered in the ivory tower that is IB?"

"Amber, aren't you a junior IB diploma candidate?"

"This isn't about me, Mark."

"You claim to be the voice of the people. It's the tagline on your blog, right? *Vox populi.* You're on the same academic track as I am. So, logically, if you can represent non-IB students, then why can't I?"

"Those are pretty words, Mark." Every time she says my name, her disdain deepens. "There's a key difference, though. The diploma program doesn't start until junior year. I grew up here. I went to elementary school with these students. I took PE with them freshman year. Only half of my sophomore Honors World History class went on to IB History of the Americas. I know the junior class intimately. I'm not stuck inside the IB bubble, but you are. Because you started here as a junior, literally *all* your classes have been IB. You've been cloistered apart from the bulk of your class. Not to mention underclassmen, who have absolutely no idea who you are because you have no life outside of IB. Care to comment?"

"You're right, Amber."

"I am?" She jolts upright. "I mean, I am."

"I have been isolated here, but I'm trying to change that now."

"How, exactly?"

"There's one week before this election. I'm committed to spending it getting to know all of UHS. I want to talk to as many students as possible. I want to hear their concerns, as well as their ideas for making this school as great as it has the potential to be."

"So you're not trying to Make Utopia Great Again?"

"No." I laugh. "Like you said, I'm still new here. I can't make claims as to whether UHS has ever been 'great.' But I do know that *utopia* is a promise. It's a promise to work toward a school we can all call 'great.' It's a promise to build a safe, inclusive community for all our students, where we can all strive toward achieving our fullest potential."

Amber stops typing. She's really looking at me now, studying every pimple and pore. "Well." She clears her throat. "What made you decide to run for office?"

I practice the smile Jenny told me to use. The one I learned during Dad's first two campaigns, when he took me on the trail, and Mom showed me how to rub Vaseline on my teeth. "Your blog, actually."

"*Really?*" Somehow, she manages to sound skeptical and giddy all at once.

"Benji Dean's statement, to be exact."

"Do you know Benji? I didn't think you ran in the same circles."

"I do have friends outside the IB bubble." I keep smiling, polite as can be. "And I am *proud* to call Benji my friend. His refusal to apologize to his bullies gave me the courage to speak up and speak out."

"That's why you're entering the electoral fray in the eleventh hour?"

I lay out my case. I can almost pretend I'm back in JSA, debating a resolution on my own terms. Except instead of passing pretend resolutions for accepting Syrian refugees or against drilling in the ANWR, I'm advocating for issues that affect my peers in the here and now. I'm making my case against the biases in the student handbook, the malicious incompetence of our administration, and the unchecked bigotry on our campus. Sitting across from Amber, talking about structural inequality, I'm starting to believe that maybe, just maybe, I could use this platform to effect real change.

"I have to ask," she says, utterly shattering my illusions. "What's your stake in this?"

I owe Ralph an In-N-Out milkshake.

"Like I said, Benji's my friend, and we all have a stake in making this school safe. But that's not what you're really asking, Amber."

She feigns surprise. "What do you think I'm asking?"

"You want to know if I'm speaking up for queer rights because I'm gay. But you know you can't come out and ask me outright."

"Well, I don't believe in outing anyone without their

consent," she replies, too eager and not at all chagrined. "But do you have a comment?"

"I want you to understand that what I'm about to say has nothing to do with your indirect question. I'm not telling you because you asked, and frankly, I'm not telling you because it's relevant to my campaign. I'm telling you because if I'm going to put myself out there, for people to listen to me and maybe vote for me, then I want to put it all out there. If there are queer or questioning kids who read Benji's statement and are afraid there's no space for them here, I want them to know they're not alone. So, yeah. I'm pansexual. Care to comment?"

SIXTEEN

THE MAKE YOUR MARK CAMPAIGN TOUR COM-
mences at lunch. At the track/field I've spent my entire UHS
career avoiding. Hammerhead lights tower over Astroturf
and shiny silver bleachers. I'm keenly aware this isn't *my* turf.

"They should be right over here." Rachel points seemingly
straight up.

Nadia's tour schedule relies on her expertise as a yearbook
photographer. She also says I need to take advantage of the
web of connections our friends have beyond Club Français.
She calls it networking. I call it nerve-racking. I wouldn't be
nervous if it weren't for Dad's voice in the back of my head,
but as it is, I can't stop wiping my palms on my jeans.

Sure enough, the UHS girls' soccer team sits at the peak of
the home bleachers, just where Rachel said they'd be. There's
maybe a dozen of them. They sport an unofficial uniform of
athletic shorts and racerbacks. They all stop talking as we
approach.

"Hey, ladies," Rachel says, settling in beside a girl with light brown skin and a top knot. "Have a minute?"

Top Knot looks me up and down. Her bubble gum squelches when she speaks. "Sure."

"Cool," Rachel says. "I want to introduce you to a friend of mine. The one I was telling you about."

Top Knot pops a bubble. She must be the team captain, because all the girls defer to her.

"Remember," Nadia whispers in my ear. We're still a few steps down on the bleachers, far enough that they shouldn't be able to hear. "Stick to the Jenny-approved talking points. Don't go off script—"

"Don't worry," I mutter, though I am definitely worrying. "I've got this."

I climb up the steps and put on that Vaseline smile. I stick my hand out, and Top Knot shakes it, her grip bone-breaking. "Hi." It takes every ounce of bravado I have to get that word out steady. "I'm Mark Adams. I'm running for student body president. Since I'm asking for your vote, I want to know what you want your student government to do for you."

"Beatriz," Top Knot says, and then, "Are you for real?"

"Excuse me?"

Rachel frowns at Beatriz, taking her perfectly reasonable skepticism as a personal betrayal. Meanwhile, I'm over here second-guessing why I ever thought this was a good idea.

"With the hair," Beatriz elucidates, swooping her palm

over the top of her head. "And the teeth. And the butchered JFK quote."

The other girls hum their approval. High ponytails swish when they nod.

"Seriously," Beatriz continues, "all you need is one of those tiny little flag pins on your hoodie."

I'm definitely not going to tell her that I have a small collection of American flag lapel pins in the antique jewelry box my grandmother left me.

"So tell me," she says. "What makes you any different than Clary? She came out here last week, spent five minutes bragging about herself, and then promised she'd get the cheer team to perform at a couple of our games."

This isn't in the stump speech. The only script I have to go on is the truth. "I don't know what you've heard about me, but let me tell you a little about myself. I started at UHS last year, and while I've been happy to find my place here, I've also found that the school isn't the utopia promised in the name. I want to change that. I want to ensure that every student's voice is heard, so we can build an inclusive community, together." I'm out of breath when I'm done, and my hands are shaking, so I stuff them in the pockets of my hoodie. "That means I want to hear what all of you think. The girls' soccer team won the regional championships four out of the past five years, and yet you receive a fraction of the advertising and booster support our last-in-the-division football team receives. I want to know what your team needs and how I can help you get it."

"In other words," Rachel says, a smile arching across her lips, "he's for real, Beatriz."

For an impossibly tense moment, Beatriz is silent, gum lodged in her cheek, watching me sweat. Then she nods, a sharp, decisive movement. "Okay, Adams. Let's talk about where Title IX falls short."

Utterly without warning, Nadia's DSLR flashes, embalming the moment in pixels.

"So, clearly there's a learning curve to campaigning," I say, hopping down the bleacher seats.

"Don't worry, you crushed it," Rachel assures me. Over her athletic shorts, she wears a retro fanny pack decked out in silver sequins. The style choice makes sense when she pulls out a canister of hand sanitizer.

I'm grateful, despite the alcohol burn on my chapped skin. "Are you sure? Because I got the feeling Beatriz didn't like me very much."

"She just wanted to be sure you weren't another silver-tongued pretty boy who talks a good game but can't back it up."

"Like Henry," I say.

"Now you're getting it." Nadia smiles. "Hurry up, we've got another stop."

"I'm promoting you from pollster to deputy campaign manager."

"That's the job I've been doing already, but thanks, I guess?"

"Ooh, what am I?" Rachel interjects. "No, wait, I've got it. I'm, like, the cool secretary. The intern who fetches coffee and carries your coat."

"Bodywoman," I say automatically.

"Your what now?" Nadia asks skeptically.

"That's the industry term for a politician's personal aide de camp. Bodyman. Bodywoman."

"Sounds about right. Antiquated and unnecessarily gendered, just like politics," Nadia observes.

Rachel shudders. "No offense, Mark, but I'd rather be Nadia's bodywoman."

"Babe." Nadia smiles. "Same."

Out of the arena, Nadia treks off the beaten path and into the overgrown grass.

"Dare I ask where we're going?"

"So impatient," Nadia huffs. "Or are you just afraid to get a little dirt on your shiny Chuck Taylors?"

"I'm never going to live down the 'pretty boy' thing, am I?"

"Never," Rachel agrees, entirely too gleeful.

"Well. I guess there are worse things to be." Especially for a trans boy.

We round the outer shell of the track. The fence demarcating the school's outer limits comes into view, chain link against the lush flora and fauna of a well-manicured park. Between us and that fence is a grassy knoll, where a small army of outcasts has made their camp. The high ground, obscured from scouting eyes by the bleachers, has the strategic advantage of protecting these rebel combatants from all but the most dedicated assailants.

Even from a distance, they're surround by a haze—cloying, fragrant, and . . . organic. The smoke tickles my throat. I cough into my sleeve. "Nadia, you've got to be kidding."

"Don't be a snob, Mark. Their votes count as much as anyone else's."

"Unless they get suspended for possession before the election," Rachel points out. "Which is a definite possibility."

"Which is exactly why we're here," Nadia explains. "You might not agree with their life choices, but the stoners are a powerful group of influencers with legitimate concerns. Mandatory minimum sentencing for possession is two weeks' suspension. The three-strikes policy ends in academic probation. All of which is totally unethical now that marijuana is legal in the state of California."

"Not for minors," I point out, nonsensically, and I know it.

"Like I said," Nadia ignores me, "they're *influencers*. Half the student body has bought or will buy weed at some point in their student careers. So while the stoners may look like outcasts, they actually interact with an impressive cross-section of the population. You need them on your side, especially because they're currently an undecided voter bloc."

"Okay"—I raise my hands in surrender—"okay, let's talk to them. Just put your camera away."

We trudge up the knoll until we reach the encampment. The smoke is stronger here, dense and pungent.

"Hey, guys," Nadia calls. "Have a minute?"

In the sea of faded leather jackets and bad dye jobs, a leader emerges. Pale, pockmarked, and a slouchy beanie pulled down to his red-rimmed eyes. "What's it worth to you?"

"One sec." A zipper clinks, and Rachel rummages through her fanny pack. "Eureka!" Triumphantly, she pulls out a Ziploc bag stuffed full of gummy bears. "We come bearing gifts."

A few of Slouchy Beanie's friends snort and chuckle.

Slouchy Beanie snatches the bag. "All right. You can chill with us."

"Chill?" I ask, like an alien who has suddenly landed on a strange new planet where I don't speak a word of the language.

Slouchy Beanie reaches into the chest pocket of his utility jacket, from which he produces an Altoid tin. He pops it open and waves an expertly rolled joint at me. "Chill," he repeats.

"Nadia," I hiss.

Rachel's already sitting down. A girl with a purple mohawk and a matching lighter compliments her fanny pack.

Nadia's about to sit beside her, but I grab her arm. "What the hell, Mark?"

"Can I talk to you for a minute?"

"Now?"

"Yes, now."

Slouchy Beanie just shrugs, popping a green gummy bear into his mouth.

Nadia drags me aside. She's got the Angry Mom routine down to a T, hands on her hips and everything, and I feel every bit like the kid who's too scared to go on the roller coaster and chickens out after standing in line for an hour. Nadia raises her eyebrows at me and grouses, "What?"

My skin is wet and clammy. "I said I'd talk with them, not, you know."

"Are you telling me you can't even *say it*?" She flicks me on the arm. "How can you represent the average American teenager if you can't even talk about smoking?"

I'm the son of a congressman, I don't say. *My dad has a security clearance that requires him to report things like this,* I don't say. *Marijuana is still illegal on the federal level, which means Dad would disown me if he ever found out, and God knows he doesn't need another reason,* I don't say. I swallow it all down. "I've just never smoked before."

"Well, that's about to change."

"We're on campus." I look around, paranoid even though I haven't inhaled a single hit. "Someone could see."

"That's precisely the point," Nadia says, exasperated. "For the kids sitting right there to see that you're cool enough to sit down and share a joint with them. Clary'd be too concerned about getting grass stains on her pleated skirt, and we all know that Henry wants a zero-tolerance policy for drugs on this campus. These kids are looking for a reason to vote for anyone else. God, Mark, how can I explain this in terms you'll understand?"

She murmurs something that sounds like a prayer, utterly impenetrable to me. "Okay, you know how presidential candidates go around to small towns and visit greasy spoons where they're expected to bump elbows with the locals while sampling local delicacies? Like the loose meat sandwiches in Anytown, Iowa. Every candidate has to go and eat the entire loose meat sandwich with a big ol' smile, and at no point are they allowed to stop and ask what the hell 'loose meat' even is. This is your loose meat sandwich. So, God help me, you're going to sit down with Shawn and his friends, and you're going to light it up. And then, when you are politely baked, you're going to discuss the issues that matter to Shawn. Got it?"

It's not like I have a moral objection to weed. I think it should be legal everywhere, and if it weren't for Dad, I probably would have tried it before. There's nothing I can do to make Dad happy these days, so maybe it's time I stop trying. "Okay," I say, nervous but maybe a little excited, too. "I'll do it."

"Awesome. Let's get blitzed, Mr. President."

We make our way back to the group. Nadia slides down and wraps her arm around Rachel's shoulder. She's usually so careful about PDA, but out here, at the edge of the wilderness, there are no beasts to fear.

"Sit *down*, pretty boy," Rachel tugs my sleeve. She grins up at me, her smile wide, her pupils blown. I don't know how much she's had in the two minutes we've been gone, but she's enjoying herself.

I sit down next to Slouchy Beanie, who I assume is the aforementioned Shawn.

Nadia balances the joint between her fingers and takes a long, practiced drag. She keeps her lips pressed together before she exhales, smoke spilling from her mouth.

She passes the joint to me. I'm careful with it, careful not to accidentally unroll it, careful not to burn myself on the smoldering tip. I place it between my lips, just holding it there. The scent is strong. My eyes are burning. I'm thinking about that John Green line Mom likes, where you hold the killing thing between your teeth. I always thought that was a load of loose meat. "When in Iowa," I say and breathe in deep.

I cough. Of course I cough. Nadia thumps me on the back. I try again, slowly, letting the smoke settle deep in my lungs. I can feel it cauterizing my soft tissue, which I take to mean it's working. I pass the joint back to Shawn. "So," I wheeze, "I hear you want to talk about mandatory minimums?"

Shawn takes a hit. "Sure, we can talk about them, but I don't really see the point."

I don't know whether this is anarcho-libertarian bullshit or just plain teenage nihilism, but I don't want any part of it. I'm about to tell Nadia this was a waste of time, but she settles a hand on my shoulder. Probably more to keep me in place than to reassure me.

"Why don't you tell us what you mean," she says, taking the joint from Rachel.

"Well," Shawn drawls. "It's obvious the school's drug policies are pretty fucked up, yeah? But all that's in the student handbook, and that's all *Moira* cares about."

Nadia passes me the joint again. I do my civic duty; I take another hit. "Exactly. That's what I want to talk about. How can we change those policies to help you?"

"You say 'we' like it means something."

"Of course it does. We, the people, vote and elect officials to represent us and—"

"And nothing ever changes," Shawn says slowly. At least I think he says it slowly? The space between his words stretches like putty. "Because politicians make promises they can't keep."

"The corrupt ones, sure. The ones beholden to billionaire donors and PACs who want power more than they want to protect the people they've sworn to represent."

"Nah, all of them. Every election, you hear candidates

promise universal healthcare or free college, and none of it happens. Because the president doesn't actually have the power to write the laws. ZP says that's Congress's job."

The joint's back in my hand, between my lips. Smoke in my lungs, out my mouth. "That's . . . true."

"And it's the same in a high school election, yeah? You can sit here and tell me you're gonna relax drug policies, but the president doesn't get to rewrite the handbook. You just get to—what's the executive branch do, again?"

"Enforce the laws."

"And even that's Moira's job. You just get to plan some shitty dances."

I'm laughing before I realize it's happening. "You're right. Shawn, you're totally, completely right."

"He is?" Rachel asks. "Then why are we—"

"You're right," I say again, faster now. I couldn't stop myself if I tried. "My entire platform is well beyond the executive authority of the student body president. Because I don't just want to govern within the confines of the handbook; I want to challenge the handbook itself. I want to make real, institutional changes, and that means working outside the traditional confines of presidential power. Not that I want to be a dictator!" I raise my hands like I've been caught by the campus security guards I'm still half convinced will find us here.

Rachel tosses the bag of gummy bears into my open palm.

"Thanks," I say, and stuff a handful in my mouth. "If anything, the system we have now is the dictatorship, and Flynn is the dictator in chief. The president's just a puppet. Which means we have to get creative. So even though I won't have the power to make changes to the handbook directly, I'll take my concerns—*your* concerns—to the people who do. I'll camp outside Flynn's office until she listens. Enlist the PTA to join the cause. Go straight to the school board if I have to. In short, I'll use my mandate as your representative to lobby the powers that be into changing policy. I'll be a one-man pressure group, and if that doesn't work—"

"You'll burn the student handbook on the senior steps?" Shawn asks.

And then I'm laughing again, until I'm breathless, until I'm coughing, until I'm sure I've never laughed this much before. "I was going to say I'd go to the Department of Education, but I like your idea better."

"And then what?"

I lean forward and meet Shawn's bleary gaze. I'm sure the fire in my lungs has spread to my eyes, but I understand now. Maybe it's the weed, maybe it's the thrill of the campaign trail, or maybe I've known all along and this was just what it took to shake it loose. "Then we rewrite the handbook."

The Utopia Heights Health Club is an acrid mix of sweat and disinfectant.

"Are you sure you should be lifting weights in your . . . condition?" Pablo asks as we make our way up the steps to the weight room.

"Dude." I take the steps two at a time, a spring in my step. "I'm totally fine."

"You're totally high."

"Flying," I agree. "Like Icarus. The sun is within my reach."

"Um. You remember how that myth ends, right?"

I wave my hand. "That's a technicality."

"I'm pretty sure it's the moral of the story."

"I'm pretty sure there's a point to be made that the fall is *fucking worth it* because of the heights he reached. Think about it in terms of, I don't know, human innovation."

"Following that line of reasoning, you're arguing that global warming is 'effing worth it.'"

"Psh. Technicalities."

"So you said."

I feel great. The world is bright, saturated and smooth like it's been caught on film. I'm a celluloid giant, traipsing across a twenty-foot-tall screen. Everything is within my reach.

In the middle of the day, the weight room is deserted like a classroom after the final bell before summer break. There are a few physical trainers in UHHC T-shirts and a handful of retired boomers, probably poised to claim that Pablo and I are ruining gyms in addition to the economy. *They're* the ones to blame for global warming.

Today's an arm day, so we head over to the row of sleek silver torture devices. Pablo takes the rowing machine, and I take the chest press. I adjust my grip around the bars. My muscles strain, but the burn is good. I breathe in and out with each rep, watching the way my muscles ripple beneath my skin. I can finally see them, the slow but undeniable results of testosterone.

I have my binder on under a bro-typical muscle tank. Maybe it's counterintuitive, but I never feel more masculine than I do at the gym. It's the capital of male homosociality, and while that used to feel alienating, when I looked upon a kingdom that should have been mine but wasn't, it's different now that I pass. I'm still careful in the locker room, but with a packer tucked in my boxer briefs, I've got that visible penis line. My binder matches my skin tone, and no one's ever challenged me on it. Maybe it helps that I never come here without Pablo, but I think I'd be okay alone, too. The gym is a place where men are free to appreciate other men's bodies, which is really fucking gay, okay, but it's also a way to affirm my masculinity. In a way that doesn't involve obsessing over souped-up cars or doing keg stands or punching walls.

Pablo and I switch machines. We work through another set, setting a steady rhythm of breaths and grunts. Halfway through, my phone starts vibrating in my basketball shorts. I ignore it. Between the weed and the endorphins, I feel too good to kill it.

"You gonna get that?" Pablo asks.

I finish a set and roll my shoulders. "It's probably just a news alert."

"Then you should definitely get it. What if the president unilaterally declared war on Belgium over Twitter?"

"Belgium?"

"Maybe he found out french fries aren't really French."

I snort out a laugh. "Okay, now I really want french fries. Would it be totally unrealistic for us to stop at In-N-Out after this?"

"Aw," Pablo chuckles, "look who's got his first case of the munchies. We should commemorate this with an Instagram post."

"We should definitely not do that," I say, remembering Dad's strict social media policy even through the haze of my good mood. It isn't a policy so much as a doctrine of *don'ts*.

Finishing his set, Pablo takes the terry cloth towel from around his neck and wipes his brow, but from the matte finish of his skin, it's mostly for show. He isn't breaking a sweat. But it makes me feel better about wiping the salty sheen from my face and arms. Pablo's good at that, making small concessions to make me feel more comfortable.

"Dude," Pablo says. "Your phone hasn't stopped buzzing."

"Oh." I kind of stopped paying attention to it after the first jolt. "I'll put it back on silent." I retrieve my phone from the depths of my pocket and fumble with the toggle switch. I hit the power button by mistake, and the screen flashes to life. I have three missed calls from Jenny and one from an unknown number. Sure enough, there's a news alert, but I have to read it twice before I'm sure it isn't a weed-induced paranoid delusion. "What the hell?"

"What?" Pablo leans over and takes my phone.

"Please tell me I'm reading this wrong."

Pablo stares at the screen and recites verbatim the head-line I thought I hallucinated: "'WHO IS MARK ADAMS? NEWCOMER CANDIDATE "COMES OUT" OF THE SHADOWS.'" He nearly drops my phone. "Wait, since when does *Dystopia High* show up on Apple News?"

"Who knows?" Panic displaces every ounce of euphoria, crawling over my skin like something slimy. Or maybe that's just the sweat I haven't wiped off. "Oh my God, she didn't say she was posting it today. I can't read it."

"Okay." Pablo switches off the screen. "It can wait."

"No, wait." I reach out, stricken. "I can't wait. What if she wrote something horrible about me? What if she *figured out* something horrible about me? Or worse, what if she said I'm an elitist snob who's unworthy of the highest office in the land?"

"Dude, I know you're high, but you've gotta chill. Come back to earth."

I'm falling back to earth all right, just like Icarus.

We crowd together on one of the benches and read the article shoulder-to-shoulder. My screen seems small from

163

this distance, the letters like the bottom line of an optometrist's eye chart.

But it's not a total hatchet job? Sure, Amber calls attention to my lack of experience in student government, as well as my lack of experience in the UHS social scene. But there's nothing about my life before UHS, thank God, and she conveys my message about making the school a safer place for everyone pretty faithfully.

At least, that's what I'm getting from it.

Pablo claps me on the shoulder like he's about to watch the guards lead me off to death row. "Bro," he says, with the kind of sympathy that says he's sorry for me but absolutely would not trade places with me for anything, "Jenny's going to kill you."

"It's not that bad." I scratch the back of my neck. "I mean, Amber could have spent the entire profile talking about how her deep background on my history as a student at a Marin Catholic school turned up no results. That headline could have been 'WHO IS MARK ADAMS? HE DIDN'T EXIST UNTIL THIRTEEN MONTHS AGO.' It could have been all about how I'm a consummate liar who's trying to dupe the electorate on my sick, ambitious power grab."

"Yes, that might have been worse," Pablo humors me, "but you're missing the headline. Literally."

I stab my sweaty thumb against the screen and scroll back up.

"Mark, the article's a coming-out story. And not a coming-out-in-society story. Amber took your one line about being pan and made it into the whole article. You've gone from being the candidate whose name no one can remember to being the *gay* candidate."

"Not gay."

"Well, you know that, and I know that, but as far as everyone else is concerned, you're the Gay Candidate."

"Better than an *also ran*, right?"

"If it gets you elected, yeah, but Jenny didn't want you to pigeonhole yourself."

"Our platform is literally predicated on queer issues. It was always going to come up."

"There's a difference between something coming up and making that something the story."

"I'm not supposed to be the story," I insist. "Benji's not even supposed to be the story. The story is: Make Your Mark. The story is—"

"I know what the story is, buddy. The trick is making sure everyone else knows."

"Well," I say, "at least they'll know my name now."

Pablo smiles. "They won't be able to forget it."

When I check my Google News alerts that night, the latest result for "Mark Adams" is me. *Dystopia High*, Amber's byline, and my name, lit up in cobalt blue.

I know I'm supposed to do damage control, return Jenny's increasingly frantic messages, and make sure there's more to the story than my sexuality, but less than my gender.

But my name is in the news. The name I fought so hard for. A name associated with a campaign I believe in.

No matter what anyone else says, I think that's something I should be proud of.

SEVENTEEN

THE THING ABOUT C-SPAN IS IT NEVER REALLY changes. It's the same cast of interchangeable characters trapped in the same awful bottle episode day after day. A few times a year, if you're lucky, you'll get a Very Special Episode in which very angry men and a handful of very tactful women argue about a high-profile piece of legislation you've actually heard of. Usually because these are the kinds of bills that mean life or death for someone. Healthcare. Immigration reform. Taxes. But those Very Special Episodes are when C-SPAN becomes irrelevant because every major news network streams the vote alongside colorful commentary—the colors being red, blue, and fuck you.

This isn't one of those times.

I honestly don't even know what they're debating this morning. The congresswoman from Alaska mentioned something about fisheries, so maybe it's another endangered species bill. I haven't even been able to find Dad yet. He must not be sitting in his usual row, with his usual gang of left-of-the-party-line-but-not-socialists-no-sirree cronies.

Three thousand miles away from that hallowed "temple of democracy," as the video in the Capitol Visitor Center calls it, I'm alone in the kitchen. Mom got called in early again, and I'm eating my breakfast burrito in near peace. I can't focus completely on C-SPAN because, well, it's boring, and message notifications keep popping up in the corner of my screen.

Jenny: Mark
Jenny: MARK!
Jenny: MArk.
Jenny: Come on, I know you're awake. You're always awake by five and on your computer by six.
Jenny: Mark, I really need to talk to you

I haven't talked to Jenny since Amber posted the profile, and yes, that is entirely because I'm afraid of her. Because Pablo's entirely right: if Jenny's crunching the numbers, branding myself as the Gay Candidate might backfire, and I don't want to deal with it. But I'm going to deal with it. Another few bites of my burrito, another swig of coffee, and then I'm going to reply to Jenny's messages. I swear.

A glob of refried beans splats on the counter. Mom would tell me this is what I get for standing and eating like a heathen, but she's not here. Monty barks plaintively, and sure, I could just push the mess to the floor for him to gobble up, but I wipe it up. The same congresswoman, who's got a "Top 20 Surnames in America" kind of name, is still talking. She's moved on from fisheries to water-treatment facilities, so maybe this has nothing to do with endangered species after all.

There's another set of messages from Jenny, all time-stamped in the two minutes it took for me to clean up Burrito-Gate.

Jenny: Mark, I'm serious.
Jenny: Are you there?
Jenny: It's not about the interview.

I'm about to reply when another notification pops up: *Incoming email from Graham Teagan,* and I've never clicked faster. I swear I can count my heartbeats before the email fills my screen.

To: markadams2040@gmail.com
From: graham@grahamteagan.com
Subject: Interview

Dear Madison,
It has come to my attention that you participated in an

interview with one Amber Carr about your student council campaign. I have read the resulting article, and I feel it is my duty to encourage you, once more, to forget about this election.

There will be other elections. When you're older, when you've learned more about the world and yourself, when you've remembered how the system works, you'll be better equipped to run for office. At Harvard, or after. You'll have any number of opportunities when you've grown up. When you've come to your senses.

Any publicity you garner now will only tarnish your future electability. When you run for office as an adult, you need to ensure there is no evidence of your youthful indiscretions. This interview, where you speak candidly and colorfully about your sexuality, will serve as evidence of your naïveté if it ever resurfaces.

To be blunt, for I fear the situation warrants it, you will regret this. You will regret participating in this election. The delusion you've harbored these past two years will only serve to tarnish your reputation and your mother's good name.

If you persist in this charade, and if, by some miracle, you win your little electoral farce, I hope you understand the consequences. I believe I've made my position abundantly clear in the past, but in case you've forgotten, I will reiterate it now. I cannot associate with any potential scandal. I will not tolerate that risk. If that means cutting off all relations with you, then so be it. You must make your choice, and I will make mine.

You want to do good in this world. I know you do. It's clear from the interview. You could be the kind of politician this country needs, Mads, if only you remembered the needs of the republic come before your own.

Dad

PS: Please ask your mother to return my calls at her earliest convenience.

My legs give out. I slide down the length of the cabinet before I'm a puddle on the floor, as much of a mess as the one I made on the counter. Monty butts his head against my thigh, but I can't muster the strength to pet him.

Sacré fucking bleu.

What the fuck did I expect?

I'm supposed to be flattered. Flattered Dad still cares. Flattered he still pays attention. Flattered he still thinks I have what it takes to set the world on fire. I'm supposed to feel the warmth of his approval and lean toward it. Reach for it, always. Even if it means burning myself.

His manipulation is a cheap vaudeville act.

I shouldn't be surprised. It sure as hell shouldn't hurt this much.

I stand up. Tell myself to man up. I'm the one who blew up my nuclear family like an actual atom bomb so I could live as a man, so I should fucking act like it. I wipe my eyes with the cuff of my hoodie and lock my knees so they won't give out on me again.

I close Gmail, and there's C-SPAN, still streaming in all its glory. No one's speaking right now, so it's quiet. I understand now why I didn't see Dad earlier. Laptops aren't allowed on the floor of the House. If he was sending me an email—an email he waited to send until *he knew I would be awake*—then he isn't in the chamber yet.

I watch the doors and gulp my coffee. I wait the way Monty does when he hears a noise in the middle of the night, bolting upright on his bed with his hackles raised, darting his head from side to side in search of an intruder who never appears. The minutes pass, and someone who isn't the Speaker shuffles papers from the Speaker's podium, and then the doors open. He swoops in, a leather briefcase tucked under his arm, a crimson tie knotted around his neck. He's alone. I can't make out the expression in the blur of pixels that make up his face, but I can imagine it, the lines of his features pulled taut.

Because of me.

He slides into a seat, his posture stiff and rehearsed, and my fists clench on the cold granite counter.

Dad says I'll regret this election. But he told me that I'd regret coming out as trans, too.

I'm going to prove him wrong.

* * *

Henry's holding a goddamn rally on the senior steps.

It's ten minutes before the bell, and I'm cutting across campus to get my calculus textbook from my locker. I hear the shouting before I hit the quad. I'm just trying to mind my own business, but hundreds of students are packed in like sardines. I can't even elbow my way through.

I find Beatriz at the back of the crowd and whisper, "What's going on?"

Beatriz pops her bubble gum meaningfully. "Your esteemed opponent thinks he's all up in Nuremberg."

I stand on my tiptoes, tying to see over the masses of frizzled hair and backward baseball caps. There, alone on the senior steps, is Henry, with a bullhorn in his fist. "It's time for this school to put its students first," he shouts. "For far too long, the administration has pandered to the needs of a small group of students. They ask for trigger warnings and safe spaces. If they can't make it through this sheltered high school environment without crying wolf, then how are they going to survive beyond the wrought-iron gates of Utopia Heights?"

The crowd hoots and hollers. An arm shoots up as someone waves a bandanna in the air.

"And what about the rest of us?" Henry stomps his combat boots on the concrete. "The administration hasn't kept us safe from the real violence that lurks in our halls. Just last week, I saw my friend and UHS linebacker Trevor punched in the face. The assailant broke Trevor's nose, and his punishment? One week's suspension. Is that enough?"

Cries of *"Justice for Trevor!"* ring through Henry's captive audience.

Henry holds up his hand to quiet everyone. "We know that fights break out in our halls every day. Drugs pollute this campus. And yet the administration allows this behavior to continue with only a slap on the wrist for perpetrators. We need to put victims first."

Rage brings my blood to a rapid boil. My fists are clenched, my arms shaking, my vision blurred with red at the edges.

"And they're not the only victims," Henry continues. "Someone needs to check the power of the administration's favorite sons. Some of my opponents would have you believe that that means the football team or the cheerleading squad, but hear me when I say the true elites are the IB and honors students."

It's clear Henry doesn't mean to stop there, but cheers drown him out. He waits them out with a tense smile. "Trust me, I know. I'm both a quarterback and an IB diploma candidate, and I promise you, I've only ever received preferential treatment for the latter. The classes are smaller; we have the supplies we need. The administration is invested in our success, but not in yours."

He pauses for another round of boos.

"We need to make sure this school supports all its students, whether they're headed to a four-year university, junior college, or straight into the workforce. We need to make our vocational courses as much of a priority as IB courses. We need to promote extracurriculars that teach real-world skills."

The cheers shake me to the bone. They actually believe him. They don't see his performative pseudo-populism for the opportunism it is. They're going to *vote* for him.

"That's why I'm running for student body president," Henry yells, each syllable loud as a gunshot. "I'll make sure the administration remembers the needs of all students, not just the privileged few. I'll make sure Utopia High School lives up to its potential. I'll make sure we put Utopia first."

The crowd breaks out in a chant. *"HENRY. HENRY. HENRY."*

I don't realize I've taken a step forward until Beatriz's arm hooks through mine, tugging me back. "Down, boy."

"UHS is worth fighting for," Henry shouts, and his mouth does this thing that's not quite a grin but still broadcasts his pleasure loud and clear, "so let's fight for it."

Maybe it's a trick of the stage, but I swear he looks right at me.

It's a challenge, and it's so fucking on.

EIGHTEEN

HALFWAY THROUGH GUIDED STUDY, A CHORUS of dissonant vibrations rings out, the national anthem of the digital age. Mr. González, my AP Calculus BC teacher, looks up from the quizzes he's grading in red Sharpie, prepared to remind us all of the school's notorious Phones Off, Not Silent policy, but then an actual ringtone chimes from behind his desk, and Mr. González shuts his mouth.

No surprise the thing that unites students and teachers alike is a *Dystopia High* news alert. The logo alone fills me with apprehension, like a shadow in a slasher movie. I'm sure it's about me. Panic muddles my senses; I can't make out the headline. Maybe I should see an optometrist.

Pablo swivels around and taps his fingers on my desk, but I ignore him.

Gasps ring in harmony as the entire class reads the article. Someone snickers, and finally I see it.

"Mark," Pablo whispers.

The headline reads "ALL ABOUT THAT VEEP: UTO-PIA'S NEXT POWER COUPLE OR JUST ANOTHER SCANDAL?"

It's about Jenny. My Jenny.

And Dante Gomez, the other candidate for veep, who I only know by reputation. He's one of the so-called popular kids. Hangs out on the senior steps. With Henry and company. He's got a letterman jacket, but his is for basketball. He's good—the full-ride-to-the-college-basketball-program-of-his-choice kind of good. He's tall and dark and handsome and, most important, Jenny Chu's type, apparently.

There's a grainy photo under the headline, something taken with an older smartphone that wasn't meant for night photography, especially not zoomed all the way in. But the resolution's still good enough to make out Dante with his shirt off and Jenny in her strappy black bra, standing in each other's space. They're on a dock, I think, near a lake.

It shouldn't matter that Dante's the mystery man Jenny's been hooking up with. It doesn't matter to me. Sure, we hooked up a long time ago, but I'm not burning a candle for her. She's my best friend, and I love her, point-blank.

What matters to Amber, and to my entire calculus class, apparently, isn't even that Dante has a girlfriend. It's that Jenny and Dante are both running for the same office, and this affair gives a whole new meaning to "sleeping with the enemy." It shouldn't matter because this is just a stupid student council election, as Dad called it, and it shouldn't matter who Jenny does or doesn't sleep with. It shouldn't matter, but here's Amber Carr, slut-shaming Jenny and deeming her "unfit for office" because she's hooking up with the opposition.

Pablo's saying something, but I can't make out the words. My head is underwater. The sounds are warbled. I can't find the surface.

But I can feel the weight of Ralph's gaze from his seat beside me. His mouth is moving. There are words coming out. I need to listen.

"Mark," Ralph says.

"Jenny," Pablo says.

And Jenny, oh my God, *Jenny*, who sent me a dozen frantic messages I never responded to because I was too afraid of her, then too caught up in my own drama, and just generally too busy being a shitty friend.

She's right down the hall in AP Calculus AB, except the hall might as well be an ocean, and—

What the hell?

I'm across the room and to the door before Mr. González can even yell, "Mr. Adams!" I mumble an excuse about the bathroom and lurch across the linoleum. The door's closed across the hall. I peep through the little crosshatched window and survey a field of desks. There's Clary in the front row, curled over her phone. Henry's leaning back at his desk, both hands behind his head, not a care in the goddamn world. I spy Rachel in the back corner, rapidly texting.

I knock on the window. She shoots a worried glance at the teacher before she darts over and cracks the door open.

"Mark, what are you doing here? Pablo said you just ran out of class, and—"

"How do you— Never mind." Of course Pablo warned her. "Where's Jenny?"

"She ran out as soon as cell phones started dinging."

"And you didn't go after her?"

"She was gone before anyone had even read the article," Rachel whispers. "I'm pretty sure she wanted to be alone."

"Which is precisely why she shouldn't be!"

Rachel stares at me, way too cavalier about this. "I'm sure she just went to her car to cool down."

Under normal circumstances, that might be a reasonable assumption, because Jenny is unflappable. Steadfast. The definition of cool in times of crisis. Except Jenny's never been the cause of crisis before. Certainly never a sex scandal. And I know she's flapped because she tried to tell me this morning, and I ignored her when she needed me.

"I'm going to find her," I inform Rachel. "You can come with me or not."

"Mark, just wait a minute. We can—"

Except I can't wait.

* * *

Stepping into the girls' bathroom is like stepping into enemy territory. It used to make me break out in hives. I'd be freaking out if I weren't on a mission. As it is, I barely notice the museum of internalized misogyny graffitied on the walls, or the saccharine cloud of cheap perfume that doesn't do anything to hide the underlying stench of urine. None of it matters, because there's this stifled hiccup coming from one of the stalls, the kind you make when you're trying really hard not to cry. I look under the stall and recognize sheer black tights tucked into the pleather low-tops she picked out when we went to the Converse outlet store last Black Friday.

"Jenny?" I rap my knuckles against the door.

"Mark?" her voice wobbles. "You're not supposed to be in here."

"Tell that to the state of North Carolina."

She laughs, but it's hollow.

"Jen. Will you let me in?"

Her breath catches. "I don't think I can . . ." but I can fill in her blanks. She doesn't want me to see her face, not now, not like this.

"Then I'll join you." I shimmy into the neighboring stall and put down the seat. I lock the door for good measure because I don't actually want to deal with any challenges to my right to use this restroom.

It's impossible to ignore the cave paintings etched in the back of the door. I'm stuck staring at an array of slurs that

180

definitely haven't been deployed in a reclaimed feminist sense. A Dadaist rendering of a penis, by someone who has probably never seen a penis, adorns an anatomically impossible claim about someone I've never met.

I haven't missed this. I still remember what these primitive tableaus used to say about me.

Except right now there's no catty callout that could hurt me more than the recriminations I'm flinging at myself. "I'm sorry."

"What do you have to be sorry for?" Jenny asks. "Unless you're the one who snapped that photo of Dante and me at Verde Lake and gave it to Amber, in which case you have more to be sorry for than you could hope to make up for."

"I should have replied to your messages. I got caught up in my own shit, but that's no excuse. I should have responded as soon as I saw the notifications. Especially when you said it was important."

"I just wanted to give you a heads-up. Amber called me for comment at the ass crack of dawn, as she does, and nothing I said, nothing I offered her, was enough to change her mind about running the story."

"I'm sorry," I say again.

"Seriously, for what?"

For not being a better friend. For not running a cleaner campaign. For not seeing this coming, somehow. Classic Catholic guilt for original sin. "I'm just sorry."

"You have to stop saying that," she tsks. "First law of politics. Never apologize until they've got you dead to rights in front of a grand jury."

"It's not fair, though. What she did to you. What people are saying—"

"Of course it's not fair," Jenny retorts. "That's why you got into this. Because this school is infested with vultures and harpies who are just waiting for you to make one wrong move before they feast on your fetid corpse."

"Don't go all Hobbes on me." It's supposed to be a joke, but something's lost in the delivery.

"What?"

"*Bella omnium contra omnes.*" I knock my knuckles against the wall between us. "The war of all against all. That's what we're fighting against. That belief Henry was spouting on the senior steps this morning: that human existence is a war made of winners and losers."

I shut my eyes, and the slurs and sketches disappear. I try to summon up my glittering fantasy of the best of all possible worlds. "Civil society doesn't have to be a zero-sum game."

She's quiet for too long. I imagine her staring at the wall between us, trying to sketch my profile through paint-chipped metal. "You really believe that, don't you?"

"You know I do." I pause. "But you don't."

"It's not about believing in the thing."

"Then what is it about?"

Jenny knocks against the divider. "Getting things done."

"You get the best work done when you believe in what you're doing."

"Not in politics. Ideologues are always the last to compromise."

"Maybe. But there are some things you can't compromise."

"I like that you believe that."

"Even if you don't?"

"It's what makes us a good team. You have the vision. I have the wherewithal to do what it takes to get us there. Or—" Another hiccup stunts the flow of her words. "At least I thought I did."

"Jen."

"No, Mark, listen to me. It's not about me anymore. It's about *your vision*, and—"

"That doesn't matter right now. I'm here for *you*."

"And we're both *here* for the campaign."

"We'll talk about that later."

"There is no later. The election's in six days."

"At lunch."

"You're supposed to make campaign stops at lunch."

"Jenny." I laugh a little, all my exasperation bubbling up. "It's a good thing I'm the candidate, isn't it? I can just declare all campaign stops postponed until tomorrow for an emergency campaign strategy sesh."

"That's not very democratic."

"Well," I say, "then it's a good thing we don't live in a democracy."

"Don't you dare—"

"We live in a—"

"*Democratic republic,*" she finishes. "Fuck you, Mark."

"Been there, done that."

She laughs, a real one this time. Bright in spite of the grime and the stench. She sounds like the Jenny I know and love.

I reach under the divider and hold out my hand. I wait and wait. I'm convinced she's going to leave me hanging, so I start to pull back. But then her pinky hooks through mine, and we hold on even when the bell rings.

NINETEEN

"MARCUS. A WORD?"

I'm halfway out the door after the lunch bell tolls when Clary's sugar-sweet voice creeps up on me.

"It's Mark," I say, defensive. I've spent too many years fighting for my name to let someone get it wrong.

"Isn't it short for anything?"

"Nope . . . Clarissa."

She scowls. "Just come with me, will you?"

"I have somewhere to be."

"It'll only take a minute."

We end up in the janitor's closet. "It was the closest I could find to a cloakroom on short notice," Clary explains. "And we can't be seen having this conversation in public. We wouldn't want Amber reporting that we were engaged in ex parte communication, now, would we?"

A broom jabs me in the back when I try to move. "Can we at least turn a light on?"

"There isn't one," Clary replies blithely, which is either a lie to get me to focus on the reason she kidnapped me, or a depressing statement on the amount of time she spends in janitors' closets.

I stop squirming and look at her. My eyes haven't yet adjusted to make out the shape of her, but her Peter Pan collar is bone white. "So are you going to tell me the reason we're here, or is this some backhanded ploy to play Seven Minutes in Heaven? Because I'm sorry, Clary, but you're not my ty—"

"Ugh, Marcus, no." She slaps my chest. "Get your head out of the gutter. You're here because I'm going to make you an offer. One-time only. Expires when the final bell rings."

Something drips onto my nose from up above, and it takes every inch of self-restraint I possess not to look at the ceiling. "What kind of offer?"

She smiles, her pristine white teeth flashing like the reflective material on hazard vests. "Drop out of the race for president, endorse my candidacy, and I'll support your bid for vice president."

"Excuse me?"

"You heard me," Clary says. "Let's stop this petty infighting and join forces. We can run this school as a team. With my proven experience and your"—she waves her hand vaguely—"outsider appeal, we'll be the dream team. Our student government will be the most effective in UHS history.

We'll combine our platforms, fighting for my vegan school lunch options and your whole antibullying shtick."

"Shouldn't you have filled your veep vacancy days ago?"

"I was weighing my options," Clary replies carefully, which I take to mean she couldn't find anyone naive enough to join her ticket. "I decided you were the best man for the job."

"There's just one problem." There's a hell of a lot more than one, but I'm trying to keep this civil. I've already come close enough to blows with one of my opponents.

"What's that?"

"*Jenny* is running for vice president."

"Oh, Mark, you sweet summer child. Grow up. After that exposé, Jenny has about as much chance of being elected vice president of the United States of America as she does of being elected student body vice president."

"What are you even talking about?" I raise my hand, meaning to gesticulate dramatically, but I end up knocking over a box of something that might be lightbulbs. Glass shatters on impact with the dank concrete floor. "That article is a slut-shaming hit job, and as a card-carrying feminist, I thought you'd be opposed to Amber's tactics."

"All's fair in love and politics. Jenny made a mistake, and she's going to pay for it. I don't have a problem with that."

That's when I realize Clary means an entirely different mistake, one that has nothing to do with the article. Jenny turned on Clary, and because high school politics is by definition a Shakespearean tragedy, Clary's going to force Jenny out of the election, even if it goes against her personal politics. Because the political's never as personal as when you're exacting revenge on someone who stabbed you in the back. "Jenny did nothing wrong."

"Jenny's a political opportunist with all the loyalty of a blade of grass. She goes wherever the wind blows. That's not the kind of running mate you want, Mark. You're the kind of candidate who actually believes his own spin."

Unbidden, the words Jenny and I exchanged in the bathroom come rushing back. *It's not about believing in the thing*, she said. "And what kind of politician are you, Clary?"

"Oh, I'm a political animal, too. But unlike Jenny, I've never pretended to be anything other than a snake. You know what you're getting with me. You, with your righteous all-American act and your *hair*." She tugs on an errant lock of my hair to punctuate her point. "You can't trust Jenny. You can't trust me, exactly, but you *can* trust that I'll be forthright in our alliance."

"Okay, that's enough." I reach for the brass doorknob, but Clary blocks my path.

"Not until you hear me out."

"I've heard you, loud and clear." I run a hand through my hair to rectify the damage. "You still haven't explained why I'd enter into an alliance with you to begin with."

"Easy." She's still standing between me and door like she

suspects me to bolt at any moment, which, okay, I would if I had any chance of escaping. "You and I can both agree Henry McIver is a blight on our electoral landscape. You heard his performance this morning. He won't rest until he's turned UHS into a police state and instated himself as dictator in chief. Neither of us wants that. We both lose. I lose my crown, and you lose your platform." She leans forward, eyes glimmering in the dark. "In a three-way race, you and I split the vote. All the reasonable students—everyone who sees through Henry's polished fascist aesthetic—should be the ones who decide this election. They're a majority of the electorate, but neither of us can win with the other in the race. One of us needs to drop out. Unite the party."

"There is no party," I mutter, though I argued this point with Jenny mere days ago.

I realize, now, that this is the same deal she offered Jenny. Clary made a case that they had more in common with each other, and it was in their best interests to team up to take Henry down. Jenny, ever the pragmatist, took that deal because she cared about getting things done.

Until she told me to run.

"If you're so keen on uniting the student body," I counter, "then why don't *you* drop out? Take a hit for the greater good."

"Because you're the one who cares about the greater good, Mark. You kowtow to your platform before your pride. You've already showed your cards."

"Oh my God. That's it." I push past her, clawing at the doorknob, but the door jams before I can jimmy it open.

"Like I said," Clary says, "the offer expires when the bell rings."

"Go to hell, Clary."

She shrugs. "Better to reign in hell than let Henry rule in heaven."

Apparently "emergency campaign strategy sesh" is code for "requiem for Mark's campaign," because by the time I get to ZP's room, everyone looks like they're here for a candlelight vigil.

Jenny perches on the edge of a desk, a gargoyle poised at the end of the world. The cracks I saw in her facade this morning have all been concealed with plaster. She's so unnaturally still compared to her usual high-voltage, type-A electric storm. The fact that she isn't cocking an eyebrow and asking what took me so long is proof enough that she hasn't recovered.

"For God's sake," I mutter, a poor man's recitation, "let us sit upon the ground and tell sad stories of the death of kings."

"Melodramatic much?" Rachel lifts her head from Nadia's shoulder to side-eye me.

"None of you have been doing the *Richard II* reading, have you?"

"Neither have you," Nadia points out.

"Yeah, but I've read it before."

"Nerd," Pablo coughs.

"Pot, kettle."

"Yes, we're a whole cabinet of nerds, but that isn't going to change the fact that we're in hot water."

"Jen." I can only manage her name, but she has to hear me pleading with her, a whole treatise of words I can't say.

"No. We've been sitting around, waiting for you and very pointedly not talking about it, but the fact of the matter is, the campaign is imploding."

"We don't know that," I say, even though Clary's threats have infected my thoughts like venom. "It's just gossip, the same thing that's always on *Dystopia High*. People obsess over it for a fifteen-minute news cycle—"

"Maybe fifteen hours," Rachel tries.

"And then they move on to the next scandal," I say firmly. "There's no reason to believe this will be any different."

"Well, actually," Nadia interjects, "I did a quick straw poll, and about half of likely voters stated the Jenny/Dante story will influence their votes."

"When the hell did you have time to conduct a straw poll?" I ask in spite of myself.

"In the cafeteria line. I bought a bunch of those little ranch cups to hand out in exchange for responses."

"Not the headline, people," Jenny cuts in. "I should know; I *am* the headline."

"Right, sorry," I mutter, chagrined. "So, if this story is something voters care about, then we'll deal with it. We'll figure out how to *fix this*."

"There's only one fix."

"Okay." I still haven't sat down. No one has moved. I'm an intruder in a gallery of statues. I take a few steps toward Jenny. "What's the fix?"

Except Jenny shakes her head. She still won't look at me. Her hair is down, for once, and it draws a curtain around her face. "Here's the thing," she says, quiet, conspiratorial. "On *Scandal*, the solution to every sex scandal is to marry the guy because America loves a love story. Amber even alluded to it in her headline, asking if Dante and I were the next 'power couple.' But even if he were single, I still couldn't go steady with him. Not even for a high school political marriage." She full-body shudders. "I don't want to be anyone's girlfriend."

I close the distance between us and snatch up her hand. I want her to understand me. "Hey, no one's asking you to."

"You should be," she mutters, morose. "You'll lose the election with me on your ticket."

"Jenny, what are you saying?"

She looks up at me, her eyes too pink, her cheeks too blotchy. Jenny's cried in a derelict bathroom stall and maybe in the back row of our physics class and right here on a desk in ZP's room. She fishes a crumpled hall pass from her pocket and offers it up like a tithe or a sacrifice.

I smooth out the wrinkles. It's a pass for her to see the guidance counselor last week.

"Other side."

On the obverse, scribbled in gel pen, is a single sentence:

I, Jennifer Chu, hereby resign my candidacy for the office of student body vice president, effective immediately.

"Jen, no—"

"The only way you win," Jenny says, sharp as a knife on a grindstone, "is if I lose. That's the sum of the game. So if I drop out now, before this thing gets blown even further out of proportion, then maybe there's some way you can salvage this."

My friends speak up right away. Nadia's searching for a compromise. Rachel's suggesting an interview. Pablo's making the emotional appeal. They're saying all the things I should be saying, but I can't get a word out. Bees are swarming inside my skull, and all I can think is, Clary told me this would happen. Except no, that's not right, because Clary said Jenny was only in it for herself, and yet here she is, telling me she has to drop out for the sake of my campaign.

Everyone's shouting over each other, and no one's sitting on the floor anymore. The first time I say no, they don't hear me. So I say it again, louder, my voice hoarse, as if I've been screaming. Everyone stops, and they all look to me, their fearless leader.

What a fucking joke.

"I don't want you to do this," I tell Jenny. All the strength has been sapped out of me. I'm hollow and scared; I don't know how to do this without her by my side.

"Do you want to lose?"

This is where I'm supposed to say, *I don't want to win if it means you lose.* I mean to say it. I open my mouth. I call up the words. I try to follow the script, but the heroic monologue doesn't come. Someone's deleted the text. All I can think is, I *can't* lose. The stakes are too high. Henry will terrorize the school. Clary will terrorize the GSA. Benji will be vulnerable. Dad will be *right*.

"No," I whisper, and if I don't quite meet Jenny's eyes, well, that's just because I'm shaking my head. "I don't want to lose."

I'm sure someone's going to say something. Offer up some wild idea just reckless enough to work. If I just wait long enough, Jenny will take it all back and pull the fix out of her white hat.

Instead, she lets out a long, shuddering breath. I do look at her then. She steadies her breathing, one cycle at a time. She rolls her shoulders back and sets her jaw. She puts herself back together piece by piece, and then she opens her eyes. "It's settled, then. Handled."

"You'll stay on as campaign manager." I don't let myself phrase it as a question.

"If you still want me."

"Of course I do."

She nods sharply. "First order of business, then. Picking your new VP."

"Wait, what? The candidacy deadline was last Friday."

"Did you think I was just going to drop out and leave you with Dante?"

I don't know what I assumed. "Clary hasn't replaced you." But that's not quite right, because she asked me ten minutes ago.

"I already talked to ZP," Jenny says, like it's nothing. "He said you could tap someone else, given the circumstances."

"I don't . . ." My head is buzzing again, and there's a whole other menagerie of beasts in my stomach. I haven't eaten anything since the burrito I spilled this morning, abandoned after Dad's email. "We shouldn't do this now."

Jenny shakes her head. "I'm not going to let this disrupt the campaign any longer than it already has."

I hate hearing her talk like this. I hate that I'm letting her talk like this. I hate everything about this school that has led us to this place.

But that's why I'm running for office. To change it.

"Okay. Let's do this."

"Who do you want?" Jenny asks.

Well, if I can't have her, it's not even a question. I turn to Pablo, who's leaning against the whiteboard.

"Dude." He raises his hands like I've tried to drop an

electric eel into his lap rather than an unsavory job offer. "No way."

"But you're already running for treasurer. You're on the wrestling team. People know you, and they like you."

"The public knowing and liking someone is a pretty rare combination," Nadia acknowledges.

"Then why don't *you* do it?" Pablo gestures at Nadia. "We've already established that you know literally everyone. They like *you*, don't they?"

Nadia looks unimpressed. "As we've already acknowledged, yearbook staff is a full-time job."

"Actually, no, I don't think we've established that," Pablo objects.

"What we need," Nadia says, "is someone with broad appeal. Someone who, unlike Mark, has been in the Santa Julia public school system since kindergarten. Someone likable." Thoughtfully, she looks to Rachel. "Like you, babe."

"What?" Rachel stammers, her black-rimmed eyes gone wide. "Everything I know about politics, I learned from *Parks and Rec* and you guys. But mainly *Parks and Rec*."

"That's more than enough," I insist. Because when I think about it, Rachel works. She's likable and well-known. Smart, but not showy about it. Not like I am. "You'd be great."

"I'm the bodywoman, remember?" She shakes her head. "Between soccer, IB, Key Club, and French Club, I can't make it work. I'm sorry."

"Not your fault," I say. And it isn't. Of course none of my IB diploma friends have time. They're all busy fulfilling the 150-hour extracurricular requirement in highly specialized ways to accentuate their college apps.

"We might need to expand our horizons," Nadia says.

Jenny chimes in, "All we really need is a warm body. What was it LBJ said? The veep's worth about as much as a warm bucket of—"

"Okay," I cut her off quickly. I can't ask her the question I really want to ask her. *Is that what you thought you'd be to me?*

"If you think about it," Rachel muses, oblivious to the warning look Nadia's giving her, "a student body vice president's even more ornamental than an actual vice president. On a state level, you need a warm body because there's the threat of assassination. Unless I've gravely underestimated the dangers of high school politics, the only function of a student government vice president is to—"

"Stand there and look pretty," Jenny fills in. "So let's find someone pretty."

"And *strategic*," Nadia stresses. "We need a senior who's familiar with Santa Julia schools. If not well-known, then better known than Mark. Noncontroversial. Likable. Unmarred by scandal."

"And unlikely to *become* marred by scandal in the next six days."

I think through the small cross-section of the senior class

I know, not yearbook mug shots but faces I see in class every day. Maybe I'm not quite following Nadia's criteria, but I try to imagine who I could see on the stage with me next week, working beside me in the coming months. Who do I know, in the marrow of my bones, shares my values? Who will put in the work to make this school a better place?

There's only one other person I trust.

Ralph eats lunch in the chem lab. At least, that's what he told me, so that's where I go.

The hinges creak when I slip in. Ralph startles, craning his neck over his shoulder to take in the sight of me. "Mark?" From across the room, his face flickers through a series of expressions I can't quite keep up with, frames from a silent movie without the title cards.

"Hey. You got a second?"

"Yeah, of course."

The room is dim, the contrast low like an old Polaroid. Instead of desks, rows of long black laminate tables populate the room. Ralph sits in the middle, an array of neatly ordered, color-coded Tupperware spread out before him.

I go to the next row and sit backward on the table, my high-tops planted on the chair in front of me. I look at Ralph, who has a notepad and a textbook alongside everything else. He scribbles something on the pad, his eyes down rather than on me, and a lump swells in my throat, as if I've intruded on something I shouldn't. "What are you doing?"

"Calculus."

He's using the smallest graph paper I've ever seen, the blue squares so tiny the white between them fades away at a distance. I try to make sense of the upside-down scrawl of equations. "I thought this week was just reviewing derivatives."

"It is. This is from the next chapter." He sets his pencil down with a marked kind of finality. "I like to do math when I'm stressed or anxious. It helps to break the universe down into numbers and equations, a language I understand."

"That's kind of beautiful."

"Kind of," Ralph agrees with a small smile.

I'm still seeing hieroglyphics where Ralph sees something simple. Maybe that's a metaphor, and maybe it's just a matter of perspective. I'm still trying to read them upside down.

"Did you want something?" Ralph asks gently.

"Right." I cough. "That. I need to ask you a favor."

"Of course," Ralph says, too quickly. Then, "Sure. Ask away."

That's a gilded invitation if I've ever heard one, but even with my name embossed in gold flake, I can't make it over the threshold. Whatever bravado I've been clinging to so desperately for the past week has left me. Call it a by-product of female socialization, years of being shamed for asking for another cookie, let alone a space at the table, or call it campaign fatigue. Always playing a role for the sake of *la grande illusion*. Yesterday, it was JFK. Today, it's Uncle Sam. "I need you," I say, corralling my voice into something steady, "to run for student body vice president."

"I'm sorry, what?" He's so polite, even in his complete and utter confusion.

I summon a smile. Not the Vaseline one, but something small. I need to get to that place where I believe my own spin. In spite of everything that's happened today—Amber's sensationalist reporting, Henry's fascist rally, Clary's backroom dealing—I still believe I can make real change, if I fight for it. If I can convince Ralph to fight for it, too. "I'm calling on you to serve this school by running for student government. I know you care about the same issues I do, and now that Jenny's out of the race—"

"Wait, what?"

"Now that Jenny's stepping down, I need a new vice-presidential candidate who cares about this school and wants to make it a better place. So I'm asking you to do your patriotic duty and join my ticket." I let my smile grow, just a little. "Make Your Mark with Adams-Myers."

"My name shouldn't be in the slogan."

"So you'll do it?"

"Wait, no, that's not what I'm saying. That's the opposite of what I'm saying. My name shouldn't be in the slogan because I can't do it."

"Why not?"

"So many reasons," Ralph falters. "Like, time, for one."

"As a construct? Are you going to use special relativity to turn me down?"

Ralph rolls his eyes indulgently. "I'll have you know, I have a somewhat time-consuming and certainly time-sensitive job as a paper boy, which I do every morning before zero-period band. Practicing the clarinet takes up most of my so-called free time, not that I have much of that, given the whole IB diploma thing."

"What about your community service hours?"

"Mom and I volunteer with kids at the synagogue, and there's Rachel's watershed cleanup project."

"What about something that's just yours?"

Ralph shakes his head, but it's not a refutation. Just another rebuttal in an ongoing debate. "Even if I wanted to do something else," he says, not quite looking at me, "it's not that easy. I have an unspecified anxiety disorder."

"Okay." Even though it's not a revelation, even though I saw him in my therapist's office, I'm still not sure what I've done to deserve his confidence. "I don't want to pressure you to do something that's going to hurt you, but it could be good to try something new? I'll be by your side the whole time."

"I mean," Ralph starts, then stalls. "Even if I were interested, which I'm not, there are still more cons than pros," he says, and he's trying so hard to sound flippant, and I don't know why. "I'd have to rearrange my schedule to fit the class. I don't even know if ZP would let me join, let alone run, because I'm pretty sure the deadline already passed. Not to mention, I don't really care about student government."

"You care about Benji."

His flippant veneer falls away. All the lines and angles of his countenance bend to curves. "Benji has you."

"Benji stood up for himself," I say carefully. "I'm just trying to follow his example. And stand up for the kids who aren't there yet. Who can't *get* there because the world doesn't want them to."

"Mark." When he looks up, a stray beam of light catches his irises, illuminating them like a pool in summer. I can see through the depths. "Do you have any idea what you're doing for this school? Benji called out a problem. A dark, gnarly problem that everyone has been skirting around for years. His statement shone a light on it, but in a day or two? After a week of exile via suspension? People here would've been all too eager to go back to ignoring the ugliest parts of this town. But you're not letting them. The more you talk about it, you're forcing them to confront their own privilege and biases. By running for office, you're pushing for solutions to problems everyone else was willing to let fester. I think that's really brave." He smiles at me, his dimples like divots at the corners of his mouth.

Something clenches tight in my chest, and I'm pretty sure

men have gone to war for this.

Then his smile wavers, and he says, "And that's precisely the problem. If I run as your VP, I'll ruin all of that."

"What do you mean?"

"I'm not popular. I'm not attractive. I'm not an asset. I'm the weird kid who does calculus for stress relief and likes *Star Trek* unironically and doesn't talk in class unless a teacher holds a participation grade–shaped gun to my head."

"Ralph, you're—"

"No, it's okay. I'm not bitter. Sure, I have a checklist of things I'd like to change about myself, but those aren't on it. I want to be a better son, brother, and Jew. I want to honor the mitzvah of tikkun olam. I want that desire to do good and work bravely toward it to be something innate, rather than something I constantly have to remind myself to do. But my comfort with being the geeky, anxious, weird kid doesn't change the fact that I am. Which is fine, most of the time. All the time, up until this exact moment, when you're here asking me to put myself out in front of the student body. You're asking for my help, but the truth is, I'm a liability. You don't want me."

He says it so earnestly, the surface tension in his eyes rippling the way water does when you skip a rock. I understand now that everything else has been leading up to this. All his excuses about time and anxiety were desperate stopgap measures. He ducks his head because he really, truly believes this false narrative he's constructed for himself.

I can't let that stand. "Bullshit," I tell him. "That's such bullshit. You're articulate and genuine and you care, so much. Maybe you're not good at letting other people see that, but it's there." Like a light he's tried to dim, like the sun straining against the curtains. "I see it."

"I don't know."

"You don't have to know. You just have to trust me."

Ralph looks at me. "I trust you."

TWENTY

PABLO MANEUVERS HIS RANGE ROVER THROUGH the morning commuter rush with the deft skill of a fighter pilot. He's ditching wrestling practice, and I'm avoiding my independent study. We're rebelling, but not because we were desperate for a Starbucks run.

We have an extra passenger on board, sloshing across the back seat even with his seat belt on. Benji has his caramel macchiato anchored between both hands, but despite all Pablo's cautionary sermons, I think he's more worried about spilling on his white denim jacket than the car's interior. Today's his first day back after his weeklong suspension, and even though I can't promise he'll be safe, I can make sure he's not alone.

Pablo agreed, and that's why we journeyed to the edge of Utopia Heights and back again during rush hour and braved the Starbucks drive-through. I have a tray of pumpkin-spice lattes and s'mores Frappuccinos in my lap, though I'm not sure how much of them will be left by the time we make it through this fitful stop-and-go traffic.

Pablo slams on the brakes, the car lurching to a halt as a fickle stoplight screws us over. I catch Benji's gaze in the rearview mirror. "You're sure about this?"

"God, you're overprotective." He rolls his eyes theatrically. A faint dusting of gold eyeshadow shimmers from afar. He's rocking it, but God, it makes me worry.

"With good reason."

"Right now the only thing I'm at risk for is whiplash."

"Benji." Pablo sighs. "You know it's okay to be not okay, right? You experienced a trauma. You're allowed to feel hurt or scared or however you're feeling."

"What if what I'm feeling is fine?"

"What is this, some 'real men don't talk about their feelings' thing? I expect that from Mark—"

"Hey, *excuse you*—"

"But you're better than that, Benji. This is a safe space. Tell us what you're really feeling."

"I'm feeling like I'd really rather work on the campaign. Here, Mark." It's a juggling act, getting Benji's phone from his pocket to my palm without spilling anything in the process. "I need you to approve the typography on the new campaign posters."

"What new campaign posters?"

"Look, I love glitter paint as much as the next gay, but you're the only one with handmade posters. Jenny asked me to design something more professional. We narrowed it down to the top five. We just need your sign-off."

I swipe through the images. All of them read MAKE YOUR MARK, crisp white letters set on a bright red background, with a few patriotic banners to spice it up. ADAMS-MYERS 2021 is set beneath the slogan. The font varies from image to image, but I quickly find a favorite. "This one."

"Great. Nadia and I can use the art room printer during Guided Study. I'm thinking fifty to start—"

"You're hopeless," Pablo moans. "Both of you. Emotionally stunted and completely hopeless."

We turn into the parking lot ten minutes before the bell. We're lucky to find a space right near the fence.

When we've unloaded our backpacks and our drinks, ready to embark on the perilous trek to campus, Pablo stops Benji with a hand on his shoulder. "You sure you're ready for this?"

"Guys." He looks from me to Pablo and back again, then slips on a pair of gold aviators. "You're more nervous than I am. I've got this."

And he does.

The English hall goes dead silent when we walk in. Every idle conversation flickers out. Freshmen and seniors alike stop and stare at Benji, strutting between the heavyweight wrestler and the latecomer presidential candidate.

Everyone gawks. A few kids point. Others whisper to each other. But no one snickers. No one sneers. No one hurls a single slur all the long way down to Benji's Honors English class. In the classroom, one boy nods in staid approval. A girl wolf-whistles. A few smile. Someone claps, and I hope, I pray, none of this is in jest.

I still want to believe some good can come of this.

"About this weekend," Pablo says as we all march across campus in a cluster like royal penguins. "We're still on for Operation Birthday Extravaganza, right?"

We're all headed to lunch. Or, rather, we're all skipping lunch to bother regular students who are enjoying their lunches.

And by *all*, I do mean all of us, for once. However reluctant he seemed about the campaign, Benji is fully invested now, conferring with Nadia about branding and messaging and how it all plays into our social media campaign. Which is a little confusing, because I wasn't aware we had a social media campaign. Maybe that's the point.

Ralph's with us, too, shoulders hunched so high his neck disappears into his shirt collar like a frightened turtle. But not like Mitch McConnell. That would be entirely unfair and also extremely weird, because I've never once looked at Mitch McConnell and thought "cute."

Not that I'm thinking that now or anything. About anyone.

"Yes, yes, *yes*," Nadia gushes. "Operation Birthday Extravaganza is a go."

"I said I didn't want to do anything major," Rachel groans. She's in the process of passing out war rations from her fanny pack. I take a bag of Flamin' Hot Cheetos when she offers them to me. "No Gatsby-esque blowouts, or whatever you guys are planning."

"If we're going to Pablo's," Benji chimes in, "it's gonna be Gatsby-esque."

Pablo sighs, beleaguered. "If this is because we have a pool—"

"Dude," I say, "it's not about the pool."

"Don't worry, babe," Nadia assures Rachel. "Pablo and I have everything under control. It'll be like our usual coed sleepovers, except with cake and better booze."

"Please no more mudslides," I beg, thinking back to the historic Whiskey-Kahlúa Rebellion last winter. I'm about to bite into my first Cheeto when Jenny sneaks up beside me and snatches the bag away. "Hey!"

"Do you have any idea how many breath mints you'd need to counteract just one of those abominations?"

Deliberately obtuse, I ask, "Do you mean the Cheetos or the mudslides?"

"Screw you," Nadia says. Despite growing up in a dry household, she's the best bartender among us—*best* being a relative term. "Those who have never attempted to bartend are always the harshest drink critics."

"And drunk critics," Rachel giggles.

Picking up on the silence that suddenly feels as deafening as everyone else's easy banter, I fall a few steps back, where Ralph's bringing up the rear of our little party. "It's your birthday, too, isn't it?" I feel like an idiot even before he raises an eyebrow while keeping an otherwise straight face, all Spock-like. "Of course it is. Twins. I know how biology works, I promise." Even though a sizable caucus of faith-based conservatives would beg to differ. "Shouldn't you have a say in Operation Birthday Extravaganza?"

"I'm not really a birthday person."

"You know, people say that, but they never really mean it."

Ralph shrugs. I'm half waiting for him to say birthdays are an illogical human tradition.

"You're planning to come to Pablo's on Saturday, right? We'll eat fancy rich-people cheese, watch bad movies on a projector television, and play the world's queerest edition of Never Have I Ever. If Pablo lets us break out his parents' good wine, this party will exceed your wildest dreams."

"Never have I ever dreamed about attending a party described as 'Gatsby-esque.' 'Kafka-esque,' maybe, but that was definitely not a dream I ever wanted to live out."

"I can guarantee you're not going to wake up on Sunday morning to find you've been transformed into a gigantic insect. I can't, however, make any promises about finding yourself mired in an endless deluge of bureaucratic quicksand."

"Is hacking through the red tape not part of your platform?" he teases.

"*Our* platform," I correct.

"Oy vey, thanks for reminding me that I know next to nothing about our platform."

"We should fix that," I say, always the politician, offering up a solution to every problem, and just as self-serving.

"We should," Ralph agrees.

I smile. I can't help wanting to spend time with Ralph without the whole campaign team trailing along. For purely professional reasons, of course. A president and his veep need to establish a rapport.

But any and all plan-making is interrupted by Jenny calling my name. She and Nadia are arguing and waving a tablet around, likely to smack an innocent bystander, which definitely wouldn't play well on *Dystopia High*.

So, I offer Ralph an apologetic smile and put myself in the line of fire. For the greater good, obviously.

Nadia calls it our Full Grassley, named for the gamut populists run in Iowa by visiting each of the state's ninety-nine counties. Our goal is to make an appearance with every clique before the final bell on Monday. Well, every clique except those in hostile territory. Like Henry's football team, Dante's basketball squad, and, unfortunately, Clary's GSA. Which kind of defeats the purpose of calling it a Full Grassley, but what do I know? Even Senator Chuck Grassley's Iowa constituents think the tour is a load of loose meat.

First up, Benji introduces us to a group of underclassmen who hang out by the planter at the edge of the quad. Ralph and I shake hands with these pimply kids, fresh out of middle school. Thanks to the state-mandated Health and Life Skills class, half of them are cradling plastic babies, who blink their creepy doll eyes and cry when you forget to feed them. Cristian and Luis, a pair of freshmen in color-coordinated polos, introduce me to Abigail, wrapped in a sequin blanket. They've been dating since last winter, but the kids in their class still make jokes about how Abigail has two dads. I tell them Abigail has nothing to be ashamed of, and neither do they. Cristian says he's excited to vote for a candidate like him. Luis asks me to pray for Abigail, because that's what parents ask politicians on TV. I press a kiss to Abigail's forehead, and then everyone else is clamoring for my blessing. Which is how Ralph and I end up kissing fake babies while Nadia snaps photos.

Then we stump with the junior class IB kids, who hang out on the steps outside the performing arts auditorium. Except it's barely a stump speech because we just commiserate about the woes of the #IBLyfe—their hashtag, not mine. They pelt us with questions about exams, Extended Essay topics, and details about our college application strategies, even more than we'll get from our families at Thanksgiving. Amber is conspicuously absent, but her best frenemy, Megan, flips through an intimidating color-coded binder, tabbed and indexed, with an appendix or three. She's so serious as she extols the necessity of school-sponsored college prep events, like alumni talks and weekend peer-led SAT prep classes.

Inside the auditorium, Ralph and I brave a treacherous catwalk to speak with Xander, president of our state-runner-up show choir and stage manager for the fall play. He's a tiny guy with an electric-blue pompadour who demands we petition to make show choir a class. I make the mistake of laughing, because I honestly believe it's a joke. But Xander bristles and counters that we have separate beginner, intermediate, and advanced choirs. To my surprise, Ralph puts his hand on my arm, and if my heart stutters, it's only because it's the first time he's really engaged with our constituents. He points out that we also have two bands, symphonic and jazz, and those count as courses, so why shouldn't our award-winning show choir get academic credit for their work, too? I'm smiling at him rather than Xander when I promise to take it to Flynn.

Then Jenny introduces us to the Asian and Pacific Islander Student Association, who congregate at the picnic tables outside the gym. Nadia spends precious minutes gushing in mutual admiration with Linh, who, I learn, is internet famous for her Instagram and YouTube channel, where she reviews makeup products with a focus on cosmetics for women of color. Finally, Nadia arranges us for a photo op, and Linh and I get down to negotiations. It's immediately clear Linh doesn't just care about makeup and fashion in the traditional sense. In addition to concerns about garden-variety racism and discrimination, she vents about school spirit days that encourage students to wear other people's cultures as costumes. Henry would categorically dismiss Linh and her friends as snowflakes; Clary would remind them of her Latinx heritage while ultimately cleaving to respectability politics because challenging beloved school traditions would upset the popular kids she's courting. But I shut up and listen.

With far less trepidation than me, Nadia follows Pablo, Ralph, and me into the boys' locker room for our meet-and-greet with the wrestling team. "Gender is a construct," Nadia says, and while I agree on a theoretical level, footballs are also constructs that can hit you in the face. We meet Kai, better known as "The Wave." Fat and confident, with warm brown skin and a man bun, he welcomes us with open arms—and a bro hug for Pablo—before he names the football team as his primary grievance. I'm prepared with a snarky remark about how they're better funded than the mythical border wall, but Kai is actually more worried about the preferential treatment players receive. When Nadia's camera flashes a few minutes later, my hand locked in Kai's stranglehold of a handshake, I'm not thinking about Benji.

I'm thinking about winning.

TWENTY-ONE

CHRISTIAN CLUB HAS LEMON BARS. ON FRIDAY, Grace greets us with a Listerine smile and a tray of home-made confections dusted in powdered sugar. I don't know if baked goods are a weekly tradition or a sign of goodwill, but I take a square and summon up a smile. "Thank you for this, and for inviting us here today."

"Of course." Grace, who looks ready to pluck wildflowers in a hayfield, with her blond hair and summer sundress, loses a bit of the skip in her step. "Our doors are open to everyone."

I'm sure Grace believes that, but there's a reason only Ralph and Benji are here with me right now, and neither of them looks particularly comfortable. Ralph's posture is yearbook-portrait perfect. Benji's still-split lip is set in a thin, defiant line. He came because he still goes to church every Sunday and might have joined a club like this if he'd thought he could find shelter in a crowd of kids who probably view abortion as a wedge issue. They're both safest out of the line of fire, sitting up on the counters by the windows.

I stand on the front line while Grace introduces me to her acolytes. She was very clear with me that she's their group leader, not their president, but she sounds more like a preacher. "'For there is no authority except from God, and those which exist are established by God.' Romans, chapter three, verse one," she recites with a smile. "Without further ado, here's Mark!"

My smile isn't as easy. Now I feel like I'm campaigning for God's vote, too.

But it's okay. I make it through my stump speech without stumbling; I've given it enough times now that I can say it with the alacrity of the Hail Mary. Then it's over, and Grace is still smiling when she joins me to moderate the Q&A.

First up, she calls on a guy with a bowl cut who may or may not have been in my French class last year, but I wouldn't testify to his identity under oath. "What's your stance on religious expression in public schools? Prayer, for example."

"I absolutely support the right of all students to express their religious beliefs however they see fit, including private prayer and groups like this."

"Shouldn't prayer be built into school hours?"

"The Supreme Court ruled mandatory prayer unconstitutional in 1962 in *Engel v. Vitale.* But I certainly believe the school is obligated under the First Amendment to make accommodations for prayer during school days—like the salah, for example."

Bowl Cut's eyes are glazed like marbles.

"My running mate's Jewish." I look to Ralph, praying he'll chime in, because I know he practices the religion he was assigned at birth, but he blanches the moment I make eye contact. "The High Holy days are coming up, and he'll miss a few days of class. No student should be penalized for that."

"But what about you?" A guy sitting on a desk in the back sneers. In his polo and salmon shorts, he looks like a frat bro in training.

"What about me?"

"You're talking about Muslims, Jews, and the separation of church and state. Everything and everyone except the people this club is for. So tell us, *Mark*. What do you believe?"

"J'accuse!" Bowl Cut wags his finger at me. "Back in Madame Lavoisier's class, you stood for the pledge every morning, but you never *said anything*, let alone 'under God.'"

I never expected anyone to challenge me on my record with the Pledge of Allegiance, of all things, but I have a ready answer. "I don't believe in blind allegiance to the flag, or anything else. I'd rather prove my faith in this country—and in God—through my actions. As you've probably guessed, I don't believe 'under God' should be part of the pledge. As you so astutely put it"—I nod graciously to Salmon Shorts—"it's a question of church and state. But if you're asking about my religious affiliation, I'm Catholic."

"Everyone says they're religious on the campaign trail," says a mousy girl in the front row. The gold cross around her neck glitters against her lumpy sweater. "But I've never seen you at St. Julia's Cathedral. When was the last time you went to confession? Or the last time you took Communion?"

"Martha," Grace chides, so gentle you could almost miss the rebuke. "Everyone's entitled to express their faith in their own way." Her smile strains, a rubber band poised to snap. "Or not at all."

"I don't mind," I reply, though I do. But I can't say I didn't know this was part of the gig. I know why Dad goes to Mass every Sunday. "I'm still trying to find my place in the Santa Julia Catholic community. I can tell you that I was confirmed two years ago." Under a name I'll never repeat. "I went to confession the last time I was in Marin." Over a year ago. "I still believe." Maybe.

It doesn't take a seismograph to detect the discontent rumbling beneath these stony faces. I get it, I do. These kids don't just wear their faith on their sleeves, but with crosses around their necks, rosaries circling their wrists, and promise rings on their fingers. I talk a big game about performing my patriotism through actions rather than mindless loyalty oaths, but everyone here performs their faith in a way I can't.

"Look," I say, mouth full of mothballs, "I know what it feels like to get flak for who you are. For what you believe. We're in high school, where nihilism is always on trend. It's never *cool* to care about something too much, whether it's *Star Trek*, constitutional law, or God. My esteemed opponents disparage me for caring too much about all of you, but I do. That's why I'm running—to ensure this school doesn't just protect us but *celebrate* everything that makes us different."

For one shining moment, the weathervanes stop spinning; the wind chimes stop rattling. Martha clutches her pendant in her fist. Grace nods, sincerer than any of her smiles. I *have* them.

Until Salmon Shorts snorts. "Is no one going to say it? Your idea of 'utopia' sounds a lot like Sodom and Gomorrah. Your campaign is full of heathens and infidels. If that wasn't bad enough, you flaunt your *alternative lifestyle* like it's something to be proud of, like it's something the rest of us should aspire to. Your friends are dykes, fags, and whores. You say you want to protect all students, but you're the poison, Mark. *Your kind* are the real threat."

Then he's quiet, and so is everyone else.

My jaw is wired shut. I was prepared for hecklers and detractors, but not for this. I should have known better. This spark is from the same fire that jump-started my campaign, but maybe I've been complacent, too. Or maybe it's just been too long since I felt that ire directed at *me*.

"Jared," Grace hisses. "You know we don't allow that kind of language in this room."

"Language." Benji chuckles, drawing every set of eyes toward him. "What about that kind of *hate*?"

"Compassion," Grace stammers, "is the cornerstone of our faith."

"You're right," Benji agrees. "'God is love.' First John,

chapter four, verse eight. But it isn't that simple, is it? That bedrock's stained with blood."

Ralph slips down, trembling and utterly graceless, from his place on the vents. He darts past me, skin gone sallow under the guttering fluorescents, and out the door.

Benji's too tense, rearing for another fight, and I'm taut, in the middle of summer camp tug-of-war. I said I'd take the front line, but I forgot about the shrapnel.

Benji catches my gaze and cocks his head toward the door. *Go*, he says without saying it. *I've got this.*

I leave him to read the riot act to Grace's flock.

Running water occludes all signs of life, but its presence proves everything. This isn't like before, when Ralph was easy to find, with his tiny Tupperware town sprawled on black laminate. He's nowhere to be seen in the classroom. However, although we call this whole torture chamber the chem "lab," the lab itself is an adjoining room.

Every faucet is running, each stream amplifying the next. I find Ralph crowded in the corner, shaking and curled in on himself.

"Ralph," I say. *"Ralph."* My knees hit the linoleum, jolting my system, but not as much as the sight itself. Sweat lacquers his forehead. Every breath sounds like it's been squeezed from a tube of toothpaste. His eyes are glued shut, and though silent sobs rack his body, he doesn't cry.

My first instinct is to reach out and touch, but I'm not sure it would be a comfort. My fingers extend and contract. "Ralph." I'm not sure if he even knows I'm here, or if he's just stuck in his own personal hell.

Hell, I'm not even sure if Jews believe in hell.

"Mark?" he croaks. He pries his eyes open, just wide enough for me to see the bleary bogs beneath.

"I'm here."

His eyelids flicker shut.

I still don't know the protocol. For all my emotional rollercoasters—depressive drop towers and manic Tilt-A-Whirls—I've only had a handful of anxiety attacks. Those were county fair Ferris wheels compared to this. "I can leave, if you want. I'll text Rachel, or—"

"Stay."

I can't help it. I rest my hand on his arm, gentle, but firm enough for him to know I'm still here. His breathing doesn't slow; his tremors don't still. But he doesn't jerk away, so I massage tiny circles through his scratchy sweater. It's stupid and useless, but if he's seeing a therapist, he doesn't need me to tell him to focus on his breathing. There's nothing I can do except stay here with him.

"Do you remember Charles Sumner?" I ask, apropos of nothing, but also everything. Jared, Trevor, every bigoted line item in the ledger of human history. "It was just a foot-note in the textbook. The spring of 1856, when Kansas was quote-unquote 'bleeding,' Sumner stood up on the Senate floor and denounced slavery in incendiary rhetoric. Two days later, Preston Brooks, this nobody congressman from South Carolina, beat Sumner over the head with his gold-tipped cane right there in the Senate chambers. The story was all over the news; everybody saw the symbolism in blood spilled on the literal bedrock of our democracy. It was uncanny foreshadowing. Just five years before the war, an elected official attempted murder right there in the Capitol."

"Now they just bludgeon each other with words," Ralph wheezes.

"And pork-barrel legislation." I can't keep the smile out of my voice that he's back here with me.

Some of the tension bleeds from his posture, limbs unspooling and head lolling back against the cabinets. His breaths are steady, metronomic.

"Hey," I whisper. "Feeling better?"

"Kind of."

The impulse strikes me like a bolt of lightning. I want to reach up and cup his cheek with my hand. I want to wipe away the small battalion of tears that broke past his defenses. I want to feel his skin beneath mine, even if it's clammy, even if it's feverish. Instead, I drop my hand as if I've been electrocuted.

I slide off my knees and into that leg-tuck side-lean position they always told us girls to do when sitting on the floor, when the impropriety of skirts in crisscross applesauce might have made the nuns faint. I lean back beside him.

"Do you want to talk about it?"

"It's just brain chemistry. My limbic system—"

"I know." And I do, just with fewer details about my limbic system. Without my permission, my hand migrates to his thigh, just above the knee, just where the hem of my uniform skirts used to fall. "But that's not what I meant."

"It's stupid," he mutters. "Illogical."

"It's really not."

He looks at me. "The day before our b'nei mitzvah, my grandfather took Rachel and me to the park. We didn't see our dad's parents very often because they lived in New York. Rach and I thought he just wanted to impart some sage wisdom about coming of age. But I'll never forget." He swallows a hiccup to stop the panic from surging back up. "I'll never forget how he hooked elbows with us on either side, and we walked halfway around Verde Lake in total silence. Then, he told us about his childhood in Vienna.

"I'd always known the facts in the abstract. But he'd never talked about it. About the other boys pelting him with rocks on his first day of kindergarten. His violin teacher canceling their lessons. Hiding under a table with his thumbs pressed in his ears on Kristallnacht. Watching Hitler's victory parade after the Anschluss, when his sister pulled him so close he thought she was going to hide him in her coat. He was seven.

And then the war came, but his life had always been a war zone. That day, we stopped at a bench. He always wore turtlenecks, and he rolled up the sleeve of the one he was wearing and showed us the numbers they'd inked on his arm at Mauthausen. I ran my fingers over the figures, whorled by his aging skin, and pressed tight enough to feel his pulse."

I want to say something, but this isn't my tragedy. I squeeze his knee a little tighter to let him know I'm still here.

"That was when I understood. That tattoo hadn't just stained his epithelial cells; it had seeped into his DNA. I carry that trauma in my body, too. And I feel it, all the time, when kids say they're jealous I get to take days off school for holidays they know nothing about or that I get eight days of Hanukkah, never realizing they get two months of Christmas. They joke about how I spend my money, or how I shouldn't say anything about wanting more Jewish characters on TV because Jews run Hollywood, don't you know? And I'm supposed to keep my mouth shut, even in liberal circles, when literal Nazis march through the streets of American cities or Democrats imply 'Jew' is synonymous with 'Zionist.' I know the weight of microaggressions, I do. I feel antisemitism in my bones, and even though I'm not *out*-out, homophobia's this omnipresent ache, like muscle tension. But it's—"

He looks away, and I feel that loss in my body, too.

"The hurt is so constant, you learn to live with it. But what Jared said? It's not like watching foreign wars on the television, thinking, from the comfort of your living room, 'It can't happen here.' This is a mortar in my neighborhood, and—"

I want to stop him, press my hands over the wounds to stanch the bleeding, but there's nothing to cover. Nothing to fix.

"And it's stupid. Because I have it so much better than everyone else, not being out enough for anyone to care. Rachel's waterproof; slurs just sluice right off her. For years, Nadia didn't go a day without someone pulling on her hijab or calling her a terrorist; it's only her social capital on yearbook staff that keeps her safer now. People still tell Pablo to go back to Mexico, but he channels his anger into wrestling. You saw what Amber did to Jenny, and Benji—oh God, Benji. We left him there, alone, with those assholes—"

"Ralph, oppression isn't a contest. Having a reaction—feeling the hurt—isn't a weakness."

He's shaking again, vibrating like his atoms are about to burst. No amount of pressure I can exert through force of touch can hold him together, but damned if I don't try.

"Becoming numb, accepting hate as an inalienable fact of the human condition—that normalizes it. Complacency in the face of oppression codifies it. That's what stops us from changing anything. Not fear of repercussions, but fear we'll let ourselves hurt and fight and still lose. But we have to. Fight the good fight, knowing it's good even when we know it's a Hail Mary. Because what happened today? Everything that's been happening?"

I choke back that stupid Catholic guilt surging up my throat. "It's not okay. It's never okay. That's why I'm doing this—why I'm going to keep doing this, even if it's a lost cause. I'll make a martyr of myself if that's what it takes."

"That isn't what it takes," he says, quiet but firm. The only thing left shaking is his head. He whispers something else, soft like a prayer, in a language I don't recognize. When he registers my confusion, he enunciates, "Olam chesed yibaneh. In Hebrew, it means, 'the world is built from loving kindness.' Those words aren't just a prayer but a call to action." He looks down, where my hand still rests on his thigh, as if he hasn't noticed it until now. "We must build this world from love."

I'm not sure I understand the distinction, but there's a whole universe of things I don't understand. Ralph's just one constellation, and this is a single star that isn't visible to the naked eye. I could spend a lifetime of cloudless nights with a telescope and still not understand.

But maybe I don't need to. "Okay," I promise. "That's what we'll do."

TWENTY-TWO

RALPH'S HOUSE IS EMPTY AFTER SCHOOL, SILENT
as a model home. The house is different without half a dozen
teenagers stomping over the geometric rugs and occasionally
shattering the glass terrariums dangling from the windows.
Everything is pristinely picturesque, fit for a West Elm catalog, not a fixture out of place.

Until a tiny, feisty, furry meteor zips into the foyer. The
kitten orbits my leg, brushing up against my jeans. "Who's
this, and why have I never met them?" I ask. "Where have
you been hiding them?"

"Ariel's not good with crowds, so Rach puts her in one of
the bedrooms whenever she has people over."

I crouch down to get a closer look.

Her long coat is mostly white, with patches of black and
orange blotted like watercolor paint. She looks so soft, but I
don't want to spook her. I stretch out my palm. Ariel stares
up at me with inquisitive eyes. She sniffs my hand, her cold

pink nose just barely brushing my skin, then immediately turns tail and scurries away.

"Ariel," Ralph chides. "Be polite. We have company."

"It's okay." I smile. "I probably smell like dog."

"You have a dog?"

I forget how much we don't know about each other.

"Jack Russell terrier. Monty."

"Short for Montgomery?"

"Montesquieu."

"Like the French philosopher?"

"To whom we owe our branches of government, yes."

God, this boy's laugh could eclipse the sun. It's just as rare but all the more magical for it, and oh. *Oh.* I'm crouching on the floor laughing about pet names, and I don't know when Ralph went from being the quiet-weird kid I found interesting to my running mate whom I find attractive. But we're laughing together, and I don't know if it's the unabashed dimples or the oversize glasses or the hard-won laugh, but I know, now. I didn't realize I was falling until I broke my bones on the ground.

The laughter fades, and the moment passes, and then we're just two boys huddled a little too close for the Bro Code bylaws. Ralph straightens up, his arms knit across his chest, self-conscious and closed off and afraid he's let me see too much. I want to reassure him, offer up some truth or trinket of myself, but he doesn't let the silence linger before he says,

"We should probably get to work."

After everything that happened this afternoon, I asked him if he wanted to reschedule our policy briefing, but he insisted. I thought he might need the normalcy, so I agreed.

We go upstairs to the room at the end of the hall. The first thought that strikes me is how empty it is. Even in a small room, the birch furniture set leaves so much negative space. Beyond the bed, a tower of cardboard boxes peeks through an open closet door. The robin's-egg-blue walls are free of the usual band posters and photo collages that adorn most teenagers' walls. Instead of movie tickets or photo-booth selfie strips, the bulletin board by the bookcase is papered in newspaper clippings. Actual, physical newspaper clippings, yellowed with age. I tiptoe over the carpet. There's a line of shadowboxes above the desk. I peer closer at the collection of butterflies within them, embalmed in glass. They're beautiful and still, each so alone in its own wooden tomb.

Ralph watches me silently while I try to make sense of these disparate data points. He has dried, dead things on his wall and sealed boxes in his closet, and I want to understand.

"We moved a few years ago," Ralph explains. He gestures for me to take the desk chair, then sinks down on the edge of the bed like Earth's gravitational field has suddenly doubled in force. The panic attack took so much out of him, but I didn't realize how completely it destroyed his shields. "You know about my dad, right?"

I nod. Rachel never talks about him, but Pablo filled me in on the pertinent details. Mr. Myers was diagnosed with an aggressive brain cancer when they were in middle school. He died a few months later.

"We've always lived in Utopia Heights," Ralph says, "but we used to live higher up. On your street, to be exact. That was the house I grew up in; that was *home*. Then Dad was gone, but his medical bills weren't. Mom tried to keep everything together. She didn't want Rach and me to lose our home along with everything else, but no sum of pretending could make the math work out. So we moved here, the summer before freshman year. And I always meant to unpack, to decorate this room with all the attenuating fixtures of my old room, as if glow-in-the-dark stars and *Enterprise* schematic posters were the alchemy that could make it *home*, but I got busy with school. Or I got busy with the idea of being busy, and I never quite . . . got around to fixing it. Months went by, and in the spring, we read *Great Expectations* in English, and I thought, this is how it's going to be. I'll grow old sitting on the edge of this bed, in this unfinished replica of my childhood bedroom, waiting for my dad to walk through that door and take me to a Giants game."

I lean forward, teetering on the edge of the chair. "There's nothing wrong with you for grieving," I say, which is stupid and inadequate, but I need him to know there's nothing wrong with *him*, point blank.

"Even if it means I'm becoming Miss Havisham, alone in a disintegrating wedding dress, stuck in the same room while the whole world keeps on turning?" His eyes are so bright, shining with all the tears he didn't spill this afternoon.

"I wasn't like this before, you know. Or, you don't know because you weren't here. But before we lost him, things were different. *I* was different. I had friends besides my sister. I did things outside of school. I wasn't afraid to talk in class or put myself out there. I felt capable of imagining a life for myself. But after he died, I'd try to think about the future, and all I could see was that blank spot where Dad was supposed to be, like a photograph where someone had cut him out. I didn't know how to come out to Mom because I always thought I'd tell them both when they were across from me on that awful love seat in the living room. He won't cheer when they call my name at graduation. He won't cry when he sends me off to college. Any and every milestone is one I'll mark without him. So I keep the articles he wrote for the paper up on my wall. I wear his bow ties. I'm a living monument to his memory. And, you know, in Jewish tradition, we don't say, 'Rest in peace.' We say, 'May his memory be a blessing,' but I don't feel blessed. It's this thing I carry, always, but sometimes it's a burden, and I'm tired, but I don't know how to put it down, even for a moment."

He carries so many invisible burdens on his sweater-clad shoulders. Secrets he doesn't let anyone see. Except, through some work of calculus I'll never solve, he's showing me. And I don't deserve it because I can't reveal anything in return. "He wouldn't want that for you. I mean, I didn't know him, but I know *that*."

"I know," he whispers. "I know."

"And you don't have to carry any of this alone."

He looks at me. Golden light streams through the window, glinting off desiccated butterfly wings.

I want him to believe me, but there's no equation to solve, no theorem to invoke, to prove it to him. All I can do is stay.

Maybe that's enough.

We polish our platform until the sun lolls deep in the sky and the garage door groans. Ralph's mom finds us huddled on the floor, watching *Parks and Rec*. Ariel's snoozing on Ralph's lap and Ralph doesn't seem to care that she's shedding long white hairs on his navy blue chinos.

"Hard at work?" Mrs. Myers asks from the doorway.

I straighten up, startled, as if we've been caught doing something a lot more scandalous than watching old sitcoms with a kitten.

"Mom." Ralph smiles, but even he seems a little uptight. Or more than a little uptight, since uptight is Ralph's factory setting. "You know Mark."

"Hi, Mark." Mrs. Myers smiles back, a little indulgent. We've met a few times in the past but always through Rachel.

"You'll stay for dinner, won't you?"

Ralph sputters out a polemic on the reasons why I shouldn't feel obligated to stay for dinner, but I accept without ever making the connection between the setting sun on this Friday afternoon in this very Jewish household.

Which is how I end up staying for Shabbat.

Rachel comes home from soccer practice with Nadia in tow, and we all crowd around the counter. Ralph wears a kippah embroidered with a silver star of David. Nadia whispers in my ear, explaining the pieces of the ritual she's picked up as Rachel's habitual plus-one. Mrs. Myers lights two spindly candles, and the scent of freshly baked challah wafts through the kitchen. I nod along to melodious prayers I don't understand. They're beautiful and opaque, like spheres of blown glass.

Then there's brisket over the butcher-block table, and Ariel begs at our heels. Maybe I drop a morsel for her, and maybe Ralph kicks me under the table. But we all laugh and eat and sip grape kombucha, and it's so much easier than I ever thought it could be.

I'd forgotten what it felt like for family not to hurt.

TWENTY-THREE

I HITCH A RIDE TO OPERATION BIRTHDAY Extravaganza with Jenny, the logical choice since we live closest to each other and she's my best friend. At least, it seems logical until we're in the car together, cruising along private dirt roads, listening to shiny bubblegum pop about how men are trash. We haven't really been alone together since that morning in the girls' bathroom. I consider asking how she's doing, but she wouldn't see it as a kindness. And if her personal life is off-limits, gossiping about my inconvenient crush would be impolitic.

But at least we still have politics.

"So," I half shout over the music, "I briefed Ralph on the platform. He's ready to stump on Monday."

"Because that went so well yesterday," Jenny says.

I'm not prepared for the barbed-wire sarcasm in her tone. "What happened with the Christian Club wasn't Ralph's fault. He isn't the one who started—"

"But he *is* the one who ran out of the room."

A surge of protectiveness wells up in my chest. "You weren't there, Jen. You didn't hear the things they said."

"What did you expect? The campaign trail isn't lined with daisies; it isn't just about preaching to your base. A good candidate doesn't run out when the voters disagree with them. They don't give up when things get tough. They fight for what they believe in."

This isn't an indictment of Ralph; it's an indictment of me. "Okay, you're right. I shouldn't have run out, either. But Benji had it covered. He didn't need me speaking over him."

Jenny laughs, something jagged and brittle. "Benji spoke out because you just stood there while they hurled slurs at your campaign team—your *friends*. When they came for your own, you had a responsibility to say *something*."

The way she says it—the vitriol like lighter fluid, where one wrong word from me would spark a four-alarm fire—makes me think I'm missing something. Some explanation for why she's taking this so personally when she wasn't even in the room.

"You're right," I say again.

"Of course I am," she says, flippant. She tosses her braid over her shoulder, signaling an end to the conversation, when I'm still trying to figure out what the hell just happened.

We drive up to Olympus Crest in silence. The houses are so far apart you can barely see the neighboring mansions.

Horses gallop in a field, and Jenny revs the engine to outrace them. Past the Navarro estate's open gates, gravel crunches under the tires. Beyond the stables and the man-made lake, the house is a literal Disney castle.

Everyone else is already assembled in one of the sitting rooms, laughing about something that has nothing to do with the election, for once. The moment I step in, Rachel—feather boa, sparkly tiara, and all—throws her arms around me. "No shop talk," she says, when I kiss her on the cheek and wish her a happy birthday.

For his part, Ralph's bow tie has gold foil stars overlaid on blue velvet. I settle in next to him on the couch and whisper birthday wishes in his ear. He smiles at me, and that little gesture shouldn't make me feel warm all over, but it does, like I've spent a whole afternoon lazing in the sun. It's enough to melt any of my lingering unease from the conversation with Jenny in the car.

Pablo's parents make a brief appearance in their California-casual rendition of evening wear before they head off to rub elbows with the Santa Julia elite. They do the whole wink-wink-nudge-nudge routine about not doing anything they wouldn't do, but given the stories they've regaled us with at past sleepovers, they definitely know we'll be drinking later, and they don't have a problem with it. They'd rather have us drink here than at some random house party.

When they're gone, we annex the kitchen. We make our

own pizzas: heirloom tomatoes, lush, verdant herbs from the Navarros' garden, and fresh mozzarella from happy California cows whose world-renowned dairy is a few properties over. Dozens of neatly chopped toppings in glass bowls are spread out over the marble countertops, and we each get our own wooden paddle and ball of dough to personalize as we please. I have no idea what I'm doing. I spread my dough thin and coat it in pesto, then layer it with three kinds of cheese. I add jalapeños and chorizo and these fragrant, freshly picked olives. I have no idea how the flavors will mesh together, but at least it will be a beautiful, bold disaster.

We load the pizzas into the wood-fired oven three at a time, and we power up the state-of-the art sound system. At Rachel's request, we blast queer anthems loud enough that we'd have to worry about noise complaints if we were anywhere else. We dance in the kitchen like the total nerds we are. Benji vogues. Pablo moonwalks. Nadia gives Rachel a twirl. Jenny outclasses us all with actual moves, the same ones that drew me to her at that JSA convention so many years ago. Ralph's stiff and wooden at first, barely bopping his head to the beat. But the bass is thumping, and so is my heart. I catch Ralph's hand. He's startled, eyes flickering wide, but he doesn't let go. So I lead him in an improvised jitterbug. We don't know what we're doing, but he smiles, and the song keeps going.

Even though there's a perfectly serviceable dining room,

we squeeze into the round booth in the kitchen nook. We're all on top of each other, a tangle of elbows and knees. I'm squished between Jenny and Benji. We pretend we're food critics, offering up intentionally pretentious reviews of our meals and sampling each other's creations, dietary restrictions permitting. Everyone teases Rachel for adding pineapple. Pablo tastes mine and praises its "exemplary mouthfeel," the way the earthiness of the pesto mixes with the sharp bite of the jalapeño, and the subtle tang of the Asiago. We're all still snickering from *mouthfeel*, but Pablo gets defensive, insisting it's real culinary jargon.

I don't care if it's real as long as I can have this moment— here, now, always.

We take a brief intermission from our culinary adventures to watch a bad teen movie. We all talk through it, except Benji, who shushes us despite his initial, vigorous protests about wanting to watch something of a higher artistic caliber.

Downstairs, Nadia magically extracts a round, squat cake frosted to look like a soccer ball from the fridge. "It's a Sachertorte," she smirks.

"A soccer what?" Benji frowns.

"Sachertorte," Nadia says again.

"It's Viennese," Jenny explains.

"Like your grandparents, babe," Nadia adds, slinging her arm around Rachel's waist. Rachel smiles and whispers something against the fold of Nadia's hijab.

Ralph's standing next to me on the far side of the island, one hand circled around his wrist, watching Pablo painstakingly arrange eighteen rainbow candles along the hexagonal ley lines. Maybe he only hears the *soccer* in Sachertorte, in this room full of people who are more Rachel's friends than his.

When the scene is set, Nadia strikes a match and lights the candles. I push Ralph forward, and he shouldn't be surprised, not then. Not when Rachel pulls him the rest of the way and tucks him under her arm even though he's half a foot taller.

After we sing happy birthday to *both* of them, Rachel plucks out the candles, licking a few of them, and hands the knife to Ralph, who cuts the cake into twelve endearingly precise fractions. While he serves the slices on gold-rimmed plates, Rachel asks, "Would it be in bad taste to say 'Let them eat cake'?"

"Yes," I hiss. "Marie Antoinette was—"

"Let *us* eat cake?"

"Since we actually *have* cake, I'll allow it," Pablo says.

Benji shakes his head. "Y'all are taking this way too seriously when there's a whole cake ripe for the taking."

So we sit on the floor with fine china and cloth napkins, and we eat cake.

* * *

We squeeze into the hot tub with margarita glasses filled with pinot noir from the Navarros' personal label.

Those of us accustomed to Navarro sleepovers all knew to pack swimwear. But no one remembered to warn Ralph and Benji, so they borrow swim trunks from the drawer of spares in the pool house.

And me?

I wear a rash guard over my binder. I always worry someone's going to call me on it—why do I need a rash guard in a hot tub in the middle of the night, safe from sun and surf—but they never do, just like no one would ever think to question Nadia's burkini. They probably assume the rash guard is a body image issue. Technically, they're not wrong.

The stars stand out like blackout poetry. The bubbling water scalds my skin, but I don't object. Because I'm sitting next to Ralph, who is shirtless and warm and giddy from the wine, which heats my blood like water set to simmer on the stove.

When there's a lull in the conversation, Nadia takes a long swig of her wine, then announces, "So, in the spirit of our biannual big queer heart-to-heart, there's something I've been meaning to tell you guys. It's not a big deal or anything, but . . ." Nadia pauses, an uncharacteristic tremor in her voice. "Well, okay, maybe it is. I don't know. But I thought you should know. I've been doing a lot of thinking lately, about myself, and how I fit into this ineffably weird world, and I realized something." She takes a breath. "I'm nonbinary. Genderqueer. Possibly a demigirl? Definitely still femme. Details forthcoming, or maybe not. I'm honestly okay with not having it all figured out."

A jet of hot water stabs my lower back. My binder is too tight, clinging to my skin, contracting around my lungs. It hurts to breathe.

Rachel rests her head on Nadia's shoulder. She looks up at Nadia, soft, supportive. She doesn't say a word, but it's clear she already knew. Benji and Ralph murmur words of unequivocal support. Jenny's gaze is fixed steadily on Nadia, and she nods and smiles right on cue. Only Pablo is looking at me, concern brimming in his eyes. Because he understands, even before I do, the whirlpool forming where my stomach is supposed to be.

I've spent this whole last year acting like me being trans and stealth was the most important secret in the universe. Like my identity had the power to bring down empires. But I'm not some lost prince; I'm not even the prodigal son. I'm just the selfish, rich trans boy who thinks the entire fucking universe revolves around him. Maybe I'm just the black hole at the center of the galaxy, swallowing up all the brightest stars around me.

I should know better than to assume everyone around me is cisgender. This is the paradigm that hurt me so much before I came out. It still harms me, every time I go outside, every time I use the boys' bathroom or the men's locker room, every single time I have to measure myself against the masculinity metric of this fucked-up patriarchal society. Even though I live in this suffocating, Stepford suburb in this backwater town, I never should have assumed I was the only transgender person here. I've been acting like I have a monopoly on the Santa Julia trans struggle, and here's one of my closest friends, my deputy campaign manager, and I never once considered the possibility. I never gave it any thought that any of my friends, queer as they may be, might be trans, too. Because I talk a big game about a better future where you're not cis until proven trans, but I still assume cis as the default.

And here I am, making someone else's coming out all about myself. Like the self-centered supermassive black hole of a friend I am.

Meanwhile, Benji's asking about pronouns.

Nadia smiles and says, "She/her still feels comfortable right now, like an old sweater I've worn in. Maybe I'll grow out of it in the future, but not yet. I'll let you know when or if that changes."

I grit my teeth. I stretch my lips. It's a Picasso smile, grotesque and abstract. I can only hope the dark smooths out the jagged edges. I need to say something. Offer up my support. Let Nadia know I'm on her side, even if I'm throwing off the gravitational balance of the whole damn cosmos. But I can't summon up a single word.

Luckily everyone else is loud enough to drown out my silence. Pablo still shoots me the occasional furtive glance, but no one else has realized anything is amiss, not even Ralph.

Nadia says she's grateful for us, and that's when I have the presence of mind to say, "You don't have to be grateful. Acceptance is what you deserve. Anything less would be—" But I can't finish that thought. If I follow it to its conclusion, it will suck me in, past my own event horizon.

"Anything less," Jenny says, glancing inscrutably at me, "would be unacceptable."

"And an indictment of *them*," Pablo adds, "not you."

Then Benji's saying, "So, this might be weird, but I want to clarify something. Because we've talked about how hetero-normativity forces queer kids and only queer kids to do this whole coming out song and dance, and cisnormativity works twice as hard against trans kids. It reinforces all these bull-shit ideas about gender stereotypes and what marginalized folks owe to everyone else, and we shouldn't owe anyone any-thing. No one should have to come out. But until people stop assuming cis and straight as the default, allies can disrupt the cis-tem by normalizing coming out. So, Nadia, I don't want to steal your spotlight—"

"The mic's all yours, honey."

"So, I thought y'all should know I'm definitely cis. No

matter what Trevor and company believe, I'm totally fine being a boy who likes the things I like. I reject toxic masculinity, but I'm comfortable with *my* masculinity, pastel and marshmallow-soft."

Nadia's got this wobbly smile on her face, and she looks like she wants to say something profound, but the only word she can get out is "C'mere." So Benji floats across the hot tub, and Nadia wraps him up in a solidarity hug.

Then everybody's talking all at once, and I'm still staring at Benji. This kid is fifteen, and his praxis is better than 99 percent of the adult "progressives" I've met. It's sure as hell better than mine. This is why he's Tumblr-famous. His social justice blog isn't just Discourse but real talk. Not the empty gestures I use to get by.

Here I am, this colossal fraud. I'm the balloon person they blow up at car dealerships, all hot air and bravado and not an ounce of substance. These are my best friends in the whole world, and only two of them know this part of me. Benji's right about the epistemology of visibility, and I know, intellectually, that trans people shouldn't be forced to wear their gender on their sleeve. I know, too, that there's privilege in the way I live. I'm lucky to pass. So many trans people would kill to be stealth.

But I'm not one of them.

I want to be out and loud and proud. I want to be visible. I want to be seen for everything I am.

I want the people I love to know all of me.

I should tell them.

I should tell them.

I should *tell* them.

I clench the stem of my margarita glass in my white-knuckled fist. I knock back this top-shelf wine as if I'm taking a shot of bottom-shelf tequila. And I don't say a word.

TWENTY-FOUR

MORNING SUNLIGHT PAINTS STRIPES ACROSS my face. I grimace, groaning when the first tinges of a hangover slam against my skull. My limbs are heavy, weighted with lead, but it's nothing ibuprofen won't cure.

I force my sleep-addled body into motion. Sit up. Stretch my arms. Keep quiet, so as not to wake Pablo and Jenny.

Although this place has plenty of bedrooms—Pablo has four older siblings, after all—we sleep in a few separate clumps to preserve the slumber-party feel. Pablo's liberal, forward-thinking parents prefer for us to determine sleeping arrangements by orientation rather than gender. We take that as a rough guideline, but it doesn't really work, what with some of us being attracted to multiple genders. The Gold Standard Trio, as ZP once dubbed us, have claimed Pablo's room ever since Jenny and I stopped hooking up last fall— with the exception of one drunken New Year's Eve fumble. Ever the hospitable host, Pablo cedes his bed to Jenny and the trundle to me, and rolls out a sleeping bag for himself.

His stupid blinds are half-open, which explains why it's ungodly bright for just past sunrise. According to my watch, I shouldn't be awake. Pablo's snoring, and Jenny has her head buried under her pillow.

There's no way I'm going to fall back asleep.

In the bathroom, I slip my packer into my boxer briefs and adjust my joggers until the bulge sits just right. I strip off my BARTLET FOR AMERICA T-shirt, shimmy into my binder, then layer the shirt back on. I study my reflection in the mirror. Today I see an algebra problem where the two sides of the equation don't match up. I splash water on my face and run a hand through my hair, but I still can't reconcile the flaw in my genetic code.

I head down to the kitchen with plans to wrangle the Navarros' espresso machine before everyone else wakes up, but the kitchen isn't empty. Water gurgles from the faucet. There's a figure at the sink, tall with dark, tousled bedhead, clad in *Star Wars* pajama bottoms and a collared shirt. "Ralph."

"Oh." He smiles over his shoulder. "Hey. I wasn't expecting anyone else to be up this early."

"Me neither." I cross the room, unsure how close to get. "I couldn't sleep. What's your excuse?"

"Paper boy, remember?"

"Right."

Ralph has his sleeves rolled up to his elbows. Soap suds cling to his forearms. He's already cleaned up the mess we made of the kitchen, and now he's washing the last remnants. "You don't have to do that."

Ralph shrugs. "I don't mind."

"Pablo would literally wrestle those plates away from you."

"Then it's a good thing he's not up yet, right?"

"Here." I sidle over to the dishwasher. "Let me help."

So he rinses, and I load. When he hand-washes the last few holdouts, I towel them dry. We make a good team.

Ralph looks to me. "Now what?"

"We could start breakfast."

"Do you know your way around this starship masquerading as a kitchen?"

I stifle a laugh. "I think I can manage."

"What do you have in mind?"

"Pancakes with dark chocolate chips."

"Would it be blasphemy to add coconut flakes to the mix?"

"I might have to consult the legal precedent." I take a moment, weighing this decision with the utmost seriousness. "But I like the way you think."

We divide and conquer. Ralph scours the fridge for the wet ingredients; I scavenge the walk-in pantry for the dry ones. After realizing it would take an engineering degree to work the espresso machine, I fire up the coffee maker. Ralph starts a teakettle on the stove. We reconvene at the marble island, bumping elbows over a pair of stainless-steel mixing bowls.

I'm quiet as I parcel out the flour. I don't know if it's muscle memory of rounding off powder in measuring cups or sense memory of alcohol-sweet vanilla extract, but something triggers a cascade failure. A thousand memories of mornings not quite like this but close enough. Sleeves rolled up. Laboring over a hot stove. Standing on a stool or my tiptoes to watch Dad do the heavy lifting. We used to wager how many chocolate chips we could sneak in without Mom complaining.

"So," Ralph starts, slow and a little hesitant, "why pancakes?"

"Aside from the fact that they're fluffy and delicious and one of the few meals I can cook from memory?" I quip, making light when I shouldn't. "I used to make dark chocolate chip pancakes with my dad. Every Sunday, after Mass."

"Used to?" he echoes, a prayer in an empty cathedral. "You never talk about your dad."

"My dad's gone," I say, without thinking it through.

"Oh," Ralph says. Then, "I'm sorry. I didn't realize."

That's when I realize the array of possible interpretations my careless words invite. Ralph has made a perfectly reasonable inference, erroneous as it is, and I need to correct him.

But.

This is Ralph I'm talking to. Chronically grieving Ralph, who hasn't stopped sitting shiva for the father he lost four years ago. I don't want to lie to him, but I can't tell him the truth. I can't admit my dad represents this town and its neighbors in Congress, not when one Google search would blow my secret identity. For someone so terrified of a scandal, Dad never gave me a good enough cover story. So what lie am I supposed to invent? What fake campaign sob story am I supposed to concoct? My dad is a dirtbag who left me? He and my mom separated for all the right reasons? How do I spin that yarn without specifying that I'm the "irreconcilable difference" between them?

Moments speed past me, a blur in the window of opportunity I have to fess up. I'm so practiced in the art of lying that I can't summon up even an ounce of truth when I need it.

Then it's too late, because Ralph has already mistaken my awkward silence for genuine grief, and he's looking at me with something that isn't quite pity. He sees his pain reflected back in me. "What . . ." He measures the weight of the question he thinks I can bear. "What was he like?"

I shouldn't dig myself deeper in this hole, but I'm already six feet under. Which is a morbidly ironic choice of words here, but I'm up to my elbows in dirt. I don't know how to walk this back.

"I looked up to him," I say, and even as I'm committing to this lie, I realize it doesn't feel like one. The words ring true. Because the man who threatens me every Sunday afternoon, the stranger whose face I watch on C-SPAN—that isn't the father I loved. That man is as dead as the tragic hero in the myth I'm telling. "More than anyone, he was my blueprint for the kind of man I wanted to be. And it wasn't just that he was brilliant and eloquent and charismatic, or that he was as comfortable bumping elbows with Ivy League economists as he was joking around with local farmers. He celebrated the Fourth of July like it was the most important day of the year, before Christmas or Thanksgiving. He said democracy was the only gift he needed, but God, he loved the fireworks. And . . . and he loved me, too. Every Sunday, we made pancakes. No matter how busy he got, he'd always find time to talk with me about what I was reading and give me another list of recommendations. He taught me everything I know, starting with how to think for myself. He told me it was my civic duty to fight every injustice I met, no matter how small."

"What did your dad do?" Ralph asks softly as he cracks eggs against the rim of the mixing bowl.

"He was a lawyer." The past tense still isn't a lie. Dad doesn't practice law anymore; he writes it. "A prosecutor."

Ralph looks at me—really *looks* at me—in that way he has, as if his glasses are microscopes and he can see through the mirage of my skin, past the lies my body tells, right to the heart of me. He makes me feel *seen*, in a way no one else can, and under any other circumstance, I'd revel in it. But now I'm terrified his scrutiny will reveal the deception under my skin, bright white tumors on an X-ray. "If he's your blueprint," he says, "then his memory is already a blessing."

I can't look at him. Not like this. So I focus my attention on the task at hand, beating the eggs with more vigor than I should. The whisk clangs against the sides of the bowl. The yolks burst and divide into tiny trails, comets circling a central star before their orbits decay.

Then Ralph's hand is on mine, gently prying the whisk from my viselike grip. He doesn't say anything, and I'm grateful. The kitchen is silent but for the drip of the coffee, the hiss of the kettle, and the first sizzle of butter in the skillet.

Ralph folds coconut flakes and bittersweet chocolate into the batter. He pauses with the second bag poised over the rim. "More?"

"Definitely," I manage, my voice miraculously steady.

As we scoop the chocolate-studded batter into the pan, Ralph regales me with a story about how he asked Mr. González how to derive one of the theorems we learned last week, and Mr. González demurred, insisting that the proof was "much too complicated." Ralph's pretty sure Mr. González was just saving face.

I know he's trying to distract me, but I don't mind. I want to be distracted. I want to think about anything other than my emotionally deadbeat dad. I want to hold on to this morning and these pancakes and this quiet closeness. I don't want to ruin this. "Is that your thing, then?" I ask. "Calculus?"

Ralph wrinkles his nose. "What gave you that idea?"

"You do it for fun."

"Not for fun. Stress relief." He fidgets with a flake of loose silicone on the spatula handle. "I'm not a math genius like a Pablo. It's not some profound passion. It's a coping mechanism at best."

"So what do you want to do?" Maybe it's gauche to ask; maybe it's selfish. There's still so much I don't know about him, things I suspect *no one* knows about him. I want to hoard every truth he's willing to give me, even if I can't return them in kind.

Bubbles erupt in the batter like tiny volcanoes, leaving yawning craters in their wake. Ralph wiggles the spatula under each pancake, flipping them with careful precision, before he hazards a glance at me. "Is it bad if I say I don't know?"

"Not at all."

"I know I'm supposed to know. It's the question every high school senior gets from every extended family member, every nosy yenta, every single bystander. 'What are you going to do after high school? Where do you want to go to college? Tell me, where do you see yourself in ten years?' And I should have an answer, but I don't. Usually, I tell people I'm thinking about med school, like Rachel, because it sounds practical. 'Doctor' sounds like something I could be. It doesn't matter that I don't dream about the cardiovascular system or how to repair it because 'doctor' is the safe answer. I can even imagine the college application essay I could write, about how I want to grow up to save people like my dad."

He looks away again, focusing his full attention on the browning pancakes. "What I *can't* imagine is living that life. As a kid, when I thought about the future, I thought about seders around our butcher-block table, all of us sharing wine and matzo. We'd swap work anecdotes, and we'd be together. I know I should be able to picture a future without him, but I still can't."

I buy myself time by stealing the spatula. It's for the best that I didn't correct him about Dad. It's the whitest of lies, easier than the truth.

"You don't have to have everything figured out. Hell, you don't have to have anything figured out. You've been eighteen for one day. Cut yourself some slack."

He rubs the back of his neck. "I'm not very good at that."

"I know. But you have time for that, too. So cut yourself some slack about not being good at cutting yourself slack."

Then he's just *looking* at me again, and fuck, I am so far gone.

He smiles. "I'll make it my Rosh Hashanah resolution."

Jenny's phone is dead when she drives me home, so the car stays silent because she hates all local radio stations with equal fervor. She rebuffs all my attempts at small talk with monosyllabic answers, so I quit trying. I'm not sure where we stand after yesterday afternoon, and I'm too afraid to ask.

Maybe, if this were a normal morning, I'd ask her if she knew about Nadia. I'd ask her if I'm a terrible person for not confiding in our friends. I'd ask her if it makes me a coward that I can't stand up to my dad, even in this.

Maybe she'd reassure me, and maybe she wouldn't. I've been around Jenny at her most brutally honest, and even when she bruised my ego, I'd prefer that over this gaping hole in the reliable missile defense grid that has always protected our friendship.

Maybe it makes me a terrible friend for not pressing the issue with her, but I'm still fixating on my conversation with Ralph.

By the time Jenny pulls up in front of the house, I'm already late for my FaceTime date with Dad. But for the first time in a long time, I'm not sure I want to accept the call. It's not only that I metaphorically killed him off a few hours ago, but also the secret moral of that story. If the father I loved is dead and gone, maybe it's foolish to chase after this power-hungry ghost. Maybe I don't need his approval.

For the first time since we moved here, I'm imagining what it would be like to spend my Sunday without him. Mom and I could go for a drive. Maybe take Monty to the river, or even the beach. For the first time, I can imagine a single, shining day where I don't need *him*.

My key clicks in the lock. Monty rushes up to me, yipping until I duck down to scratch his head.

Voices emanate from somewhere down the hall, low and garbled, like a radio talk show. I follow the noise to the kitchen. Mom does that sometimes, listens to the radio while she cooks. Maybe she's making hot cocoa. We could take it out back to the yard we never use, sit on the chaise lounges with the price tags still pasted on, and just talk. I could talk about Nadia, or Jenny—or maybe even Ralph.

Except the only scents wafting down the hall are coffee and sandalwood, and the voices are pitched too low for song.

My pulse picks up. I barely noticed Mom's SUV in the driveway instead of the garage. She hasn't mentioned the possibility of dating post-Dad, but maybe she, too, can imagine a future without him.

"Mark, honey?" she calls, hazy and distant. "Is that you?"

"Yeah."

"We're in here."

In the kitchen, two figures sit at the granite counter, coffee mugs and Atelier croissants artfully arranged between them. My mother smiles when she sees me, waving me in. Her hair is done up in a loose bun, a few stray strands framing her face. She's wearing a sheer chiffon blouse over a satin camisole. She looks nice. Date-nice.

Sure enough, there's a man across from her, his back to me as I enter the room. I take in the shape of him. Broad shoulders. Slim build. Light pink polo shirt. Dark blond hair, slicked back. Sandalwood cologne with a dash of leather.

He turns around at his stool, looking back at me over his shoulder. Hazel eyes meet mine. Dad stretches his mouth around his teeth, political and practiced, but it looks nothing like a smile. "Hello, Mads."

TWENTY-FIVE

WHEN DAD TOLD ME HE WAS RUNNING FOR CON-
gress, he took me for a drive. He didn't tell me where we were
going, just that it was a highly classified, top-secret mission
for just the two of us. We rolled the windows down in his
Cadillac and blasted Bruce Springsteen as we drove up north.
We took scenic backroads and crossed the Marin County
line into Sonoma, passing miles of patchwork fields and nee-
dlepoint vineyards. He told me stories about the history of
California, all as if to say, *This, too, could be yours.*

We ended up in Santa Julia. He said it was the largest city
between San Francisco and Sacramento, but it had none of
the trappings of a city. The tallest building was fourteen stories, and its town square was the only nod to an urban grid.
But Santa Julia had *history*, and Dad took me to a museum
dedicated to one of America's most prolific cartoonists, then
a greenhouse owned by a world-renowned botanist, both of
whom once called Santa Julia home. "Northern California is

a cradle of innovation," Dad told me, "the Mesopotamia of the Digital Age."

Then he took me to a hole-in-the-wall taqueria in the heart of the Main Street–style downtown. We carried our carnitas tacos to the old train station and set up camp at a refurbished picnic table alongside the derelict tracks. Pork juice and chipotle salsa dripped down our faces, and Dad laughed like he didn't care who was watching. We watched locals and tourists alike stroll through the square. The sun beat down on us, even in December. Then Dad looked at me and said he had something important to ask me. "I want to run for Congress," he told me, "but I won't unless I have your blessing."

I imagined him riding into Washington on a white horse, slaying fire-breathing corporation-dragons and vanquishing armies of Republicans. "Yes," I said. "Of course," I said. "Run," I said.

When Dad tells me now, six years later, in the kitchen of a house he doesn't live in, that he's running for governor, he doesn't ask my permission. He just looks at me, his face enveloped by shadow as the afternoon light cuts swaths through the room, and informs me. "As you know, I'm running for governor."

Except I don't know, really. I know his twenty-year plan always included the Sacramento Governor's Mansion as a stepping-stone to the White House. I know the press have been circling the wagons for months, speculating when one of the Hill's most brazen Democrats would announce. I know he wants power more than he ever wanted me.

But this is the first time he's really said the words.

When I don't say anything, Dad sighs, a long, drawn-out, theatrical affair. It's a parody of parental concern, as if my silence is normal teenage histrionics and he really thought I'd grown out of this by now. "I'm announcing my candidacy on Wednesday."

This is the part where I'm supposed to offer my seal of approval. He wants me to ask how I can help, like I did for every other campaign. I went on tour with him and stood by his side in every photo op. I phone banked; I canvassed door-to-door. I did my homework in the campaign office when I was too young to do anything else. I wanted to be as close as I could to the magic; I should have listened better when he told me it was all a trick.

"We need to discuss what we're going to do about"—he gestures at me, at the two-body problem he sees in place of his child—"*this.*"

Mom worries her lip between her teeth. She doesn't know how to stop this. Any sway she once held over Dad disappeared the day she chose me over him.

"I'm holding the press conference here in Santa Julia," Dad continues, "at the old train depot."

The train depot isn't derelict anymore. Thanks in part to

Dad's earmarks to secure federal funding for local infrastructure programs, an energy-efficient commuter train now runs from Santa Julia to San Rafael. Of course he wants to showcase one of his greatest achievements.

When Dad announced his first congressional run, he did it in front of the Marin Convention Center, a building so futuristic it was once used as a location in a big-budget science-fiction film. It was unseasonably cold for a California winter, and though the sun was shining, I shivered in my peacoat. Mom and I bookended his Lucite podium as he told a cadre of reporters and a handful of civic-minded citizens about the shimmering future he could herald for the Second District. I believed him, then.

"I want you there," Dad says now, though he isn't quite looking at me. He's looking past me, as if he'll be able to see the afterimage of that preteen girl in the peacoat if he just looks hard enough.

"Do you?"

"Of course I do, Mads."

"But you don't, really. You don't want Mark Adams; you want Madison Amelia Teagan, your prodigal daughter. You want me to wear a skirt and a sweater set and the strand of pearls you gave me for my thirteenth birthday. You want me to do my makeup and contour away the harsh new angles of my face. Curl my hair, maybe, to make the cut look more feminine. Slip into a pair of designer heels. That's the price of admission, isn't it? That's what I'd have to do to earn the honor of appearing by your side again."

"Madison," he snarls. Blood rushes his face, dousing it in red. His knuckles throttle one of Mom's gold-flecked mugs. The scent of espresso mingles, faintly, with the tang of whiskey.

"That's not my name."

"It's the name I gave you."

"Graham," Mom says sharply.

"No, Greta, I've had enough of this. You've had a year, Madison. A year to playact and pretend, but it's time to grow up now. You don't have the luxury of living this life. Other people can live at the margins, but you're not other people. You're destined for greater things, Madison, and if you want to grow up to make the world a better place for *other people*, you don't get to be one of them. You have to be better. Not normal, but perfect. Above reproach. As Madison Teagan, you can do anything you want; the Oval Office is the limit. But *Mark Adams*? Mark Adams is a fiction."

Anger bubbles up my throat like bile. "You don't get it. Madison Teagan is a fiction. Every time I put on a dress and pretended to be someone I wasn't—that was playacting. *That* was the lie, not this. Never this. You want to talk about fiction, Dad? *Graham Teagan* is a fiction. He's a figment. The congressman and the candidate, with the trophy wife and the beautiful daughter and the best interests of the country at heart? That's a story you tell. It's a parlor trick. Now you see him; now you don't."

"You ungrateful, spoiled little—"

"*Graham*," Mom says again, not a reprimand but a threat.

Monty barks in my defense. Or the yelling has frightened him, but I choose to believe he's on my side.

Dad stops. Sets down his mug. Runs a hand through his thinning hair. His breaths rattle through him, rage still spewing from him like a steam engine. "Go to your room, Madison."

I laugh, incredulous. Reckless. "You don't *live* here."

"I'm still your father."

"Are you? Because if I'm not your son, then I think you've forfeited your parental rights."

I'm sure he's going to blow again, but Mom stops him, her hand circling his wrist. But it's me she looks at, her eyes inscrutably dark. "Go to your room, Mark."

I shoot Dad one last withering glance. Then I scoop Monty up in my arms, and I go.

In my room, above my bed, against my gunmetal-gray walls, hangs a Jasper Johns print in a heavy wooden frame. Arguably his most famous piece, it's named, simply, *Flag*. He created a whole series of flags in mixed media, newspaper decoupaged under beeswax and paint. In one, three flags nest like Russian dolls, one on top of the next. In another, the flag is a study in whitewash.

But *Flag*, first and simplest, bears the most resemblance to its subject, colors vibrant, proportions in accordance with US Flag Code, and forty-eight period-appropriate stars. From afar, stripped of its context, the flag presents an image of uncomplicated patriotism, quaint and nostalgic in its simplicity, but that's the trick of it. Take a symbol in the public memory, and the viewer imbues it with their own hopes and fears. When Johns painted *Flag*, McCarthy was hunting "commies" like it was open season, Eisenhower was adding "under God" to the Pledge of Allegiance, and schoolchildren were "ducking and covering" under their desks. Being American meant swearing unwavering loyalty to a singular definition of American life.

Named after a Revolutionary War hero, and a Korean War veteran himself, Jasper Johns is also gay. It's impossible for me to see his flag without the lens of his queerness coloring every daub of paint and wax. In the 1950s, anywhere but in the underground New York art scene, he would have been hunted, too. Called un-American. The army would have discharged him, had they known. And yet Johns painted so many flags in that era, with an obsession that must have been rooted in love.

But in my mind, it wasn't simple patriotism but critical love, a reminder that dissent itself is patriotic, and a call for the country to *do better*. I've always found it hopeful, in a bittersweet kind of way. When you're queer in America, you have to learn to love your country for what it could be, or not at all. You're always feeling forward, reaching, leaning toward a future that doesn't yet exist. That might never exist.

Today, huddled on the hardwood floor with my knees plastered against my unwieldy chest, I don't feel hopeful. Tears streak my vision. Jasper Johns's frenetic brushstrokes blur in and out of focus.

When Dad was Marin County's district attorney and I was too young to know what *transgender* meant, except in my bones, Dad prosecuted antiqueer hate crimes to the fullest extent of the law. During his campaigns, he spoke with queer activists within the community and promised to make their agenda his priority. In Congress, he has cosponsored a dozen bills designed to protect queer and trans rights, including a revamped version of the Equal Rights Amendment that included gender identity and sexual orientation. It didn't pass, but Dad sure gave good lip service about supporting queer Americans.

Maybe he doesn't realize it's not as simple as hanging a rainbow flag beside the American one at his rallies. It doesn't matter what a good ally he pretends to be when he can't show up for me. Because fighting for a better future doesn't mean shit if it means sacrificing the present.

That's the problem with a progress narrative. It says, *Wait for it.* It says, *It gets better.* It says, *Just tough it out.*

But we shouldn't have to wait. *I* shouldn't have to wait. I shouldn't have to compromise myself or pretend to be someone more electable to make myself worthy of my father's love.

When we moved to Santa Julia and I dressed up for every after-church FaceTime call, I thought Dad would come around. I thought he'd understand, eventually.

He's never going to come around. It doesn't matter if I win my election or get into Harvard or finish law school at the top of my class. Dad will only ever see *Mark Adams* as a cautionary tale where his daughter is supposed to be.

And what if he's right? What if I put myself out there—my whole self—and voters don't want me? What if I can't *be change* and *make change* all at once? What if this country I'm trying so hard to love doesn't love me back?

My country; my father. If there's a difference, I can't remember it.

Knuckles knock out a sonata on my door. I choke back my sobs and wipe my tears with my fist. I can't decide whether I'm hoping or dreading that the body on the other side of the wood is Dad.

"Mark, honey?" Mom's voice, a whisper, barely there. "Can I come in?"

At the foot of my bed, Monty rouses from his fitful slumber and barks.

Mom sighs. "Your father left."

"For good?" My voice wobbles in spite of myself.

"To cool down." Wood sags, and joints creak, but my door doesn't open.

"Did he spend the night?"

"What do you mean?"

"Last night." My words are brittle, broken glass. "While I was gone, did he—"

"Oh, Mark, no. He's staying at the Grizzly Inn."

"Oh," I mutter, more breath than word.

"He may still be part of our lives—life in the public sight lines was inevitable from the moment he announced his first campaign—but after everything that happened . . . In all the ways that matter—the matters of the heart—your father and I are done. For good."

"Okay." It doesn't sound like I believe her.

"Mark," Mom murmurs. The door jimmies open, and then she's on her knees in front of me, testing the trace evidence of my tears with her thumb.

Monty jumps down from the bed with a thud, nosing his way in, literally. He imprints his cold, wet snout against my arm and looks up at me with his black, baleful eyes until I rearrange my legs to form a lap for him to occupy.

Mom watches us. "You don't have to be part of his campaign if you don't want to, and if you do, you shouldn't have to hide. And you should know, I told him in no uncertain terms that if he doesn't let you on that stage as you are, I won't be there, either."

A fresh spring of tears wells up, just when I thought I had nothing left to give. I don't know whether to thank her for her solidarity or beg her to reconsider.

She must see my indecision because she says, "It's been a long time coming."

"Then why—" I sputter. "Why did you agree to pretend in the first place?"

"Why do you think?" She smiles wryly. "I did it for you."

"But I never asked you to—"

"You didn't have to. You're my son, and you were hurting. I did what I had to do to keep you safe."

I never let myself consider how much she gave up for me. Last year, she primped and preened and sang Dad's praises on the campaign trail. She still attends donor dinners and flies to DC whenever he snaps his fingers. She's done it all for me, and all this time, I've been taking all my cues from her. "I really thought, if we played by his rules, he'd come around. This was just the middlegame, and you always have to sacrifice a few pieces, but—chess is a game, and that's all we are to him, isn't it?"

"It's not that simple. It never is, with Graham."

"Yeah, it really is," I insist, my voice hollow. "It's what you said about the public sight lines. Dad tried to tell me, too, in his own way." *An election is an invitation.* "He knew. He realized his career meant putting his family in a glass house, and he didn't care. About us. We didn't even figure into his calculations. We were only ever political props to him, the picture-perfect would-be first family he could pose in portraits and plaster on campaign buttons. Of course he trotted me out when I wore pleated uniform skirts and had hair down to my push-up bra." I look away. Out the window, where Utopia Heights is pristinely beautiful and nothing is allowed to hurt. "Did he even want kids? Did he want me? Or did he know he'd never get elected to any higher office unless he could prove his virility?"

"Mark," Mom cuts in, sharp as a needle, and I know I've gone too far. "Honey, no. Your father loves you. Of course he loves you."

This is worse than if she'd scolded me for talking about my father that way. This needle stabs me straight in the heart. Mom's arms fold around me, and Monty wriggles between us, and over Mom's shoulder, Jasper Johns's flag blurs purple.

If Dad's a feckless narcissist who loves himself and no one but himself, then it's not really about me. His cruelty is pathological. He knows not what he does, or whatever.

It's worse if Dad loves me. It means I matter, but just not enough.

TWENTY-SIX

RALPH DOESN'T ASK ME WHAT'S WRONG. HE doesn't point out that he saw me just this morning. He doesn't stare at the tear tracks on my face. The Prius idles, and he just asks me where I want to go.

I don't know. I barely know why I texted him. I just know it was late, I couldn't sleep, and his was the only name that brought me comfort. "Can we just drive?"

Ralph nods. The engine rumbles. An indie folk ballad hums over the speakers, slow and somber.

We wind up, up, up through Utopia Heights, past my street and the turnoff to Jenny's. We barrel on by the rusted playground, just a gleam of silver in the night. We crisscross through every upper-middle-class cul-de-sac. We twist and turn on spindly two-lane roads, weaving our way up the slope.

I don't realize where we are until Ralph pulls into one of those scenic overlook parking lots, except it's not particularly scenic. From this vantage point, scour-brush evergreens

270

obscure all signs of civilization. The tree cover is precisely what makes Redwood Ridge a popular make-out destination.

The engine clicks off; the music cuts out. "Are you coming?" Ralph looks at me expectantly, and I don't understand. Does he expect me to lie down beside him on the windshield? I wouldn't object, but—

Ralph is already out of the car. I follow his lead. The night isn't too cold. Late summer in California means my hoodie is more than enough.

Ralph pops the trunk. I'm still not sure if he's going to pull out a blanket, but the supplies inside could pass for a zombie apocalypse survival kit. Toolbox, water bottles, snacks. Ralph extracts a pair of scuffed leather hiking boots and a flashlight the size of a baseball bat. He sits on the bumper and swaps out his favorite brogues for the boots and does up his turquoise laces. "Will you be okay in those? I think there's a pair of Rachel's—"

I cut him off with a sharp shake of my head. Breathe deep. Tamp down the dysphoria and the tears and all the things I want to say to him. "Where are we going?"

Ralph grins. "I know a place."

"Okay." Because even though nothing about tonight is remotely okay, I trust him.

So I follow him. Out of the parking lot, across the deserted road, to a narrow trailhead. A brown sign marks the entrance to Martin Eden State Park. The flashlight beam reflects off the surface, hitting me right in the eyes. But not before I see the fine print that says the park closes at ten p.m. It wouldn't bother me if I were alone, but I'm very keenly aware of the warm body beside me. I glance at Ralph.

"Ignore it."

In spite of everything, a spark of thrill flickers through me, seeing this rule-breaking side of Ralph, so unlike the straitlaced face he presents to the rest of the world.

We hike along a dirt trail through the boundless black of the night, until the constellations revolve overhead and Santa Julia falls away beneath us.

The trailhead dead-ends into a glade. At the apex of Utopia Heights, the redwoods thin out. The world is quiet here, windless and still.

When Ralph realizes I've fallen behind, he stops. Looks back at me. Casts his flashlight beam toward the dirt. He still doesn't ask those questions I wouldn't be able to answer. He just waits, steady and patient as those mile-high trees.

"Are we close?"

Ralph nods.

We traverse the lonely field, making our way to the summit's edge. The sky opens up before us, every star in the sky telescoping into focus. We pass a cluster of weathered picnic tables, but Ralph presses on. "Have you been here before?" His flashlight glints off a sign for PARAÍSO POINT.

"No." I've heard the name in passing, but I still don't know where *here* is, exactly.

"Dad used to take us here for picnics. Saturday mornings, after Hebrew school. He always said the name was ironic because it's the one place in Utopia Heights where you can see 'all the world at once.'"

"*Paradise Lost.* How Lucifer first sees Earth when he falls from grace." The reference rubs salt in the open gashes in my heart. "But your dad was Jewish."

"He was an English major. What's your excuse?"

"Lapsed Catholic. And my dad wanted me to read all the classics."

I stop short.

Here at Paraíso Point, the hillside drops off suddenly, giving way to rock and dirt. Below, trees carpet the foothills, fading into tidy terra-cotta tiles of suburban roofs. All of Santa Julia unfurls before us. The city's embers smolder on the horizon. "Your dad was right," I whisper. It seems like sacrilege to speak so loud in a place so holy.

"All the world at once." Ralph clicks off the flashlight. Santa Julia is a beacon; the stars are incandescent. "Shall we?"

I'm not sure what he means until he goes right up to the edge and dangles his long legs over a flat-faced boulder. He's not afraid, so neither am I.

Gingerly, I scoot down to sit beside him. The cold stone leeches heat through my jeans, but Ralph radiates warmth. He's so close, and it has nothing to do with the size of the rock.

Santa Julia flickers and glows, and in the starlight on this impossible night, the city is the most beautiful place I've ever seen.

I texted Ralph because I didn't want to be alone, and I trust him more than almost anyone. I want to trust him with this. Show him my scars. Tell him the truth.

Except Dad is the star around which the truth revolves. Dad, who swore he'd never speak to me again if I told anyone. Dad, who screamed at me for having the gall to run for student body president. Dad, who has done nothing to earn my allegiance.

If I've already burned that bridge, then all this is water under it. If Dad already hates my guts and changing his mind would cost my soul, then there's no reason to keep honoring the oath he twisted my arm to get. I can tell the truth.

Except. Ralph thinks my dad is dead. He took me to this secret, sacred place. This place where his dad used to take him. I can't ruin that by owning up to the lie I've let him believe.

So maybe the full truth, nothing but the truth, is off the table, but that doesn't mean there's nothing left. There's still one choice I can make.

"Ralph," I say. Anything could break my resolve, so I don't look at him. Stare straight ahead. Take my strength from this town that took me in.

"Mark." He says it so softly. I know he's staring at my profile, taking in the shape of me against the star-studded sky, and I have no idea if the words I'm about to say will change what he sees there.

But I trust him. More than anyone. It's not bravado so much as a leap of faith.

I breathe in the clean night air and say, "I'm trans."

And Ralph says, "Okay."

I do turn to him then, scanning the picture before me for the difference, but nothing has changed. Shadows swallow his eyes, but his gaze is steady. The line of his lips hasn't shifted.

Maybe he misunderstood.

"I'm transgender," I try again. "Transmasculine."

But Ralph says, "Okay." Same tone. Same expression. No judgment.

My shoulders roll back, and my spine creaks into alignment. My body is light, buoyant. Giddy with relief and hope—but I can't trust it. "That's it?"

"Did you think I wouldn't be okay with it?"

I saw how easily Ralph accepted Nadia, but I'm not his sister's girlfriend. What we are is deep and porous and all the more dangerous for it. "Kind of. Maybe. I don't know." I take another deep breath. "Is it really that easy?"

"It's that easy." The smile falls away when he opens his mouth, then shuts it again. I think he wants to ask me how *not easy* it's been in the past, and maybe I'm being unfair here. Jenny didn't so much as blink even as the confession tumbled out when her lips were pressed against mine. Pablo asked careful questions about a topic he didn't know much about, then called me a week later with follow-up questions about all the gender theory he'd read on the internet. Mom called me her *son* mere minutes after I came out, while Dad huffed and puffed and blew the house down.

Maybe Ralph can read these tomes of ancient history etched in my eyes. He understands that as simple as this may be for him, it still isn't easy for me. He angles his body toward me, closer than before. I could count his freckles.

Sober, solemn, soft, he says, "Tell me what you need me to know."

So I tell him that we moved here so I could transition, start fresh, stay stealth. I talk about what it feels like to be visible and invisible all at once. My therapist would call this "pressure of speech," but I'm not sure. The words flow out of me like blood from a wound. Maybe Dad nicked an artery, and all this is arterial spatter.

Ralph doesn't seem to mind the blood, guts, or viscera I'm leaving in his hands. He listens so intently, and it isn't until I've bled myself dry that he asks me, "Who else knows?" Then he cringes. "You don't have to tell me, if that's too invasive. Just stop me if I say anything—"

"Don't worry, I will." I kick my heels back against the earth. "But I don't mind you asking. The school knows, obviously. Beyond that? Just Pablo and Jenny."

"Then why—" He sucks in so much air I think he's going to give himself hiccups.

I'm not sure where he's going with this, but I trust him. "It's okay. Whatever it is, you can ask me. I can't promise I'll answer, but—"

"Why did you tell me?" It comes out so quickly, in one rushed breath.

"Ralph."

"I don't understand. You asked me to be your veep. You texted me tonight. And now you're trusting me with this part of you, and it's not that I'm not honored, I am. I just don't understand. Why *me*?"

"*Ralph*," I say again, rougher. I've been so transparent. Translucent. I haven't just worn my heart on my sleeve; I've put it on display in the National Museum of Natural History. "You *know*. You have to know . . . how I feel about you."

His eyes are wide, wild. His lips part. His brows furrow.

He doesn't know.

I know how to make speeches about hope, change, and the promise of a better future. I know how to debate policy and philosophy. I know how to argue my case, behind the podium or in the pulpit. But nothing I know about the art of rhetoric has prepared me for this. There's no speech I could give that would convey a fraction of what I feel for him.

So I kiss him. It's brash and reckless, but I crash my lips against his, the only declaration I know how to make. Except Ralph stays still, a wax model in the museum of unspoken feelings, and I'm sure I've made a terrible mistake. Dread curdles the acid in my stomach. "I'm sorry," I whisper, pulling back, desperately searching for a way to walk this back. "I didn't—"

Ralph lurches forward. Our mouths collide so suddenly I almost lose my balance, but Ralph's arm hooks my shoulder, tugging me closer. His lips part beneath mine, and I kiss him, desperate, as if he's going to pull away at any moment. I savor the taste of him, all bergamot and orange zest. My hand cradles the back of his head, fingers threading through his short, coarse curls, as if there were any way to bring him closer.

We kiss until we're breathless, and we tent our heads together, steadying ourselves at the edge of the abyss.

"Just to be clear," Ralph says, hoarse. "You're saying—"

"You're the only thing I'm sure of," I whisper. This is the bravest I've ever felt. Not bravado, not a performance, not an act. Just the truth.

I don't know what response I'm expecting, but it's not the exasperated chuckle Ralph gives me. "Why didn't you *tell* me?"

"I thought you knew!"

"I thought I had the world's most hopeless crush."

"Not hopeless."

And here, at the still point of the turning world, I kiss him again.

TWENTY-SEVEN

THE GENDER-NEUTRAL BATHROOM IN THE nurse's office feels a hell of a lot smaller with four people crammed inside.

My campaign team insisted I needed a makeover in advance of our final day of campaign stops, so Nadia forged hall passes. She's the de facto stylist because she "has her finger on the pulse," or however Jenny put it. Rachel takes her job as bodywoman very seriously, so she has a whole garment bag of style options, some pilfered from my own closet and others whose provenance I can't verify, and I don't want to know how she got any of it. As my campaign manager, Jenny's managing operations from her perch on the shag toilet lid cover, but so far her oversight has mainly consisted of staring at her phone and muttering monosyllabic responses when Nadia and Rachel ask her opinion.

Now Rachel's unbuttoning the flannel shirt she buttoned me into just moments ago before Nadia deemed it "too lumberjack" and Jenny grunted her assent. Thank God I wore an undershirt over my binder. I'm still self-conscious about the curves Rachel might unearth, but she keeps her touch perfunctory and clinical, as professional as she'll be when she earns her white coat.

"What about this?" Rachel shakes a generic white button-down by its hanger.

Nadia shrugs. "Won't know until we try it."

I spread my arms, like I've done half a dozen times already. Rachel pulls the sleeves on, and this is definitely my shirt. I know because there's a thumbnail-size hole just above the left cuff from the time Monty got a little too aggressive when I tried to take that awful elephant chew toy away from him. Rachel's sparkly nails clack against mother-of-pearl buttons. When she throws a red tie patterned with tiny blue mustaches around my neck like a noose, I grumble, "Why doesn't Ralph have to go through this?"

"Oh, he already did," Rachel assures me. "Yesterday afternoon, I tore apart his armoire. I didn't actually have to do much, because that whole grandpa-sweater aesthetic is actually pretty hipster chic. We just had to dial back the Bill Nye vibes."

Her hands are too close to my throat. I swallow, and my burgeoning Adam's apple bobs. "What's wrong with *my* look?"

Rachel tugs on the four-in-hand knot she's executed

perfectly, as if to purposely mess it up. "You're so . . . clean-cut."

"Preppy," Nadia says.

"*Pretty*," Rachel says, without the cadence of a compliment.

"Yeah, the whole pretty-boy JFK thing. You look too much like a politician they'd see on TV."

In the dingy mirror, I don't look that different. It's my shirt, the way I'd wear it except with an extra button undone, and a novelty tie loose like a punk-boy-band member might style it. "Isn't that a good thing?"

"It means you look like a liar," Jenny interjects, without looking up.

Rachel takes a step back, surveys her handiwork, and frowns. "Yeah, this is all wrong."

Nadia cocks her head, studying me askance. "What about a different tie?"

"Still wrong," Jenny comments, thumbing out what must be a dissertation on her phone. "No tie."

"We *are* trying to dress him down," Rachel agrees.

She and Nadia rummage through another garment bag. I watch Jenny's reflection in the mirror, her milkmaid braid plaited across her head like a crown. I can't see her face. I don't know what she's thinking.

Rachel summarily dismisses a fistful of sweaters, and Nadia frowns at everything plaid. Somewhere at the back of the bag, they find a black sweatshirt printed with an upside-down American flag. Grayscale and faded like the ink has chipped away through decades of use. I pull it over my head, and we all gather around my reflection. Nadia smiles, and Rachel squeals, and even Jenny nods.

Quickly, they settle on a pair of my own jeans. My skinniest pair, which I don't wear very often, because they came pre-distressed. But Nadia insists distressed skinny jeans poll well with every demographic, and I capitulate to spare myself the indignity of stripping down to my boxer briefs in front of them.

When I think we're done, Rachel asks, "What about the hair?"

"How's the speech coming along?" Pablo asks that afternoon at the gym.

"Um."

"Mark."

I can't tell him that the only line in my speech.docx file is the heading "MAKING MY MARK???" I turn up the dial on the treadmill, gears whirring under my gym shoes, but I still can't outrace Pablo the way people outrace their problems and conversational partners in the movies.

"How has Jenny not been all over you about this? Why hasn't she marked up all your drafts in gel pen?"

My breaths are coming harder now, but Pablo just notched up his speed, so I can't back down now. "Jenny's been busy."

"Not too busy for this. She lives for the thrill of the campaign."

It's not about believing in the thing, Jenny told me. She said it was about getting things done, but I can't tell anymore whether Jenny cares if I win or lose.

"Okay, out with it."

"Out with *what?*"

"Dude. C'mon. Tell me what the hell's going on with you and Jenny."

"There's nothing going on—"

"You barely said a word to each other at the sleepover, and she's gone radio silent in the group chat. You don't think that's weird?"

"I think you need to stop spamming the group chat with dog pictures."

"Half of them are pictures of *your* dog, but that's not the point. Think back. Tell me. When did Jenny step back from the campaign?"

"Obviously she's been less involved since she took her name off the ballot, but she's still campaign manager."

"But how much has she actually been *managing*?"

"Plenty."

He rolls his eyes. "Right. Have you stopped to ask yourself why?"

I'd tell him I've been a little distracted, but that would only beg more questions I can't answer. Not when Dad's hotel is next door. He could be in his suite right now, marking up the speech his communications staff wrote for him, announcing his candidacy for governor.

"You might want to try asking *her*," Pablo says.

I almost ask him if he already has, but that wouldn't be fair. Jenny and Pablo were best friends long before I came into the picture. Besides, I don't have time to worry about any of this. I have an election to win.

"I'm not going to bother Jenny with the speech," I say, desperate to get the conversation back on safer ground. "Ralph and I are going to swap drafts tonight."

Pablo stumbles over his feet. "When did *that* happen?"

"What?"

"You and Ralph. Swapping drafts. Sitting in a tree."

"I think you're barking up the *wrong* tree."

I may have misjudged the steadiness of this terrain.

Last night, Ralph and I decided not to tell anyone about us before the election. We don't need another variable complicating the political calculus, and besides, I could write the textbook on lying for the greater good.

"You're spending a lot of time with him."

"He's my running mate."

"Right."

The gym keeps the flatscreens above the treadmills set to news stations. Fox News is trashing the Clintons. MSNBC's got an economist assessing the health of our GDP. But on

CNN, they're showing live footage of the head of the Motion Picture Association announcing his candidacy for governor. He's making his speech in an orange grove, his smiling wife and two college-age daughters all in stylish floppy sun hats, and fuck, Dad's probably watching this on his hotel TV.

Think about anything else. Think about the stale stench of sweat suffusing the recirculated air. Think about the rhythmic thud my feet make on the treadmill belt. Think about the fire in my lungs and my thighs. Think about Pablo, breathing easy beside me. He asked me about Ralph. Think about Ralph.

"I like spending time with him. He's . . ."—smart and funny and sad and so much better than he knows—"interesting."

"He certainly has an interesting fashion sense."

"Hey." It comes out sharper than I intend. I try to summon up anecdotes to prove Ralph's worth, ones that won't violate his privacy. "He knows as much about *Star Trek* lore as he does about Jewish theology, and he cares so much about doing the right thing, and . . . did you know he does calc problems in his free time?"

Pablo tries to whistle, but ends up coughing because intense cardio isn't conducive to whistling. "Dude," he says after he takes a long swig from his water bottle, "even I, the presumptive theoretical math major, do not do calculus for fun."

"Well, he didn't say it was for fun." My skin itches, sweat

and something else pooling over my pores. I worry I've said too much. "He called it stress relief."

"Either way, he's voluntarily choosing to do integrals when he could be, I don't know, watching porn."

"Porn?" I ask, incredulous.

"What?"

"You're ace."

"I hear it's therapeutic." Pablo shrugs. "Besides, a lack of sexual attraction does not automatically correlate to an aversion to sex and/or porn."

"Are you telling me you watch porn?"

Pablo makes a face like he's swallowed a bug. "No, but I hear it's what the red-blooded allosexual teenage boys do. You're a red-blooded allosexual teenage boy. You tell me."

"I'm pleading the fifth." If my face is red, I can cite physical exertion in my defense.

"Oh, God, can you imagine that headline?"

"What, 'Underage Gay Candidate Watches Porn'?"

"No, about you and Ralph. Amber would have a field day with your campaign-trail romance."

"Then it's a good thing we have nothing to worry about." When my heart clenches in my chest, I tell myself it's just one more lie. One more for the greater good. But I know I'm lying to myself, too.

It's a classic Hollywood jump scare when Mom knocks on my door that night. "Um," I say, heart pounding in time with the flashing cursor on my screen. "I'm kind of busy, Mom."

"This won't take long," she says and lets herself in anyway. She switches on the lights, and I blink rapidly to readjust. "Working in the dark isn't good for your eyes, you know."

"It helps me focus."

She tsks, then sets a mug of steaming coffee on my desk that has me salivating at the scent alone. "I figured you could use this more than cocoa."

"Thanks."

She leans against the wall, right against the cheap replica of the Constitution Dad bought me at the Independence Hall visitor center's gift shop when I was eight. "So," she says diplomatically, "how's the speech coming?"

I shut my eyes. "I just cited Thomas More."

"That bad, huh?"

"In my defense, it's really hard to resist talking about *Utopia* when it's in the school's name."

"Still, your goal is to sway undecideds, not scare them away with sixteenth-century philosophy."

"I know, I know. There's just so much riding on this speech. Nadia's latest polls show Henry up by eight. I'm ahead of Clary, but ten percent are still undecided. There's always a margin of error, but . . . You see my problem here."

"I see an opportunity there."

"That's what Jenny would say."

"Isn't she helping you with this?"

I stare at my screen, wishing the letters would rearrange

themselves into the answers I need. "She's busy," I lie. "Family thing."

"Well, why don't you read it to me?"

"Seriously?"

"How do you think your father got his start? When he was an ADA, he'd pace around the living room reading his handwritten drafts of closing arguments while I played jury on the couch."

I try to imagine it—Mom still finishing her residency, Dad prosecuting low-profile cases with all that passion—but it hurts too much to hold the image in my mind. "Okay. If you want."

So I read her four paragraphs about power and privilege and all the ways UHS doesn't live up to the promise of its name. It's only in the last paragraph that I finally use the word "I." That's where I commit myself to dismantling the systems of oppression that make our school an unsafe space for so many of our students. I'm listing off all the groups I want to protect when I reach the cursor, midsentence. "And, uh, that's where I'm at."

Mom doesn't say anything, and the silence makes my skin itch. I look up at her. "Was it that bad? You can tell me."

"No, no," she says with a small smile. "It's beautifully written. It's just a little . . . hollow. I already told you philosophy won't win undecideds, but the bit after that—where you talk about everything you're going to do—it's a lot of pressure.

Such a burden to place on yourself. And I hope you know it's not all on you."

"If you think I'm not up to it—"

She raises a hand to stop my tirade. "You remember when the nurses went on strike last spring?"

I nod, unsure where she's going with this.

"I never told you, but I went to the hospital administrator. I pled their case. I tried to make her see reason—and of course it didn't work. One of the nurses pulled me aside later and told me it wasn't my fight. I could advocate and try to reason with the brass all day long, but I was just one person speaking out of turn. The real power was there on the ground, in that picket line, all those nurses who had come together to speak for themselves. They built a coalition—one that was impossible to ignore."

"That's why—"

"You've started an important conversation, but that's what it is: a conversation. Not a lecture from your bully pulpit." Mom crouches down in front of me. "There's a difference between being an activist and being an organizer. Your father never understood that. He thought he could stand up alone and do it all himself. But real change happens when regular people come together to fight for it. Your job as their candidate—or president, God willing—is to empower them to do just that. Don't just speak for them; give them the space they need to speak for themselves."

"I—" I stammer. "Of course I want that. But I need to convince them to vote for me first. And that means making the big promises."

"No, it means showing them the kind of representative you're going to be. Remember, each vote cast for you is a promise, too."

I have five minutes onstage to convince 10 percent of the electorate that I deserve their promises, and I still have no idea how the hell I'm going to do it.

TWENTY-EIGHT

ELECTION DAY COMES LIKE CHRISTMAS MORN-
ing. For me, at least.

The first Tuesday following a Monday in September, students file into the gym for the captive-audience assembly,
grumbling their way up the bleachers. It's our last chance to
sell ourselves to the electorate before they cast their votes.

There is no stage. Just a row of flimsy folding chairs
glinting where their paint has peeled away and a podium dec-
orated with patriotic bunting.

In the boys' locker room, we candidates wait for our curtain call. In one corner, Henry and Dante confer in hushed
tones and animated hand gestures. In another, Clary runs
through vocal exercises, which has a junior class representative candidate flicking peanuts in her direction.

Pablo and Ralph have staked out their own row. When I'm
done sneaking peeks through the doorway, I join them. Pablo's leaning against the lockers, arms crossed over his chest
and eyes shut. He says it never helps to go into a wrestling

match tense, but then again, he's running unopposed. For his part, Ralph is panic-attack pale. His flannel bow tie looks like a noose. He can't seem to decide whether to fidget with it or with the fidget cube in his pocket.

"Hey," I say, setting a hand on his shoulder and praying I don't startle him. I sit down next to him. "You okay?"

"No," Ralph says emphatically. "There's a reason I barely speak in class, and that reason makes speaking in front of the entire student body a very bad idea. I took double my regular dose of anxiety pills this morning, but I still feel like there's a hornets' nest right beneath my skin. And I just realized it's just me and Dante running for veep, and there's a chance I could win while you lose to Clary, and I don't know if I can handle—"

"Ralph." I wish I could *really* touch him, hold his hand, convey through the warmth of my skin against his just how much I believe in him, but there are too many watchful eyes. "Whatever happens, you can handle it. I'll be by your side in student government even if I lose. But you don't need me. You care about this school. Doing the right thing means more to you than anyone I've ever met. Here." I extract a folded slip of paper from my back pocket. "I brought you something."

"I didn't know Election Day was a gift-giving holiday."

"It's not a gift-gift."

"Yet you're giving it to me."

"Just take it."

He does, unfolding it with far more reverence than this

scrap of paper deserves. He irons it out on his thigh and presses out the creases. His glasses slip a notch down his nose as he studies the page of integrals. "Did you . . . rip this out of our calculus textbook?"

"What? No, of course not. That would be vandalism. And you know that I, an upstanding candidate for student body president, would never support—"

"You're such a politician," he says, a smile tugging at his dimples. "So full of shit."

I'm not sure I've ever heard him swear before. He acts so serious, and it's a goddamn revelation each time he shows me another side of himself. Everyone else would call him a square, but I swear he's a decahedron. "I knew you'd be anxious. So I thought this might help."

He looks at me, or, more specifically, at my mouth. Like he'd kiss me *thank you* if he could. He bites his lip and says it instead. "Do you mind if I . . . ?"

"Not at all. That was the point."

He pulls a mechanical pencil from his shirt pocket. I wish I'd brought graph paper, but Ralph just starts marking up the margins.

Meanwhile, I read over a crumpled copy of the speech I cobbled together last night with Popsicle sticks and paper clips. I didn't take Mom's advice, but at least it's finished. There's a thesis. I think Ms. Polastri would give me a solid A-.

"C'mon, candidates," ZP calls from the door. "It's showtime."

Ralph and I join Pablo in line. Pablo looks perfectly calm and collected. Everyone else is tense, rocking on the balls of their feet or gripping their friends for support.

"Ready for this?" Pablo claps me on the shoulder.

"Yep." I grin. "Totally."

Ralph must not be listening; otherwise, he'd call bullshit.

Looking around, I realize who else isn't here to call me on my shit. "Where's Jenny?" Even though she isn't running anymore, I fully expected her to muscle her way past ZP. She's still my campaign manager, and I still want her here for emotional support and constructive ass-kicking. After all, I wouldn't be here without her.

Pablo frowns. "She said she'd be here."

The lights dim, and ZP beckons us onto the basketball court to find our assigned seats. My chair squeaks when I sit down at the end of the row. Clary squirms next to me. She crosses her knee-high-clad legs quickly, as if she's afraid the decrepit old chair might give her chlamydia. Beside her, Henry leans back, cold and confident, his feet planted firmly on the ground. I do my best to mirror his posture; I can manspread with the best of them.

At the podium, under a blinding spotlight, ZP tells our listless audience that they're about to hear from some of Santa Julia's best and brightest. "Electing representatives is a solemn civic duty," he says. "Just like senior ditch day."

The candidates for lesser offices swallow up twenty

uneventful minutes before Pablo takes the podium. He effort-lessly charms the audience with casual jokes about what he's going to do with the class budget. At least, they're jokes to him. Maybe the voters really do think he's going to put vend-ing machines in every hallway and book the various former members of One Direction to play at our school dances.

Then it's time for the vice presidential candidates to say their piece. Dante's up first, and honestly, when he's done, I couldn't answer a basic comprehension question about his speech. He could have read the Gettysburg Address word for word; he could be the next Barack Obama, for all I know. Because then Ralph steps up, and all I can hear is the sound of blood rushing in my ears. I can't tear my eyes away from him. His face has gone from as white as Mike Pence's hair to as green as a dollar bill.

Ralph clutches his tablet against his chest. He steadies himself against the podium to stop his knees from buckling. He glances back over his shoulder, right at me, and I give him the warmest smile I know how to give. When he turns back to the audience, his voice doesn't quiver, doesn't quake. He talks about growing up in this neighborhood, with the people in this crowd, and how this school isn't the commu-nity he remembers from their hopscotch days. He tells them about the moment I asked him to join my campaign and how he knew it was his duty to do what he could to mend this small patch of the world. Tikkun olam, he says; in Judaism, it's everyone's responsibility to mend this world, from playground to boardroom. When he's done, I clap louder than everyone else in the gym, until my palms are red and raw. His cheeks are red, too, flushed with something like exhilaration.

ZP takes the stage again. "And now let's have a drumroll for the candidates for student body president."

Clary's first. Her voice is pitched high and sugar-sweet over the speakers. She talks for her full five minutes and says a lot of words that don't mean much of anything. She paints a picture of class trips to far-off places but doesn't make any promises. It's all rainbows and unicorns, except her horses are just coconuts clapping together, and her pride flag has a stripe just for allies. Anemic applause follows her conclusion, but according to Nadia's polls, that doesn't mean anything.

Henry, to his frustration, is second. He rips the mic from its stand and prowls the floor. He doesn't have so much as an index card but fills the gym with victim-blaming, dog-whistle rhetoric. He plays the demagogue, acting like he's going to deliver this school into the hands of the voters. His adoring fans interrupt every other sentence with applause, and Henry pauses to let them. After the daily rallies he's held across campus, he knows how to play the crowd like a professional—like my dad. He takes up his full five minutes, too, and when he finally hands over the mic, he gets a standing ovation. They keep going even after ZP clears his throat into the mic, only stopping when Henry waves them off.

He swaggers back to his seat wearing a smirk worthy of a senior superlative. "You're up," he sneers at me.

I get up. Walk to the podium. Clutch my speech in sweat-soaked fists. I've never been afraid of public speaking. I've won awards for my debate chops. But I've never done anything quite like this, especially not as Mark Adams.

And I'm fucking terrified.

From where I stand in the glare of the spotlight, the crowd is dim and blurred, but I can make out a few faces. Off to the side, Amber has a heavy-duty video camera balanced on her shoulder and a scrawny freshman carrying AV equipment. In the front row, Trevor Dalton and Kevin Guo wear T-shirts with Henry's name inked in black Sharpie and stare at me with unabashed disdain. Nadia and Rachel make themselves known halfway up the bleachers, cheering long after everyone stops. Elsewhere, with the sophomores, I find Benji, who nods solemnly. Jenny's nowhere to be seen. Besides, what chance does my message have in a room that claps like that for Henry's hate-filled homilies?

Then I catch sight of Beatriz's towering top knot beside Xander's shiny blue pompadour. Kai in his varsity jacket and Shawn in his utility jacket. At the bleachers' summit, Cristian and Luis hoist Abigail up on their shoulders to give her a better view, and I remember. I remember every minute I spent on the campaign trail, getting to know these people and talking about what I could do for them.

Except, this isn't about what I can do for them. This isn't about how I can protect them from Clary's platitudes or Henry's threats. This isn't about whether Dad will disown me if I win.

Because this isn't about *me*.

I understand now. I understand why Nadia said I shouldn't run as a populist, why Benji said he didn't want to be my cause, why Mom said a vote was a promise.

All those faces in the bleachers are counting on me. But I'm counting on them, too.

I glance at the damp speech in my hand, so many beautiful words about how I alone will dismantle systemic oppression at UHS in exchange for votes, and I crumple it up.

Then I put on my smile. Straighten my spine. Reach for the mic.

"You shouldn't vote for me.

"No, I'm serious. You don't know me. I only transferred here last year, and I've only ever taken IB classes. I didn't make an effort to introduce myself to any of you until last week, when I suddenly needed your votes. So you have no reason to believe any of the promises I've made to you.

"And you shouldn't. I got into this race because I watched our out-of-touch administrators suspend my friend for refusing to apologize to bigoted bullies. I thought I could protect kids like him. I thought I could fight the homophobia, racism, and classism that stop Utopia High School from living up to its name. I thought I had the power to make real change.

"But the truth is, I can't. Just like I can't make show choir a class or put an end to mandatory minimums for pot possession. I can't make good on any of my promises on day one, or even day one hundred, of my term.

"For one thing, the student body president doesn't have that kind of power. The student handbook doesn't exactly enumerate the powers vested in our executive branch, but I know they don't go much farther than spirit days, dances, and the senior class trip. As your president, I definitely wouldn't have the power to rewrite the handbook itself.

"And that means, despite my best efforts to be a different kind of politician, I'm just another upper-middle-class white guy standing up here asking for your vote without any way to follow through.

"But I think there is one thing that sets me apart from my opponents, and that's this:

"I want to try anyway.

"Because in the past two weeks, I've traveled across this campus and talked to more of you now than I did all of last year. I've listened to your stories. I've heard all the ugly ways this school has found to tear you down. And I've learned how much better you all are than this school deserves. You want to play soccer under the Falcon mascot even when the school doesn't promote your team as much as the others. You want to celebrate school spirit days even when some of them turn your cultures into costumes. You want to hold hands with your boyfriend even when other students snicker in the halls. In spite of everything this school has tried to take from you, you keep giving the best of yourselves.

"You deserve better.

"And I want to build something better.

"Because while you're out there giving the best of yourselves, the best I have to give you is my vision of a better UHS. A place where every student feels safe and is treated equally under the rule of law. A place where bullies are punished, but we aren't punished for being teenagers. A place where free speech is protected, but hate speech is not.

"That's my vision, but it isn't a promise. This isn't something I can give to you in exchange for your vote. It isn't something our sacred student handbook will ever authorize.

"I told you I got into this race because I thought I had the power to make real change, but I was wrong. I don't. I can't. The only way to make real change is together, whether that means delivering petitions to the administration, attending school board meetings, or calling each other out when we're wrong.

"I believe we can and should challenge Utopia High School to live up to its name. That's what I'll do as student body president, but I can't do it alone. I need your help.

"I need more than your votes; I need your commitment, too, to this school and this community. To put in the work, each and every day. To be kind and compassionate. To call me out when I'm wrong. To challenge yourself and your peers to do better. To keep on giving the best of yourselves.

"So vote for me if you share my vision for a more inclusive UHS. Vote for me because you want better from your administration. Vote for me because you know I'm not the perfect candidate, but I'll keep giving the best of myself, each and every day. And if that's not enough—

"Don't vote for me."

Total silence meets me when I walk away from the podium. Clary's lips are parted, wondering what the hell I've just done. Pablo's shaking his head, convinced I've lost it. Henry's grinning, sure that I've just handed him the election. The worst part is, I'm pretty sure they're all right.

But then, two hands clap together, and it's Ralph, smiling at me like I've done something brave, like I haven't committed career suicide.

Then more hands join in, the sound swelling all around me, and when I turn back around, people are standing in the bleachers, some whistling, others calling my name. I have no idea how it compares to Henry's reception, but it's thunderous enough for me.

Somehow ZP gets them all to quiet down, and I stumble back to my seat. I listen to his voting instructions in a daze. Everyone's supposed to go back to class to finish out first period, and they'll call groups back by homeroom to vote.

ZP holds the candidates back, explaining that our first duty as freshly minted, soon-to-be-elected-if-we're-lucky officials is to transform the gym from town hall to bona fide polling place.

First things first, I hurry over to Ralph. "See, I told you it wouldn't be so bad."

His eyes narrow behind his glasses. "If you call almost passing out in front of the entire student body *not so bad*, then sure. Absolutely."

"You were great."

He shrugs, but the blush that paints his cheeks pink gives me hope he might believe me. "You were better. But that definitely wasn't the speech you sent me this morning."

"I know. I know. But I couldn't—"

"It was *perfect*."

I want to kiss him more than anything, but in the middle of the gym, we're too exposed. I can't stop myself from reaching out. A hand on his arm is innocuous enough, right? But then he reciprocates with a hand on my shoulder, and we're hugging, right there at center circle. Close enough to feel the

302

heat bleed between us. Close enough smell his citrus after-shave and the tea on his breath. Close enough for him to feel my heartbeat. We're too close, but I don't care.

Pablo coughs, loudly, and I break away guiltily. From his arched eyebrows and amused smile, it's clear Pablo has figured us out, and he doesn't care. So I go over to him and smile, sunny as the summer day. "You were great, too, dude." I kiss him on the cheek, partially to give my relationship cover, and partially to rewrite the script of what masculinity is supposed to look like.

"You were extremely reckless," Pablo grouses. Then he rolls his eyes, grudgingly fond. "I'm proud of you."

"Guys," ZP calls. "A little help here? Please don't tell me you're planning to shirk your responsibilities on day one, or else I might be tempted to rig this election."

A chill crawls down my spine. "Don't even joke about that!"

"Hello, FEC remember?"

"Still not reassuring."

"Still not my job."

We collapse the bleachers and stow the folding chairs. Then we build a row of voting booths with PVC pipes and shower curtains. Next comes the registration table, replete with student directories for the election monitors to use to check voters off. Student IDs are required to prevent identity fraud, which is ridiculous. Even though school IDs are free, voter ID laws are something else I'll fight if I win this.

Finally, on its own card-table altar, sits the sacred ballot box. In reality, it's just a red cardboard box with a slit on top. Someone's put a layer of duct tape over the seam where the lid meets the sides to prevent tampering.

When our work's done, I stare at the setup with more awe than it deserves, thinking the gym looks more magical than it did at prom. ZP takes a seat at the registration table and kicks his feet up, revealing his Captain America high-tops. He grins up at us. "So, ready to take these ballots for a spin?"

Henry and I end up in neighboring booths. His silhouette is a ghostly shadow behind the shower curtain; he marks his ballot with such efficiency. My palms are so sweaty, I almost drop my marker. The fluorescent lights shine down on the yellow card stock in front of me.

My name, in fresh black ink. It all comes down to this. I pop the cap off my marker. Breathe in the caustic scent of Sharpie. Trace the sign of the cross over my chest before I overthink it. Make my mark.

STUDENT BODY PRESIDENT
☑ Mark Adams
❏ Clarissa Cabrera
❏ Henry McIver

TWENTY-NINE

AMBER LIVESTREAMS THE ELECTION RESULTS. No, really. ZP may have locked down the history hall where votes are being counted, but she has an inside source on the two-woman election committee.

The campaign team makes my living room our war room. Everyone's here, even Jenny, who showed up to third period as if nothing were wrong. She hangs back near the self-serve speakeasy we're running out of the kitchen, nursing a cocktail that's more vodka than cranberry. Everyone else demonstrates judicious restraint with the Bacardí Black Pablo's sister bought us and the brownies of questionable provenance Rachel brought. I limit myself to precisely one dark and stormy—just enough to dredge up some Irish courage, but not enough to lose my wits. After all, we have work to do.

Hooked up to my laptop, the TV streams direct from the *Dystopia High* website. Amber has transformed the library into her own personal newsroom. She sits smart in her polka-dot blazer, a trio of campaign surrogates at her side: Beatriz, Kevin, and Martha from Christian Club. The screen behind them displays a flashy PowerPoint where Amber's AV flunky tracks the votes as they come in.

ADAMS	CABRERA	MCIVER
32	77	69

"For the mathematically challenged," Amber announces, her grin made for television, "Clary Cabrera leads with forty-three percent of the vote. Henry McIver is close behind at thirty-nine percent. Dark horse Mark Adams is a distant third, just under eighteen percent." She turns to her panel. "So far, would you say these numbers line up with expectations?"

"Yes," Martha says, quick but quivering.

Kevin nods, making a show of pensive reflection. "These numbers will keep evolving throughout the afternoon, but there's already a clear loser here."

"You're saying the Adams camp should be worried?"

"Absolutely. Adams never had a chance. It's always been a two-man race."

Amber looks to Beatriz. "Thoughts?"

Beatriz launches into what looks like a strategic defense, punctuated with solid hand gestures, but I don't hear any of it because Nadia notches down the volume. Probably because she can see the panic on my face.

"Relax," she says. "It's early days. If Amber's numbers for absent students and spoiled ballots are accurate, we're waiting for a total of two thousand eighteen votes. Right now, we're looking at one seventy-eight. That's—"

"Eight-point-eight-two percent," Pablo says, absently, from his space next to Benji on the couch.

Nadia pointedly ignores him. "That's only six rooms reporting. Out of sixty-nine."

"Nice," Rachel chuckles.

Nadia rolls her eyes fondly and taps the wall beside the screen, where she has reconstructed a campus map with red, blue, and yellow Post-its. It's a cross between John King's Magic Map and a murder wall. Since the results come in by homeroom, and homerooms tend to correlate to demographic groups, Nadia and Pablo have been crunching the numbers on matching TI-84s with terrifying fervor. "Half the classrooms reporting are freshmen. That explains Clary's lead, though I'm sure we picked up a few votes there, too. They're young and fresh, and by and large, they aren't yet inured to Clary's patent-leather brand of bullshit. Henry's votes must be coming from the non-IB upperclassmen classes." In her Post-it color story, I'm blue, Henry's red, and Clary's yellow.

There's not a lot of blue.

Nadia scratches the back of her head. "This would be so much easier if we had exit polls."

"What were you going to do," Pablo asks, "stand outside

the gym doors and harass kids on their way back to class?"

"Actually—" Nadia starts.

Rachel lurches upright from an Eames chair. "Oh my God, babe, what did you do?"

"Nothing!" Nadia throws up her hands. "ZP sent me back to class after giving me a lecture about voter intimidation, but it was no big deal, I swear."

"Please don't get suspended," Benji says. "You wouldn't believe the things I've seen . . ."

Pablo swats him with a throw pillow. "Seriously, though. Harassing voters is no way to win a campaign."

"Says the man who won by default," I jibe.

"The night is young."

"It's midafternoon," Ralph points out from the armchair opposite Rachel. Monty's curled up in his lap, and Ralph has been giving him all the head scratches his heart desires. He calls him "Monsieur Montesquieu." His pronunciation's terrible for a prospective Club Français member, but that only makes it more endearing.

"Either way," Nadia says, "this is just getting started. Buckle up. We're gonna be here for a while."

ADAMS	CABRERA	MCIVER
162	231	218

* * *

"It's the top of the hour, and I'm Amber Carr, coming to you live from Utopia High School with the latest election updates. In the red-hot race for student body president, Clary Cabrera holds a two-point lead over Henry McIver. With nearly thirty percent of the vote counted, Mark Adams remains in third. We turn now to our panel."

"Clary is the frontrunner," Martha says, and nothing else.

"Henry's playing the long game," Kevin says. "He's had a strong first quarter, and we're not even at halftime. He just needs to keep doing what he's been doing."

"It's not just about the raw numbers," Beatriz counters, "but where they're coming from."

Amber lifts an eyebrow. "You're saying the Adams camp isn't worried?"

"Amber, according to my contacts, they haven't begun to worry."

"That's my homegirl." Rachel beams. She's the one who's been texting Beatriz sound bites.

"Why are we lying on national television?" Nadia said to buckle up, but I haven't even sat down.

"Mark, it's not even community television," says Benji.

"Same difference!" My voice cracks, high and feminine and *fuck*.

"This is fine," Nadia says, though I'm starting to wonder if she'd say that even if the whole house caught fire around

309

us. "Nearly all the freshmen homerooms have been counted now, which means Clary's pool of gullible voters is about to dry up. As for Henry, the wood shop and auto shop votes just came in, plus a sophomore PE class."

"That doesn't mean that I'm suddenly going to start getting votes."

"It does, actually," Nadia explains for what is, admittedly, not the first time. "Not a single IB class is reporting, and only a few of the freshman and sophomore honors classes. That's your base. And everyone else? The non-IB kids we've spent the past week talking to? Most of those kids are dispersed across campus. Like Shawn's friends? There's no homeroom for stoners. As long as we keep picking up small batches of votes across the board, that'll keep us competitive until our precincts get counted. Help me out here?"

She looks to Jenny, still alone at the bar, tipping another finger of vodka out of a flask. Her eyeliner is smeared. Locks of hair have come free of her French braid. There's a tear at the knee of her tights. She looks like she spent the night clubbing. She shrugs. "The numbers aren't my strong suit."

"The math is there." Pablo picks up the slack. "Clary's vote surged in quick, but it's drying up fast. This is Henry's wave. Yours is yet to come."

"But it's coming?" I can't keep the tremor from my voice.

"I'd bet my Nikon on it," Nadia swears.

* * *

ADAMS	CABRERA	MCIVER
290	255	439

"And now for a Key Race Alert!"

I swear to God Amber thinks she's Wolf Blitzer. Why anyone would aspire to be Wolf Blitzer is beyond me.

"Early frontrunner Clary Cabrera has fallen into third, just behind Mark Adams. Henry McIver, our outspoken quarterback, has surged ahead with forty-five percent of the vote and just under half of precincts reporting. In another race, *Dystopia High* is ready to make a projection."

The screen cuts to an animated graphics card, a sprawl of twinkling stars and broad stripes. "*Dystopia High* projects that latecomer candidate Ralph Myers will win student body vice president." Ralph's yearbook photo fills the screen, a gold checkmark superimposed over his shoulder. "After Jenny Chu resigned her candidacy amid scandal last week, Dante Gomez was considered a shoo-in for veep. Adams tapped Myers to fill Chu's shoes . . ."

Rachel squeals first, but I think I shout the loudest. Not that it matters, not that it's a competition—not when Ralph *won*, and we're all cheering our hearts out.

Ralph is, well, verklempt. His eyes are so bright, tropical seas under a summer sun. His lips tremble, trying to keep it all in. Ralph, who told me he'd be a liability to my campaign, who believes the whole world spins without him, who never believed he could win. I don't think he realized how much he wanted this until now.

I tug Ralph to his feet and wrap my arms around him. Then another warm body presses against my back, and I smell Rachel's cake-batter lip gloss. Everyone rushes over to join the group hug, all of us are jumbled up and tangled together, inseparable.

Except Jenny. It's only when we break apart that I realize she hasn't moved. She lifts her glass in mock salute. "Congratulations." She nods to Ralph. Jenny seems to be checking off a list of unforgivable things she can do in one day, but I don't blame her for this. There are things I need to say to her, too, but now isn't the time.

Ralph's still standing beside me. I feel the warm puff of his breath against my neck before I hear him whisper, "Well, now you *have* to win."

ADAMS	CABRERA	MCIVER
419	262	655

"With two-thirds of the vote counted, Henry McIver's lead has skyrocketed. With just under half the vote in McIver's column, Mark Adams trails by eighteen points. Clary Cabrera's been left in the dust. Martha, Beatriz, any word on when your candidates plan to concede?"

Martha is on the verge of tears, clutching her cross like a rip cord. If she's in contact with Clary right about now, I can only imagine the passive-aggressive emojis flooding her inbox. Her lower lip wobbles. "No."

"No word or no plans?"

"No."

Stubborn professionalism is the only thing that keeps Amber's smile tacked in place. "Beatriz?"

"Mark wants to see every vote counted."

Kevin barks out a laugh. "Sure. We'll play this game through to the final buzzer, but that doesn't change the reality that both your guys are gonna be calling to concede real soon."

Nadia hits mute. Kevin's lips keep moving. "Listen." Nadia tugs my shoulder until I'm facing her rather than the screen.

"I'm listening."

"I hate to steal Kevin's sports metaphors, but you need to keep your head in the game."

I could argue. I could point out that her own models and figures indicate there's only a 20 percent chance I can pull out a win. My state of mind isn't going to change the outcome. What's done is done and cannot be undone, and all that.

My campaign team's looking at me like I'm the doomed hero in a war movie on my way to the final battle, and I'd rather go AWOL.

"I need some air," I tell the murder wall. Dark and stormy's a pathetic metaphor for my mood, but I pick mine off the mantel and head outside to the patio we never use.

I slump down in a whitewashed Adirondack chair, staring sullenly out at the spacious property that makes this house a brochure-worthy manifestation of the American Dream.

It's always been more yard than we needed, a wooden deck bordering drought-resistant grass. The line of plum trees against the fence was planted by the previous tenant. Some shrubbery has survived, but weeds and wildflowers have supplanted everything else. Mom kept a garden back in Marin, but she wasn't a single mom then.

The sliding glass door squeaks open. "Mind if I join you?"

I'm expecting Pablo, but it's Ralph who slips into the chair beside me and sets his drink on an actual coaster. Mine's just sweating on the wood.

I can't look at Ralph, so I look down. My arms are crossed over my chest, another line of defense against the anomaly there. The fine gold hair dusting my forearms has multiplied in the past year. I should be happy, but all I can think is, what if I've done all this, sacrificed so much, and it still isn't enough? "Have they called it?"

"What?"

"The election. They've called it for Henry. That's why you're out here."

"No, they haven't, and that's not—"

"Right." I shut my eyes and swallow my pride because that's what you do when you have a boyfriend. "I'm sorry."

"You don't have anything to be sorry for." His fingers clasp around my wrist. My pulse hammers against the bracelet of his touch. "You're scared."

"I'm not scared—"

"There's still a third of the vote out, mostly IB kids. Besides, I beat Dante, so the odds are—"

"Ralph," I interrupt him, more forcefully than I should. But it's true. I'm not scared; I'm angry. "I'm going to *lose*." The first time I've said the words aloud, and they're every bit as painful as I thought they'd be. They sting just as much as when Dad said them. "Clary was right—we split the vote. If I'd just stayed out of this like everyone told me to, then Clary would've won, and that would've been fine. Instead, I went and handed the election to Henry."

"That's not true."

"I looked him in the eye and swore I'd stop him."

"And you will."

"You don't know that."

"Hey," Ralph says sharply. He takes my hand in his and holds on tight. "Listen. I'm not going to tell you how much I believe in you because you should already know. But I want you to remember who you believe in. Last week in TOK, when we talked about whether people are fundamentally good or bad, Henry almost tore your throat out because you had the audacity to believe the best of humanity. That there's something decent at the heart of us, and that we're capable of saving ourselves. Do you still believe that?"

"Yes." In spite of everything, somehow, I still do.

"Then you have to believe they'll do the right thing."

"What's the right thing?"

Ralph smiles. "Voting for the better man."

"Hey guys?" Benji pops his head outside. "You need to see this." There's no inflection in his voice. He's as unfazed by the sight of Ralph and me sitting out here holding hands as he is by whatever's happening inside.

This is it. Back to the battlefield, or maybe the gallows. Maybe Henry's police state has already convicted me of treason. My legs quiver when I stand. Ralph is steady and silent, and I wish I could borrow some of his strength. This may be a funeral procession, but I have to see it through.

Everyone looks up when I walk in. Maybe they know I'm about to step on a land mine. But that doesn't explain why Nadia and Pablo are still hunched over their calculators and Rachel has her phone to her ear.

In their collective silence, Amber booms, "Here, in the eleventh hour, with just fourteen percent of ballots outstanding, the unimaginable has happened."

ADAMS	CABRERA	MCIVER
736	269	734

"With twelve new classrooms reporting, insurgent candidate Mark Adams has taken the lead for the first time. Betting-market favorite Henry McIver now trails by two votes."

Amber keeps talking. Kevin and Beatriz weigh in while Martha slouches low in her seat, but all I hear is buzzing. A swarm of bees has made its hive inside my skull, and maybe I'm allergic. Maybe I'm anaphylactic. Because my vision blurs, my skin burns, and my heart must be tachycardic.

Someone calls my name, and a hand settles on my shoulder, anchoring me to the earth. Ralph is right beside me. His face resolves into a smile, dazzling, dizzying, or maybe that's just an aftershock. "I *told* you."

"I don't understand." I look from Ralph to Jenny, drinking straight from her flask, to Nadia. "I was behind by eighteen points. You and Pablo were doing your best Nate Silver impressions, and even though you were trying not to show it, I could read between the lines. The math wasn't there. It should be over by now."

"Have you listened to a single word I've said all day?" Nadia admonishes. "I told you, it's all about where the vote is coming from." She whips out a laser pointer and aims it at her murder wall. The red dot marks a sniper's target in the history hall, which was mostly empty space when I went outside. Now almost every classroom has been replaced by a blue Post-it. "They've started reporting the IB vote. Not to

317

mention, the freshman health classes just came in."

"That wave I promised?" Pablo grins. "It's here. This is the rising tide."

"But it's not raising all ships," Rachel clarifies.

"Just ours." Benji claps me on the back as he swings past me to crash on the couch.

"And if we look at which rooms are still outstanding," Nadia adds, "the math is clear."

"What are you saying, exactly?"

Her gaze is steady, dark, and deep, but she beams, brighter than anything. "I'm saying you're gonna win this."

Keys jangle. The door churns open. Mom calls, "Hi, honey. Any word yet—"

A chorus of shushes stops her short. She finds us all at the edges of our respective seats. I'm teetering on the armrest of Ralph's chair, neck craned, too close to the screen. Still glued to Amber's livestream, where Amber, Kevin, and Beatriz cycle through the same stale talking points. Only a handful of votes have come in since I took the lead. Amber said they expected the last ten rooms to come in one batch. That was half an hour ago.

That was when Jenny left.

Mom stops behind the couch, taking in the numbers on the screen, the mess we've made of her living room, and the assortment of coasterless effervescent beverages on various

318

surfaces. At least the bottle is safely tucked away in Pablo's backpack.

Just when I think Amber's about to start reading straight from her history textbook to fill the airwaves, her assistant rushes on-screen. He crouches down to whisper in Amber's ear, and she perks up.

"BREAKING NEWS!" Amber yells, so loud that Martha nearly jumps out of her seat.

Ralph clenches my arm right as I stand up. His hand slips down the length of my skin until it scrapes against mine. My fingers thread through his of their own accord. I breathe, in and out, and try to remember every prayer those catechism classes drilled into my head. Ralph's grip tightens, and I don't let go.

An illusory cursor backspaces each number on the PowerPoint.

"We've just received the final, certified vote totals. All two thousand eighteen votes have now been counted." Amber grins, feral. She's dragging this out, a cat toying with a mouse before the kill. "Finally, we're ready to name the winner of the presidential race."

The screen cuts to that insufferable DYSTOPIA HIGH PROJECTION title card and some stupid sound effect Amber probably downloaded from YouTube. I squeeze Ralph's hand so tight I can feel his bones. The graphic disintegrates, and in its place, my junior yearbook photo materializes. I look so young, still a few months pre-T, my face soft and round, but none of it matters because there's a gold checkmark sloping across my chest.

"That's right," Amber begins in voice-over. "You heard it here first, folks. *Dystopia High* can now announce that Mark Adams has won this year's presidential election."

ADAMS	CABRERA	MCIVER
947	272	799

"In our final tally, Adams has earned forty-seven percent of the vote. Football captain Henry McIver garnered forty percent. Clary Cabrera, outgoing junior class representative, received a mere thirteen percent. Adams's victory marks a shocking upset. Until he announced his candidacy two weeks ago, the IB senior was a total political outsider. He first joined the race amid the controversy surrounding sophomore Benjamin Dean's suspension . . ."

Amber goes on, but I can't hear a word she's saying against the tidal wave of sound in the living room. The tsunami nearly knocks me off my feet. Someone screams; it might be Mom. Everyone whoops and cheers, and I'm pretty sure Rachel throws a handful of glitter confetti at me. It gets in my hair and maybe my eyes, but I don't care. I don't care.

For a second all I can think is, thank God there's no

Electoral College to fuck this up.

Then Ralph's arms are around me and he's beaming, and we must be at the eye of a hurricane because he says, *"I told you,"* again, and I can hear him perfectly despite the chaos around us.

I haven't said a word but I'm already hoarse. Everything I mean to say is caught in the wreckage of my throat. Maybe I don't need words. All I could summon up would be flotsam and jetsam against the roaring ocean in me.

Hands and arms tangle around me, an octopus of sensation I can't begin to trace. My campaign team—my *friends*—are on their feet, congratulating me, sharing this with me, savoring this impossible thing we salvaged together from the deep. We're probably going to be cited for noise complaints, but I don't care.

Because I won.

I won.

I *won.*

THIRTY

LATER—AFTER THE SHOCK LOSES ITS SHEEN, after we celebrate over a trio of extra-large pizzas, after another round of hugs and tears when everyone leaves—Mom and I convene in the kitchen over hot cocoa and macarons.

"Just so you know," Mom informs me, serious as if she were telling me someone has died, "I expect you to vacuum all the glitter out of that rug."

It'd be easier to take her seriously if she didn't have a chocolate milk mustache. "I'll try, but I'm not sure how much good it will do. I think we might just have to accept this as our new reality. We're glitter people now."

She snorts out a laugh. "I certainly hope not."

"It's not so bad." I sip my hot cocoa.

Mom's brows knit together, like the scarves she starts but never finishes. I can't decode her gaze any more than I could count stitches. She used to ask for my help when I was little. She would wind skeins of yarn around my hands, but I could never keep still. Sometimes those memories are as distant as another life, past and buried, and sometimes, when she looks at me like this, I wonder if she's still there.

Then a smile pulls at Mom's lips, the way a magician pulls an endless handkerchief from a sleeve. Except this isn't a trick. "I'm proud of you."

I duck my head. "You would've said that even if I lost."

"Doesn't make it any less true."

"I didn't *do* anything. It wasn't up to me. Other people—"

"Honey, don't you understand? You put yourself out there, when no one knew who you were, despite the personal risk. You ran a spectacular campaign. You did your absolute best, and that's why they voted for you. But even if they hadn't, you'd still have everything to be proud of."

I mull it over, running my hand through my wayward hair. My hand comes out covered in glitter. "Maybe you're right."

"I'm your mother; I'm always right. It's in the job description."

"I think I'm proud of me, too." Maybe it's sacrilegious; maybe I'm a sinner. Pride may be a deadly sin, but I don't feel damned.

"You should be," Mom insists.

Finally, I believe her.

That is, until fervent knocks pelt our front door like hail.

Mom and I have been chatting about the election and my

friends, all the gossip and ephemera I didn't have time for on the campaign trail.

Then the knocking starts and doesn't let up as Mom and I wait, silent and still. Nothing good comes knocking this late, not in suburbia.

The lights are on. The windows are open. Anyone can see that we're home.

Mom retrieves her tablet from the credenza. She angles the screen away from me as she navigates to the app that controls this entire house, right down to the surveillance cameras on our front porch. Her expression is more guarded than our state-of-the-art alarm system. Her lips twist, then she rolls her shoulders back and marches to the foyer.

I hear the rumble before anything else. Hushed entreaties drowned out by formless bluster. Heavy footfalls send earthquake tremors through the hardwood floors.

Dad is a thunderstorm, drenched in whiskey, doused in kerosene. His silhouette is a black cloud darkening the hallway. The sight of him is a lightning strike, the blinding flash of rage illuminating his every pore. There's a delay before the boom comes, yawning seconds that I count under my breath to measure the distance between the danger. Then he opens his mouth, and the thunderclap shakes me to my bones. "What *the hell* have you done?"

It doesn't take bravado to tell him, "I won."

"*You won,*" he mimics in falsetto. He's close now, right on the other side of the island. His sweat could start a distill-ery. He peers down at me, and I've never felt so small. Not like a child, nothing so mundane. He sees me now the way he sees his constituents—as problems to *handle* on his way to greener pastures like the South Lawn. "You don't have any idea, do you? Foolish girl, you haven't begun to consider what *winning* means."

Wild and uncoordinated, he fishes for something in his pants pocket. Sweat steeps the gussets of his rumpled shirt. He lobs his phone at me, the case skidding across the pol-ished granite countertop.

I don't touch the phone. I keep my distance. I just stare down and try to make sense of the political calculus he sees there.

There, in his news alerts, two links glimmer for MARK ADAMS. Amber's presence at the top of the feed defies all known laws of physics, but there she is. *Dystopia High* proclaims "PRESIDENT-ELECT MARK ADAMS: WILD-CARD CANDIDATE CLAIMS VICTORY." But this can't be the article Dad means.

The next entry is from the *Santa Julia Herald*, the town's century-old daily. It may be a subsidiary of the *New York Times* these days, the bulk of its content identical to those of every major national paper, but there's still an EMPIRE NEWS section. This is where Ralph's dad published local interest stories about the reformed hoarder who donated thousands of books to an elementary school and the straw-berry farmer whose crops withered in the drought.

Except this isn't a profile; it's a feature, destined for prime real estate above tomorrow's fold: "GAY TEEN WINS LOCAL STUDENT COUNCIL ELECTION."

Dad's arms make a shield across his chest, which doesn't make any sense when he's the one on the offensive. His brows slope in an indignant ridge, so much like this holier-than-thou hill. "Go ahead," he sneers. "Read it."

The words are half taunt, half dare, and undoubtedly a command. If he could imbue it with the authority of Congress—pass a law decreeing I participate in my own scolding—he would.

Mom hangs back, at the border between the kitchen and the hall. She sways like a ghostly apparition, betwixt and between, unsure how to intervene.

Halogen track lights reflect and refract tiny rainbows off the screen. I glance back at Dad—imperious, impervious—and jab the hyperlink.

I skim the article. Whatever I was expecting, this isn't the declaration of war Dad made it out to be. It's a puff piece, not a hit job. Human interest, not investigative journalism. They haven't clocked me. Hell, they didn't even contact me for a comment. There's just a mild-mannered if passive-aggressive quote from Jenny about how she plucked me out of faceless obscurity. It's just feel-good inspiration porn about how the queer new kid made a heroic stand against a well-watered army. It's no worse than anything Amber's already written or broadcast.

Except the blood vessel throbbing on Dad's temple says it is. Red suffuses his face like blood seeping into a cloth. "It was bad enough you decided to run," he says, more measured than I expect. "It was foolish to run, but if you'd stayed a single-issue sideshow, you could have survived this. Novelty candidates are footnotes. Forgettable. They'd have written you off, and you could have written all of this off when you came to your senses. But it wasn't enough to stage your petty little protest. You had to go and—"

"Win?" A laugh bubbles up, unbidden. "You're upset that I had the audacity to *win* an election?"

Dad braces his palms flat against the island. "You think this was a real campaign, Madison? You think your little student council election bears any resemblance to the career I've built in public service? I didn't raise you to be that naive. This 'election' you participated in was a reenactment. It wasn't democracy so much as a beauty pageant. Children's theater. Those *children* voted for you because you became a fad. You were the next shiny object for them to fixate on."

His anger is infectious. I smooth my hands over my jeans to stop from clenching them into fists. I time my breaths like my therapist taught me. But I feel the rage rising like a fever. Sweat slicks my skin. My blood-splotched face must mirror his. "I won because the voters liked what I had to say. I talked to them; I *listened* to them. I told them UHS could be a better place if we worked together, and they believed me."

"You think you prevailed on the merit of your precious ideals?" Dad laughs, deep and barrel-chested. "Please. I taught you better than that. Your Social Justice Warrior mystique appealed to their hashtag-resistance brand of activism. Voting for you was a box they could check off to feel good about their progressive credentials. How many of them Snapchatted your speech or Instagrammed their ballots? Did you know they were tweeting about you? Don't you dare tell me you sparked a movement. This is nothing more than performative activism for your generation of social media–obsessed acolytes."

"That's not true."

"You still don't understand, do you? You're here playacting politics as if what you do as a small-town student body president means something. As if you're going to make a real difference here. And here's the secret, Madison: it does mean something, but not what you think. If you were anyone else, it wouldn't matter. You could do as you pleased, pretend all you liked. You wouldn't make a difference, but you'd do no harm, either. Except this game of make-believe does matter, because you're my daughter. You're a Teagan. You have a place not only in a political dynasty but also in the halls of history."

"I'm *not* your *daughter*."

Dad ignores me, ignores my trembling voice and clenched fists. "I warned you. I told you what would happen. I predicted all of this."

"You predicted I'd lose."

"You're still missing the headline, even when it's right in front of you. It hasn't even been five hours, and the *Herald* has already picked up the story. You're a hashtag. Has it even occurred to you what will happen if the Bay Area news stations or papers pick this up? How deep they'll dig?"

I dig deep. Meet his bluster with bravado. "If it's just a silly small-town student council election, like you said, then why should they care?"

"You won. You're the novelty that keeps on giving, and now you've given them something to write about." His neck is crimson, redder than his face. "Do you remember what I told you?"

"An election is an invitation," I recite by rote, before I can stop myself.

"You've led the bloodhounds right to our yard and left the door open for them to wander in. Pick up the scent of the bodies beneath the floorboards and the skeletons in the closets. They'll catch the whiff of rot and lies and tear you apart."

"Tear *us* apart, you mean. That's what you're worried about. You don't care what they do to me. You care what they'll do to you."

Dad laughs again, primal, between a bark and a snarl. "So what if I do? Why shouldn't I care when your frivolous popularity contest threatens my governorship? Everything I've worked for is at risk because you wanted to play the hero and wear the white hat. My career for your game of dress-up. Your vanity will cost us everything."

"*My* vanity? You may think high school politics are frivolous, but I didn't get into this for my vanity. I did it to—"

"Help your friend?" Another belly laugh. "Yes, I read the interview. I've seen your spin. But if you truly believe that yarn you spun, you're even more naive than I thought you were."

For a moment, I can't hear anything beyond the blood roaring in my ears. "Of course I did this because of Benji."

Hazel eyes narrow to letterbox slits. They're so much like mine, except I've never seen such cruelty etched in my irises. "You did it for the spotlight. You wanted to make a name for yourself—not just any name but this spurious pseudonym you've been using. It wasn't enough for you to come here and pretend. You couldn't abide by the terms of our agreement. You wanted *more*. Your name in lights; the soapbox under your feet; the gavel in your hand. You did this to get back at me."

If rage is a virus, it has nothing on the defibrillator jolt of indignation that surges through me now. My heart pummels my rib cage. I see red. "My life," I seethe, sixteen months of resentment threading through every word, "isn't about *you.*"

I get up. Every inch of me is shaking, but I fight through it. Force my muscles into motion, even as the gears grind and the cogs creak. Push past Dad, out of the kitchen, up the stairs to my room. I lock the door and push my chair against it as a barricade. I sink to the floor.

My phone wriggles from my sweaty palm. My knuckles turn white against the curve of my fist. I swipe through my contacts. Tears blur the names, but I find him. There, last on my favorites list.

And then I call him.

"Ralph." I choke out his name, and that, more than anything—more than me FaceTiming him three hours after he left my house—gives me away. That, or the tear tracks streaking my cheeks.

"Mark?" The furrow of his brow signals he's already entered Concerned Boyfriend Mode. "What's wrong? Did something happen? I can come get you. I'll be there in ten minutes."

The image jerks as he gets up. I can practically hear the clang of his keys as he prepares to swoop in on his white horse, storm the castle, and slay whatever dragons await. Except there's no barricade to break but the one I made at my door, and if he crossed the moat, he'd only see a self-anointed king where the dragon is supposed to be.

"No," I whisper from my place under my desk. "I mean, yes, something happened, but no, you don't need to come get me."

"But I *want* to be there. If you need me."

"You're already here." All I want is for him to stay, but I'm afraid that's just another line item on the ledger of things I can't have.

"Mark, you're scaring me. Just tell me what happened." He says it so plaintively; he doesn't have the faintest idea what he's asking.

But I have to answer. I called him because I needed him, but I knew where this would go. I set this trap for myself. Dad didn't teach me chess for me to ignore the endgame, and the only way this ends is with me in checkmate.

Unless, somehow, that tenuous thing we forged Sunday night is strong enough to survive the awful lie I set in motion.

"I want to tell you," I say at last, "but there's something you don't know about me."

"You can tell me anything." He sounds so desperate, and I want so desperately to believe him.

"When I told you I was trans, I didn't tell you that Adams is my mom's maiden name."

"Okay."

"No, it's really not." It's all I can do not to bury my face between my knees. "You don't understand."

"Then *tell* me."

"There's a reason I didn't keep my dad's name, and it's not what you think."

He doesn't say anything. Just looks at me with those patient, caring eyes, and as hard as Dad tried to break me, this is what does me in.

My heart is a grenade, primed and loaded. All that's left to do is pull the pin. "My dad's name is Teagan."

"Is that supposed to mean something—"

"*Graham* Teagan."

"Graham Teagan," Ralph repeats. He blinks before recognition sparks in his eyes. "Like the congressman?"

Knowing this is the last time he'll look at me with any kind of warmth, I memorize his face. His high cheekbones. His sharp chin. His freckled skin. "Yes."

"But your dad—"

"Isn't dead."

His image jerks on my screen, like his hand is shaking. His face is ashen, as pale as human remains after cremation. "*You told me,*" he whispers. "You told me—"

"I don't expect you to understand, let alone forgive me. But I need you to know—"

"You let me believe he was dead," Ralph says, too hoarse to shout. "We bonded over it. Shared grief. And you . . . you were just lying?"

Now that he's gone, I feel his touch like a phantom limb. I wish I'd let him whisk me away, if only so I could kiss him one last time. "It wasn't all a lie. Graham Teagan may be alive, but the man I knew . . . he's dead to me," I insist, futilely tilting at windmills, desperate to make him believe me.

"But he's here. You can see him. You can hug him. You can tell him you won an election and kissed a boy and—" Suddenly, all I see is the ceiling. Maybe he dropped the phone. Or he can't bear the sight of my face. "Tell me. If he's dead to you, then when was the last time you talked to him?"

I shut my eyes. "He's downstairs. That's why I called you. He showed up and started screaming and—"

"Downstairs," he whispers, bloodless. I've seen so many sides of Ralph, but I've never heard him so cold. "That's what I thought."

A thousand protests wither and die on my lips.

And then he hangs up.

THIRTY-ONE

"I'M GOING TO STEAL THE DECLARATION OF Independence."

My head jerks up, then back against the headrest.

Pablo's eyes stay on the road. "That got your attention, didn't it?"

"*National Treasure* is no joking matter."

Except Pablo doesn't look like he's joking. As he brakes for a stop sign, he shakes his head at me. "Have you even heard a word I've said?"

Honestly, I haven't. I woke up after a few fitful nightmares, and I've barely been keeping it together. Testosterone makes it harder to cry, but I've drained my tear ducts.

I clear my throat. "Sorry, I just have a lot on my mind. With Dad announcing later and all." It's only half a lie. I'm pointedly *not* thinking about Dad's announcement. "What were you saying?"

"I was asking if you'd talked to Jenny."

Another person I'm pointedly ignoring. "Not since she left yesterday. Have you?"

The turn signal clicks, clicks, clicks. Pablo's silence is confirmation enough. "You need to talk to her."

"I don't think she wants to talk to me."

"I don't care what either of you wants right now. You're best friends; you're *my* best friends. I know you know she's hurting, and if you haven't already guessed, you're the reason. I know you're hurting, too—no, don't give me that look; I can tell—but that's no excuse."

I look away, out the window. "If Jenny has something to say to me—"

"No, no, I'm not going to play ambassador and ferry messages between you. You're the politician, so be the diplomat. Extend an olive branch. Negotiate a ceasefire, before anyone else ends up as collateral damage—"

Be the better man.

Except I don't know what that means anymore. Is it the man the voters see or the one Dad says I'll never be? Why should I owe my allegiance to people who don't repay it in kind?

"Mark."

I'm in my usual seat on the back counter in ZP's room. I'm supposed to be reading excerpts from *Les Misérables* in the original French, but I'm not sure I'd be able to stay awake reading the Brick in English. So instead of notes on the

336

revolutionary shenanigans of Les Amis de l'ABC, my note-book is full of abortive apology letters to Ralph, all scribbled out, all *wrong*.

I'm not prepared for the sight of Henry McIver, blocking the doorway like a tank. He scans the room with the precision of a heat-seeking missile before locking on me. "We need to talk."

Everyone else looks at me, too, while I study Henry. I can't remember the last time I saw him without his letterman jacket or gel slicking back his hair. Even though the anger wafts off him like a stench, I'm not afraid of him. I cock an eyebrow. "Well, I'm right here, Henry. Say whatever you need to say."

"Outside."

ZP peers over the brim of his Ms. Marvel comic book, darting between Henry and me with unfettered concern.

"Fine." I squeeze through the narrow space between two columns of desks. When I get to the door, Henry doesn't move right away. He stands there as I step into his personal space, staring down at me with visceral contempt. "Shall we?"

The boys' bathroom hasn't changed. Same enigmatic odor of stale urine, rancid sweat, and toxic masculinity. The door slams shut behind us, and Henry verifies that the stalls are empty. "Lock the door."

He says it like an order, but I've never been good with authority.

When he realizes I'm not moving, Henry rolls his eyes

and does it himself. He stares me down, rage festering in his eyes like an open wound.

"Well?" I clear my throat to hide how badly he's unsettled me. "You're the one who wanted to talk."

Henry steps closer, silent and a little rabid. He's usually so contained, even if that thing he's containing is anger he's left to ferment. Now that anger is spilling from him like wine from a cask. This close, it's not just the laundry-day outfit and the artless bedhead. It's the veins streaking his bloodshot eyes and the circles under them.

"This is a hell of a way to concede, Henry. Clary just sent me a text."

Henry smirks, his teeth neat like a row of tombstones. "I'm not conceding."

There's a difference between not conceding and locking your opponent in a bathroom. The difference is I'm pissed. "What are you going to do? Demand a recount?"

"I'm not contesting the result because unlike you, I actually respect the students at this school. What I'm contesting, Mark, are your methods."

"My methods?" Genuine confusion pollutes my anger. "What exactly is it you take issue with, Henry? The way I went around campus and talked to the voters instead of just stomping my boots on the senior steps and telling them what they want?"

"There you go, proving my point. You don't even see it, do

you? You're a walking case study in pretension, so far up on your high horse you can't even recognize your own hypocrisy. You talk so much shit about the blinders everyone else wears, but you can't see past your own."

"What are you trying to say?"

"You've invested all your political capital pretending to be a populist, but you call the kids at this school *voters* rather than students. They're your *constituents* before they're your peers. I know where you live, Mark. Up in Utopia Heights, so far above the ground you need a fucking oxygen tank. You talk about the common man, the every-student, but what do you know about school lunches? The library? The bus?"

He's close enough I can smell Irish Spring again. I'm dizzy with the scent of it cloying his words. "You think you're any better? You're enrolled here, too."

When Henry laughs, it comes out a howl. "And here I thought you'd done your oppo research. I live in Cantera Valley, did you know that? I had to apply for an intra-district transfer, citing the poor quality of academics at Cantera High School so they'd let me do IB here. So I'd have a shot at getting out of this fucking town. They rejected me, you know that? So I enrolled using the address of my dad's old supervisor, from the vineyard where he used to work before it burned down. Not everyone here fits into the neat little roles you've cast us in." He flicks his eyes to the checkerboard tiles. "With friends like yours, I thought you would've known better."

At first I'm not sure who he means. Then I remember Benji's tract house at the outskirts of Utopia Heights, cracked wood under fresh paint, where I sat beside him on a creaking swing as he tried to warn me. It's my fault for ignoring him.

I look at Henry. Try to see him anew. Reconcile cheap cotton, scuffed leather, and ratty denim with what I know to be true. But I can't see past that day by the gym, him standing there while his friends tormented mine. "So what?" I demand. "That gives you an excuse to turn this school into an oligarchy for the football team and terrorize vulnerable students while you're at it?"

"You think that's what this is about?"

"Isn't it? How else do you explain what you did to Benji? What message were you trying to send to queer kids at this school?"

Henry blinks at me, his eyes glassy and unfocused. "You think you know everything about me, even now, don't you? Well, let me reiterate. Some of us don't have the *privilege* of doing as we please. We do what we have to do to get by. Sometimes that means keeping quiet for the greater good of our own damn futures."

"That's what—"

"What you're trying to change?" Henry scoffs. "You may not know anything about me, but I know you, Mark. I know your kind. Whatever lies you tell yourself to sleep at night, you're not in this to make UHS a better place. You don't give a shit about Santa Julia. You're not from here; you're not going to stick around. Utopia Heights is a thought experiment to you, and so was this election."

"That's not true," I whisper, though my lips are trembling. My nails curl into the meat of my palms.

"What happened to Benji was just an excuse. An opportunity for you to leverage your way out of the shadows. You paraded around campus and talked to people you'll forget as soon as you take the oath of office. You played the campaign trail like a game, because that's what it was for you."

Every word ricochets through my skull, bullets in a panic room.

"That's all it ever is for people like you."

"People like me?"

"Privileged rich kids who have the whole world handed to them, then decide to stomp on it because they think their parents will just buy them another. Spoiled brats who've never had to learn—"

I never learn what Henry was going to say because my fist slams into his jaw. Pain blossoms through my knuckles and out to my wrist. I stagger back, breathing heavy as shock washes out the rage. I look at Henry, his hand cupping his chin, blood smarting at the corner of his parted lips. He can't believe it any more than I can.

Then his mouth twists into a grimace, and he lunges.

My shoulder blades crash against the wall before I realize

Henry's pushed me. He follows with his fist. The world goes dark, and I pitch blows in the black. Henry groans, and I pry my good eye open. His hand brackets my throat. He catches one of my wrists, and even if I wanted to fight back with the other, his palm presses down on my windpipe. My vision falters at the edges, dark vignettes closing in.

Henry leans in. Blood dribbles down his chin, over his graveyard of teeth. "What was it you told me, Mark? About how humans are better than beasts?"

His grip lets up, just enough for me to suck in a torrent of cold, putrid air. He's waiting for an answer, so I rasp, "We're not."

Then I knee him in the groin and prove him right.

THIRTY-TWO

CARS HAVE ONLY JUST BEGUN TO SWARM THE parking lot when I flee campus. ZP will wonder where I've gone, but he'll give me the benefit of the doubt. Mr. González won't, when class starts, but I don't care. Add cutting class to my record; it won't make a difference. I've already done the damage.

Morning traffic chugs along, parallel to the narrow sidewalk. As I hustle past Hearst Village, I consider banging on my therapist's door or hiding out in Atelier, but I don't have the guts to show my face, bruised and bloody, to anyone who knows me. That counts for God, too, as I pass St. Julia's Cathedral.

They'd be so ashamed. All of them. I don't need my selfie camera to know what I look like. The golden boy with the black eye. I had the whole world in the palm of my hand, and I crushed it with the clench of my fist.

I trek through the foothills, one middle-class subdivision

after the next. So many rows of postwar houses, some renovated, some original. Wood and stucco and brick. Actual white picket fences. What do I know about the American Dream?

Roots have upended the sidewalk. The worn soles of my high-tops detect every irregularity in the concrete. My shins are still sore from the hike the other night, and now they ache with each step I take.

So does my face.

This isn't like what happened to Benji. Henry provoked me, but it wasn't bullying. He wasn't punching down. He didn't say anything that wasn't completely true, and I knew it. I played right into his hand and succumbed to my baser instincts, the rage pulsing through my bloodstream and the Hobbesian call of my lizard brain. No amount of spin can change the fact that I shot first. It wasn't self-defense; it was my fault.

Henry's probably already in Flynn's office, offering up his split lip as testimony. Cutting class doesn't matter because I'm not going to apologize. Flynn's going to call for my suspension like my head on a platter. Just like that, a single indelible line on my transcript, and everything I've worked for—no, everything that's been handed to me—will evaporate. So much for the presidency I just won. So much for Harvard. So much for the political career I thought I could build somewhere far, far away from this stupid backwoods town.

Here comes the creek that demarcates the unofficial border between Utopia Heights and everything else. I stand on the old steel footbridge, wind whipping my face. Water gushes on beneath me, so like the irascible white-water rapids within me. Sirens shriek and wail en route to the hospital across the way.

Past the bridge, I have a choice to make. If I veer left, I'll sink into Cantera Valley. If I keep straight, I'll end up downtown.

Henry was right about everything, and if he's right—

So is Dad.

Behind the gray stone train depot, the new bottle-nosed commuter train gleams on the tracks. Its svelte chassis sports a banner: GRAHAM FOR GOLDEN STATE GOVERNOR. Rows of wooden folding chairs line the neatly trimmed lawn, every last one full. An entire class of elementary school kids crowds the front; the press corps sits at the back. The rest of the seats are reserved for a diverse cast of dairy farmers, grape pickers, and homemakers who clap on cue like a studio audience.

I hang back near the video cameras. They're not just from Bay Area stations but a few national networks, too. Maybe I should have anticipated that. California's the largest state in the nation, with a history of sending governors to the White House. It was stupid to come here. Foolish and self-indulgent, just like I always am. I tug the drawstrings on my hood until it's tight around my face and pray no one will recognize me.

Least of all Dad, up there in the front of the crowd. He doesn't have a podium or even a microphone. There must be a lavalier clipped to his lapel, right beside the American flag pin. There's no teleprompter in sight as he expounds on his vision for the state. "California has always been and must continue to be a city upon a hill," he says. "A beacon for the rest of the nation, lighting the path to the future even in our darkest hours."

I look up at him, alone on the slate walkway. The press must be buzzing with questions about where Mom and I are. I wonder what they see when they look at him. Do they see past his blue-and-gold-striped tie, clean-shaven jaw, and slick blond hair? Do they hear the Boston posh in his accent, or just the California cool? When they look at him, is it the congressman or the future governor they see? If they peer into his reflection in the shiny train windows, can they see him in DC, hand on the Bible, swearing to *preserve, protect, and defend*?

"I believe in the promise," Dad says, "of this Golden State. Here at frontier's end, our families chased the American Dream in search of a better life when the rest of the country—or the world—left them huddled and poor. California has always promised to do better."

The crowd cheers, and I try to see what they see. If this is all they know of Dad, just his pretty speeches and patterned pocket squares, what separates him from anyone else vying for their votes?

"This is a sacred promise," Dad says, "we must work to uphold for ourselves and our posterity."

I stare and I stare, but I can't line up the cryptogram with my decoder ring. Whatever the world sees is Greek to me. When I look at the figure Graham Teagan cuts against the celluloid-blue California sky, I don't see my dad or even a politician so much as a colony of bats in a bespoke suit.

"It's a promise *I* will work to uphold."

All I hear is the ghost of every promise he ever made to me.

"Through my tenure as Marin County's district attorney and the Second District's congressional representative—"

To love me unconditionally.

"I've done my best to honor the will of the great people of this state."

To protect and defend me.

"And, if you'll have me, I want to continue to honor the promises I've made to you. That's why I'm announcing my candidacy for governor of the great state of California—so we can continue to ensure this promised land delivers that promise to all. Thank you, and God bless you."

Applause goes off like fireworks, gunpowder-deafening. They give him a standing ovation, and I—

Shut my eyes. Breathe, desperately. Don't let my legs give out.

"Hey, kid." A hand descends on my shoulder, rough and heavy like the voice it accompanies. "Are you okay?"

I open my eyes. The cameraman from one of the San Francisco stations is watching me. *Frowning* at me, to be exact.

"I'm fine."

He points to my eye, still throbbing like a second heart. "You don't look it."

I shake my head. Try to remember how to lie like a politician and come up short. "You ever read Kafka?"

"Are you telling me a giant cockroach gave you that shiner?"

I try to laugh, but pain ripples through my skin. My smile comes out a grimace. "There's this story about a villager who's waiting for a personal message from the kaiser. Day after day, they wait by their window for a messenger who never comes. It's supposed to be an allegory for God, the futility of endlessly, faithfully waiting for a sign from a higher power who is never going to answer your prayers. But maybe it's just a sad parable for representative democracy— the hopeless, baseless faith that the people you put in office will remember you as an individual with a face and a name and hopes and dreams rather than as just another statistic. The evening comes, and you wait for the change they promised you, but they never deliver."

"What's that got to do—"

"Nothing," I say quickly, finally registering the arachnid eye of the camera trained on me. "It's nothing."

Civilians wander the sidewalks of Railroad Square. It's after nine a.m. now. The good citizens of Santa Julia should be at work or in school. White hair and wrinkles denote some as retirees, heading into Sunnyside Express for their eggs sunny-side up. Among a throng of selfie sticks, I hear lilting snippets of Japanese, presumably from tourists. A clique of stay-at-home moms power walks with their strollers.

None of them notice me. I'm just an anonymous teenage delinquent. No need to report me for truancy when my dirt-caked sneakers and swollen bruises tell them everything they need to know.

I walk quickly, desperate to get away from the train depot before the press conference breaks up. I look for the stall where Dad and I got tacos all those years ago, but the store-front's been boarded up between an Asian fusion restaurant and a cold-press juice bar. I'm still dizzy, so I buy an over-priced bottle of pomegranate tonic.

At the far end of the square, which is really more of a rectangle, looms the old courthouse building, which is due to reopen as a boutique hotel next spring. I stare up at the sign, illustrating the urban planner's vision of this space revital-ized. Gentrified.

My legs give out beneath me like matchsticks.

Let us sit upon the ground and tell sad stories of the death of kings.

I unscrew the stubborn bottle cap. The glass sweats in my hand. I knock back the bloodred juice like cold medicine and gag at the bitter tang of an unfamiliar spice.

In my back pocket, my phone buzzes for the tenth or hundredth time. ZP, asking where I went. Pablo, asking if he needs to be concerned. Nadia, asking if I'm okay. I toss the phone away and watch it skip across the grass. I don't have answers for any of them. At least not answers they'll like.

Henry was right. Dad was right.

I don't know how I never saw it before. Once I grew up, once I realized what Dad meant when he called it all a magic trick, I chose better idols. Politicians who were articulate and idealistic. Obama. JFK. FDR. And where reality fell short— because even the best of our past presidents have been complicit in imperialism, racism, capitalism—there was Jed Bartlet, Leslie Knope, and even Mellie Grant. Those were the archetypes I've tried to emulate. The kind of man I've tried to be.

But before that, before I saw the gears behind the curtain, before I understood what any of it meant, I was enthralled by the illusion. All Dad's speeches and promises and that imperial message from the castle on the hill. I used to hope I'd grow up to be just like him, and I did. I did. I didn't realize how similar we'd become.

I entered this election thinking I could make a difference. But I can't change the school, let alone this town. I can't win hearts and minds. I can't protect queer kids or anyone else.

I gave speeches drenched in saccharine platitudes. I made promises far beyond the executive authority of a student body president. I conjured up the illusion of a populist leader who would put their constituents first.

My constituents. What a fucking joke.

I should have realized; I should have recognized the signs. Once I saw them in Dad, why couldn't I see them in myself? I wanted the crown. I wanted the throne. I wanted to be *seen.*

Everything else was just a carnival sideshow.

My greatest trick of all was fooling myself.

THIRTY-THREE

AT LUNCH HOUR, THE DOWNTOWN BRANCH OF the public library is primarily occupied by the homeless, demarcated by unkempt hair, threadbare thrift-store attire, and canvas duffel bags. I offer up meager smiles, but my heart's not in it. It's just a sprained muscle, throbbing in my chest.

I weave through the stacks, which smell of mildew, must, and, somehow, inexplicably, the '70s. The history section is deserted, and between tomes on the rise and fall of empires, I sink down to the ground. Cracked spines recording the abdication of kings carve notches in my back.

When I pull my dirt-speckled phone from my pocket, it lights up with a flurry of notifications. Everyone wants to know if I've forgotten about today's French Club meeting. Still no word from Ralph, not that I'm surprised.

Like most people under the age of thirty, my call history is nearly nonexistent. It's not hard to find the incoming call from last week. Local area code, unlike my own, for a number I didn't bother adding to my address book.

"Mark!" exclaims Amber. "Just the man I was looking for—"

"Look," I cut her off, feeling sick. I shut my eyes, but the nausea doesn't dissipate. "I need to schedule an interview. Are you interested?"

When I texted Jenny to meet me at our park, I planned to wait at the swings. That's always been our place, which is precisely why I couldn't sit there when there's so much razed ground between us. So I take the high ground. Sit on the perforated platform above the slide. Station myself as sentry. Look out for incoming armies from the safety of my tower.

The sun slouches below the tree line. Pastel watercolor splotches paint the sky. Jenny marches through the sand, a gladiator come to her last stand. It's impossible to miss the cant of her frown.

She hoists herself up the fireman's pole to meet me in the turret. When she catches sight of me, her mask of indifference slips, just for a moment. Then she's hard again, immovable marble and fountains of sarcasm. "What the hell happened to your face?"

"*Now* you care what happens to me."

"Dare I ask where you've been all day?"

My knuckles sting. "Dare I ask where you were yesterday?"

Jenny blinks, and I curse under my breath. So much for calling off the hostilities.

"So that's what this is about." Jenny stands there, two steps apart but a thousand miles away. "Did you call me here just to berate me?"

"Christ, no." Even when I'm trying to do the right thing, I still get it wrong. "I'm sorry. Sit with me?"

So we sit. Jenny tugs the frayed hem of her jean shorts. I test the tensile strength of my bruises beneath my fingertips. I called this summit; it's my responsibility to start this conversation. "If you don't want to tell me where you've been the past few days, I won't ask again. But this whole campaign was your idea, so you deserve to know."

Jenny leans forward, her back curved like a shark's fin. "Know *what*, exactly?"

Here's the moment of truth. All that's left is for me to say the words and make them real. "I'm resigning."

"Resigning *what*, Mark?" Sharp and shrill, Jenny's words have teeth.

"The presidency."

She slaps me. I don't know what kind of reaction I was expecting, but it's not a smarting cheek below my black eye.

"What the hell, Jen?"

"No, I'm the one who should be asking you that question. What the ever-loving fuck, Mark? Is this some kind of joke? After everything we've been through—everything I've *done* for you—you decide to just throw it away?"

"It was never mine to begin with. I don't expect you to understand."

"No, explain it to me. Please. Try to make me understand how you could be this fucking stupid."

It hurts to see her like this, hands on her hips and fury on her lips. "I got into this for the wrong reasons. I'm a fraud. A charlatan. A snake-oil salesman."

"What did you think politics was? This isn't Cub Scouts."

"I didn't get to be a Cub Scout." My arms cross over my chest. I should have taken my binder off hours ago, but I couldn't handle more than a quick stretch in the library's sole single-stall bathroom.

"I swear to God, Mark, don't make this about something it isn't."

"Then what *is* it about? You're the one who asked me to do this."

"Because you wanted a different kind of candidate. Don't you remember sitting on those swings, bemoaning Clary's crocodile tears and Henry's iron fist, calling on some political knight in shining armor to save us all?"

"Why didn't you tell me to stop believing in fairy tales?"

Jenny stills. Wind wrenches flyaway strands free from her plaits. Even marble cracks. "Maybe I wanted to believe in the magic, too."

"Jen." Gravity weighs me down, but I don't sit. I brace

myself on the railing instead. Cold metal steals the heat of my anger.

She swats the hair out of her eyes. "Here's the part I don't understand. Everything you said on the campaign trail? You believe. Every promise you made, you intend to keep. What about that makes you a 'snake-oil salesman,' as you so colloquially put it?"

"I'm not the man they think I am." I'm selfish and privileged and so caught up in my own head—

"'They'?"

"The voters—the students," I amend.

"Because they don't know you're trans? Or soon-to-be-Governor Teagan's son?"

"Because I'm not from here. Utopia Heights doesn't belong to me. I shouldn't get to show up and pretend to be a populist, act like I care about this place and these people, when it wasn't ever about any of that. I wanted to do the Right Thing, capital letters, and maybe make a name for myself along the way. It was always about me. What I wanted. What I thought was best. What I could do to remake this world in my own image."

"What a load of sanctimonious crap." Any sympathy in Jenny's eyes has dried up. "You want to do the right thing? Stop making everything about yourself? Then finish what you started. Don't give up on the people you promised to help."

"They don't need me—"

"Maybe not. But they put their faith in you."

"Since when do you care about faith?"

"Since I put my faith in you, and you let me down." She looks away, out over this deserted kingdom of slides and monkey bars, toward the trail that leads to Verde Lake.

Every self-deprecating talking point I meant to hit vanishes from my mental teleprompter. I may be a feckless narcissist, but even I can recognize I've gotten the script wrong. All this time, I've been wondering if Jenny and I were okay, when I should have been asking if *she* was okay.

"You didn't even *realize*"—Jenny's voice breaks—"you let me down."

Every part of me is aching, and I don't know how to fashion splints and tourniquets from the fabric of my hoodie. I'm utterly defenseless against the truth I've been too oblivious—too self-absorbed—to recognize. Helplessly, I insist, "You resigned."

"You weren't supposed to accept." Jenny looks back over her shoulder. Her eyes are pitch-black, like tar pits, and I can't begin to excavate the fossils in their depths. "Think back on all those political shows you love so much, the ones full of power, responsibility, and life-or-death stakes. Think back on the scandals and screw-ups. Think back on every well-intentioned resignation scene where an underling tries to fall on their sword. After three rounds of feints and parries, the politician rejects the resignation. They take the road less traveled. They *fight*."

"You *told* me," I protest. "You told me I wouldn't win unless I accepted your resignation."

"Yes, I did. It was the right decision for the campaign. For the cause. For your good fight. If I was going to be a good soldier, I had to fall on my sword." Teardrops percolate at the corners of her eyes. She wipes them away. "But I wanted to believe your good fight wasn't a single-issue crusade. I wanted—"

"You wanted me to believe in you."

"I wanted you to *fight* for me. The way you fought for Benji. The way I fought for you." She shakes her head. "It was selfish, I know. It's selfish to hold it against you. *I'm* selfish, and that's how I know, Mark. For all your many flaws, as self-centered and self-righteous as you are, you're still the least selfish politician I've ever met."

Jenny looks at me, unflinching, as if she can see right through to the bones of what I believe, and she still, somehow, believes in me. "You're only selfish if you back out now."

THIRTY-FOUR

MOM'S WAITING FOR ME IN THE LIVING ROOM when I get home. The Eames chair swivels toward the foyer the moment the lock clicks. She has a glass of red wine poised between her fingertips. "Mark Teagan Adams, where have you—"

Then she sees me.

"Mark." My name loses its bite. All the angry angles on her face lose their edges. Every reproach falls away.

I just stand there in the foyer. My backpack thumps the floor before I realize I've dropped it. My face crumples. The dam I've built around my pain cracks, and all the tears I've held back—about Dad, Henry, Jenny, Ralph, and every other sin I've committed—rush forth.

Before I know it, Mom is beside me, wrapping her arms around me as if she can hold me together through sheer force of will.

But I still fall apart. I bury my face in her shoulder, muffling my sobs against her cardigan. Mom holds me through the tremors that rack through me like the San Andreas Fault. She strokes my back. She rests her cheek against the crown of my head. She whispers sweet nothings like fairy tales in my hair. And I know they're platitudes—I know they're lies—but she says them with the conviction of facts from peer-reviewed studies, and I want to believe her.

When I wake, Mom's fingers are carding through my hair, and Monty is sprawled across my feet. The room is dark. My head throbs. Everything aches.

I jerk up. I don't how I got here.

"Honey," Mom murmurs, bleary.

I look at her. Worry has carved caverns in her features. It's my fault, again. "I'm sorry," I whisper. "I'm so sorry."

She purses her lips and shakes her head, but she can't summon the words to brush it off and tell me all's forgiven. "Hot cocoa?"

My watch glows in the dark. It's after midnight. "Yeah, okay."

Mom heats milk on the stove. I pull Monty into my lap as I take a seat at the granite counter. I run my hands over his Brillo pad fur. Cacao and cinnamon bloom in the air, and Mom doesn't say a word. I'm grateful for the respite. I need the silence to corral my thoughts into any kind of parent-worthy excuse.

I stare at my mug. I watch the tiny specks of spice sink into the foam. None of my paltry explanations come close to excusing my behavior.

"I prepared a hell of a lecture," Mom muses. "I had charts and graphs and a whole cartridge of bullet points. But I wasn't prepared for the black eye."

I look up. She winces, seeing it anew. "The school didn't call?" I ask.

"Oh, the school called. I received a series of lovely robo-calls informing me you missed all your classes."

"But you didn't hear from Principal Flynn? Or Vice Principal Chakrabarti? Not even a message from a secretary politely demanding you call back at your earliest convenience?"

Mom shakes her head.

"No one called you about a fight or"—I gulp—"suspension?"

Mom doesn't panic. She doesn't get angry, not like Dad would. She just asks, "Were you suspended?"

"I thought it was a foregone conclusion. That's why—"

"Why you left." Mom nods.

If Mom didn't get a call, it's only because Flynn doesn't know. After everything I've done to criticize the handbook, there's no way she wouldn't take any opportunity to use it against me. And if Flynn doesn't know, that can only mean . . . Henry didn't tell her.

"You tell me, then. What should I ask first? What happened, or where you went when you left?"

Monty squirms in my lap, so I let him go. "I went to see Dad."

"He didn't mention—"

"Not to talk. I went to watch him announce. I stayed in the back. I made sure he didn't see me."

"Why?"

"I needed to know. After what happened with Henry— after everything he said about how I have the whole world on a string but treat it like a yo-yo—I needed to hear what Dad would say."

Mom waits for the confession I don't want to give.

"I should have known. I should have seen it, in the way you look at me sometimes. I'm just like him. Just like Dad, just like I always wanted to be, but it isn't what I want anymore, and I—"

"Mark," Mom says sharply, scolding me for the first time since I broke down. "Honey, stop. Slow down. Breathe."

I do. I breathe. I didn't realize I was hyperventilating behind the pressure of speech. She leans in to sweep the hair from my eyes, and I shut them. "I'm sorry."

"No." She sighs. "I am. If I ever let you think . . ."

I blink at her, struggling to unravel the knots in her brow and the dropped stitches in her speech.

The backs of her knuckles graze my cheek. "You and your

father are cut from the same cloth, it's true. But when I look at you, I don't see the man he is today. I see the ghost of the man I married. The man I loved. The man I met at a Harvard grad student mixer, who spent the whole night talking about universal healthcare with a glimmer in his eye after I told him I was in med school. You know we moved out west for my residency, but when it was over, I told Graham it was his turn. Wherever he wanted to go—Boston or somewhere new—I'd follow him. But he took me to the revolving bar at the top of the Hyatt in San Francisco, where we could see the whole city turning beneath us, and he told me he didn't want to go anywhere else. He loved this state. This was the place he wanted to keep safe, and these were the people he wanted to represent. He really, truly believed he could make Marin 'a city on a hill,' as he always said."

They're the same words Dad used today when spelling out California's place in the nation. Words used by Kennedy and Reagan alike to celebrate American exceptionalism. Words used by John Winthrop in 1630 to extoll the Massachusetts Bay Colony as a model Puritan society.

"The man you're becoming," Mom murmurs, "is so much like the man he was. But the man your father has become? I barely recognize him anymore."

"But he was *right*," I insist. "I've been selfish and angry, and I wanted to prove him wrong."

"And you have. He's been in the wrong every moment

since the day you trusted us with your identity. He was wrong about the election, and he's wrong about *you*."

"But—"

"Honey." Mom takes my hand. The same one I used to punch Henry. The same one Ralph held. Except she turns it over, bypassing my bruises, and presses her thumb against my pulse point. "What do I have to say to make you understand? The sins of the father aren't your burden to carry."

THIRTY-FIVE

THE BLARING HONK CATCHES ME OFF GUARD. Partly because Pablo never honks, but mainly because I wasn't expecting him at all. Not after the way I ignored him yesterday. Not after how I ditched. Not after what I told Jenny.

I'm not ready. It's taken twice as long as usual to put myself together, which went about as well as piecing together a broken vase with a glue stick. I've tried to make myself presentable for my interview with Amber. Mom helped me paste concealer over my bruises. She gives me a questioning look when Pablo announces his presence, but I know I'm in no position to turn down olive branches when they're offered.

So I get it together, let Mom hug me and assure me she'll love me no matter what I decide, and greet my fate.

"What are you doing here?" I shut the door gently, the way Pablo likes, because I don't dare rock the boat, or the car, as the case may be.

"Best-friend duty. Or maybe second-best-friend duty, now that Jenny's reclaimed the title."

"Co-best friend," I amend, relieved and grateful and not at all sure what I did to deserve forgiveness. "If you're not—"

"Mad at you?" Pablo asks. "No. Irked, yes. But we don't need to talk about that right now."

"Are you kidding? You're always trying to get me talk about my feelings, and now that I'm trying to apologize, you don't want to hear it?"

"You have a few other apologies to make first, and I don't want you to strain yourself."

"Hey—" We've reached the bottom of the hill, and Pablo makes a right instead of a left. "This isn't the way to school."

"Very observant for someone who doesn't drive."

I study the storefronts we pass, trying to discern a pattern in the data. "Are you going to tell me where we're going?"

Pablo shrugs. "We'll be there soon enough."

True to his word, a few minutes later he pulls into a narrow parking lot in front of a wooden facade. Our destination is Ike's Creekside Diner, which literally moonlights as a gourmet bistro.

"As much as I could use a chorizo omelet right about now," I ask, hesitant, "are you sure this is the best idea? Won't you miss wrestling practice?"

"There are more important things," Pablo says sagely, "than executing the perfect fireman's carry."

Well. I can't disagree with that.

We head in. The bells above the door chime. I'm expecting truckers and tourists looking for some local color. What I'm not expecting is two tables pushed together in the center of the dining room, the entire French Club convened around them as if this were a cabinet meeting or maybe an international peace treaty negotiation.

Everyone's here. I study my friends' faces, Jenny looking blasé at the head of the table, Rachel bleary-eyed and resting her head on Nadia's shoulder, and Benji sipping from a rustic tin mug with his pinky out like a true Southern gentleman. Suspicion sends prickles of fear through me. "Is this an ambush?"

"I prefer 'intervention,'" Jenny says, leaning back like she owns this place. It's her party, and we're all guests here.

Except me. I'm pretty sure I'm not the guest of honor so much as a prisoner of war. Reluctantly, I take the seat at the foot of the table.

Pablo slides in next to Benji. I'm a little concerned he would try out that famed fireman's carry on me if I tried to run. "Look, Mark, we're all here because Jenny told us what you're planning."

"We're concerned," Rachel says, punctuating the sentiment with a yawn.

"More like pissed," Nadia adds. Her winged eyeliner is sharp enough to kill a man.

"Mostly, we're confused," Benji says. "Not so much about Henry. None of us blame you for giving Henry a taste of his own medicine, but we don't understand why you'd want to give up now. For the past two weeks, this campaign has been your whole life—and ours, too. You started this because you believed in your cause, and you won because your belief was infectious. So what we need to know is, what changed?"

The coffee isn't bitter so much as burnt, and it has the texture of soot. I down half my mug in one gulp.

Across the table, Jenny catches my gaze and holds it without letting go. "They deserve to know."

She's right—they do. They deserve to know what changed. I owe it to them. But if I'm going to tell that sordid story, then maybe I should tell the *whole* story. Not because I owe it to them, not because I owe it to anyone—except, maybe, myself.

Truckers and tourists chatter among themselves. A lone waitress calls out orders to the line cooks. Hardcore country music screeches over the radio. No one else will hear me if I come out here and now. Honestly, I'm not sure I'd care if they did.

I look at my friends, who have been by my side every step of the way. And finally, *finally*, I tell them.

No one judges me.

Rachel cries when I talk about Dad. Nadia's relieved not to be the only trans kid in Santa Julia. And Benji . . . for someone so expressive, I can't read the look on his face.

They're all so supportive and sympathetic and, frankly, suffocating. I can't breathe, and it's not about my binder. I make an excuse about going to the restroom but head to the deck out back, which overlooks the creek in the café's name. I brace my elbows on the splintering railing and lean out over the rushing water. I close my eyes and pretend I can feel sea breeze against my skin.

"Your omelet's getting cold."

"I'll be in soon."

Benji comes up beside me, pulling down the rolled cuffs of his white denim jacket. It might not be sea breeze, but there is a chill swirling in the air, the first portent of fall to hit California yet. "So," he says, staring out at the ducks paddling through the water. "Are you going to tell me what this is really about?"

"I already told you everything there is to tell."

"You said a lot of things in there, Mark, but you didn't name one real reason to renounce the mandate the student body gave you."

I look at him. Study his lower lip. Search for the scab where the tissue is still knitting itself back together. "Even if everything he said about me is wrong, I should be suspended. Ineligible for office."

"If he hasn't already, then Henry's not going to press charges."

"I know," I mutter, the words bitter like soap in my mouth. "And it's not fair."

"No, it isn't," Benji agrees, blithe. "It wasn't fair when it happened to me, but letting the same thing happen to you isn't justice."

"But it isn't the same. Henry wasn't threatening me. I started it."

Benji taps the bruise peeking over my collar. It smarts even under his featherlight touch. "Sure looks like Henry gave as good as he got. Pretty hard to claim self-defense if he throttled you."

"That's not what happened."

"And that's not the *point*, Mark. If Henry's not going to snitch, accept his silence as the gift it is. If the system is broken, you're not obliged to abide by its laws. Don't put yourself between the rock and the hard place."

I shake my head. Tiny eddies churn the water below us. "I guess I'm still looking for the crowbar."

"You already have it. *That's* the mandate the student body gave you. You told them you were going to change the system, so do it. *Use this*," he bites. "Take that guilt you feel that the system granted you a mercy you don't deserve, and *earn it*. Fight for the people you promised to protect. Give them a voice; give them justice."

"I don't know if that's a promise I can keep."

"Then promise me you'll think about it?"

"I owe you that much, at least."

Benji smiles, small and sad. "You know, Mark, not everything is a debt. All we owe to each other is the best we have to give."

Holy water has never felt so cold. It sluices from my forehead to my nose and drips from my fingertips when I make the sign of the cross. When I enter the chapel of St. Julia's Cathedral, I don't feel anything like pure.

The early-bird service is long over now. The chapel is empty. There's no confessor, and I'm grateful for that small mercy.

The pews are cold and sterile. Uninviting. I don't have it in me to sit or kneel. All I can do is stand, plant my battered high-tops on the carpet, and stare down the long, lonely aisle to the altar.

There's no one to hear me—my prayers, confessions, or recriminations.

"I never blamed you, you know." I take one step forward, then another. "The doting, devoted father I loved turned on me, cast me out, came as close as he could to disowning me without causing a national scandal, but I never blamed you. I knew his hate didn't come from you because I know *he* doesn't believe in you."

My voice rises with each step forward.

"But me? I was never sure what I believed. 'God is love,'

they said in one breath, then 'fags burn in hell' in the next. Leibniz said this is the best of all possible worlds, because you don't make mistakes, but you made a mistake when you gave me this body. You made a mistake when you left this world an unweeded garden that grows to seed. You made a mistake when you revealed the promise of heaven. That's always been the original 'It Gets Better' movement, hasn't it? Endure whatever suffering this mortal coil prescribes, and ye faithful shall be rewarded."

The closer I get, the farther away the answers seem, and the louder my heart chimes in my chest.

"Maybe I haven't done enough to earn a reward, but what the hell have I done to deserve your wrath? Tell me. Was this body a punishment? What about the hate your gospel planted in this world? Did I deserve the hurt that bloomed in me? I'll plead guilty to pride and wrath and lust. Hear this as my confession: I may be broken and flawed, but legend has it, you made me in your image. If I'm imperfect, then what does that say about you?"

I'm at the altar now, faced with relics of martyrs and a crucifix to drive the point home. Pillars of marble meet my gaze. I've never felt more alone.

"I've done my best to atone. I've made my tithes and said my prayers. I've tried so hard to earn your love, but it's never enough. Maybe that's the only revelation you'll give me. Nothing I do in this life or the next will ever be enough.

It doesn't matter if I burn down this world and build a new Eden in its place—you'll never forgive me for the indelible facts you inscribed in my soul. Because my mere existence bears testimony to the mistakes you've made. I'm incontrovertible evidence of the imperfect world you built. *Loving me* would mean facing your own flaws, and God knows you'd never do that."

Variegated light breaks through the stained-glass windows. A kaleidoscope of colors projects onto my skin, but it doesn't feel like a sign.

"So take this as my revelation, my gospel, my holy sacrament. I can't make amends for original sin. I can't absolve the world of the fire you lit under it. I can't earn your love, and I'm done trying. I'm *done*."

THIRTY-SIX

IF YOU DON'T HEAR FROM ME AGAIN, KNOW THE culprit behind my untimely demise was Amber Carr, in the library, with her laptop.

I'm all too aware of the furtive glances students and librarians alike send through the glass wall. Even though it's quiet here, I'm exposed.

If Amber sees through the concealer or my cavalier performance, she doesn't mention it. "Well, you called this press conference, so I'll let you kick things off."

I stop squirming. Sit up straight. Summon up the dregs of my bravado from the bottom of the well inside me. "I called you here today to announce my resignation."

Amber nearly jerks her laptop off the table. "You're doing what now?"

"That's why I called you yesterday. After reflecting on the past two weeks, I questioned whether I had any right to represent the honorable students who put their faith in me, when, I'm sorry to say, I haven't put my full faith in them."

"So *are* you resigning?"

I breathe in deep. "No. I realized that's no way to honor the promises I've made. The best I can do is to say now what I wish I'd said before the election. I want to tell the student body: I'm putting my faith in you today. And if you don't like what I have to say—if you feel I've betrayed you—then demand a recall election. Until then, I'll be honored to serve as your president."

I'm done waiting for a message from on high, or even down the road. I know what I believe.

This is my choice. Through and through. I know being stealth isn't a betrayal; the student body doesn't have a right to know my medical history. But I want them to know the fires that forged me. I need to tell them this story because *this is why I fight*, for myself as well as for them.

"This is what I've wanted to say since the beginning. I wanted to say it in my speech, announce it during my first interview, scream it from the rooftops when I moved to Santa Julia. I didn't stay quiet because I'm ashamed. This isn't a secret, and I'm *not* ashamed. I stayed quiet because I made a promise to someone, and I've always tried to keep my promises. Except I understand, now, that this was a promise I never should've been forced to make. So here it is. This is who I am. I'm—"

Amber holds up her hand and shuts her laptop.

"Amber, what are you—"

"Off the record." She cringes. I doubt she's ever voluntarily taken a conversation off record. "Are you sure you want to do this?"

I study her, searching for the ulterior motive hidden behind her careful speech, but all I see is compassion. Open eyes and a delicate frown spell sympathy and concern. None of it adds up with the ruthless girl I've talked to in the past. If she's not pursuing the truth, then she must already have it. "How do you—"

"Please," she sighs, dragging two syllables from the word. "Unlike the *Herald*, I do my research. After our first interview, I made some follow-up calls, and when those left me with more questions than answers, I went digging for bodies."

Maybe I've misjudged Amber this whole time. I always thought she was a gossip blogger full of hot air, but she does have a knack for investigative journalism, maybe even worthy of the Pulitzer she's after. Or, at least, one of the student journalism awards the *Herald* gives out each spring.

"So you know . . ." I pause, remembering there are two stories here, twin trees whose roots and branches have twined together. "How much do you know, exactly?"

Amber meets my gaze, steady, steely. "I know the name you used in Marin, and I know what it means."

Fear lights up my amygdala like fireworks on the Fourth

of July. Even though I know what I'm about to do, I can't stop the fight-or-flight reflex from paralyzing me in place. "How long have you known?"

"A week, give or take."

"Then . . . *why?*"

"Journalistic integrity," Amber says. Shrugging, like it's nothing.

Common human decency. The proof that we're rational animals rather than senseless beasts. We can choose not to tear each other apart. "You didn't think the electorate had a right to know?"

"I don't believe in outing," she says. "Especially not after what happened to Benji, and whatever role I unwittingly played in it."

"Okay," I say, wondering whether I should bite my tongue. I owe Amber my gratitude, but I owe Jenny my faith. "Then how do you explain what you did to Jenny?"

Amber blinks. "*Dystopia High* policy has always been that sex, lies, and videotape are fair game."

"Jenny's personal life wasn't yours to use as cannon fodder."

"I had legitimate concerns about campaign ethics. Who knows what Jenny and Dante considered appropriate pillow talk? Besides, you're one to talk. You cut her loose."

"That was a mistake."

"Look, Mark, we can debate journalistic ethics another

day, but Guided Study's almost over. Do you want to do this or not? You know I'd love to break a story with national impact, but I want you to be sure. Do you know what kind of powder keg you're about to set afire?"

"I do, and I'm ready for it." So ready for it that I ask, "Do you want to film this?"

Amber grins, wolfish, but for today, at least, this wolf is on my side. "Consider it your inaugural address."

"That's supposed to come *after* the oath of office."

"God, you're so pedantic. It makes me question why I voted for you."

"Well, "—I smile, in spite of the bubbles in my throat—"it's too late to take it back now."

She spins the laptop around, and I wait for the green light.

I put on my smile. Strengthen my resolve. Think *bravado* like a mantra. I've come out before, and I'll do it again. But it'll never be quite like this again. This is the moment I broadcast on all frequencies, to as much of the world as I can. From this day forward, I'll be out to everyone I know and so many I don't. I'll be visible; I'll finally be seen as exactly the man I want to be.

Amber hits record, and I tell the world who I am.

The Grizzly Inn lives up to its name. At either end of the lobby, twin taxidermied bears balance on their hind paws, baring their claws as well as their teeth. Their bristly brown fur stands on end, and their glassy marble eyes follow me wherever I walk.

I make my way to the front desk, strutting in like I own the place. "I'm looking for Graham Teagan."

Shutters close off the concierge's face. "I'm sorry, I'm not allowed to give out information like that."

"Not even for his kid?" I whip out my wallet and take out the state ID I avoid using whenever possible.

The concierge studies the ringlets and pearls of the girl I used to be. "This doesn't look anything like you."

I take that as a compliment, then take the creaking cage elevator to the top floor. All the way down the long hall, I find the brass number plate I'm looking for. I should've known he'd book the inn's only suite.

I knock. A fresh wave of pain crashes through my knuckles.

Dad opens the door. Whiskey wafts out. "Mads. What are you doing here?"

"Do you mind?"

He steps aside. Burlap curtains blot out the afternoon light. It makes the dark-walled room even more claustrophobic. Tangled bedsheets cover the king-size bed. His suitcase is open on the dresser, but his suits are in disarray, bits and pieces littered across the carpet.

Dad goes to the desk, where he pours himself one last tumbler from a depleted crystal decanter. "Well, have you come here to apologize?"

"Not exactly."

"Then why are you here, Mads?"

A day's worth of stubble coats his jaw. An unknotted tie hangs loose around his neck. His feet are bare. His movements are loose and fluid, sloshing just like the amber liquid in his glass.

This isn't the man who took me to see the fireworks from the steps of the Jefferson Memorial, or made me dark chocolate chip pancakes on Sundays after Mass, or drove me through the California countryside with the windows down and Springsteen blaring over the speakers. Maybe that man isn't dead and buried, but the one standing before me now sure as hell doesn't want to be saved.

"This is a courtesy call," I say, my mouth cotton-dry. "Since you were kind enough to tell me before you announced, I thought I'd give you a heads-up."

I liberate my phone from my back pocket and hand it to him with the site cued up. Amber scheduled the post to go live right before lunch, and I headed here right after the bell.

Dad's fist clenches around the phone.

My voice resounds, bellowing off these ever-shrinking walls. I sound deep and sure as I declare to the world that I'm Graham Teagan's son, formerly known as Madison Teagan.

Blood wicks up from Dad's neck, until his face is steeped in red.

"Don't bother asking me what I've done," I say when the

380

recording fades out. "Don't even try to threaten me. What-ever blackmail's on the tip of your tongue, emotional or otherwise, it won't work. The story's out there, and there's nothing you can do to kill it."

Dad quivers and quakes, a house caught up in the center of a tornado, but he hasn't begun to howl.

"I always understood the terms of our agreement. I knew what would happen if I broke our contract. I'm not here to bargain or beg for your forgiveness." I'm amazed at how calm I sound, a seasoned lawyer reasoning my case in a court of law. "In a few minutes, I'll walk out that door, and I'll never ask anything of you again. But before I go, I have one last question for you."

Dad doesn't respond. Maybe fire and fury have choked out his capacity for speech.

"I just need you to tell me *why.*" It's here my voice breaks, all the hurt I can't hold back spilling into that one little word. "Please. Just tell me. The way you reacted that Memorial Day and everything you've done since . . . is it even transphobia? Because if that was it, maybe I could understand. I know it isn't always easy. It's one thing for you to publicly support transgender causes, but it's another to find one in your own home."

Dad opens his mouth to interject, but I don't let him. Not until I've said my piece.

"If you said what you said and did what you did because

you didn't want to lose your little girl, then tell me. Tell me you were afraid of the suicide rate and the hate crimes and the uncertain status of my civil rights. Tell me you lashed out because you loved me and didn't want to send me into a world that might hate me for this choice I didn't make. Tell me you still love me, and you believe me, and you're sorry for the hate you let loose in my world."

"Mads," he says, gruff. "Of course I love you."

I wait, and I wait, and the world revolves beneath my feet.

"But you can't say the rest of it, can you?" I whisper. "Because it'd be a lie. It was never even about me. It wasn't that you couldn't believe I was a boy; it was that me being a boy didn't fit into your twenty-year plan. You never even tried. Because trying might have meant admitting some things are more important than the Oval Office."

Dad sets his glass down on the desk. He takes a step toward me. "Mads—"

I recoil, stumbling back until my calves hit the mattress. "I want to hear you say my name. My real one. Just once, and then you can go back to pretending your denial has any sway over me."

A beat passes, then another. The words don't come, so I turn around and gather the courage to walk out that door.

"Mark," Dad murmurs, grabbing me by the shoulder, yanking me toward him.

The tourniquet around my heart eases up, and I'm sure

he's going to pull me into a hug. He's closer than he's been in months, and the warmth of him thaws something in me. Beneath whiskey and sweat, I can make out the sandalwood in his cologne, and he still smells like home, he does.

But he doesn't hug me. He settles both hands on my shoulders, keeping me at arm's length. He stares straight into my eyes. "Mark," he says again. "Son, we can fix this. We can go to the press together. The *San Francisco Chronicle*, or the *Herald*, if it'll make you more comfortable. We'll tell them we kept quiet to give you space to explore your identity without having your every haircut and fashion choice dissected under the public eye. We'll explain the truth, that we made this choice together." His mouth stretches, teeth peeking beneath slanted lips in a poor reenactment of a smile. "You wanted the spotlight, son? We'll make you a national icon. You'd like that, wouldn't you? You could fight for transgender rights on the national stage. You could make a real difference, just like you always wanted."

"You're right," I say, nodding as I break his grip. "I can. And I can do it without you."

THIRTY-SEVEN

I'M DOING HOMEWORK WHEN THE TEXT COMES.
Yes, actual homework. Now that the campaign's over and
I've tended to my war wounds, I have time to sprawl across
the couch with Monty cuddled against my side as I thumb
through my calculus textbook. With a pad of graph paper
balanced on the armrest and a pencil tucked behind my ear,
I blast music over my headphones, loud enough to drown out
the ravenous world.

My phone's on silent. I've turned off notifications for everything except calls and texts. I don't dare brave social media.
My friends and even Amber have texted their unequivocal
support. Dad kept calling on my walk home, so I blocked
his number. I did call Mom to give her fair warning, and she
assured me we'll weather any and every storm together.

So when the alert chimes through my headphones, I'm not
expecting it. There's no one else who has my number who
would want to talk to me.

Except there's his name, crystallized on my screen.

Ralph: What are you doing right now?
Mark: homework?
Ralph: Is that a question?
Mark: don't sound so surprised
Ralph: You always surprise me.

If I looked up my symptoms on WebMD—heart palpitations, sweaty palms, stomach cramps—what diagnosis would I find?

I flip forward in my textbook and run my index finger along the jagged perforation where I ripped out a page for him.

I don't dare get my hopes up.

Ralph: Any chance the homework can wait?
Mark: why?
Ralph: I'm kind of in your driveway.
Mark: how can you be "kind of" in my driveway?
Ralph: Come outside.

I yank my headphones off and toss the textbook to the floor. Monty grouses when I push him off the cushions. I hurry to the door, keeping pace to the beat of my noisy heart. There's Ralph, leaning against the hood of his Prius, and I'm standing on the porch in my pride-flag tube socks. "You're in my driveway," I inform him.

"That's what I told you."

"No 'kind of' about it."

"Unless we're talking about Heisenberg's uncertainty principle, in which case determining my exact position could become a dicey proposition."

A smile comes to my lips, unbidden, but I bite it back. "Is that your only dicey proposition?"

He sobers up, too. "Come for a drive with me."

I want to say yes, but I know it's not that easy. "Are you sure that's a good idea?"

"I'm not sure if it's a *good* idea, but it feels like a necessary one." Ralph hesitates, like it costs him something to ask, "Please?"

I don't have it in me to deny him this, not when he's so earnest and anxious and still the same boy I fell for. I nod. Then I disappear behind the door to gather my shoes, wallet, and keys. I shoot off a quick text to Mom, who hasn't technically grounded me yet, even though I suspect it's coming.

I join Ralph in his car, engine running. "I'd ask where we're going, but I have a feeling you wouldn't tell me."

"You like surprises, don't you?"

"Usually," I admit, "but it's been a weird day."

Ralph frowns. He keeps his eyes on the road even when we reach the stoplight at the bottom of Hythloday Court. A soft, acoustic indie song floods the car; the unfamiliar female vocalist mourns her broken heart.

"Listen, Ralph, I'm—"

"Not yet," he murmurs.

After we merge onto the freeway, a southbound overpass carries us over Cantera Valley. The tract houses and mobile-home parks look like squares on a chessboard. I've been a passenger on this stretch of freeway so many times, but I could count the hours I've spent in the Valley on my hands. It's one of my blind spots, and I need to do better. If I'm going to represent anyone in this town, then I need to acquaint myself with each and every nook and cranny. Maybe it's not a debt I owe so much as the knowledge I have more to give.

We cross the town line to Santa Julia's slightly smaller, slightly flatter neighbor. Right down the street from a blocky casino, a strip of fast-food restaurants with flashing neon signs beckons. I know exactly where we're going. A yellow arrow affixed to a red sign over a white building. If there were ever an example of Californian exceptionalism, it's In-N-Out. The parking lot might be worse than Los Angeles traffic, but that's part of the charm. So is the grease permeating the recirculating air and the harsh fluorescents glaring off bright white décor. I breathe everything in, from the sizzling grills to the bubbling fryer. Guests chatter in the overcrowded dining room, and employees shout order numbers out of sequence over the loudspeaker.

The line starts all the way back at the double doors, but it clips along at a brisk pace. When it's our turn, Ralph makes for the open register, but I hold out an arm to stop him. He looks at me, but he doesn't object. So I smile at the perky cashier in a debonair tissue paper hat and ask for two shakes, one strawberry and one chocolate, and two orders of fries, please.

Just as I'm finishing up, a booth opens up on the far side of the room. I run over and seize it, sliding across the shiny white plastic in victory.

Ralph smiles a little at the childish glee on my face. "I'll wait for our food."

It doesn't take long; without burgers, we're an easy order. Ralph returns with the red plastic tray and sets it down between us.

I douse a fry in ketchup and pop it in my mouth. It's warm and fresh and a little soft, just the texture I like.

Ralph goes for his milkshake. His pert pink lips wrap around the straw. His Adam's apple bobs as he swallows. "You were right," he says. "You were one hundred percent, totally, completely right. This is worth skipping the burger."

I don't say, *I told you.* I don't reach for my milkshake. I don't whisper the prayer that comes to the tip of my tongue, unbidden. I just look at him. Regret might as well be written on my forehead in permanent marker.

Ralph's smile disappears, and God. It hurts to lose the

light of the sun. "I wanted to tell you in person," he says. "I'm sorry. For the way I reacted."

I shake my head, a violent rebuttal. "I'm the one who should be apologizing. Not you."

"Maybe," he concedes, "but I should've heard you out. I should've trusted you had your reasons." He ducks his head. The restaurant buzzes around us, but here in our booth, the world has gone still. "I saw your interview."

"I figured."

"I should've listened."

I shake my head again. I'm going to give myself whiplash if I keep this up. "I shouldn't have lied. I didn't mean to. I've never been good at talking *around* him, so I usually restrict myself to euphemisms. But then you assumed, and I didn't know how to tell you, not when . . ."

"Not when I've built my whole identity around my grief." Ralph nods. "It isn't your fault I put you in that position. I know I'm fragile; it's why I've avoided the Authentic High School Experience. But when I was around you, you never treated me like I was going to break."

"Then I went and lied because I thought the truth might break you."

"I understand why you did it," Ralph says, so softly I can barely hear him. "I understand why you couldn't tell me the truth. After watching the interview, I don't blame you. Because in spite of everything, I still think you're a good person. Maybe the best person I know."

If ever there were a case of perjury, it's this. "I'm really not. You should know that better than anyone."

Ralph looks me in the eye. His are clear and bright. "You're a good man."

"But not superlative." This time he doesn't disagree, and I suck in a shallow breath. "But you . . . you might be the best man I know, and you make me want to be the best man I can possibly be." He shakes his head and starts to contradict me, but I don't let him. "I know you don't see it, and maybe that's part of what makes you good. But I've never met anyone who cares so much about doing the right thing, who's loyal without fail, and who has such a steadfast sense of duty."

"I don't know what I ever did to give you that impression," Ralph mutters. He takes his glasses off and polishes them with the sleeve of his sweater.

I remember that day in the chem lab, when I asked him to serve, and he looked up at me with such doubt in his eyes. That night at Paraíso Point, when I asked for more than I deserved. "It wasn't just one thing."

He puts his glasses on, and something shifts in his expression. "You don't see it either, do you?"

"See what?"

"You don't see what I mean when I say you're a good person."

I deny the charges. "I'm a work in progress."

"You believe in everyone and everything but yourself. You believe the best of people, even when they don't deserve it. And you really, truly believe this world can be a better place if we band together to fight for it."

"I know I'm kind of a bleeding heart, but—"

"Only kind of?" Ralph squints.

"Point taken," I say. "But being a bleeding heart doesn't make me a good person."

"Being an idealist and an optimist in a world like this? That takes strength most people can't even imagine." He must see the doubt clouding my face, because he presses, "You don't have to believe me, but know that I believe in you."

I shut my eyes. "You shouldn't say things like that."

"Why not?"

"Because I don't know what any of this means for us."

"Neither do I," Ralph admits.

"Maybe we started too soon." It kills me to say it, but I do. "It's only been two weeks, and I know we've been in the trenches, but maybe we still don't know each other well enough. Maybe we should just—"

"Maybe we should start over," Ralph suggests, firm in the eddies of my indecision. "Go on dates. Get to know each other outside the foxhole. Pretend we're normal people."

"I'd like that." His smile is contagious, and I don't want to be cured. "Does that make this our first date?"

"Well, we never really had a first date to begin with."

"What about the romantic night hike?"

"Not technically a date. Dates require planning. Intention."

"Did you plan this?"

Ralph opens his mouth, presumably to say he took me here, didn't he? But I stand up and lean across the table, until my thighs dig into the edge, and I kiss him, here and now. It's fast and it's awkward, but Ralph's lips chase mine when I pull back. "Was that too soon?"

"Not soon enough."

"Is it too soon to call you my kind-of boyfriend if we're just starting to date?"

"I've always been a traditionalist at heart," Ralph says. "So if you're asking me to be your boyfriend, I'm saying yes. Nothing 'kind of' about it."

I sip my milkshake. It's already started to melt, and so have the glaciers, but this right here—the smile tugging at Ralph's lips—this is proof entropy can be reversed. Mistakes can be mended. A broken world can be rebuilt.

So we sit, and we eat, and we hold hands across the expanse of the table.

THIRTY-EIGHT

I CHECK MY NEWS ALERTS IN THE MORNING. I mean to go in reverse order, but after seeing that the first hit for *Mark Adams* is from the *Los Angeles Times*, I realize I've stumbled on a national three-for-one special.

It's everywhere. All the major California dailies have it, and so do the political blogs. I'm on *Politico* and NPR. They've even lifted my video, with due credit to Amber, thankfully. It's only a matter of time before the national networks pick it up. Dad might be a rural wine country congressman, but there's nothing the media loves more than a scandal.

If political intrigue is the media's meat and potatoes, then this is some grade-A beef. Already, the *Sacramento Bee* has declared Dad's gubernatorial campaign "dead in the water." *FiveThirtyEight*'s chief political correspondent tweeted Dad's chances of winning next fall are officially 0 percent. *The Hill* quotes a congresswoman from upstate New York saying she intends to call for an ethics investigation into Dad and, quite possibly, his expulsion from the House.

Half a dozen outlets have called me *brave*. They all praise Congressman Teagan's son for having the "courage" to speak out. I've seen cis people use that language to talk about trans people more times than I can count, but it's strange to see it leveled at me. Because coming out as trans is simultaneously the easiest and hardest thing I've ever done.

I'm halfway through the *Chronicle*'s Teagan takedown when a message notification flashes at the corner of my screen.

Jenny: I can't believe I'm about to say this, but you need to look at Dystopia High.

Mark: already looked. amber hasn't posted anything since the original article

Jenny: That's what you need to look at.

Mark: i'm pretty familiar with the content

Jenny: Oh my god, would you just listen for once in your life?

Jenny: Read the comments.

Jenny: I can't believe I just said that.

Jenny: What fresh circle of hell have we unearthed.

There are over five hundred comments.

The oldest ones are from self-proclaimed UHS students, all variations on the same theme. They support me; they don't hold it against me. Most are anonymous, but Beatriz says I'm still her president. Shawn invites me to chill with him on the knoll any time. Kai calls me his "bro," followed by a fist bump emoji. Xander offers show choir's services for my first state dinner. Cristian and Luis promise to ask their Life Skills teacher if they can do a presentation on parenting queer kids. Clary declares that if she had to lose, she's glad it was to a worthy opponent.

I choke back tears as I keep on scrolling. The next batch are from students at other Santa Julia high schools. Teachers. Parents. Then total strangers. People from Peoria to Poughkeepsie tell me they stand with me.

Mark: this has to be fake

Jenny: You're looking at it?

Mark: these are russian bots, right? this has to be an info war. actual #fakenews.

Jenny: I know you're knee-deep in the actual news, so why did you expect the denizens of our self-congratulatory liberal hamlet to react any differently?

Mark: amber must be moderating the trolls

Jenny: Probably, but so what? It doesn't negate what's there.

Mark: i don't deserve this.

Jenny: Yes, you do.

Jenny: Unflinching support is exactly what you deserve. Unconditional love. Unequivocal acceptance.

Mark: it's what we all deserve. every queer kid in america.

I know what I believe.

And I know I need to do better to back it up.

Mark: i'm sorry i didn't fight for you
Jenny: I know.
Jenny: But we both would've lost if you had. I never thought I'd martyr myself for a cause, but I'm glad it was yours.
Mark: if i had it to do again, i'd gladly go down with the ship
Jenny: God, stop, no one needs any more ammunition about shipping us.

I stifle a laugh with my fist.

Mark: i do love you, you know
Mark: and before your aro spidey senses start to tingle, I mean platonically
Jenny: I know.
Jenny: And I love you, too.

Mom took the day off to deal with the fallout and keep the paparazzi away. She pulls me aside as I'm on my way out the door and starts adjusting the knot on the black skinny tie I've selected for this auspicious occasion.

"Mom," I whine, sounding about half my age. "Pablo's waiting for me."

"This will just take a minute." From the pocket of her robe, she extracts a small velvet box, the kind that usually comes with a ring and a marriage proposal. "Open it."

The hinges creak, and there, its butterfly back tucked into the ring slot, is an American flag lapel pin. Except it's not like the ones I already own, flat flags with gold poles. Here, brass articulates the enamel, raised lines between every stripe and studding every star. The metal has started to tarnish, but I recognize the wear as a sign of love.

"I tried looking up props and costumes," Mom's saying fondly. "I thought I might be able to find one Martin Sheen wore, but wouldn't you know, *West Wing* memorabilia is hard to come by. Then I remembered that being a congressman's wife does have its advantages." She taps the folded note pinned to the upper lining of the case. "Read it."

The paper is crisp, heavyweight. I don't believe the presidential seal at the top of the page, let alone the stark penmanship that indents the paper with each stroke. But I know the loops and whorls of that signature as well as my own. "You didn't—" I sputter. "Mom, did you forge Obama's signature? Because that's a felony, and—"

"I called in a few favors," she says, smug. "I know it's not Jed Bartlet, but I thought you might settle for your favorite *nonfictional* president."

I fumble the pin with shaking fingers. "Oh my God, *Mom*—"

"Here, let me." With steady hands, Mom takes the pin and fastens it through my starched collar. "There, now you're ready for the ball."

"There's no inaugural ball."

"Well, there should be."

She turns me by the shoulders until I meet my reflection in the mirror. I look at myself. Swooping hair. Wrinkle-free shirt. Evenly knotted tie. Lapel pin. My classic hoodie, worn jeans, and trademark high-tops to dress it all down. I look like the man I want to be.

Mom hovers behind me, tears in her eyes, hands gently resting on my shoulders.

I whirl around and wrap my arms around her. "Thank you," I whisper, struggling to imbue the words with everything I should've told her months ago. "Not just for this, but for all of it. For taking my side, for choosing me, for never doubting—"

"Honey," Mom murmurs, "you don't need to thank me for any of that."

I said before that there's privilege in being stealth, but the truth is, there's privilege in coming out, too. I may have lost Dad, but unlike so many other trans teens, I've never had to worry about being kicked out. I've never had to fear for my safety at home. I've never had to doubt that I have someone who loves me unconditionally. And maybe, in the best of all possible worlds, I wouldn't need to thank Mom for that, but in this one? I am thankful. So thankful.

So I hold her tighter, unwilling to let go, until Pablo honks the national anthem.

Mom ruffles my hair as we pull apart. There goes the perfect swoop. "You're still grounded, you know."

And I laugh, knowing I don't need Dad, not when I have this.

Henry's lounging against the brick wall when I get to the main office. He's put himself together again except for the split lip I gave him. The scabs are stark against his pale skin. He can't cover it with concealer like I can with my bruises, and I feel a pang of guilt.

But it isn't strong enough to stop me from snarking at him. "Here to crash the party?"

"No, actually." He levers the sole of his boot against the wall to straighten up. "Have a minute? And don't worry, you won't be late to your inauguration."

I look around. Although students have started to scurry through the halls, none of my friends are here yet. "A minute. But for the love of God, no more bathrooms."

He laughs, and unlike every other callous bark I've ever heard from him, this one is genuine. Warm, even.

We end up outside the auditorium, just a stone's throw from the office, on a raised concrete platform outside the entrance. Henry leans back against the railing, tilting his head up toward the dazzling blue sky. I lean forward, bracing my arms on the poles, staring out at the kingdom below us. Kids running through the halls. Teachers hopscotching between them. The flagpole standing tall. *All the light touches.*

"I owe you an apology," I say, before I can think better of it.

"So do I." Henry shrugs. "So how about a ceasefire?"

I hazard a glance at him. His backlit profile cuts a jagged line across the sky. "I'm not in the habit of appeasing fascists."

"Relax, Mark, I'm not asking for us to be friends, or even allies. But we're going to be working together, and we might as well be civil." He glances at me out of the corner of his eye. "Besides, I may have misjudged you."

"You saw the interview, then."

"Difficult to miss." His gaze drifts back to the vast, indifferent heavens. "I called you a hypocrite, but I was, too. I accused you of acting like you knew everything about me when you never bothered to learn, but I made my own assumptions."

"You weren't wrong about everything."

"But neither were you."

Is this what it feels like to find common ground in no-man's-land? I keep looking at him, trying to reconcile the contrite man before me with the one who stomped his boots on the senior steps, who choked me in the boys' bathroom, who stood by while his friends hurled insults and fists at Benji.

"Look." Henry sighs. "For what it's worth, I'll make sure Trevor and Kevin don't give you any trouble."

"What about Benji? Or the next kid to come along who doesn't fit into their boxes?"

"I'll talk to them."

"Is that the best you can do?"

"I thought you didn't want to be allies."

"Not if I can't trust you to do everything in your power to stop this."

Henry shrugs. "I can't make any promises."

"Can you at least tell me why the sudden change of heart? Why didn't you go to Flynn and get me suspended?"

"I told you the other day," he says. "Some of us don't have the privilege of doing as we please."

The tract houses and mobile homes in Cantera Valley. His threadbare clothes and Irish Spring. The IB program and the football scholarship. I connect the dots, finally, and I understand. The constellation of Henry's options has never looked like mine. That's what privilege means. And it doesn't absolve him, but maybe it's enough to make me understand.

"We can't all be," Henry mumbles, "who we want to be."

I hear him. I hear the spaces between his words and the ones he can't say, clear as the void between the stars. I hear what he doesn't yet know *how* to say.

"That's what I'm trying to change." I look right at him and make it a promise.

Henry nods, curt. "Then I won't get in your way."

We crowd around the microphone in the main office. Principal Flynn hangs back by her office, staring us all down in distaste.

It's not traditional for the student body president–elect to invite guests to the kitschy swearing-in ceremony, but nothing about my campaign has been traditional. ZP didn't have a problem when I asked him about it, so all my friends are here. This is as much their victory as it is mine.

Rachel and Nadia have tears in their eyes. Pablo claps me on the back. Jenny gives me a steady nod. Benji studies me, then asks, "You ready for this?"

I open my mouth, but no words come out. My throat is desert dry, while my armpits could pass for swamps.

Then Ralph's hand slides into mine.

Despite what I believed, I've never been in this alone.

"Yeah." I smile. "I'm ready."

ZP claps his hands together like a game show host. "Then let's get started." He presses the button and clears his throat as the PA system crackles to life. "Good morning, Utopia High School! Today, we're here to perform the time-honored tradition of swearing in our chief elected official. You put your faith in him when you elected him, so

402

your president-elect is here to make a vow to you."

ZP adjusts the microphone and beckons me over.

Ralph squeezes my hand before he lets go. Then he holds the student handbook like I asked him to. I place my right palm on the vinyl cover and raise my left.

ZP says, "Repeat after me: I do solemnly swear . . ."

And I say, "I do solemnly swear . . ."

"That I will faithfully execute the Office of Student Body President of Utopia High School . . ."

"That I will faithfully execute the Office of Student Body President of Utopia High School . . ."

"And will, to the best of my ability, preserve, protect, and defend the UHS Student Handbook."

"And will, to the best of my ability—"

I stop short. I know the words, but I can't make myself say them. Not when this handbook failed Benji and Jenny and so many others. I got in this to change the handbook, not carry on its broken tenets.

ZP nudges me and prompts me with a whispered, "Preserve, protect, and defend . . ."

I take a breath. Take everything the world said when they called me brave, and do my best to earn it. "I will, to the best of my ability, preserve, protect, and defend the UHS *student body*." My voice doesn't quiver; it doesn't crack.

ZP's jaw drops, but he doesn't correct me.

Ralph beams. Jenny smiles. Benji starts a slow clap.

"Well," ZP says, grinning in spite of himself, "congratulations, Mr. President. I'll hand it over to you for your first official duty: morning announcements! The floor is, officially, yours."

The floor, and maybe the ceiling, too.

I wrap my hand around the mic. "Hi." My voice echoes not just through the office but through the entire school. It's not bravado when I say, "I'm Mark Adams, and I'm your student body president."

ACKNOWLEDGMENTS

Anyone who knows me knows that I don't know how to write a thank-you note. But I have never been as thankful for anything as I am for the fact that this book—this story that grew up with me—is making its way into the world. I've never been as thankful as I am now, to everyone who has loved and supported my weird, queer, glittery *West Wing* rip-off. So thankful that, for once, this thank-you note writes itself.

To Claire Friedman, who is everything I wanted in an agent and so much I didn't know I needed. In one of our earliest emails, I wrote, "I'm convinced you love this book more than I do," and I swear it's still true. Thank you for loving this book from page fourteen. For understanding what I was trying to do even when it was a 99,000-word behemoth. For talking me down from every panic spiral. For reading faster than literally anyone I've ever met. And for fighting for this book and for me, every step of the way.

To Mabel Hsu, my brilliant editor, for your passion, patience, and profound insight, all of which have shaped this book in ways I never could have imagined—but now can't imagine it without. Thank you for pushing me to define and refine the politics underpinning the narrative (and sending me peer-reviewed academic articles on "utopia" along the way—truly, the way to my heart). For helping me make the hard changes even when they hurt. For encouraging me to rewrite the election speech again and again, until it was nothing like I'd planned but everything it needed to be. For somehow always uncannily knowing when I have more to give. And for the box of books you sent after our first call—I may have forgotten to send a thank-you note.

To everyone at Katherine Tegen/HarperCollins who has had a hand in making this book a *book* and championing it to the world: Lindsay M. Wagner, Gweneth Morton, David L. DeWitt, Amy Ryan, Kristen Eckhardt, Lauren Levite, Michael D'Angelo, Ebony LaDelle, Jane Lee, Tanu Srivastava, and Katherine Tegen. Ivy McFadden, for catching the most mortifying typo I have ever made in my life. Anna Prendella, for insights that radically changed my thinking— and made the narrative so much stronger for it. Max Wittert, for bringing Mark, Jenny, and Ralph to life in your beautiful cover art.

To Jorge Alvarado, for asking me, "What would it have been like?" For sitting with me every time we were home from college or #adulting, drinking iced Aromas next to that telltale copy of *Heather Has Two Mommies*, and imagining what could have been and what should have been, and always knowing the difference. For telling me to write this story, even when I insisted I'd never write about our hometown. I've said this before, and I'll keep saying it until you believe it: This book would not exist without you.

To the Writer Collective. First, Nico Grey, for being my very first reader and the very first person to tell me—in the most tear-jerking note possible—that this book mattered. Crystalyn Bryan, Olivia Rose Faulkner, Danni Jorgenson, Ben Kaestner-Frenchman, Geetha Krishnan, Kayla Matt, Steph Matthiesen Avilés, Jess Mueller, and Aud Simmons, for sprints, glitter bombs, and, as Mark calls it, constructive ass-kicking. And everyone else who's ever kept me company at three a.m. in our weird little panopticon Discord server, thank you. BAT DAD forever.

To the friends who stayed. Sarah Schelde, for always, always being there when I need you and for being a better friend than I deserve. Kristen Miller, for reading the earliest, ugliest iterations of Mark in the Notebook and for always knowing me better than I know myself. Natalie Holt, for late nights writing trans political fantasies and for saying "I told you so." Alex Haupt, for teaching me the difference between a blunt and a joint. Molly Deis, for keeping me in touch with my Sonoma County roots while living this Seattle life. Jane Mac-Donald, for listening to me read too many drafts of the same damn scenes on our lunch breaks. Additional shout-outs to Brendan Aronoff, Nick Burton, Kelly Cai, Adrienne Cousar, Neal Kosaly-Meyer, Kathleen Lawton, Carlos Marquez, and

Lindsay Roiz. This book owes a debt to all of you, whether you realize it or not.

To Tatra-Li de la Rosa, for believing in me so much more than I believed in myself. For going so far beyond the call of duty. For reading my short story drafts and highlighting your favorite lines. For telling me to take risks. For knowing, before I did, that I could really do this.

To my family. This thank-you note is long overdue. Dad, for reading me bedtime stories and then reading everything I'd give you. Mom, for proving that making art is always worthwhile, even when no one's watching. My grandparents, whose memories are certainly a blessing: I wish you'd gotten to know this part of me. And, perhaps most important, my cat, Simon, for literally sleeping on my manuscript and eating my revision notes; you just encouraged me to work that much harder.

Finally, to all the trans, queer, and questioning kids reading this. If you've made it this far, you know I don't believe in progress narratives. I don't believe things get better unless we put in the work, each and every day. But I have to tell you the truth: I didn't write this book as some courageous act of literary resistance. I wrote it for a girl with a peacock feather in her hair, who went to a terrible high school dance the night she finished drafting her first novel—the one where President Mark Adams was a forty-four-year-old allocishet Republican (I'm so sorry). That girl lived in a supposedly liberal suburban town, where you were supposed to accept everyone, but you were also supposed to be *normal*. That girl knew the words *lesbian*, *gay*, *bisexual*, and *transgender*; she knew they were words for other people. That girl deserved a better story. I'm sorry it took me ten years to write it.

What I'm trying to tell you is I wrote the story I needed when I was fourteen. And I hope you find something you need in these pages, be it comfort, catharsis, or courage. I hope it's courage.

Because the story doesn't end here. I'm not the hero of this story. I'm not the savior, passing down representation from on high. It's like Mark and Benji. I want to stand with you as you tell your own stories. To make space for you, until you're ready to claim it for yourself. I'm not doing this for you; I'm doing this with you.